Patricia Angadi was born in London in 1914. After an upbringing that included a presentation at Court, she married Ayana Angadi, an Indian writer and lecturer, Trotskyite and intellectual. Together they founded the Asian Music Circle and played an important role in shaping British interest in Indian culture, presenting Ravi Shankar and other artists in England. At the same time, Patricia Angadi was establishing herself as a portrait painter. Among her subjects were Yehudi Menuhin, Lord Brockway, Barbara Castle and George Harrison. In 1964 she took a teacher-training course and subsequently taught all subjects at a Primary School for thirteen years. She is the author of *The Governess*, also available in Black Swan. She now writes and gardens full-time.

The Done Thing

Patricia Angadi

BLACK SWAN

THE DONE THING

A BLACK SWAN BOOK 0 552 99248 8

Originally published in Great Britain by
Victor Gollancz Ltd.

PRINTING HISTORY

Victor Gollancz edition published 1986
Black Swan edition published 1987

All the characters in this book are imaginary. Though
some of the situations are based on actual situations, the
actions and reactions of the people in my novel have very
little foundation in reality. An autobiographical
description would have been much too boring. But
looking back on the era from a distance of some forty
years, I have tried to invent a story which portrays the
general attitude of various sections of the British public
towards an Anglo-Indian marriage at that time, and also
to give an idea of some of the expectations of marriage
one young woman of the period might have had.

P.A.

This book is set in 11/12 pt Century
Schoolbook
by Colset Private Limited, Singapore.

Black Swan Books are published by
Transworld Publishers Ltd., 61–63
Uxbridge Road, Ealing, London W5 5SA, in
Australia by Transworld Publishers
(Australia) Pty. Ltd., 15–23 Helles Avenue,
Moorebank, NSW 2170, and in
New Zealand by Transworld Publishers
(N.Z.) Ltd., Cnr. Moselle and Waipareira
Avenues, Henderson, Auckland.

Made and printed in Great Britain by
The Guernsey Press Co. Ltd.,
Guernsey, Channel Islands.

For Ayana, with love
August 1985

Contents

THE BEGINNING

THE MIDDLE

THE END

The Beginning

I Burning the Boat

September 1942

You could call the room sordid, I suppose, just slightly sordid. It had, among other things, dirty, cream-coloured walls, a very solid chest of drawers, one sagging arm chair and a trestle table. The bed was like a hospital bed, iron, with a hair mattress, but the sheets were fairly clean, and they slept soundly enough on it.

Heather had never imagined being able to sleep in a single bed with someone else before she had actually done so, but strangely enough, she had found it easy from the very start. She lay on her back, that September morning, looking at the shaft of sunlight that slanted through the curtains patterning the wall with a slim, elegant line of gold. Occasionally the breeze disturbed the tranquillity of the shape into a sudden zigzagging dance before reverting to the sharp stillness again.

There was a certain peace, just lying there on her back and pretending everything was normal. Peace after the storm – or was it before? – she was uncertain which. Probably it was just in between two storms, and only an illusion anyway. A sudden burst of excitement raced through her, followed immediately by a surge of heart-numbing anxiety. Go back to sleep – the whole thing's a dream, and she was sitting in dream stalls in a

11

dream theatre. Dimming lights, overture, hushed expectancy, then the breathtaking vista revealed by the rising curtain, of hills floating away into the distance of a pink dawn sky. Violins playing of course.

The alarm went off, crudely and with vulgar abandon. She leaned across the inert Mohendra to douse the discord. In the ensuing silence, and as she lay sprawled across him, they kissed.

'How you can sleep on,' she said, 'on this day of days. To have to be woken up by an *alarm* on your *wedding* day – it's monstrous.'

Is this really me saying this, she thought, after all the heinous things that have happened over the last few months? What in God's name am I doing? She felt, in that instant, as though she was stepping inevitably into disaster. She was kicking away the chair, leaping finally off the cliff; burning her boats.

She climbed over the crumpled, folded body on the bed and lit the single gas ring.

'Here am I,' she said as she filled the kettle, 'used to much better things than padding naked across the room to make tea. Where are my minions of yesteryear?'

He propped himself on an elbow and looked at her rather seriously as though about to make a solemn pronouncement. 'You shall have them, my darling, I promise you. The very first thing we'll get when we're married is a minion.'

They sat together on the bed and she suddenly and unexpectedly felt the tears well up again behind her eyes. She had cried such a lot in the last few weeks.

'Are you really going to love me in sickness and in health as long as we both shall live?'

'Longer than that.'

'A likely story. What an anti-climax it all seems, doesn't it?'

12

'That's only because you let yourself get so worked up about it, my darling. This is only an ordinary day, like every other day; we shouldn't make so much of just signing a register. And think of the party at Istvan and Hugh's afterwards, that won't be an anti-climax.'

Heather felt a wave of love for him go through her. He never failed to reassure her, there was such a certainty about him. She, on the other hand, was a flippant, shallow socialite with no conception of life as it really was. She cringed at the thought of it, but there could be no going wrong with him beside her. There should be no misgivings on her part, here was someone on whom she could rely absolutely. He was strong, he was gentle and he was immensely clever. She allowed the relief and pleasure to flood back through her. No room at all for doubt.

The Town Hall was very clean with a war-time stringency. A 'business as usual' look after three years of war. Inside, Heather felt the disinterest of the place take over. Her heartbeats sounded audibly, and again there was this sensation of stepping off into the void.

In the waiting room a small bundle of a figure got up as they came in, and Heather slipped from despair into delight.

'Nanny, you came! How wonderful you are! So early in the morning and everything. I never thought you would be able to.'

Nanny was sixty-four and had been with Heather's family from 1909 when the elder boy, Malcolm, was born, two years before his brother Bobbie, and had stayed until 1923 when Heather's first governess was engaged.

Mohendra watched with a certain distaste as Heather greeted her. English nurses were an institution which he found interesting, if a little sinister. He

13

considered them to be one of the main causes of the strained English mother-daughter relationship that had grown up in this country since the Great War. His thoughts ordered themselves into neat paragraphs and he saw them printed on a page. Not having the traditional respect for the mother which was inherent in Indian culture, the English allowed the nurse to take over the role of mother. So different from the Indian family system where the Ayah remained a servant, and never more than that. Interesting point; he felt in his pocket for a pencil and notebook, but found, to his irritation, that there was neither. Careless oversight.

'I couldn't miss my little girl's wedding, now could I?' Nanny had her arm round Heather's waist and tears ran down her cheeks.

'And how are you, Mr Hiremath? Very excited, I'll be bound.'

Mohendra took her outstretched hand. 'Splendid, splendid. Yes, a very exciting day for us all, and you came to see the knot well and truly tied; that's good, very good of you.'

He watched the two sit down together with their hands clasped. Heather wiped Nanny's face with her hand, and he gave a small movement of impatience.

'Don't cry, Nan. I know you always do at weddings, but you just can't at mine because then I might, and I don't want to. In fact it's essential that I don't because I'm actually feeling very happy.' She wondered if she were telling Nanny this or herself.

A small man came into the room and asked if they would follow him. The corridors were long and had an air of faded splendour, but the stairs had kept their full glory, marbled and carpeted, with a fine balustrade. A gilded mirror confronted them half-way up with carved figures entwined, and here the staircase divided and curved on upwards to join again on the next floor.

14

Heather found her war-trained mind condemning the indulgence; how wasteful to have two staircases when one would do.

She put her hand in Mohendra's and saw herself approach the ornate looking glass. Again the sensation of watching a play. Enter the principal characters. Who on earth had designed the costumes? Mohendra looked impeccable. Tall, with a head like an eagle; she never failed to be bowled over by his really dazzling good looks. Dressed up, as he was today, in his brown shervani jacket, white trousers and with a Gandhi cap on his head, she felt a sharp tremor of pride and pleasure as she looked at him. But she – a bit over the top perhaps?

She had refused to be completely done out of a white wedding, and had designed a white linen outfit with sharp, military-style pleats splaying out into the skirt, the bum-freezer jacket caught in tightly at the waist. The shoulders jutted out wide and square, and on one of the sharply pointed lapels was the spray of green and beige orchids she had bought the day before. She had brushed her uncontrollable red hair up into a bunch of curls on top of her head, held there by a tortoiseshell and silver comb of her mother's, and then wrapped round an olive green scarf of Indian silk shot with gold. She had tied the knot slightly to one side, and left the ends standing up in points. 'Rather like ears,' she thought glumly. 'Donkey's ears.' She wore a pair of heavy gold Indian ear-rings, hung about with pale, uncut, semi-precious stones. Mohendra's wedding present to her. He wore hers, a rock-like jade ring, on his little finger. She saw with some dismay that the Martinique-style turban made her slightly taller than his six-foot height. Two ten foot bean poles, she thought with growing displeasure.

A handsome couple? An outrageous couple? A black

15

and white couple? Shocking, of course; disgusting even? She tripped on the last step, and Mohendra pulled her up sharply with a disapproving tut of his tongue. An extraordinarily un-English tut, Heather had always noticed. She could never make a noise with her tongue like that, just as she could never squat on her haunches like he could. Yet another example of the gulf between the races. She gave an explosion of laughter.

'You and your Eastern tuts of disapproval.'

'You shouldn't be Westernly careless then; you should constantly aspire to perfection and the nirvana of putting each foot exactly in the right place always. And what do you mean, Eastern tuts?'

'Even your tuts have an Indian accent. They sound ridiculous.'

'What a lot of stairs,' said Nanny. 'Wherever are we going?'

The small official in his dark blue suit ignored them respectfully, but paused at the top of the flight so that they might catch their breath.

'Was there another witness?' he asked softly. 'Two witnesses are regulation, you know.'

'I told most people the time of the wedding when I asked them to the party,' Heather said, looking at Mohendra to check for further disapproval, 'but I do think I may have forgotten to tell them where it was and Louise couldn't get down in time to come to this.'

'It doesn't matter.' Mohendra sounded authoritative. 'We have one, that should be quite enough, I'm sure. Or perhaps you could act for us?' He smiled warmly at the neat little man. 'You wouldn't mind helping to push a poor unsuspecting couple into the abyss would you?'

There was absolutely no visible response.

'I have other duties,' he said, 'but I dare say one of our lady typists might oblige.'

Heather wondered if he was offended; or perhaps he

16

was showing disapproval of the whole thing. Perhaps the Registrar would refuse to marry them. Her cheeks suddenly warmed and reddened. But how ridiculous, of course he wouldn't.

At that same moment, they heard a slight disturbance downstairs.

'Oh but I'm sure – oh please, I may be late you see – it was the buses, and I wasn't sure – upstairs you think?'

They looked back down the staircase and saw a hurrying, wraithlike figure seeming actually to fly up the stairs. Things appeared to float out behind her; wispy hair, gossamer scarf, even her flower-patterned dress looked as though it had wings. She dropped a glove and two pieces of paper in her flight, but they went unnoticed.

'Miss *Beadle!*' Heather was at once astounded and embarrassed at the vision of her one-time governess. 'How marvellous of you to come.'

'Heather, dear child, am I yet in time? I do so hope – for this momentous occasion – "Now fair Hippolyta, our nuptial hour draws on apace".' Her laugh was, naturally, silvery.

'Of course you're in time. You can be the other witness.'

They were shown into a large room that seemed to be filled with palms in pots. A man with very little hair, a drooping moustache and rimless pince-nez rose from his chair behind a very large desk to greet them, and then leant towards Heather in a grave but rather confidential manner. She had the sudden horrifying thought that he was going to kiss her. She noticed that he had cotton wool stuffed in both ears. How could he hear?

'Miss Heather Sylvia Hamilton Jones?' he asked, and when Heather nodded he continued, 'Would you come with me a moment, please?'

They walked slowly and silently along a corridor which turned several corners before coming up against an ornate mahogany door. She found herself admiring the finger plates and handsome brass handle. Inside, the Registrar placed himself behind another desk before addressing her.

'Miss Jones, you do know, do you not, that Mr Hiremath's religion allows him to take more than one wife?'

Heather stared at him in disbelief and then gave a compulsive giggle. 'Of course I know,' she said, allowing the laughter to take over. 'Of course I know that he *could;* just let him try, that's all.'

A wan attempt at an embarrassed smile crossed the sad gentleman's face. 'It's a part of my duty to warn you,' he said, 'just a part of my duty. In case, you know, just in case.'

Back with the palms, Mohendra, Nanny and Miss Beadle sat in chairs in front of the desk. Mohendra was frowning angrily, Miss Beadle looked rapt and earnest, and Nanny was crying. The ceremony proceeded gravely and without further incident. Heather remembered very little about it afterwards. In fact the only real thing that stayed with her was the photograph taken, but not published, by the local newspaper's photographer, on the steps of the registry office when they came out. In it the handsome couple smiled at each other ecstatically as though oblivious of anything else in the world. And so I was, Heather thought to herself, wasn't I?

The rest of the day was spent preparing for the evening party at Hugh and Istvan's studio in the Boltons.

'We must remember it's a reception,' Istvan said. 'That means we could dress someone up and have them announce everybody. That would be terribly grand.

Does anyone have the slightest idea who's coming?'

'I have a list here.' Mohendra brought it out of his pocket. 'They haven't all replied, but there are ninety-seven that I have asked personally, including the Mayor of Kensington.'

'Are you mad?' Hugh's mouth dropped open. 'Since when was the Mayor of Kensington a friend of yours?'

'I met him when I was lecturing to the Rotary Club. A nice man, fairly left wing.'

'Shall I do some egg sandwiches?' Nanny came out of the kitchen drying her hands. 'They always go down well.'

Istvan caught her round the waist and waltzed her round the easels and canvases. 'My darling Nanny, why didn't I meet you before today? You could have married me and spent the rest of your life making me egg sandwiches for breakfast, lunch and tea. Wouldn't that have been nice?'

'Nice for some, I don't doubt,' said Nanny breathlessly and smiling a little. 'But not the sort of thing I'd like to make a habit of.'

'That's what you said to me last night,' Istvan said, kissing her.

Heather lay back among the cushions on one of the sofas and laughed uproariously. 'Bags I do absolutely nothing,' she said, 'because it's my wedding day.'

'We should really be allowed to disappear discreetly up into the gallery,' Mohendra said, 'and let all you nice people get on with everything down here.'

'Don't be filthy,' said Istvan. 'I'll have you know I keep a good clean studio here.'

'It's all so exciting,' Miss Beadle said tremulously. 'So completely Chelsea and artistic.'

By seven o'clock in the evening the studio was packed, and Heather found herself actively involved in the excitement and gaiety of the situation. There were

19

no thoughts of yesterday or tomorrow, and today was most fulfilling. Mohendra was urging Miss Beadle to recite some poems of Rabindranath Tagore.

'Of course, of *course* you must recite them to us. So very appropriate, everyone would be delighted – I will announce it.'

How could he think that a recitation by Miss Beadle could ever be appropriate?

'Stop him, Hugh! For goodness' sake stop him, it would be a disaster.'

'Rubbish, my dear, anything goes at this party.'

It was at that moment that Heather saw her mother and her younger brother, Bobbie, at the door, and the world stopped with a jolt.

'Mummy, you *came!*'

'Insisted I should bring her,' her brother said rather grimly.

Sylvia Hamilton Jones was dressed in black: a long, clinging black skirt and a jacket-top decorated with sequins. She leant heavily on her son's arm and gave Heather a tragic smile.

'I had to be with you on this special day, my darling,' she said, 'however much my heart is bleeding. I must be with my children when they are in trouble.'

Mohendra approached. 'I'm so glad you could come,' he said, and he took Bobbie's hand and shook it too heartily. 'I am delighted to meet you at last. Let me get you both a drink.'

Heather stared at the scene from a great distance, and the laughter in her fought its way to the surface. She found the fact that these two strange men were now brothers-in-law excruciatingly funny.

'Come and sit down, Mummy,' she said, struggling with the desire to laugh. 'Miss Beadle is about to recite.'

'Miss *Beadle?*' said her mother in a handbag sort of voice. 'How very strange.'

20

Heather burst into a gale of laughter. It really wasn't fair to her mother to be so frivolous in the midst of her suffering, but somehow at that moment she found it hard to recall the misery, and hard to believe that the world was ending – or beginning, she wasn't sure which.

'If your braided hair has loosened, if the parting of your hair be not straight, if the ribbons of your bodice be not fastened, do not mind. Come as you are; do not loiter over your toilet,' said Miss Beadle in a voice full of pent up emotion, and Heather's laughter bubbled up even more out of control. She looked across the room at Hugh, and saw that he was standing by the door with a handkerchief stuffed in his mouth. She caught his eye, but they managed to keep their hysteria silent. Mohendra was sitting cross-legged with other guests at Miss Beadle's feet, rapt and attentive. Bobbie stood next to Sylvia, scarlet with embarrassment and staring down into his empty glass, while Sylvia gazed at Miss Beadle in astonishment.

The tableau imprinted itself upon Heather's mind as she sat there watching, but still somehow not taking part. She was waiting for the curtain to come down (or was it perhaps going up?) on this extraordinary play being acted out all round her. Could it perhaps be a dress rehearsal? Or a curtain raiser? And was it a tragedy or a farce? She never did discover which.

2 *Curtain Up*

Heather's mother was born in Manchester in 1882. Christened Sylvia Rose, she found herself immediately saddled with two uncompromising facts with which she could never quite come to terms. To start with, a name like Rose was a serious handicap and she resented it bitterly. Such a common, working-class name, especially as her father called her Rosie. She dropped the name herself and also tried to forget the second unpleasant fact, that her father had left Scotland before she was born to make his fortune in Manchester. Such an unattractive place for her and her younger brother to be brought up in, especially when they had such an historically Scottish heritage. Right back to Robert the Bruce, their mother told them. Luckily, it had been impressed upon them all through their childhood that they should take great care to speak properly and decently, as their parents did. The horror of picking up even a trace of the Manchester accent was so dreadful that Sylvia went out of her way to affect the Edinburgh inflexion which was so marked in her mother's speech.

She had not really improved the name situation by marrying Robert Jones in 1904, though she mitigated the effect by adding her own maiden name. Hamilton Jones sounded more dignified and had a Scottish ring about it. Their two sons, Malcolm and Bobbie, were handsome, clever boys. Sylvia smiled as she thought of them, feeling that they were her own, personal achievement. But darling Heather was not quite so clever, she felt, and had to be given the best possible start in life. Every opportunity to make the very most of herself so that she might find a good, decent man to take care of her and keep her in the comfort she was used to. Such a happy child she had always been, so enthusiastic and so warm with this great love of life that she radiated wherever she went, but somehow vulnerable. She would always need looking after, that child.

Sylvia felt a glow of happy satisfaction warm her as she thought about her children. They really were a credit to her, she had to admit. A satisfactory outcome of all the love and care she had put into their upbringing. She enjoyed talking about them whenever she could.

'Growing up fast now, of course. Time just seems to fly by, doesn't it? Seems no time at all that Nanny was taking them out in the pram, the dear wee things. Ah yes, babies are my passion I'm afraid; they grow up too soon for my liking. You see there's Malcolm now, he's already eighteen. Oh yes, going into the family business. Quite keen he is. Yes, did very well at school, was gym champion for the last two years you know, quite an athlete. Very proud of him we are. Yes, a well-made boy. Of course, Robert was always a sportsman, so those two have a great deal in common. Oh yes, he'll go into the territorials like his father. The London Scottish we think; yes, well we like to keep up the Scottish connection you know, even though Robert's business means we cannot actually live there. But my brother does have a very lovely estate there so we are able to visit quite regularly.' Her eyes took on a far away look; regret flickered there for a moment perhaps but was quickly covered by laughter. 'I think Robert actually feels a wee bit Scottish himself now. He always says he's Scottish on his wife's side. His little joke you know. A great joker he is.'

And indeed he was. A rather larger than life figure with sparse sandy hair brushed sleekly back with Yardley's solid brilliantine, and a short moustache which he crimped every morning with curling tongs heated over a small spirit lamp. The smell of methylated spirit had a nostalgic effect on Heather even now. When despatched from the nursery by Nanny in those distant days at eight thirty sharp to say good morning to her parents, she was first assailed by chemist shop smells of powders and scents at her mother's dressing table and later by the sharp, pungent methylated spirit smell of her father's dressing room. She loved to watch the delicate curling operation, and her own lips used to draw back in dread anticipation that he might one day burn himself with the hot tongs. But he never did, he was far too clever. He was also a very jolly father who laughed a lot and liked having friends round him all the time.

The family lived in a large, Edwardian house in Stoke Poges. Heather had learned Gray's Elegy from one of her governesses, a Rossetti, pre-Raphaelite type of lady called Miss Beadle. Heather was devoted to her and shared with her the sombre realization of how privileged she was to walk through Gray's churchyard every time she went to church on Sundays. They imagined together which tombstone he had sat on to compose the Elegy, and Heather would sometimes, when she was alone, sit on the same tombstone to see if inspiration would come to her as it had come to him.

At this time it was her greatest wish to become a poet, mainly in order to please Miss Beadle, but also because she had discovered the satisfaction of reading or reciting what she had written. She wrote diaries, poems and stories continuously, and illustrated them all with tiny, precise drawings, mostly of flowers, fairies and princesses. Miss Beadle was enchanted by her output and Sylvia showed indulgent amusement.

'Very nice, darling, very nice, and what pretty little drawings.' Then turning to Miss Beadle, 'But what about her history, geography and arithmetic? Poems and tales are a splendid hobby, but they are not the most important things in life are they?'

Miss Beadle clasped her hands dramatically and her long beads swung forward as if in added emphasis. 'But Mrs Jones, Heather has so much talent in the arts, it would seem wicked not to foster it to its full flowering!'

Miss Beadle did not last very long after that, and Heather's future poetry writing had to go underground and into obscurity. She was distraught that both her beloved Miss Beadle and the encouragement and inspiration she provided were snatched from her at one fell swoop. They agreed to correspond regularly, but Heather cried in secret for two days and wrote seven dirges starting with such lines as:

> Gone is my muse of yesteryear
> And I am left in darkness drear.
> I cannot pen my erstwhile poem
> Oh come, oh come, oh come back home.

She was not entirely satisfied with the rhyming of the last two lines.

Miss Beadle's successor allowed no time at all for poetry writing, but a whole hour a week for art.

'Copying nature is a most educational pursuit,' she told Heather. 'There is something to be learned from every one of God's masterpieces.'

Heather adjusted without much difficulty because everyone remarked on her ability to draw well and it was so good to be praised. She drew flowers and insects

25

meticulously and with a great deal of pleasure, but usually made up secret poetry as she drew. She decided then that even if her family thought both poetry and Miss Beadle were embarrassing and unnecessary, she, herself, would still rather be a poet when she grew up.

The house at Stoke Poges was a great centre for parties and house parties in the twenties. There were always people staying when Heather was growing up, bringing the smell of cigar smoke and noise and laughter and the clink of glasses. Heather remembered looking down on it all from the first floor landing. A scene through the banisters and from the gallery. Something rather exciting, of which she was not a part. She was just an onlooker, fascinated and excited by all that she saw, and longing to join in, but the right moment never seemed to come. Even when the boys grew up and gradually became part of the scene downstairs, she remained, still watching from the gallery.

It was an exciting and confusing time with a great deal of noise and chatter everywhere. When the visitors started to arrive, usually about tea-time on Friday, the house seemed to take on a different personality with different noises, different smells and the feeling of invasion. Heather was expected to be downstairs in the library to be introduced and to hand round the sandwiches. She enjoyed being on show and revelled in her father's comments which punctuated her mother's continuous burble on the other side of the room.

'. . . her father's red hair, though I prefer to call it corn-coloured, really more golden I think. Of course my mother had very fair skin you know, luckily without the freckles . . .'

'. . . and this is my little copper nob, the freckled one.' Laughs resounded round him, and Heather blushed with pleasure at being the centre of his world for a moment. He hugged her to him. 'Great blusher, aren't you my pet? This lovely lady here –' he took the hand of the stranger beside him – 'is a famous actress. One of these days you will no doubt worship at her feet along with the rest of us, but you'll have to wait a bit. Not quite old enough yet, eh?' He winked at the lovely lady. 'Wouldn't quite appreciate all the naughty bits, eh?' There were more gales of laughter, through which Heather heard her mother's voice carrying on like an endlessly running tap: 'Now my brother's children, they are more the dark, sultry type if you know what I mean. Nearly black, their hair is. Can be very attractive of course, but I always preferred the fair-haired English type, or I should say Scottish because my family is Scottish you know – oh yes, a very old family . . .'

Heather's brothers, Malcolm and Bobbie, always seemed to her to be quite adult. She scarcely knew them because they were usually away at school when she herself was growing up. She was full of admiration for the way they seemed to be able to attach themselves to the outer edges of their parents' sophisticated parties with a facility that Heather felt she would never be able to emulate, no matter how old she was. She could not imagine ever being able to attain the ease of manner, the charm and above all the glamour of this illustrious circle of her parents' friends.

'. . . no, Heather doesn't go away to school. We prefer to keep her here with us,' said her mother. 'We have a governess for her and we may later send her to Paris to learn French. I think a sensitive little girl like Heather might tend to feel a little lost in the rough hurly-burly of school life. She's bright enough, mind you, but I do like to keep an eye on what she is being taught. They pick up some extraordinary ideas these days I find. I must say some of these women who have the temerity to call themselves governesses also leave a lot to be desired.'

She took Heather's hand and drew her into the aura of her group of guests, straightening out imaginary creases in Heather's clothes. 'I don't really approve of all this competitive learning with exams and tests. Not for girls anyway; I mean there's no need for it, is there? There's no need for a girl to prove how clever she is. As long as she knows how to behave, that's all that matters.'

And the polite ripple of agreement that followed this remark sounded extraordinarily different from the noisy outburst at the other side of the room that exploded at the end of one of Robert's funny stories. It was sometimes difficult to understand what the joke was about, but Heather always laughed because it made her feel part of a happy family, which she considered very important. She often felt inadequate, being not as clever as her brothers, nor as happy as her parents.

Her father, after all, had all those numberless friends who loved him and thought him quite amazingly funny, while her mother was unfailingly right in every situation. Heather never remembered her ever saying that she did not know something. She was the encyclopaedia that provided all knowledge and answered every question you cared to ask. Invincible somehow, and yet not hard like rock. Heather sought in her mind for a better description of something so impregnable that was not hard, but she only came up with India rubber, which sounded worse.

'Oh no pet, you can't wear a blue jumper with a green skirt, they just don't go together. There's a wee rhyme to help you remember. Pink and green is fit for a queen, but blue and green should never be seen.'

But Heather still found it difficult to remember because you could always say it the other way round, and she considered pink looked dreadful with green, whereas blue and green made her think of the sea or of trees against the sky. She realized that she had no instinct for what was or was not done, but had to learn the hard way. You could not, for instance, split infinitives, whatever that meant, nor must you use words like note-paper or serviette, or dinner when you meant lunch, nor supper when you spoke of the grown-ups' evening meal, which of course was dinner. Except on Sunday evenings when the maids had the evening off and everyone served themselves from the cold buffet laid out on the sideboard. That was supper.

This failing in herself showed up even more during the yearly visits to her Scottish cousins. That whole family struck her as being infinitely superior to her own: Sylvia was constantly saying so. They were richer, for one thing, and they had the easy, relaxed air of self-confidence which positively glowed all round them, making them somehow untouchable and remote.

The older she got the more inferior she felt. 'Mummy, can't I have a proper long dress for Scotland this year? I am fifteen and Anna and Diana always look so good at the dances and I look so *awful.*'

'What nonsense you talk, pet. You never look awful and you can't class yourself with your two cousins because they are quite grown-up and you are not. But I suppose I shall have to start to think of you as a young lady now, more's the pity.' She cuddled Heather towards her. 'So I'm to lose my wee baby then?'

Heather tried to lose a little of her height, which was considerably more than her mother's, in order to conform to her mother's idea of what she was.

'Can we go up to Harrods one day? Tomorrow? Can we?'

'Wait a while, sweetheart. There's no rush, no rush at all.' Was it possible to consider this child an adult already? 'You could have your hair set, perhaps, it's a

29

wee bit wild; it would look better if it were set prettily.'
She pinched and pushed Heather's hair to bring it over
her forehead. 'You shouldn't scrape it back like that,
lovey, it's not becoming.' Leaning back to see the
effect, she smiled. 'But there, you're as pretty as a picture whatever way I look at you.' And leaning forward
again, and in a confidential whisper: 'Far prettier than
those two cousins of yours.'

Heather knew she didn't really mean it, but it was
nice of her to say so. 'Oh Mummy, you know I'm not.
I'm hideous and ugly and gauche and stupid. Can I
really have it set? Gosh, that would be frightfully nice.'

The trip to London was not a great success. There
was only one dress in Harrods which Heather thought
suited her perfectly. It was red velvet with a train.

'But darling, that is dreadful, quite dreadful. Apart
from the fact that you *cannot* wear red with your red
hair, it would make you look forty.'

They finally picked a white chiffon.

'But Mummy, it's babyish and it makes me look so
big.'

'You *are* a big girl, dear heart, but none the worse for
that, and white is pretty for a young girl. She's done
your hair very nicely, has she not? You look quite
grown-up. Put a few grips in at night and it should stay
tidy for quite a few days.'

Heather's gloom did not lift all through the holiday.
Both the hair and the dress caused her continuous
embarrassment. However am I going to cope with
being grown-up, she thought, if I persist in liking all the
wrong things? How on earth am I going to learn?

3 Waiting for Leap Year

It was difficult for Heather to imagine what life would have been like if it had not been for Louise. 'The Inseparables' Sylvia called them, and it was true that each clung to the other with anxious tenacity, at least where Heather was concerned, for Louise was everything she herself would have liked to be. 'A sweetly pretty girl,' Sylvia called her. 'Just like a wee fairy. You'd think she'd waft away like thistle-down.' Heather almost felt herself grow as her mother spoke, like a massive, ungainly giant. But she had loved Louise with a slavish devotion ever since they first met on her own fifth birthday.

It was all very clear in her mind, that particular party. Everyone was to come as a fairy, with the boys as elves or gnomes, and when the door opened to Louise and her nurse, Heather was convinced that a true fairy had accepted the invitation she had posted in the cedar tree. Louise had silver gauze wings and swansdown pompoms all over her. It was breathtaking, and Heather was struck dumb.

Nanny gave her a little shove from behind. 'Come on now, Bluebell fairy, where are your manners? Aren't you going to welcome your new friend? Say how do you do and take her into the party.'

Heather held out her hand in awe. 'I'm Bluebell,' she said, 'But I'm not a real fairy, are you?'

'Yes,' said Louise. 'I'm Thistledown, only I can't fly yet, I'm just learning.'

Louise was the eldest of the large family who lived down the road in the big house where nannies and nursemaids and butlers and grooms and maids seemed to outnumber the family by many dozens. Sir William Bell was a baronet, and his wife Laura had to produce six daughters before managing an heir. They were a gracious and well-mannered group who looked after their land and employees with a care that could not be criticized. Sylvia was not the only neighbour who was delighted in being able to call Lady Bell her friend.

'So nice for Heather to have a little playmate nearby,' she told Robert. 'And such a lovely house they have. In those surroundings you just couldn't help picking up beautiful manners and an appreciation of the good things of life.'

'As long as she doesn't go getting ideas above her station, eh pet?' Robert tickled Heather under the chin and laughed. 'Don't think I'll ever attain titled rank or a stately home, so don't you grow up expecting it, sweetheart.'

Heather, as usual, wondered what he meant and smiled at him happily.

'Don't be so obtuse, Robert,' Sylvia said. 'You know I didn't mean that; I'm not a snob, you know that perfectly well.' She did not notice the movement of his eyebrow. 'And anyway they are no better than we are if it comes to that. I've been told that the grandfather, who made all the money, was a publican!'

'And a sinner?' But she was not listening.

For once Heather fell in with her mother's idea for her. Usually the children of her mother's friends filled her with horror and shyness; but Louise was different, and for both of them it was love at first sight.

'Would you like to see my dolls' house?' Louise asked

32

the first time Nannie took Heather to tea. 'It has a lavatory and a bathroom and electric light.'

Heather had never seen a dolls' house so impressive, nor anything as beautiful as Louise, and her enthusiasm bubbled over.

'Oh isn't it pretty! Look at the carpets and the kitchen. Is that the cook? What's her name? How many children are there? Are they good children? I have got a family at home, only most of them are very naughty except Phyllis and she's very good but I usually keep her in a cupboard because I don't like her much. My Auntie Elizabeth gave her to me and I don't like her much either, only Mummy said that it was a very special doll so I would have to take special care of her, so I put her in the cupboard so she can't get broken. But I have a rabbit called Peter and he is very naughty indeed and often quite rude so that I have to smack him. Do you have to smack any of your dolls?'

Louise was astounded by the flow of conversation. 'No,' she whispered.

'Oh I do, consterly. There's Nancy, she's very naughty, and then I have a boy doll called Dickie but he's only a baby and he cries sometimes. You've got a real baby, haven't you? I wish I had a real one. Does he cry?'

'Our new baby is a girl. She cries all the time. I don't like her very much because she's rather ugly.'

From this first conversation there grew a friendship that scarcely wavered in intensity through the years, even when Louise was sent to boarding school and Heather had a succession of governesses who came to live with them for various lengths of time. When the holidays came round, it was as if they had not been parted. The conversation that had ended when term started went right on from where it had left off.

'I do envy you going to school, you're so lucky. Can't

think why Mummy doesn't let me. She's so odd in some ways.'

'My dearest Het, you are potty, just don't know when you're well off. School is loathsome, totally loathsome.'

'But you like it sometimes, don't you?'

'I suppose one could say there are times – but not many, really not many. Oh it's just *topping* to be back, you've no idea. And these hols are going to be pretty galumptious I think; I suppose you've heard that we're having a dance?'

'Yes, Mummy talks of nothing else.'

'But you're always having parties at your house; such glamorous ones too with all those famous actors and things. My parents just love your parties.'

'But they're always for them and never for us, at least not for me because I can never talk to famous people. Malcolm and Bobbie can'

'Didn't you get a prince to come to the last one?'

'Yes, but only a Russian one so he didn't count really.'

'Mummy and Daddy were terribly impressed.'

'Ditto ditto about Mummy and yours. She thinks it will be much more dignified and worthwhile.'

'Oh rot – I hope to goodness it won't be dignified. Can you imagine anything more ghastly?'

'I bet I don't get anyone to dance with me.'

'Oh yes you will – I shall see that your programme is absolutely filled up and I shall find you someone grue-somely nice for the supper dance!'

'Really? Do you promise? Who will you find me? Have you thought of someone? I shan't know anyone and I shall look frightful, I know I shall. I shall have the curse and lots of spots and even if you get people to book up my programme, they'll all cut my dances, I know they will.'

'You ass, of course they won't.'

'You don't have to bother, you're so *pretty*, everyone will be mad about you. I shall probably be three times the

34

height of all the boys put together, and my feet are so big.'

She held both feet in the air hopelessly.

'I hate being small,' Louise said. 'Everyone thinks I'm helpless and they all try to do things for me.'

'But I would love that. I wouldn't even mind them thinking I'm completely non compos mentis because then they'd feel sorry for me, even though I am a horsey giantess, and they might come rushing to my aid. But anyway I *am* pretty stupid, you know. Useless really, when you come to think of it. Bet I'd come bottom of the class if I had a class to come bottom of.'

'You're quite mad. You're absolutely frightfully good at drawing and writing stories and making up poems and things.'

'But I can't very well do that at parties, can I?' Heather giggled. 'And anyway, Mummy says that that sort of talent is all very well as a social grace, but that I ought to know how to add up or I won't know what tradesmen are diddling me or how much I ought to pay the maids.'

They wandered out on to the terrace of the big house and looked down over lawns and a lake to the fields beyond.

'We're going to have a monumental type marquee out here,' Louise said, 'and five hundred gold chairs.'

Impressed as she was with the magnitude of the forthcoming dance, Heather remained unconvinced that she would actually enjoy it and approached the day with increasing trepidation. She disliked the blue taffeta dress Sylvia had bought for her. It was pretty but her hands looked so big and red. 'And I haven't any chest,' she moaned to Louise. 'You've got a much better one than I have,'

'It's not bad as long as it doesn't get any bigger,' Louise admitted. 'But supposing it does and I don't get any taller, I shall just look ridiculously top heavy. I find it embarrassing enough as it is.'

'I think it's a super chest, not like mine which is just a couple of pimples.'

There were a lot of Louise's school friends at the dance, with whom Heather could make no contact. They were staying in the house and took on the intimate friend quality. Heather imagined she saw I-am-Louise's-special-friend-who-are-you gimleting out of their eyes when they looked at her. Would Louise remember what she had promised? Would she find partners for her?

Her dance programme, its tiny pink pencil attached with pink silk, already felt limp from the heat of her hand. Whether to hold it out for all to see or hide it from sight was something that was difficult to decide. To display it in full view might seem too obvious; might show up the anxiety she was feeling. But then not to show it at all might imply that all the dances on it were already booked. Or they might think she didn't want to dance at all. She held the programme up and pretended to study it seriously, making imaginary marks with the pencil. At her anxious insistence, her brothers had booked two dances each, grumbling a little as they did so.

'Hold on, hold on – one dance is enough, surely? There are some rather tasty little dishes here, don't you think?'

'Bit *young* though. And far too many mothers around for my liking.'

They're so sophisticated, Heather thought to herself in proud admiration. Shall I ever be able to cope with situations like this with such nonchalant ease? And as she thought it, she wondered whether to put the accent on the first syllable or the last; or even the second. *Non*chalant; non*chal*ant; nonchal*ant*. And do you

36

sound the last 't'? She repeated the word with the varying emphases under her breath until she saw a boy at the other side of the room staring at her with intense interest. She turned the muttering operation into a fit of coughing so that she could cover her mouth. How embarrassing – he must have thought she was talking to herself, which of course she was.

She looked round wildly for Louise and saw that she was surrounded by a noisy group; all intimate friends, she felt sure. She stood on one foot and stared at the closely packed group with a mixture of envy and admiration, until Louise looked up and saw her.

'Oh Heather, you're here – you look divine, you do honestly. Come over here and let me introduce you. Chaps, meet my very bestest friend in the world.' She hugged Heather towards her. 'Since we were so high, honestly. Like a sister really only much nicer than all those little brats that are my real sisters.'

Heather glowed with delight, and some of it was for the discomfiture in the eyes of the previously threatening cronies. She looked down at them kindly. It was sometimes good to be tall. And in no time at all her programme was practically filled up and became an asset instead of a liability, dangling there on her wrist by its pink silk cord. Dangling there jauntily for all to see with boys' names scrawled over nearly all of it. In fact, she would only have to go upstairs and powder her nose twice during the whole evening.

So the party could really be called a success where she was concerned, and one she could talk over and discuss with Louise for many days after with a great deal of enjoyment.

'That Meecham boy's a blissful dancer, isn't he?'

'Yes, but a bit wet don't you think? I *mean* – can't really say much, can he? Only really talks about dogs and horses, doesn't he?'

'Did you like that boy who came with him?'

'The one with red hair? That's Hugh Dawson, the one who never talks at all. At least he doesn't to me; I've met him before at other parties. He just stands around and looks. All sort of mysterious and odd. Can't make him out really, when he looks at you you're never sure he sees you, are you?'

Heather blushed. She had not found him like that.

'I had the supper dance with him.'

'*No!* Honestly? Did you really? Do tell – did he talk at all? I mean did he talk at *all*?'

'Yes, a bit.'

He was the boy who had watched her mouthing the word nonchalant, and for the first five silent minutes of the dance, Heather was in an agony of doubt as to whether to pretend she hadn't noticed him staring at her or whether to plunge into an explanation of why she had been talking to herself.

'You were talking to yourself before we were introduced,' he said finally, in a voice full of disinterest. 'I was trying to imagine what you were saying.'

In spite of her efforts to have prepared an answer, Heather felt her blush rise right up from her shoulders, through her hair to the very top of her head.

'I recite poetry when I'm nervous,' she lied. 'I didn't seem to see anyone I knew when I came in so I started reciting poetry. "At Flores in the Azores, Sir Richard Grenville lay, and a pinnace like a fluttered bird came flying from far away." '

His eyes brightened and he gave a short laugh.

' "I would count myself the coward if I left them, my Lord Howard, to these inquisition dogs and the devil-doms of Spain." I don't know the middle bits any more.'

'How funny, those are just the same bits that I remember. Do you know "Time was when meadow, grove and stream, the earth and every common sight to me did seem apparelled in celestial light"'?'

' "The glory and the freshness of a dream," ' he said.

'Yes and then there's that nice bit, "It is not now as it hath been of yore . . ." '

' "Turn wheresoe'er I may . . ." '

' "The things which I have seen I now can see no more." It's so frightfully true, isn't it? I mean things do seem so absolutely different when you're grown up.'

'So utterly ordinary, don't they?'

'Absolutely.'

They scarcely noticed what they ate or drank at supper because of the pleasure of the combined recitations. They managed almost all 'The Ancient Mariner' and 'Kubla Khan', and snatches of Wordsworth and Milton, but by the time the band started to play again they were becoming a little flippant with Kipling and A. A. Milne.

'I wrote some rather good limericks the other day,' Heather said.

'Oh go on, do tell . . .'

'Well it's really got to be written down because of the spelling but – There was a young lady of Chiswick, Who flatly refused to take phiswick (p.h.i.s.w.i.c.k. you know), When 'twas forced down her throat, She put on her coat, And said, "Now I shall go out and biswick." '

They collapsed together into helpless laughter. Heather's chin dug into his shoulder and she tripped over his feet.

'Oh God – that's frightfully good. Let's sit this one out, shall we? We're making a ghastly spectacle of ourselves on the dance floor.'

Still laughing, they found a vacant stair and Heather realized with a sense of acute pride that she had cut someone's dance without actually noticing it. She saw her true partner trying to make out her name on his

39

programme and then looking anxiously round to find her.

She put her head down on Hugh's lap. 'Hide me, oh my great redeemer,' she said. 'I should be dancing with that wandering boy over there.'

Hugh took the folded handkerchief from his breast pocket and spread it over her head. 'Safe in the arms of Jesus,' he said. 'Your head is now completely buried in sand, no one would ever dream that you were here.'

But when she sat up again, there was suddenly nothing to talk about and nothing seemed remotely funny any more. There was a long, embarrassed silence between them, until he finally said, 'I'm frightfully sorry, but I just can't cut the next dance. It's ... it's ...'

'Nor can I. But it was really awfully nice. Thanks awfully.'

She ran down the stairs into the hall, looking expectantly round as if searching for someone. There was no name on her programme for that dance, so as soon as she was sure that Hugh had moved off on to the floor with his next partner, she walked purposefully back up the stairs smiling what she hoped was a radiant, confident smile and tried the door of the lavatory, which was locked.

Swinging the programme round on her wrist and humming a tuneless little tune, she wandered slowly back into the bedroom where coats and cloaks were hung on racks and piled on the bed and there were pink shaded lights on the dressing table. She saw with consternation that a loop of hair had somehow taken on an absurd angle. So, she had been looking ridiculous all this time. She licked the palm of her hand and smoothed it down, untangled the chain that hung her bag on her arm from the silk string of her programme and took out her powder compact. Her face looked very

40

shiny and ugly, and her spirits drooped.

After a measured period of time she descended the stairs with what she hoped was a gracious dignity and saw her next partner approaching her, rather gloomily she imagined.

'Ours, I believe?'

He was fat and his hair was straight and greasy. He came up to her shoulder. Not at all attractive, but he can't help that, Heather reminded herself; mustn't hold that against him because I myself am tall, thin and very unattractive. They moved off among the other dancers.

'The first part of the party has been tremendous fun, hasn't it?' she said defensively and a little shrilly. 'My last partner and I didn't have much to talk about so we quoted poetry at each other all through supper. I can't begin to explain how much fun it was because we knew all the same things and so it was a sort of literary communication, if you see what I mean. But then I don't suppose you do, do you?' She pulled back and looked into the young man's face. There was an expression of incredulous fear showing.

'Well, I . . .'

'No, of course you don't – why should you? I mean, if I said "Time was when meadow, grove and stream . . ." ' She looked at him again. No, no. It would never work a second time. 'But I do find conversation difficult because I seem to have absolutely nothing to talk about, even though I am sixteen years old – nearly seventeen, in fact – so should at least have learned some of the social graces by now my mother says. And I do realize that I am not at all sexy either, so we can't even fall back on that.'

He grasped quickly at something he could recognize.

'Who says you're not sexy?'

Heather glanced at him in astonishment. 'Well, no

one; but then no one has said I am, so I thought . . .'

'I think you are.' And he tightened his arm round her waist.

'That's nice,' Heather said, feeling a rising tide of excitement. 'I like that.'

'So do I,' he said into her ear so that his voice sounded loud and breathy.

'Hot breath of desire, stifling mind with its all-engulfing fire,' Heather mused silently, and immediately saw herself on a tigerskin rug in front of a blazing fire, cool and calm in the midst of a sea of passion.

He removed his mouth from her ear. 'Can't we sit this one out somewhere?'

The passion evaporated and of course there was nowhere very private, but she enjoyed the kisses behind the library door. They were a very good substitute for conversation.

'I like sex,' she told her partner as they returned to the dance floor, and wondered what it would be like to be married to someone who was fat and had greasy brown hair. But there was still nothing much to talk about.

When Louise pressed her after the dance concerning Hugh Dawson, Heather was rather at a loss as to what to say. Louise obviously had such a very different idea about him so that she felt her own impression must somehow be faulty.

'He's never talked to me,' Louise said, 'not even when he danced with me. He just puts his name down on your programme and looks terribly miserable, as though he's thinking of a dead dog or something, and then he just never *talks*. Sort of makes me go all quisby really. But didn't I see you two positively shrieking with laughter at one point? I couldn't believe it.'

Heather thought for a moment or two, wondering

42

whether she could pass off the idea that he had found her conversation both stimulating and witty, but finally decided that it was better to be honest with Louise; she would never be able to keep up a lie.

'We were reciting poetry.'

'You were *what*?'

'Reciting poetry.' She suddenly exploded into a shout of laughter. 'It was so *funny*, you can't imagine, he knew just all the poems I knew. You know, the ones Miss Beadle taught me. She was a bit mad because she didn't know anything except poetry and she just got me to learn yards and yards of it.'

Lovely Miss Beadle, she thought, and remembered the time they had lain in the long grass beside a stream and she had heard *La Belle Dame sans Merci* for the first time. She had been very much in love with Miss Beadle.

'You and your governesses,' said Louise. 'I wish you could have come to school with me. I'm leaving at the end of the summer and being sent to Paris to be finished.'

'Mummy won't even let me do that now. She's decided that she can't spare me after all. Isn't it silly? Though I wouldn't really want to go, much too frightened. It's all right for you having been away to school, you'd know how to behave with everyone. I wouldn't.'

'Oh rot, of course you would.'

Heather knew that she was wrong, but there was no sense in making an issue of it, so she switched her thoughts from failure and the conversation to surer ground.

'It was an absolutely divine dance.'

'It *was* rather marvellous, wasn't it? Specially for me because your own parties are always best, aren't they?' Heather could not imagine having her own party. Who would she ask? 'Did you see the person I had the supper

43

dance with? He's an absolute angel you know; I'm quite in love with him and I think he is with me a bit.'

'I just don't know what being in love is, I can't really imagine I shall fall in love with anyone. I mean what's it like? Is it like having a crush on people? I had a crush on Miss Beadle, that's why I know so much poetry. Is it like that?'

'Exactly like that; you just feel above yourself the whole time. It's – oh, I don't know, but it's pretty heavenly.'

'That fat boy, I can't remember his name, rather awful really, he kissed me behind the library door.'

Louise giggled. 'Oh he *always* does that, but he really is a bit addled, don't you think? I just can't imagine anyone being in love with *him*, can you?'

Heather felt the heat rising in her face. She had not been kissed before. 'Absolutely *not*,' she said, remembering the excitement of the moment. 'But he does kiss quite well.'

'What, properly you mean?'

Heather was nonplussed. 'Absolutely,' she said. 'What about your one?'

'Divinely and he kisses you just everywhere too.'

'What *everywhere*?'

The idea was preposterous, and Louise exploded with laughter. 'Well not *everywhere* you idiot, but quite far down your neck.'

'*Really*? Will you marry him?'

'*I* don't know; I mean, he may not ask me.'

'Wouldn't it be awful if no one asked you. Just think, supposing you never met anyone who liked you enough to ask you.'

'Or if you never met anyone you liked enough to say yes to.'

Heather paused to consider the possibility of such an unlikely situation. 'I think I would say yes to anybody if I'm not married by the time I'm twenty-five.'

'What sort of a person do you want?'

Heather put her chin on her hands and stared into the fire. Louise's bedroom was so cosy with that fire. Heather only had a gas fire in her bedroom, but sometimes she stayed with Louise, and the winter evenings as they lay in bed talking before they went to sleep were magical times she would remember for the rest of her life. The gentle hissing and crackling of the flames, the orange light flickering across the ceiling, it was full of mysterious unreality.

'Tall,' she said, 'but not terribly good-looking, with fair hair; and he'll be the most marvellous pianist and be very good at dancing. He'll be very quiet and rather shy, and he'll play to me in the winter evenings. He'll be about five years older than me and he'll be frightfully kind and simply adore me.'

'Why not good-looking?'

'That would be too good to be true, wouldn't it? And anyway, the good-looking ones are usually so pleased with themselves because everyone's after them and you could easily lose them when they got tired of you.'

She rolled over on her back and watched the fire patterns on the ceiling. How beautiful they were.

'We won't have much money,' she said, 'but enough to have a little cottage in the country somewhere which will be very modern inside and I shall have two maids and a gardener, but we'll drive our own car. I shall have four children, two boys and two girls. Twin boys first and then about two years later a girl and eighteen months later another girl. I shall call the boys Stuart Mark and Howard Charles and the girls Cora Clare and Cherry April.'

'Ugh,' said Louise. 'How revolting. I shall call my children good solid English names like George and William.'

45

Heather let out a shriek of laughter. 'Oh Louise, you *can't* – not George! I mean you might as well say Algernon or Sebastian or something! And I suppose you'll call the girls Matilda or Emma?'

Louise threw a pillow at her, and the coal in the fire shifted itself and fell into new positions, with red caverns forming themselves in the changing pattern. The flames died and the ceiling glowed in a wavering, fiery sea of orange.

'What's going to happen I wonder; where will we be in twenty years?'

The ceiling became suddenly ominous, and Heather turned over and laid her cheek on the pillow. 'It's a bit frightening, isn't it?'

'I'm not frightened,' Louise said. 'We shall both be respectable married ladies with lots of lovely children and dashing, splendid husbands. Can't see what there is to be frightened of in that.'

'Yes, but supposing it doesn't happen like that. Suppose nobody does ask us.'

'Then we'll just have to wait for Leap Year and ask them, that's all.'

pride and joy of our dearest mother. Your way is clear, God has given you good brains, the future lies with you.'

'You must stand first in I.C.S. examination in order to get best possible job on your return,' his second brother added, 'and at the same time sit for engineering degree so that no stone is left unturned and you have advantage in more than one field.'

They spoke in their mother tongue of Kannada with the Western phrases or words added in English. Mohendra wagged his head from side to side. 'Indeed indeed,' he sobbed, 'can I ever forget the sacrifice that all have made for me to give me this chance? Never fear brothers, I have the most strong realization of my great responsibilities and my even greater indebtedness towards all of you for offering this great chance. I will not let you down, this I promise you. I am filled with the most excellent resolution to achieve and with God's help I will grasp my opportunity with both hands.'

England he found to be cold, strange and unfriendly. Through Indian connections from home he found digs in Shepherds Bush with an amiable, if limited, English couple with two adult daughters. He and another Indian student, Ram Seth, occupied the two attic rooms which were small and cheerless. But I will not complain, he wrote in his diary, for these stringent conditions are merely ordeals to be borne with fortitude and patience, the better to test out and build up the character. Unfortunately, the family in which I am living here is more of a low class than of a high or aristocratic one, so the company I have to mix with is not so propitious to me. Doesn't matter; at least it is better than a boarding house. I must try to use these people to my benefit and advantage. I must impose my solidity and character on each of them and keep in my mind the many warnings I have received from home about the habits of the English people as a whole.

He talked occasionally with Ram Seth in the next room, but insisted that their conversation should be in English and not Hindi.

'I have to improve my hand in English language,' he said, 'and learn to speak fluently with all the idioms and turns of phrase so popular over here. I wish to make myself very perfect in this way.'

'You are indeed perfectionist, my friend,' Ram Seth told him. 'For me, I will learn enough to get by and that is all. As long as I know all engineering terms for my exam, then that is enough.'

'But do you not see,' Mohendra said, 'that there is already bias against Indian getting really good job in any profession? We have to beat the Englishman at his own game if we are to succeed.'

'I do not have your ambition nor your good brains,' Ram Seth replied. 'I shall be very content to serve my country by being good engineer.'

Too easy going, these people, Mohendra thought, they will accept second fiddle role too meekly. What hope of ousting British rulers while this attitude exists?

As time went on, he found two things constantly getting in the way of his studies. One was politics and the other was women. In spite of several timetables which he drew up for himself regularly, and solemn vows which he enumerated in his diary, there seemed less and less time at his disposal for solid study. The first I.C.S. exam came and went before he had finished even half the necessary reading or attended a quarter of the obligatory lectures. On the engineering side he discovered that he had first to pass elementary exams in physics and chemistry for which he had not been prepared, imagining that the letters of recommendation from his Indian professors would be enough proof of his ability. He was incensed by these petty rules and regulations.

'Such a waste of time,' he told Seth, 'when so many important things are happening all round us, so much to be done in the world. We should take full advantage of being in the centre of everything. To hear the views of these writers and politicians first hand is very worth-while and to discuss with them is most important.'

Seth was flattered to be in the company of such an eminent intellectual, but realizing that his own mental capacity was not in the same class, he was careful to prepare for his particular exams and pass them regularly without too much difficulty.

'I cannot take them this time,' Mohendra told him, 'because I have not had the time to do proper preparation in order to stand first. To be less successful would be a shame for my family.'

Seth was glad that he had no such handicap to contend with. It made life a great deal easier.

Mohendra considered Seth's attitude to sex and women very lax and immoral. 'You seem to have adopted the Western lack of morality,' he scolded. 'Can you not see what a waste of time and energy it all is? Nearly every night with a different woman – such degradation and low living with these worthless trollops. Don't think I don't understand these baser appetites of life or that I do not feel them myself. Of course I do, but I try to treat these necessary forays as a satiating of an appetite rather than an enjoyable pastime.'

'English girls are good for sex,' he told Seth, 'and many of them have excellent brains and are anxious to learn, but they are not gentle and pliant as our Indian girls are. I cannot imagine one single one giving herself completely to her husband as our wives do. They do not have that wonderful selfless quality of Indian womanhood.'

'Good for mistress,' Seth agreed, 'but impossible as

wife. Thank Gods I have a good girl waiting for marriage next year. My parents found her some two years back and she fulfils all the most important stipulations. We were very lucky.'

'You have seen her?'

'Oh yes, I went there to meet the family. We are not old-fashioned; if I had not liked we might have called the whole thing off. When will be your marriage year?'

'Oh, marriage. I am not yet ready for that. So much to be done first, I must not waste opportunities. And in any case the girl they have chosen for me is not congenial. She is very dark and does not have sufficient education. Without education these girls cannot be true companions.'

That evening, he wrote in his diary: 'Marriage' and underlined it. He considered a moment or two before continuing, then –

I am thinking of when I should marry and what should be my views of conjugal life. The following are a few jottings which are shaped by both principles and the likes:

(i) Co-habitation, for its own sake, is the last consideration in choosing a mate, and I don't like to have more than two daughters and two sons.

(ii) Sanitary rules should be heeded to. The consort I would like should be three to four years younger (nor more younger because then education is incomplete or not up to standard; nor any more aged becaused I don't like elder mate apart from other considerations). She must be perfectly healthy and cheerful; I don't want to outline the beauty of such a girl, yet she must be the golden mean, rather thick than thin, middle height, always gay. Not only clean but liking cleanliness.

(iii) Moral considerations, which include religious ones, are fundamental. I don't at all like English type where humbug of mistaken equality discards the

51

sanctity of married life. This, and similar things compel me to choose a mate in my own country; even the Mohammedan girl is excluded on account of different range of ideas, angle of vision, outlook etc., which are essential to lead the couple in the same groove. Indian womanhood as it was, and not as it is now, is preferred.

(iv) Intellectual demands from the girl are Culture, Art and Taste. So judging from the present circumstances in my country, I must choose a girl from Matric upwards. She must always be studious and anxious to know more of the world and other things, grasping many subjects, reading a lot of books on social and political questions of the country; trying to contribute her share to the amelioration of the Nation by writing articles and taking part in public activities. If I come home from outside, she must tease me with a volley of religious and philosophical questions and intricacies. She must be a good housekeeper, and without herself doing anything, should be able to manage things at home by her timely reserve, smiles and familiarity, so that peace and calm should reign in the household.

I have still many things to consider before I choose a suitable consort; but I cannot relate them now on account of the pressing time. This is not at all an 'impracticable' ideal. Of course, if I don't get such a girl in my community I shall have no hesitation in seeking her from another. I have no love with Brahmin girls somehow or other. I will, if it be necessary, try to find one from Poona side. Marriage is essentially a joining of hearts, a wedlock of souls. In the hearts there are no barriers of Religions. God is omnipresent. If I don't get a girl to the Standard or approximating this standard, I would rather remain a bachelor (I *can* remain a bachelor though I don't advocate it as a principle, for I have a kind and soft heart which seeks and finds pleasure in the company of friends and relatives) than marry a girl whom I don't like. Unequal wheels hinder the progress of a carriage and sometimes stop it completely.

As for dowry system, it is not a condition of marriage at all. Its origin is different altogether and cannot justify its being continued now. Still, the dowry can be viewed as a compensating element, and then it might be justifiable. If the girl has some social flaw or other, she might be very dark or very thin or in some other way not very presentable, perhaps ill-educated or sickly. But for me, I would rather have no dowry at all than have to accept any of these disadvantages.

But with the passage of time he found himself becoming more and more obsessed, not only with the appetite, but with the girls themselves who were so plentiful and so available. After trying to limit himself to the occasional but regular use of prostitutes, he found himself becoming increasingly attracted to the more intellectual and independent type of girl he was now meeting every day. He enjoyed the respect they showed to him, and the way they listened to and argued with his theories. They were so ignorant in Indian philosophy and Indian art but so eager to learn. He was pleased to enlighten them and complimented by the fact that they all seemed noticeably attracted to him. At the same time he fought a losing battle against becoming too involved.

He learned the subtleties of love-making by slow degrees over the ensuing months which extended into years. Examination times came and went and still there seemed more crucial books to read, more immediate discussions to take part in and more vital articles to write. His own convictions on political theory formed themselves round his almost continuous presence in the reading room of the British Museum and in his arguments and discussions with groups of socially conscious students over endless cups of tea or coffee. And still the examination times came and went.

Almost imperceptibly, it seemed, the Indian family ceased to support him. He railed a little at their short-sighted lack of faith, but after a while he stopped writing his excuses – in fact he stopped writing at all. This omission stayed with him as a shrouded part of his existence which he did not like to think about. It surfaced occasionally and caused him great and oppressive suffering. Never mind, one day he would be far greater than the tuppeny ha'penny civil servant or engineer they had hoped for. He would repay the debt and fulfil the ambition one hundredfold before very long. They would be proud enough of him then.

Meanwhile he had to exist on what he could beg, borrow or, with luck, even earn from writing political articles and pamphlets, pawning anything of value he owned, selling books borrowed from libraries or any other source or, best of all, living with a congenial person of either sex who would support him for any length of time.

After all, Engels supported Marx didn't he? There was no shame in it. It could even be considered a privilege.

5 Anything for the Freezing Indian?

Heather and Mohendra met in 1941. Looking back on it, the extraordinary business of growing up in the years before then seemed like a dream to Heather. A crowded and excited dream concentrated on enjoying anything and everything life had to offer. While Louise was sent to the Monkey Club in London to add domestic polish to the Parisian finish, for Heather it was private art lessons in the studio of a member of the local art society.

'Couldn't I go to a proper art school?' she asked, but Sylvia was adamant.

'While we can pay for private lessons for you, darling, I can't see why you'd want to take your chance among hundreds of others at some overcrowded art school. And anyway, all the places near to here have a dreadful reputation. I mean just anyone can go there. Miss Huntsman is a dear lady and she does the most exquisite little watercolours. Her flower paintings are some of the prettiest I have seen, which was why I chose her for you, seeing how fond you are of painting flowers. Why, you might start to sell some one of these days, and be able to keep me in my old age.' Heather joined in the daughter.

There were plenty of things to enjoy in that dream period before the war, and Heather and Louise both set about enjoying them. It was like a continuous party –

as long as they didn't read the papers or get involved in political discussions.

'I feel very ineffectual when I listen in to the news sometimes,' Heather said. 'I mean it's all so inevitable, isn't it?'

'It's not as if we could really have any influence,' Louise agreed. 'It's as though things are being arranged by everybody else and you just have to sit back and trust them.'

'I *hate* politics, everything is hopeless when you start to think about it.'

'Exactly.'

But these were little sombre moments in between the tennis parties and the cocktail parties and the dances. Unwelcome thoughts flickering through the Busby Berkeley sets and the Fred Astaire songs. Something there and yet not there, which could, with sufficient determination, be swept under the carpet and dismissed from the mind by thoughts of long holidays in the sun, or visits to Wimbledon, or the Eton and Harrow match, or the Chelsea Flower Show.

It was only after the Munich crisis in 1938, and the digging of air raid shelters in Hyde Park, that these dark thoughts refused to go away – even though Chamberlain had waved his piece of paper at them. When war broke out, the Joneses sold their Rolls cheaply, to aid the war effort, but kept the Austin and the Hillman Minx, and hoped that the chauffeur would not be called up. Malcolm and Bobbie joined up at once, and were both officers in the London Scottish regiment, while Sylvia became deeply involved with the Women's Voluntary Service organization.

'Doing my tiny bit,' she said, 'to help those poor dear darlings overseas.' She cut and buttered bread at a local forces' canteen for troops billeted in and around Slough.

'Salmon or tomato we give them, but you wouldn't believe how mean that Mrs Page from Fulmer is. I can't tell you how mean. But I always thought she had a mean look, didn't you? People with such narrow noses are always mean. Their noses always look as if they'd blown them so often that they'd pinched their nostrils in for ever, don't you think?' She pealed with laughter. 'She actually said the other day that Mrs Hamilton Jones must think our canteen was made of margarine and salmon the way she piled it on the bread! Not to me, of course, not to my face, but it got back to me naturally, so I put it on extra thick that evening, just to show her. Fancy her begrudging our brave boys anything! I suppose she was brought up on bread and scrape herself and just can't rise above it. You feel sorry for such people, don't you? I mean to say, if you can't be generous *now*, then when can you? Don't you agree with me Robert?'

Robert looked up with a slight start. 'Yes – er – well not exactly *agree* with you, darling. There is a thing called rationing, and if there isn't enough . . .'

'Oh, blow rationing! I would give all, *all* my coupons to help the war effort if one dear soldier could eat the better for it.'

Heather looked at Sylvia and wondered how she could ever have once considered her to be right about everything.

'Oh Mummy, you're so silly,' she said.

Sylvia's eyes brimmed with tears. 'That's not kind, Heather. Not at all kind.' She put down her knitting and began to search in her bag for a handkerchief. 'You never used to be unkind. The sweetest wee girl you were, never could I say that you were unkind. You've changed so much lately, and it's not one bit for the better. More than a year into the war and still no war work. It's not natural. I wish you would come with me

57

one evening and see what a grand job the WVS are doing. Perhaps you'd be inspired to join us instead of mooning about doing nothing to help the country in its need.'

'They'll call me up soon enough when they want me,' Heather said gloomily. She felt desolated by the horror of the war and the kind of jolly bonhomie which was showing itself among so many people. As far as her own feelings were concerned, she felt a kind of unreasoning terror as to what might happen and found herself paralysed into a slough of non-activity. All she wanted to do was to go for long, lonely walks, sit by herself somewhere out under the sky where no one could see and draw interminably. There was a dark chasm ahead and seemingly no way to avoid it, but the discipline of the meticulous draughtsmanship helped to fill in the fearful blankness. Sometimes she sat in her room where ideas for poetry would fill her mind and she would paint black and grey and white ink shapes round the words.

When Louise got married in the March of 1941 to one of the many young men who had always seemed to surround her, Heather felt her isolation was complete. There was no longer anyone with whom she could share her surface layer.

'I shall miss you horribly.'

'Oh rot, there are masses of people around and you'll probably get swept up into some fearfully exciting and important war job before very long.'

'But you're the only one I've ever been really able to talk to. Now I've got no one. You're so lucky to be getting married so that you'll never be on your own again.'

She compressed her lips together in an agony of confusion. Louise's fiancé might be going to the war. He might get killed. How tactless she was. But Louise was somehow shielded by her immediate happiness, it seemed to allow no room for doubt.

'Yes I *am* lucky, aren't I? Can't really believe it all. To have found somebody so perfect as Johnnie, just an amazing piece of luck really. I mean it's all so suitable, isn't it? Having the same sort of ideas and everything. He's so absolutely right for me and he gets on frightfully well with the family. And because he farms his own land up in Yorkshire he might not even get called up because food's so important. But of course he's dead keen to go.'

Heather suddenly allowed herself to cry. 'Oh it's all so awful you going and me being left. I'm never going to get married. I mean I just can't seem to like people enough, or mostly the right ones don't like me.'

'But Het you have millions of affairs.'

'Affairs, yes. They're such *fun*, and every time I think to myself this might be the one, but it never is.'

'But you haven't actually *done* it yet have you?'

'Oh no. I want to keep that for the wedding night, like you. I tell them all, right at the start, that I'm a virgin and all the English men behave terribly well and don't try. A Swede once told me that I was unnatural and left me flat. But as soon as anyone starts getting a bit het up I clam up like a limpet because I'm so petrified of pain and babies and everything.'

'I'm pretty petrified myself.'

'But it *must* be easier when you're married because of not having to worry about being found out and having enough time and the right place. It must be heaven then I should think.'

'I suppose so. Did you ever have an affair with that Hugh Dawson?'

'No, of course I didn't. I've hardly seen him since your dance all those years ago, even though he lives so near.'

'He's sort of dropped out of our set, hasn't he?'

'I sometimes see him at cocktail parties but he always looks as though he disapproves of me. Specially when I'm getting off with someone.'

'Probably wants you himself but too shy to approach.'

'Absolutely not, I've given him my best come hither looks and he doesn't respond at all.'

The depression lifted and they both laughed, but Heather nevertheless felt as though a prop was being removed, and that her own life was now balanced precariously over the black crevasse.

'I bet I'll be an old maid,' she said, as she thought sadly about the reasons for her inability to attract men like Johnnie.

'Oh piffle!' Louise laughed uneasily. 'Things are uncertain for everyone just now. I mean, even though I was lucky enough to find Johnnie, one can never be sure of anything with this war on, can one? All the separations and things.' Her voice wavered. 'You will come and stay with me, won't you?'

Heather hugged her and they both cried a little because the obvious was out in the open. It would never be the same again.

Louise was swept up in the trappings of a white wedding in the country church, and Heather was bridesmaid, dressed in corn-coloured silk with a wreath of jonquils, and the job of keeping Louise's four sisters and brother in order during the service. She watched this lifetime friend being borne away in a gust of kisses and cheers to a separate life, far removed from the one they had known together.

The morning after the wedding, reaction to the previous day's excitement drowned her, and Heather woke slowly, feeling sick from the champagne and a sense of doom. She dragged herself out of bed and drew back the curtains. The March day was breathless, and her spirits revived at once. The sound of a singing thrush was so uplifting that she found it impossible not to be uplifted. Tomorrow was out there, waiting to be grasped, and she dressed in a rush and ran downstairs, colliding with Sylvia on the way.

'Oh my word, whatever's the matter? I thought you were asleep after all that excitement. Where are you off to in such a hurry?'

'Just out,' Heather called back over her shoulder. 'It's so beautiful out there, I just can't waste it.'

'But what about your breakfast?' Sylvia had been looking forward to a chat about the wedding; Robert was so unresponsive in the mornings and it had been such a grand affair. So many people there. If only Heather . . .

'You're so boisterous, pet,' she said in an aggrieved tone, but the front door slammed and she was gone. Sylvia turned, and made her way down the stairs again. What a let-down after the exhilaration of yesterday.

Heather, meanwhile, bounded across the lawn in front of the house and out through the gate. She felt the need to throw off any sort of restriction and any thoughts of yesterday. A clean sweep, off with the old and on with the new. The triteness made her laugh and she slowed down, breathless, to a long, fast stride up the lane, into the field and on up the ridge of the gentle slope towards the small spinney of bare trees on top. She wished it were higher; Buckinghamshire was such an enclosed county, too gentle. She felt she needed space today, and vistas.

She reached the trees and sat down at the edge of the spinney looking down the slope into English countryside. The smell of things around her produced a surge of new excitement near the base of her spine. It was all going to be different from now on. Brave new world, she thought, brave new world, and it's wonderful. It's March, things are beginning and I can begin too. There's so much to do. Louise in her Yorkshire castle, married and settled and safe, and me down here, unmarried, unsettled and unsafe and I like it.

Lying on her back on the cold ground that the sun

was only just touching, she looked through the lace-work of twigs above her. Words raced through her head, jumbling in torrents like shingle under a wave, queuing up, waiting to be put into poetry. She felt drunk with the abundance. But before it could really take hold clouds came and she sat up in the ordinary world and saw it was time for lunch. One couldn't be late for lunch, it wasn't done.

She started to walk quickly and awkwardly down the hill again. A return to restriction and the ordinariness of every day. A pulling on of a tight jumper. But slow down a little, no need to get there before it was absolutely necessary. Walk slowly back into the dull security of every day.

She slowed down to a disconsolate amble, slipping on stones and turning her ankle over every now and then. Bringing her mind back to uncomfortable things like reality. Oh to be certain and sure of things, like Louise, she thought. To be able to do the right thing, like she does. All I can do is talk nonsense incessantly when I'm shy, and nobody likes that.

Deep in her melancholy soliloquy, she was suddenly riveted with the shock of seeing Hugh Dawson in the distance. He was approaching her through the trees of a small wood and she stopped abruptly, looking round for escape, even considering hiding behind a tree. But he must have seen me, she thought, I can't do that, and to turn aside would be too obvious. Her mind switched back to the sharp anxiety of Louise's dance all those myriad years ago. This was a stranger approaching her. He's a man now, she thought, not a boy, and yet I don't seem to have moved at all. Still the same awkward idiot I was then without a sensible word to say for myself. I'll just have to say hallo and hope he doesn't stop. Must seem natural. Nonchalant was the word, it came bubbling up from her memory with a burst of laughter.

She still didn't know how to pronounce it. She started to walk again. Needn't say more than that. Just smile and say hello. Stop being so silly.

Embarrassment increased with every step. When should she start smiling? Should she pretend not to see him until the last moment? A long drawn out smile would be much too difficult to maintain. But where to look in the meantime? Up in the air as though bird-watching? She kept her eyes on her shoes.

'Hallo,' he said, stopping exactly in front of her.

She looked up with a bright, surprised smile, 'Hal*lo*' she said, as though astonished to see him, and there was an intense silence.

'Haven't seen you for ages,' he said at last. 'Thought you must have been swept up in the war effort or something.'

'No, I haven't.' Why wasn't he in uniform? Did one ask? Or was that prying?

'So what have you been doing all this time?'

Nothing. Nothing at all, but you couldn't say that could you? 'Just sort of – sort of – waiting around, really. I mean – sort of – '

'Marking time?' He smiled very broadly and she was conscious he was laughing at her. Strangely, though, it didn't seem to matter, and she found herself inclined to laugh right back at him.

'I've done quite a bit of drawing,' she said.

'You have? I never knew you drew. Thought it was only poetry.'

'Oh that – that was just one of my governesses. The next one got me into drawing.'

'I was just going to Stoke Poges to draw tombstones myself,' he said. 'Why don't you come too? We could draw together.'

Heather's embarrassment evaporated. 'I'd love to come! I used to go there a lot when I was young – because of liking Gray's Elegy you see.' But why should he see? He was no longer a school boy and he would hardly remember the encounter at Louise's dance.

'And did the curfew toll the knell of parting day?' he said. 'That was one of the very few we didn't get on to at Louise's dance, wasn't it?'

'And I actually think it's one of the best, don't you?' This was no stranger; Heather's relief liberated her tongue. 'So sort of lugubrious in the nicest possible way. I mean what could be nicer than "The ploughman homeward plods his weary way, and leaves the world to darkness and to me" unless it's "Save where the beetle wheels his droning flight, and drowsy tinklings lull the distant folds". I just *love* it, and I haven't been back to the churchyard for years so it would be sort of like stepping back in time and I absolutely love that too, don't you?' Why can't I shut up? she thought. Are there no degrees between silence and verbal diarrhoea? And she snapped her mouth shut with determination.

'How nice.' Hugh sounded as though he would really enjoy her company, and they walked through the turned earth of the spring field where larks were beginning to rise and soar into their new spring songs.

'And you?' Heather ventured. 'Have you been called up?'

'They tried to, but I'm C3. Had rheumatic fever when I was a child. Father can't forgive me for that. He wanted me to volunteer as cannon-fodder as soon as I left school.'

'But you didn't?'

'No, I got a scholarship to the Slade and have just finished my three years there.'

Heather was impressed. Both by the fact that he had defied his parents and won a scholarship and that he had had rheumatic fever. He sounded so in charge of

himself and his own destiny. She had only had thing[s]
like chicken pox and measles, was completely dominated by her parents and seemed to have no idea what
she was doing with her life.

'What will happen to you now?' she asked.

Hugh shrugged. 'Don't know really. The powers that
be are trying to get me into some respectable war work,
but I shall resist to the death. All I do know is that I
just have to paint and that I can't live at home, so
tomorrow I'm going up to London to stay in a friend's
studio in Fulham in order to paint and soak up culture
for a bit. You could come and visit me and we could do it
together.'

'But what about the bombs? And hasn't culture gone
underground for the duration?'

'Blow the bombs, you could get killed anywhere. And
there's quite a bit of culture left above ground. Exhibitions and concerts and things. And above all there are
people to talk to.'

'It sounds wonderful. I wish I could make decisions
and follow them up like you seem to do.'

'Well you could.'

'No I couldn't. I am incapable of making my own
decisions. I have to be told what to do, otherwise I can't
function.'

'Right. Well, open that gate for me this minute.'

She laughed, and pushed open the gate into the
churchyard. It looked much bleaker than she remembered it. Was this really where she and Miss Beadle had
sat, deep in the long, waving grass, barely visible to
each other through the feather fronds? It was too early
for the cow parsley and the willow herb to mask the
hard edges of the grey tombs. No daisies, no butter-
cups, no poppies; no two ways of looking at it, just cold
statements of dead facts.

'It's beautiful, isn't it?' Hugh said.

...hinking – I mean, it looks so different in

...e it lush,' said Hugh, and Heather at
...inadequate and childish. She liked it

...t always,' she said defensively.

Hugh bent down to set his pad and pencils on a stone,
and when he stood up she saw that his face was a deep
red. Was he blushing? But why? A wave of compassion
swept through her; there was nothing she didn't know
about the agonies of blushing. But perhaps it was just
because he had been bending down.

'I didn't mean to criticize you,' he said.

'Oh no, I know.' She rushed in to deny that she was in
any way upset. 'I know you didn't.'

Hugh suddenly laughed. 'So now that we've both
fallen over ourselves to apologize for possibly hurting
each other's feelings, we can probably be considered to
be good friends. Are you going to draw too?'

She became panic-stricken. How could she presume
to sit down and draw with someone fresh from three
years at the Slade? 'Oh – well, I haven't any paper.
And anyway, I'm no good. I only do flowers.'

'What's good?' he said. 'And tombstones are much
easier than flowers.'

She thought it better not to argue, and instead, borrowed block and charcoal and moved off to sit opposite
a marble angel. She was filled with misgiving and
anxiety. Suppose she made a mess of it? She had only
drawn with an HB pencil before, because Miss Huntsman advised it, and she found the charcoal clumsy and
awkward at first. But it didn't take long for her to start
enjoying herself, and her enthusiasm surged up to the
surface. They both worked silently for some time. The
absorption was so complete, that she jumped violently
when he spoke over her shoulder.

'That's superb,' he said, with pronounced admiration in his voice.

She leaned back and looked with distaste at the heavy, rather messy smudges of her charcoal angel, and then round at Hugh to see if he was joking. 'It's revolting,' she said. 'I'm only good at drawing things in detail and writing poetry I don't show anyone.'

'So you do still write poetry?'

'A bit. Can't do it so well now somehow. And I've never done any painting or anything. I mean I know absolutely nothing about art with a capital A. Nor about anything else really.'

'Stop being apologetic. You don't know anything about anything because you've never moved out of your little cocoon, that's all. To carry the Elegy a lugubrious bit further, remember that "Full many a flower is born to blush unseen and waste its sweetness on the desert air." '

'Come to think of it, I do think my sweetness is just a tiny bit wasted.'

'So why don't you come up to London and see what you're missing? You could do some painting with us in the studio. We can share a model, that makes it cheaper.'

The old fear engulfed her again. This time of physical hurt. 'I should be frightened by the raids. I get terrified when I even think about it.'

'But that's just it. Thinking about it is the most frightening thing of all, like it is with everything. When you're in it, it's not the same at all, it really isn't. When you are doing something, it's not nearly so bad. Like now I've actually decided to leave home and be an artist, everything is much easier.'

'I would so like to.' The idea suddenly filled her with a sharp excitement. She saw herself striding through London dressed in fire-fighting gear. Ready for bombs;

ready for anything. 'Will you be a fire-fighter? I could help you on your night watch.'

'You're an idiot.' Hugh said it kindly. 'If there's a raid while you're up there, we'll sit under the stairs and hold hands; except that there aren't any stairs because it's a studio with just a ladder up to the gallery.'

'We could sit under the ladder.'

She was already fired with enthusiasm. The whole conversation excited her. 'I'll definitely come,' she said, and her mind churned with the new thoughts until she suddenly leaped to her feet with a scream. 'Oh my God!'

Hugh jumped to his feet as well. 'What is it? What's the matter? Did you sit on a bee?'

'It's lunch time, I forgot.'

'Does hunger usually strike you with this extraordinary intensity?'

'No you fool, but I'm *late*. Daddy will be livid.'

'Does it matter, I ask myself, if Daddy is livid?'

'Well he'll shout and Mummy's eyes will fill with tears and it will be all my fault. But I will come to London, I don't know how I'll manage it, but I will come. Give me the telephone number and the address and I'll be there. Dear Hugh, you've really made me feel that there's some hope for me after all. Why am I so *feeble*?'

'I don't think you're feeble, just dominated by the family and convention, like we all are.'

'You're not.'

'I was, but the war helped me to break free, like it could help you if you let it.'

'I don't see that being swept into the ATS would do any good. I would much rather be dominated by Mummy and Daddy than by a lady sergeant major.'

'We'll argue about it in London.'

On the spur of a sudden involuntary delight, she put

68

her arms round his neck and kissed him. 'Might do, might not,' she said, and she ran through the tombs and down the lane, full of the exhilaration of the new idea, and the belief that everything from now on might, after all, be marvellous fun.

It took time before Heather could bring herself to suggest it to the family.

Hugh's departure for London was discussed one breakfast time. Sylvia was pouring coffee.

'You know what Ethel told me yesterday?'

'Uh?' Robert reached for the marmalade.

'She said that Dawson boy – you know, only boy in the family – has defied his father and said that he intends to become an artist! Can you believe it? Poor Mrs Dawson is terribly upset, Ethel says. He's been such a disappointment to them, that boy, though the girls couldn't be nicer. Such a disaster it is, they were counting on his going into the family business. Now it means it will have to go to some nephew or other. The business must be making millions now, what with the war and everything. I mean, what is there in art nowadays? And I'm sure he'll expect his father to support him. You'd think he'd be keen to join up if he doesn't want to go into the business, but not a bit of it. I believe he's got himself mixed up with some disreputable arty crowd in London. After all his parents have done for him. Such ingratitude!'

'I'm going up to London to see him next Wednesday,' Heather said, the idea forming itself in her head as she spoke.

Robert looked up from his paper for the first time. He always managed to spread and eat his toast without ever taking his eyes from the paper.

'Going up to see him? Whatever for?'

'He's taking me round the galleries.'

'What galleries?'

69

'Art galleries. I know nothing about art, and I want to.'

'But you go to the Academy every year and Miss Beadle took you to the National Gallery twice.'

Heather laughed. 'But that was hundreds of years ago, and anyway, I want to know about now, what's happening now.'

'I can tell you what's happening now,' Robert said. 'They're producing disgraceful rubbish. You can't want to go all the way up to London to look at junk. You can see that at the nearest rubbish dump.'

'And you can't go on Wednesday,' Sylvia said, 'that's the day you take me into Slough to do the shopping.'

Heather took the train to London on the following Thursday, having first telephoned Hugh. He met her at the station.

'You just wouldn't believe the fuss,' she said. 'I might have been going to the North Pole. Mummy said that she'd worry all day in case there was a raid and that I'd got to be back by teatime.'

'But you're not going to be are you?'

'Well I . . .'

'Of course you're not going to be, because you're going to have tea with me, it's all arranged. You can catch the six something this time, and the next time you can catch the seven something so they can get used to the emancipation of their daughter by degrees. You just mustn't let yourself be manipulated you know, not any longer.'

'But you're manipulating me now.'

'Only just a little, until you learn how to manipulate yourself. First I'm going to introduce you to my friend Istvan whose studio I'm living in. He's a very excellent Hungarian painter.'

Istvan was lean and dark and fortyish, and he welcomed Heather effusively. 'Come in, come in, my darling! Coffee is on the boil, bubbling away on the hob, even if it is made of dandelions or acorns these days. And my favourite grocer found me some biscuits under the counter yesterday. A positive feast laid out for you. Hugh darling, get the mugs, the Japanese ones, dear, not the common Woolworth ones, or she might think I don't have the exquisite taste for which I am so well known.' He talked on in an endless flow, covering such various topics as war-time restrictions, air raids, Hugh, artists in London and his life in Hungary before he came to England.

'It was no use staying there, dear, I was just another of those myriad peasants who didn't know his arse from his armpit, and of course everyone disapproved of me and thought I was mad because I painted these strange and disgusting surrealist pictures instead of tilling and sowing and turning sods and things. They couldn't make me out at all so I ran away from it all and finally landed up here.'

'You don't want to believe a word,' Hugh said. 'He actually comes from an aristocratic Hungarian family with pots of money.'

'Dreadfully degenerate I am,' Istvan agreed, 'like all aristocrats. Enormously inbred and unmentionable.'

Hugh watched the first shock of the new vocabulary have its effect on Heather and saw her warm to the experience of being included in Istvan's immediate aura.

'I *love* him,' Heather said to Hugh afterwards. 'How did you get to know him? Mummy said the other day that you have got yourself mixed up with some disreputable arty lot; are there any more like him?'

'We have a lot of friends, some a bit eccentric I have to admit. Istvan is just an incredibly good painter. I've learned so much from him.'

71

'Really? Is he really a good painter? I don't understand his pictures. Why is he a good painter?'

Hugh expounded and Heather took in the words.

'I still don't altogether see, but I do like some of his things, probably for the wrong reasons. I'm still horribly uneducated, aren't I?'

'Give me a chance, we haven't started on your education proper yet. What about your poetry? Written anything good lately?'

'No, of course I haven't. I don't know what poetry is. Like I don't know what art is.' She hunched her shoulders. 'Like I don't know what anything is.'

'Come on then, let's set about your education right now.' He looked at his watch. 'Half-past eleven; the whole day is ahead of us, I have it all mapped out. I'll be your guru.'

'What's a guru?'

'Indian word for teacher, ignoramus.'

It was the first of many such expeditions. All through the summer and autumn of that year, they visited galleries, concerts and exhibitions. Sometimes they painted or drew in Istvan's studio or among the rubble of bombed London. The inhibitions began to crack. They sat for hours, alone or with others, discussing, drinking coffee, listening to records. Heather found herself in a completely new, Cinderella world, which of course was not the real world. When the clock struck twelve she would have to go back to reality, or disaster might strike.

It was late on a very cold December afternoon, when the three of them were bunched round the black studio stove, toasting bread and drinking coffee, that Heather saw Mohendra for the first time. When Istvan answered the knock at the door, she heard Mohendra say, 'Is there a crust and a coffee for the freezing Indian?'

'Come in, dear, come in. Where on earth have you been for the past epoch? You haven't begged a meal since spring. Is this a record we ask ourselves? I'm sure we can find a few crumbs, but for pity's sake don't ask me for money. I haven't a penny, and certainly not enough to keep either you or the wolf from the door. But come in and sweep up some crumbs for yourself. The dust on the floor is full of good, healthy vitamins and is guaranteed to cure night blindness so that you can see in the blackout. Heather, my dear child, this is my favourite Indian, and he is called Mohendra. He is very erudite and very pretty, but maddeningly hetero-sexual. Mohendra, dear boy, meet Heather.'

Heather shook his hand and wondered what erudite and heterosexual meant. She thought she had never seen such a superbly handsome man before. Words coursed through her mind in her attempt to describe him: aquiline, eagle, hawklike, bold, beautiful, proud paragon – *magnificent*.

'Hallo,' she said.

'I never knew Istvan and Hugh had such attractive friends,' he said, and the first overpowering impression of nobility and regality faded a fraction. There was something not quite noble in the voice and something not quite illustrious in the brilliance of the smile.

But whatever small disappointment flickered through her mind at that moment, it was dispersed during the ensuing hour or so. The cosy and lethargic conversation the three of them had been having before was transformed into a sharp and exhilarating discus-sion. Heather listened with growing interest and admi-ration to Mohendra's extraordinary flow of words. This was someone completely sure of himself, she thought, someone who was not in awe of life nor of any person in it. She was fascinated, though quite unable to join in the conversation between Mohendra and the other two, which seemed to relate to the apparently unpardonable decision of the British Government to bring India into the war without prior consultation with the Indian people. She found herself becoming indignant that such a thing could have been allowed to happen. She was so intensely interested that she forgot the time and only suddenly noticed that it was almost too late to catch her train back to Slough.

'I've got to go, I've got to go.' She ran round the studio picking up her coat, her bag, her torch. 'Where are my gloves? And my scarf?' She snatched the scarf from Hugh's hand. 'Bye – phone me soon again or I'll stagnate to death.' She kissed him, and Istvan crushed her to him in an affectionate embrace.

'Bye darling, come again very soon.'

Mohendra got up, 'I'll take you to the station,' he said. 'Which one is it? When does your train go?'

'Could you take me? That would be wonderful.' Heather felt relieved. 'It goes at 7.20 because after that it does get a bit late the other end. I have quite a way to bicycle from the station.'

'Plenty of time,' Mohendra said. 'We could almost walk it and still get there,' and together they ran out of the studio and into Fulham Road, Heather following just behind him so that he could lead the way to where he had parked his car.

'Quick,' he shouted suddenly, 'there's a bus, what a bit of luck.'

Of course he had just meant he could accompany her to the station. Silly of her to take if for granted that he had a car. Silly of her to be disappointed.

Breathless on the blacked-out bus that crawled ponderously through the traffic, she looked at her watch. 'We can't possibly make it at this rate,' she said. 'We'd better look out for a taxi.'

'Nonsense!' How had she found fault in that smile?

74

Even if it was a little over effusive, it was at the same time completely disarming. 'I promise I will get you there on time. What do they say in the scouts? Cub's honour isn't it?' and he saluted with two fingers. It was like a child making a bad joke and Heather felt embarrassed. 'Anyway, why is it so important that you should catch such an early train? We could have dinner together. You could stay the night and go tomorrow morning. Why not? I have a flat and there is room for you there.'

'No, I couldn't possibly do that. My parents are expecting me home.'

'You could phone them.'

'No I couldn't.' How to explain the impossibility? To him just a telephone call, to her the overthrowing and breaking down of an impenetrable barrier. 'They like me to get home before the bombs start if possible. So do I.'

'The bombs can start any time and I have an excellent air raid shelter in the basement under the stairs. Or we could go down the tube. It's quite jolly there I believe.'

He put his arm through hers and took her hand. 'I should like to show you my flat. It's not very grand, but I could cook you a nice curry and my bed is very comfortable.

The rush of excitement that Heather felt was overpowering. Here was no suggestion of kisses behind the door or petting in the back of the car. Here was a straightforward proposition from an overwhelmingly attractive Indian wanting to make love to her after knowing her for two short hours. Assuming that any small inconvenience could be easily overcome. Not even considering that there could be any really good reason for her to refuse. What an unbelievable situation to find herself in! It might never happen again.

75

'It's just not possible,' she said, listening to her heart beating in her ears. 'And certainly not tonight.' Leave it open just in case there was another opportunity. Don't let him go. If she got to know him better she might lose this unreasoning fear that clamped down on the excitement.

'What about tomorrow then?'

She laughed. 'No, of course not tomorrow. I don't come up to London every day.'

'But now that you've met me you could start coming up every day or you might come up tomorrow and stay, now that you have met me.'

'But I only laid eyes on you for the first time about two hours ago. I'm scarcely going to fall into bed with you at the first opportunity.'

'Why not?'

'Well, because I'm not in the habit of throwing up my life as soon as somebody suggests it.'

'Throwing up your life? I never said anything about that. What are you doing down in the country that you don't wish to throw up?'

Absolutely nothing, of course. What an awkward question. She was handling this very badly. Now that she thought about it, he hadn't even mentioned going to bed with her, just that his bed was comfortable. Suppose he was just being friendly and offering her a bed for the night? The heat rushed into her face.

'What do you do?' he said again, and she found herself with a rising panic of not knowing how to explain herself.

'Well I – I don't do anything much at the moment. I suppose I shall have to get into some sort of war work before I get called up.'

'But you will surely object conscientiously if you are called up, will you not?'

She saw the possibility of escape in the taxi that

pulled up beside the bus at the lights. 'Look, there's a taxi, I'm going to catch it.'

She jumped out of her seat and swung round the back of the bus to the taxi. 'I want to go to Paddington please.'

He was behind her and together they fell into the back seat as the traffic moved on.

'There was absolutely no need, you know,' he said. 'We could easily have got there on time. But this is nice because I can kiss you here.'

It was a long, passionate kiss which Heather found unaccountably sensuous. The fact that he was Indian added greatly to the pleasure. Why? she wondered. Just something different? Slightly wicked? Something other people didn't do? There was a sense of daring, of being special and set apart. She returned the kisses with an abandoned delight and was startled when the cab pulled up at the station.

'We're there, look, we're there.' She pulled her scarf tight and fumbled to get out. 'How much?'

'Three and nine, dear.'

Mohendra turned and shut the door while Heather searched for her purse in the semi-darkness. Why on earth *should* he pay? She had suggested the taxi. He obviously had far less money than she had.

They were there with ten minutes to spare.

'I told you, didn't I? You silly girl, wasting money like that. You should take my advice, you know. Why not stay here with me tonight? That little taste has set up a quite unquenchable desire in me.'

'I know just how you feel,' she said. 'But I can't stay tonight.'

'But you'll come back tomorrow?'

'No, I won't come back tomorrow, but I will come back. Hugh wants to take me to the London Group show where he's exhibiting.'

He made a long drawn-out clicking with his teeth and tongue. He sounded like a shocked maiden aunt.

'Not to see Hugh, to see *me*. I will take you to the London Group or the Paris Group or the Moscow Group – any group you like, but you must come and see me so that I can make love to you all day, and all night too.'

He put his arm round her as they walked up the over-crowded platform. Soldiers were everywhere, all with their arms round girls. For the first time Heather found herself included in a crowd of ordinary people doing just what everyone else was doing. When she fought her way on to the train, then squeezed herself round to lean out of the window, he pulled her forward just as the whistle blew and kissed her passionately again. As the train began to move, she detached herself in an agony of embarrassment, because she was no longer one of a crowd. All the other girls were kissing Englishmen or Frenchmen or Poles; she was kissing an Indian. She glanced round guiltily to see whether there was disapproval on the faces of the people round her. She imagined there was, and pushed her way back into the jammed corridor to hide herself a little.

But what did it matter, after all? It was not as if there was anyone there she knew, and it was good to bring a little shock into the lives of all these drab people. Anyway, what was wrong with kissing an Indian in public?

6   *You Cannot be Serious*

As Mohendra walked back from the station, it began to snow lightly, leaving melting grey blotches on the pavement and wet feathers on his hair and eyebrows. Damn this cold, he thought. I can't very well go back to Istvan's studio. Silly of me to leave like that before we'd had anything to eat, but she was very attractive; a little thin, perhaps, but so very elegant and full of warmth. He felt much in need of warmth at that moment, both inside and out. Pity she didn't stay, she was bound to have had a shilling for the gas and they could have been cosy together; could have gone out for a meal. But he rather admired her unwillingness to stay, in spite of the inconvenience to himself. Showed spirit; and her blunt way of putting it was amusing and forthright. Obviously came from a good family; well brought up.

He paused on the corner of the road and looked up towards the Boltons, where Istvan had his studio. I could borrow some bread and cheese and get her address and phone number, he thought. Help to fill the gap that Ursula has left. His emotions gave a lurch as he thought of Ursula. What a girl, but so damned obstinate. My gods but I miss her; she could easily have taken me to the States with her. I could have done so much over there, given half a chance. Much easier to get books published there and they pay so well for lectures. He made an impatient gesture with his clenched fists. What a chance wasted. Could easily have paid my way and then paid Ursula back for the fare as well. She was sometimes mean about things, she could easily have paid the fare. Much too influenced by that wretched Lesbian set. Silly girl.

He walked briskly up Gilston Road and turned into the Bolton Studios. Hugh opened the door to him.

'Hallo, did she spurn your advances then?'

'Not at all, not at all, quite the opposite in fact. But she had to get home to her Mummy.'

'Yes, she does tend to do what they tell her. Shame really, because they're not very nice, and not at all intelligent. Poor Heather, she was born into the wrong environment. She's a talented, and very sweet girl who's just beginning to realize that there's another way of life. Did you like her?'

'Yes I did, very much. Just my type if I may say so, and I want her address and phone number. Can I come in?' He began to shiver, and the smell of toast and coffee irritated the void in his stomach.

'Of course, of course, come in out of all that revolting weather, and mind you treat my sweet protégée well. I feel very responsible for her and wouldn't ever want her to get hurt.'

'What a suggestion, my dear Hugh. What do you take me for? Some sort of Don Juan?'

Hugh put his arm round Mohendra's shoulders. 'I take you for what I think you are, my dear friend, a lovable and brilliant personality who never fails to bowl us all over with his remarkable charm. Wish I knew how you do it.'

'You are a flatterer,' Mohendra's smile showed his satisfaction. The obvious admiration Hugh had for him, mingled with the warmth of the studio, the comfort of the chaotic clutter of paintings, easel, brushes and old, dirty armchairs had rather the same effect that alcohol might have done. He sank down among cushions, lengths of material and a paint-stained overall, and closed his eyes.

'This is what I call living,' he said.

Istvan brought beans on toast and a cup of cocoa. 'There you are, inveterate sponger. Eat, drink and be merry because you never know, I might not feed you again.'

'Very good of you, Istvan, to tide me over like this, but it is only temporary you know, because I am waiting for them to pay me for two articles I wrote for *Tribune*. These wretched papers have no thought for the starving millions, in spite of all their rosy idealism. You and Hugh must come round and have a real Indian curry with me as soon as I get my money. What about the day after tomorrow?'

'I would rather die, dear boy. Come to think of it, that's probably what we would do if we ate your curry.'

'Come now, that's not fair. It would be better than the stuff they serve up as curry at the British Restaurants.'

'Darling boy, you *don't* mean to say you support those gruesome national monstrosities? They may supply a cheap wartime substitute for food, but they are so alarmingly full of large English matrons dressed in green all doing a tremendous amount of good that I feel swamped whenever I walk past one. The smell emanating from them is full of rich English gravy. It's all too much.'

'It's a good cheap fill-up, nevertheless,' Hugh said. 'We can't all be rich like you.'

'True, true. I never stop thanking God for the good old Hungarian aristocracy.'

'Shame on you and down with the ruling classes; to the guillotine with the lot of you,' Mohendra said with his mouth full.

'What? And forgo those baked beans? You're such a hypocrite, you dear, time-honoured lotus-eater.'

'Me a hypocrite? But no, not at all. How can you say that? It is not at all true. Where can you say that I have ever shown this sort of characteristic? For instance . . .'

Istvan turned up the gramophone record of Beethoven's Ninth. 'La la la la . . .' he sang to the Song of Joy. '*Mohendra* will not convince me *he* is not a hypocrite,' he sang to the melody. 'But then so are all Indians.'

What stupid things this man sometimes comes out with, Mohendra thought, but he ate his beans in silence.

Heather picked up her bicycle from Slough station and started to ride back through the pitch-black night.

'It's just not safe for you to be out late these days,' Sylvia had insisted. 'Anything might happen with all these soldiers around, not to mention the bombs.'

Heather enjoyed, as a rule, the heavy blackness of the night during those cycle rides from the station, split, as they were occasionally, by the unearthly beauty of the searchlight beams. But snow had fallen heavily that evening and large drifts had built up on the country roads so that progress was slow and difficult. From the warmth and safety of the small studio group, this exhausting struggle seemed frighteningly remote.

It was an hour-and-a-half later, instead of the usual twenty minutes, that she finally put her key in the lock of the blacked-out house. The relief of walking into warmth and light reduced her to a crumpled, crying heap on the carpet.

Sylvia and Robert came out of the sitting room.

'Heather, my pet, where *have* you been? I've been frantic with worry. There, there darling, don't cry,

82

Mummy's here. But you're quite frozen – Robert, get some brandy, the child's a block of ice, no less. Out of your wet things now, sweetheart. My poor wee scone, whatever happened? I told you not to go, now, didn't I? It's just not safe up there. Look at the state of you.'

Heather's sobs turned back into hysterical giggles: the relief of the return to childhood and Mummy was mixed in her mind with the illogicality of the words that trickled on in an endless, silly stream. 'If only you would listen to Mummy, pet, instead of going gallivanting about like you do . . .' But Mummy couldn't kiss it better because she was hopelessly, childishly wrong. The danger was here, not there. Up there was warmth, freedom, fun and unbelievably exciting possibilities. Down here there were snowdrifts and smothering, all-enveloping care.

He telephoned her the next morning at quarter to nine. Mary, the old parlour-maid, stumped up the stairs slowly and knocked on Heather's door. The telephone never rang before nine.

'A gentleman on the phone for you, Miss Heather.'

'For me?' She leaped out of bed and looked underneath for her slippers. Her dressing gown was on the floor, and she ran down the stairs trying to untangle the belt and do it up.

'Hallo.'

'Good morning. How did you sleep?'

'Like a log, after nearly freezing to death in a snow drift.'

'One of the reasons I phoned you; all that snow about, I was anxious. I told you not to go back, didn't I? You'd have been much safer here with me. I didn't sleep at all well. I was very cold and lonely.'

Sylvia was almost bound to be listening on the extension. How to stop him?

'There's very deep snow out here.'

'Then come back to London, it's nearly all melted here.'

'No, I can't possibly.' But of course she could.

'Anything is possible if you make it possible. When will you come?'

'I really don't know, I'm very busy this week.'

'Doing what?'

She hesitated. 'I'm helping with the Church jumble sale.' There was a short silence. 'It's in aid of parcels for the refugees.'

'There's so much important work you could be doing up here you know, meetings to be organized, pamphlets to be written. You could be so much use up here. Please come because I want you – now.'

She felt panic engulf her. If someone had picked up the extension, they hadn't put it down yet because there had been no click.

'I'll try to come up again soon; I'll let Hugh know when I'm coming.'

'Let *me* know, I need you much more than Hugh does.'

'All right.' Anything to get him off the phone. 'All right, I'll come up very soon.'

'This week?'

'No, not this week, next week perhaps.'

'That's seven days away.'

Mary passed through the hall carrying toast and coffee into the dining room and staring straight in front of her. The gong for breakfast would go when she came back again.

'I've got to go, it's breakfast time.'

'I had mine at six o'clock. I've been working since five.'

There was absolutely no reason why she should feel at fault for not having done the same. Mary returned from the dining room and swung the gong stick. Starting softly, the sound rose to a booming crescendo before dying away.

'That's the gong, I've got to go.'

'The *gong*?'

'Yes, for breakfast.'

'All right, you silly girl, go and eat your breakfast, and think of me with every mouthful.'

She put the receiver down with relief and ran upstairs again. How much she would have enjoyed that call in privacy. As it was, she brushed her hair in a state of tense anxiety as she wondered what might be said at breakfast. Had Sylvia heard it all? Or had her father picked it up? Perhaps neither of them had, then all this worry for nothing. Hurriedly pulling on her clothes and giving herself a peremptory wash, she walked downstairs again, prepared for battle.

'Feeling better, pet?' Sylvia was pink and bright and smiling. It was possible that she hadn't listened, but then she could not admit to having done so; listening in to other people's conversations just wasn't done, even if it was your own daughter. 'What a dreadful blizzard! Did you feel warm again after your bath last night, darling? I hope you won't catch cold. What an experience to have. I was terribly worried, you know, when you didn't come home on an earlier train. You really must give up these wild expeditions to London, anyway during the winter. I mean, there's just no point, is there? You must think seriously about it. There's so much you could do down here too. If you joined the Land Army that nice Mr Morley would be only too glad to have you on his farm, I know, he told Daddy so only the other day. It would be such a good idea because then you wouldn't have to go away at all.'

'Mummy, I would hate to join the Land Army, and anyway, I'm frightened of cows.'

'A great many people have to do disagreeable things they don't want to do when there is a war on, dear. You don't think I enjoy helping at the hospital, do you? Or sorting out all those old clothes for refugees?'

You love it, Heather thought, you love every minute of it because it makes you feel important and worthwhile. I suppose that's why I like going up to London; Hugh's friends make me feel worthwhile. So I shouldn't really blame her.

Robert came into the dining room, rubbing his hands. 'And how's my little moorland flower this morning after her adventures in the blizzard?'

'I'm all right.' Heather winced under the jollity. 'But it was very frightening.'

'I should darn well think so, but I'm sure you weathered it like a trooper, eh?'

How does a trooper weather things? Not by bursting into tears, she surmised. But Robert was enjoying the idea of her being a heroine soldiering on against unprecedented odds.

'Of course you did.' He took the coffee poured out for him by Sylvia. 'Thank you dear. Who on earth was that telephoning at some unearthly hour this morning?'

Heather looked at him. Had he heard?

'It was for me, someone for me.'

'Someone for you? At that time in the morning? What was so urgent?'

'It was a friend of Hugh's . Hugh wants me to go up for the private view of his show next week.'

'Heather, dear.' Sylvia took a small sip of coffee and put the cup very carefully and quietly back on the saucer. She was apprehensive of confrontation. 'I do think you should not keep going up to London like this. I've just said as much. Do my words mean so little to you? Are my wishes and my worries for you as nothing?' Her lips drew together so that they would not tremble.

86

'But Mummy, the blizzard happened here, not in London.'

'That's not the point, pet, not the point at all. We would never have let you out in that storm if you had been here.'

Let me out, let me out – Heather thought furiously. What am I? A pet dog or something?

Robert looked at her angrily. 'Can't understand what you see in this Hugh fellow. I really can't. Of all the decent chaps round the neighbourhood why on earth are you so keen on him? Great disappointment to his family, you know. Never done a decent day's work in his life. And why hasn't he joined up? Wouldn't be at all surprised to hear he was a conchie.'

'He's C3,' Heather said. 'He didn't pass his medical.'

'Stuff! You can always pass your medical if you want to. More likely turned him down because he's a pansy. They don't want perverts in the British Army.'

Heather was stunned for a moment, not so much by her father's attitude, which was typical of him, but because it only dawned on her at that moment that Hugh and Istvan were lovers. What an interesting realization and how obtuse of her not to have grasped it until then!

'You don't want to get mixed up with that sort,' Robert said. 'You want to keep well away.'

Heather's temper mounted again; how appalling these ideas were. How dare they talk of Hugh in this way? She controlled her voice with some difficulty. 'Hugh is my very dear friend,' she said, 'and he always will be. He is one of the kindest and most intelligent people I have ever met.'

'You're a loyal wee soul,' Sylvia squeezed Heather's hand, 'and we wouldn't want you otherwise for the world. Daddy just means that Hugh may have got mixed up with the wrong sort of people, and we wouldn't like you to get into that set in case you might come to some harm because of them.'

'I have met just two of Hugh's friends so far and they are not the sort that are likely to do me any sort of harm at all. One is an amazingly clever Indian and the other is a painter whose studio Hugh's sharing.'

'Damn it girl!' Robert pushed his chair back from the table and got up. 'Do we have to discuss this sort of thing at the breakfast table? Two men living together! It's disgusting. Case for police action, even. I don't want any daughter of mine mixed up in some sordid police prosecution, just you remember that,' and he strode out of the room.

'Now you've upset your father,' Sylvia said tearfully as she followed him out.

Heather sat on at the dining table in a pall of depression, and later in the day phoned Hugh from a phone box in the village to say that she would be coming up the following day.

'Can you put me up?'

'Of course we can. We can put her up, can't we Istvan?'

'Darling,' Istvan came on the phone, 'I have been *dying* to put someone up on my put-u-up, and there's that divine *chaise-longue* I got the other day for twenty-five shillings. You could recline on that like Madame Recamier.'

'Mohendra will be delighted,' Hugh came back. 'He was very smitten.'

'So was I. I think he was quite the most beautiful man I've ever seen *and* so intelligent.'

'I suspect he'll take over your education from now on.'

'Do you think he would?'

'Just give him half a chance and I shan't get a look in.'

'Don't be silly, I'm coming up to see your exhibition, remember? But I must say, he is terribly attractive, isn't he?'

'Yes, I have to admit that too, though not really my type.'

'Your time is up, caller, do you wish . . .'

'No, no, I haven't any more pennies – see you tomorrow, Hugh.'

So, the precedent was created, the step taken. From now on it must surely be easier.

7 Train Journey

Dear Louise, February 1942

May I come and stay please? Things are so difficult here at the moment, and I feel I must get away to
be able to see things clearly. I have so much to tell
you. My life seems to have taken an incredible turn
and I must talk to someone about it all.

Love,
Heather.

Dear Heather,

How wonderful! You are exactly what I need.
Come at once and stay for ever. Just wire time of
train and I'll be there to meet you.

In haste,
Ever thine,
L.

Louise sealed the envelope with an unprecedented feeling of excitement. She told herself that it was all very
unreasonable and silly. Her sisters were forever visiting and school friends had come and gone. So what was
so special about Heather? There was no satisfactory
answer except that the reminiscences that the letter
had brought with it evoked an unexpected flash of light
in an otherwise sombre monotony. Something about
the recollection of Heather brought on a buoyancy that
was not evident in Louise's everyday existence.

There followed a sudden rush of forbidden emotion and fear, for Johnnie had just gone to the war, leaving her alone and in charge. A sense of fury and frustration too, but fear was the dominant sensation. Heather's proposed visit had momentarily brought all the hidden desperation to the surface. No use dwelling on gloom and despondency though, plenty to take your mind off despair.

In spite of having got to King's Cross early, the fight for a seat on the train to Yorkshire was fierce. Heather won through in the end, and found herself wedged into a corner next to the window, with bodies jammed solid from door to window in every compartment and along the corridor. Sitting, standing, leaning, there seemed no room for movement other than occasional shifts in position, which would set up a ripple through the whole mass. But the panic which always overtook her in the struggle to get in and get seated before the train took off without her had begun to die down, and the crush of massed bodies seemed instead to be a solid, safe alternative to the anxiety of being left behind.

There was something about train journeys. The stab of excitement at the long-drawn out sound of the whistle followed by the almost imperceptible movement that was soundless. Platform people moving minutely backwards; fluttering hands and handkerchiefs, retreating out of sight. Strange exhilaration as the train took charge. How nice, she thought, to be carried away, confidently and surely, from my world of anxieties and responsibilities. Like being picked up and carried away as a child. All you had to do was sit back and let others take over. How restful.

She shut her eyes and was swept away over fields and through stations, with wire lines switch-swaying beside thick, invisible windows. Ahead, the fussing of steam and pistons, but back here only the obedient jiggedy dum, jiggedy dum, and the swish of telegraph poles and other sound amplifiers. Trains were places where words always crowded into her mind.

She clenched her fists inside her fur gloves and thrust them up her coat sleeves for warmth. In spite of the massed bodies all round her, breath hung about the carriage in small mists, and her feet were numb and frozen. In her head Miss Beadle's earnest reciting voice sounded nostalgically and insistently in time with the rhythm of the wheels: Faster than fairies, faster than witches, Bridges and houses, hedges and ditches.

There were primroses then, all along the banks. Gone now, because I'm grown up, she thought.

The girl standing in front of her suddenly sat down on her knee. 'Do you mind? Just for a bit?'

'No, of course not.'

The girl was quite small. There was a jab of conscience as to whether she should offer to change places for a while. All those posters telling you to give up your seat to a member of the Armed Forces. She stared at the unfocused rush of houses and gardens beside the railway line and thought: house backs house backs all the same. Are there real people in them?

That town there beneath me, she thought, ticking slowly over under God. Bus following car following bus, intent on their own crawling business. Woolworths and Boots and the clock tower, all exactly the same everywhere, and people plodding home with their shopping. All oblivious of the surging train above them except for that one woman who glanced up for a flashed second and immediately became aware of me on the outside looking in.

She pulled her hand out of her glove and fought, in the restricted space, to find her pocket and a pencil and notebook. The girl on her lap jumped up. 'So sorry, am I getting too heavy? So sorry.'

'No, please don't move, really.' Embarrassment at being the comfortably seated one, but if she talked it might all go before she could get it down. 'Please sit down again and then I can use your back as a writing desk.' Light-hearted banter to be polite, yet at the same time all this poetry to be got down on paper before it went away. The girl remained standing, increasing Heather's feeling of guilt, and giving her nothing hard to write on. The pencil jigged and slid across the paper with the swaying of the train. She leaned forward, in an attempt to control it, and the sleeping soldier beside her collapsed into the space she had left. She wrote on her knee, laboriously and jerkily. The pencil formed line after line of words. Poetry? Or pretentious rubbish? She couldn't tell. How freezing cold it was. She felt suddenly exhausted, and the inspiration died as immediately as it had been born, but she was able to sleep some of the time in companionable intimacy with the soldier next to her.

Louise and Johnnie lived in a Jacobean manor house. Heather wondered why he had joined up when farming was a reserved occupation.

Louise seemed overjoyed to see her. 'I'm so fearfully glad you've come,' she said as they drove back from the station. 'You can't imagine how glad. One doesn't have many people to talk to these days.'

But she was surely surrounded by people. Heather imagined a continuous group of friends, all dressed in tweeds and brogues and jodhpurs, milling in and out of the baronial-type hall, but although the hall was baronial in size, it was conspicuously empty of anything other than three cocker spaniels. It was also outstandingly cold.

'What a superb house,' she said, overawed by the splendour of it all. So exactly what her own mother had wanted for her. She felt suddenly intensely sorry that she would never be able to come up with anything like it; Sylvia would be so disappointed.

'Yes, it is rather divine isn't it? I keep telling myself I'm terribly lucky really. But I do sometimes envy people who live in a cottage. It's easier to heat and you don't get evacuees. Thank goodness Harvey's too old to be called up and Mrs Blanding, she's the house-keeper, is an angel and organizes things like evacuees and their keepers, and she makes do and mends superbly and finds staff from absolutely nowhere. I don't know how she does it because everyone wants to work in munitions these days and they make you feel so guilty if you want to keep them as maids.'

Heather felt out of her depth and had a vision of Louise sitting on a throne giving everyone their orders.

'And the baby?'

'Oh she's an absolute angel, and Nanny is old and terribly efficient and loyal and that sort of thing, so she'll stay with me for ever, thank God.'

I couldn't bear anyone to bring up my children, Heather thought. I shall do it all myself. 'I'm dying to have children,' she said. 'It's the only real ambition I've ever had. I want at least six.'

Louise turned right round to see if she was serious. '*Six?* Why for heaven's sake? Just you wait till you've had the first. I mean, you just can't imagine the agony. The idea of any more fills me with gloom. And then all this feeding business, so *bovine* somehow – or does that only refer to bulls? Anyway, cow-like.'

Heather was abashed. 'Was it agony?'

'Unbelievable; and they won't give you anything if they can help it and anyway not until you're about dead from pain.'

'Really?' Heather felt her stomach seize up as she envisaged the pain. But how could Louise feel that way about feeding her baby? This was impossible to understand because it was something Heather had always considered must be the ultimate pleasure in life. She felt a small, cold distance slide between Louise and herself.

'Can I see her?'

'But of course,' the old Louise warmth returned. 'I was going to take you up to the nursery straight away because I'm quite dotty over her and most terribly proud, but I didn't want to be a bore. Mothers can be terribly boring about their children.'

I'm sure I shall be, Heather thought. I must remember to guard against it when I have children. *If* I have children. A spasm shot through her. Suppose I don't ? Too awful to consider. She felt a flash of envy when she saw Louise's baby who was pretty, friendly and well-behaved, She would have liked to stay in the nursery to get to know her. But the nurse obviously did not expect this.

Louise took her arm. 'You must be ravenous and freezing and tired. Would you like tea? Or a drink?'

Were they going to be able to get together again? There was an embarrassed barrier between them, in spite of letters. They were circling each other with polite exchanges because neither knew whether the separation had been too long. Louise had always been accessible before, Heather thought, but with these surroundings there must have been some change. But it was always possible to leave after a day or two if things didn't work out.

They ate dinner off trays in one of the small rooms off the main hall.

'Would you mind awfully?' Louise asked. 'We really only use this room because we can keep it warm and we shut up everything else we can so that we don't have to dust and clean all the time, and Harvey just serves it up and then we wash up in the pantry so he can go to bed or do his Home Guard training or whatever he wants.'

'Of course I don't mind.'

'We can get a great old fug up in here, you see, and it's frightfully cosy with the log fire and everything, don't you think? I listen to the wireless when I'm alone and when I'm not out on some ghastly committee thing, knitting for the troops and such-like.'

The wine they were drinking seeped through gradually, and Heather began to feel relaxed and warm.

'What do you do all day?' she asked. 'Do you sit on a throne and order your subjects around?'

'You could say that. I run the estate because the bailiff was called up and there's a farm and the upkeep of the place and a few things like that.'

'But do you know how to do it?'

'Not really. Johnnie and the bailiff always did it so I was pretty much at sea when they both went.'

'Did Johnnie have to go?'

Louise drew her eyebrows together and put her finger on the furrow they made. 'No he didn't, he really didn't. All this bloody patriotism bosh and he couldn't stand the idea that his friends might think he was opting out. And his family too, they just took it for granted he'd join up like his father did in the other war. So bloody silly, the whole thing.' Tears appeared in her eyes but were not allowed to fall. 'But I'm being boring and I want to know all about you. What are these things that are difficult at home? I must know everything. Tell all. Are you in love? Have you gone the whole hog or anything? It's such ages since I *talked* to anyone. I mean I don't talk to anyone up here really, I just behave and do the right thing.'

Heather felt diffident about plunging in straight

away. 'I know what you mean about talking to people,' she said. 'I need an outside opinion about something.' She hesitated by taking an overlarge gulp of her wine. Louise was bound to be shocked but probably wouldn't show it. There would be no unbiased opinion, so what *was* the use? It was just a case of telling someone who was not intimately involved. Of unloading some of the confusion. She made a cautious approach. 'You remember Hugh Dawson?'

'The well-kept grave? Of course I do. He used to talk to you, didn't he? Could never get a word out of him myself.' Louise clapped her hands. 'You don't mean – you're *not* in love with Hugh Dawson? Is this the difficulty?'

'No, no . . .' How to explain? It was like the apprehension before plunging into cold water. How stupid to have started out on this unburdening. What was she doing in this uncongenial atmosphere? 'No, it's not that. He's queer anyway.'

'*No* – really? *That's* what it was of course, but I never suspected it at the time.'

'He lives with this Hungarian artist in Fulham.'

'You're joking! Does he really? I mean – sort of openly? Same bed and everything? What do they do, do you think? Do you know what they do?'

The plunge-in was deeper and more disastrous every minute. These were her friends Louise was discussing. But it was only what she herself might have said a year ago. The self-mortification had to go on, a true purging away of original sin.

'I have fallen in love with one of their friends, an Indian revolutionary writer who is the most beautiful, the most intelligent and the most attractive man in the world. He seems to be taking up more of my life every minute, and I'm not sure what I'm going to do about it.'

There, it was out, and much better out than in. She

poured herself another glass of wine and drank half of it with a bravado she did not feel.

'An affair with an Indian!' Louise lay back among the cushions of her chair with the expectant air of one about to be lavishly entertained. 'But what on earth do the parents say? How tremendously mad you are, Heather. You're like a salutary dose of salts in my boring existence. Personally, I just couldn't, but I suppose that's only me having a colour prejudice, which I'm quite sure is a very wicked thing to have and I expect I'm missing a great deal. What's he like? I mean what's he *like*? Have you done it yet? Have you gone all the way?'

'No, not the whole way. I'm so petrified of pain and of illegitimate babies that I think I shall probably stay a virgin for the rest of my life.' She felt a little guilty at fraternizing with the enemy.

'But I thought', Louise filled her glass again, 'that men from the East were insatiable and wouldn't be said nay to.'

This was really too ridiculous. She should be very angry with Louise and never speak to her again. Instead, she sighed and said, 'Louise, don't be silly. I'm serious about this,' and wondered whether it was true.

'You're not? Are you really? But you'll be cut off and drummed out of the regiment and everything. You *can't* be serious about it – can you?'

'I don't know yet. I didn't think I was at all at first. Just thought of it as a very exciting affair, specially because he was Indian, of course. You know, sort of different.'

'You can leave out the sort of for a start.'

Heather laughed. Alcohol was a splendid thing – She had not been able to consider the situation as remotely funny before.

'Actually he's not different at all except that he's

98

nicer than anyone I know and terribly clever. Amazingly clever. Makes me feel very ignorant. Trouble is, he seems to take it for granted that he and I are made for each other.'

'And are you?'

'Well, yes, I think we probably are. He's got everything I ever wanted – superb looks, unbelievable brain, super intelligence and he's quite overpoweringly sexy.'

'*Much* too good to be true. You're obviously starry-eyed and bowled over. You must get out while the going's good. You can't possibly marry him, now can you?'

'This is the difficulty.' Heather paused and looked into the fire. 'I can't see myself being a pioneer and a trail-blazer. I haven't the courage or the guts, but I somehow find myself being swept along, willy-nilly. He's so plausible and right about everything.'

'Terribly suspect. What does he actually do?'

'He's a writer, I told you.'

'But that doesn't mean anything unless you're a famous writer. How does he make his money?'

'He does make some with his writing,' Heather said, remembering that he had borrowed ten pounds off her last week and how shocked she had been that he had asked. Men never borrow money off women. But what a stupid concept that was, as he had pointed out. Those who have can surely help out those who have not, whatever sex they might be. 'And he earns quite a bit by lecturing; on politics mostly.'

Louise laughed and Heather felt defensive. 'Yes I know how I've always steered clear of politics but it's only because I didn't know anything and so was afraid of it. Being slightly more informed makes you realize you *can* actually do something about the state of things, and that you should.'

'Oh calamity! You're well and truly hooked aren't you? What a disaster.'

Heather bridled and again felt the surge of annoyance. 'I'm not hooked,' she said. 'I'm just a little undecided, that's all. But even if I do consider marrying him, it wouldn't be the end of the world, would it?' There was a moment's silence.

'Of course it would be. The end of your world in any case.'

'Doesn't necessarily follow, and anyway, I don't fit in very well with our sort of world.'

'Oh rot, and you certainly don't fit into *his* sort of world, now do you?'

'Oddly enough, I do sort of feel I belong much more with the Hughs and the arty lot, even though I'm such an uneducated simpleton at the moment.'

'For God's sake, stop being so humble,' Louise said crossly. 'You're ten times better than any long-haired, dotty intellectual I've ever met. All sandals and dirt under the toenails and all that rubbish. You've got breeding, my dear Heather, and you can't just toss that over your shoulder at the drop of a hat. Upbringing is all-important and stays with you for the rest of your life, no matter how much you try to disown it. And it's the same with him; totally different heritages. Can't possibly mix them. And what about religion? Don't they worship idols or something?'

Heather looked at her in exasperation, but reminded herself that less than a year ago she would have thought the same. 'No more than I worship a crucifix,' she said, 'or actually believe I'm drinking real blood at Holy Communion, stupid. We're both at about the same point of belief or disbelief, whatever you like to call it.'

'We have some wonderful brandy,' Louise said, jumping up, 'that Johnnie's father laid down years ago, and we have it for special occasions. This is definitely a special occasion.'

100

The brandy was certainly wonderful; Heather felt the glow of relaxation almost at once. Why had she thought this atmosphere hostile a short time ago? 'Whenever we are apart he writes me these amazing letters practically every day,' she said. 'He gets fearfully upset if I don't reply straight away. Listen . . .' she searched in her bag. 'I've got at least three in here that I haven't answered yet. You've got to hear his side of things. That's fair. Listen: "Why don't you answer my letters you heartless, too-busy-with-flippant-nonentities sort of person? On Wednesday I caught the 4.15 post so that you would be sure to get a letter in the morning, and then again I rose early to write yet another note before the post came, in the hope that I might have something from you." '

'My God,' Louise said, 'what obsessive meticulosity. The man's a freak.'

'It's just that he's so well organized and I'm not.'

'But do you actually *love* him?'

'Well, yes. I mean how can you help it? If someone as god-like as him seems to be devoting his life and his thoughts and his love towards you, you can't really help responding, can you?'

'I think I could. I should feel so inadequate, I couldn't possibly spend my life trying to live up to him.'

'That's just it. He makes me feel absolutely capable and worthwhile. When I'm with him I feel I'm invincible and talented and wanted and sexy. But *do* I love him? I really don't know. Of course I *say* I love him, and I mean it; then. Anyway, shut up and listen: "I am eagerly awaiting your decision to come here *soon* and stay for a few days so that we could be together continuously for some time. Why are you so afraid of staying with me? I find this impossible to understand. It is very hurtful to me and really very silly of you. I would so love to take you to meet my friends (not just

101

Hugh and Istvan and their friends) because I am sure they will all be impressed by your charm, and with your polish you would soon become the cynosure . . ." '

'Polish? What's he talking about? Mansion or Bluebell? And what does cynosure mean?'

'I don't know,' laughter began to take over, 'just shut up and *listen*: ". . . you'd soon become the cynosure of my own small circle. Please do organize this. I am now myself making arrangements to leave this awful bombing and go and stay at that colony I told you about near Stroud." '

'A colony? Colonies are surely full of lepers, aren't they?'

Heather shouted with laughter. 'Be *quiet*, you great cow, it's a place called Whiteway Colony which is a sort of a village run on Tolstoyan lines . . .'

'Oh God, now you're quoting; what does that mean? Remember, I'm one of your ignorant friends. Things have to be explained to me in words of one syllable.'

'Well, it's a group of people who got together and built their own homes on a piece of land they own jointly, at least they don't own it because they burnt the deeds or something and Mohendra has been asked to stay in someone's chicken hut.'

'And he wants you to share his chicken hut?'

'Yes.' Heather became hysterical with laughter and tears dripped down her cheeks.

'Have the chickens been evacuated to somewhere more comfortable?'

'Be serious, you fool. Just because you live in the lap of luxury gives you absolutely no right to mock.' She put her head back into the cushions of her chair and groaned with the effort to control her laughter. It all seemed so hilarious now where before it had been tense and anxious. She continued reading, through spasms of giggles. "You could very easily say that you are visiting friends in the country as your Mummy and Daddy do not seem to quibble when you visit your friend Lewis for instance . . ." '

'Lewis?'

'He means you – he gets his names mixed sometimes. He usually calls you Lucy. "They will surely not be so unreasonable as you, with that disturbingly prolific imagination of yours, think that they will be. You imagine all sorts of difficulties and thus exaggerate the eternal tension – the contradictory nature of Mama for instance. If only, darling, you can cultivate more self-confidence – based on the solid basis of wide and useful reading, right understanding of things and persons – you'll have more patience and forbearance, and – may I add? – a little more tact in handling problems which seem impossible to you now. I'll love you even more if you could do that (though strictly between ourselves, Miss Heather Jones, I can't see how I could possibly love you more than I already do)." '

Louise gave a long drawn out snore. 'Boring,' she said. 'So he loves you infinitely, that's nice. But how can you be sure that his love is true and unshakeable and everlasting and the sort that never runs smooth?'

'Very hard to tell. Oh, Louise or Lewis or Lucy, whatever your name is, whatever shall I do?'

Louise put her glass on the table and leant over the side of the chair, her head resting on her arms. 'I think an affair with a ravishing sexy Indian would be absolutely splendid and an enormous boost to morale as long as you can keep quiet about it, but more than that, no, a thousand times, no. You couldn't stand the hoo-ha; you're not the type. Too family orientated. Can you *imagine* what everyone would say? You're just not the bold, brassy bohemian type, whatever you may say to the contrary. Much too conventional; like me.'

'Am I? Yes, of course I am. Can't bear shocking

people; don't like embarrassing them even.' It was true. Louise was absolutely right. 'So you think I should have an exciting, undercover affair with him, while at the same time I should look out for my titled Lord Right who will naturally be inundated with money. Yes?'

'Absolutely. No question. I'll take your word for it that your Indian is a sexy Adonis with an excess of brain,' Louise added, 'but his letter sounds as though he is a self-righteous, self-opinionated, crashing bore.'

'That's just because you are a prejudiced, philistine ignoramus,' Heather said comfortably. 'Just you wait till you meet him. He's phenomenal, really he is. A prodigious paragon, in fact, and impossible to resist. If I don't find Lord Right fairly soon, I can't really see that there is much hope for me.'

'Heather you *can't*, you just can't' Louise stared unhappily into her glass and considered in the long, somnolent silence that ensued the appalling disaster her friend might be plunging into. She felt tearful and racked with a sentimental desire to rescue this same friend from a fate which was, without doubt, far worse than death. 'It just isn't done, old girl,' she said. But Heather lay smilingly and obliviously asleep.

8 Mules are Sad, Bad-tempered Creatures

Stoke Poges,
February 1942

My dear Mohendra,

I have not had time to answer all your splendid letters to me because I have been staying with my friend Louise in her great big Yorkshire mansion. I shall never be able to match your letter-writing ability anyway. Words just seem to flow out of you as though you were some sort of word-machine. I have a lot of words inside me too, but my machine doesn't contain as much knowledge as yours, added to which, I seem so busy doing things all day that I find it difficult to sit myself down to write.

I spent a lovely week with Louise, just talking and talking and catching up on a whole year of separation. And when I got home I went to a big dance at the RAF base here, where I danced and flirted with dozens of handsome RAF types. Then brother Malcolm came home on embarkation leave and I talked to him about you.

Heather put down her pen and pressed her hands together, biting at the knuckles of her fingers. How to express it? Not possible to put it down as he actually said it. Much too insulting. She had been shocked at the affront herself, how much more would he feel it? And yet a year ago it would just have been a joke between friends, a smart conversation piece.

Malcolm had looked impressive in his uniform, and she felt proud and fond at the same time.

'Hallo, little sister,' he said. 'And what did *you* do in the Great War Grandmamma? When are you going to don the uniform, you slacker? Please not the ATS, the colour wouldn't suit you, but you'd make a lovely WAAF.'

Sylvia swept him up in a wash of pride. 'Oh my darling boy, what a joy to see you! Come in now, out of the cold and put your things down. Mary, take Mr Malcolm's things up to his room. You'll be needing a drink, I'm sure. Robert, get the boy a drink, dear. Dinner won't be all that long and it's your favourite soup. Cook's made mulligatawny, we both remembered, you see.'

The menace of embarkation hovered, and there was a degree of hysteria.

Heather had him to herself only once during the three days, when they drove together to visit friends nearby. It wasn't easy to talk to him. She seemed to know him so little, and the officer in the kilt sitting beside her was even more of a stranger than her civilian eldest brother had been. She was glad that he started the conversation.

'What have you been doing with yourself then?' Did he find it difficult too? It was impossible for her to imagine that either of her brothers could ever find themselves at a loss for words.

'Finding things out, growing up, educating myself,' she said.

'About time too, not that education will do you any good. How are you setting about it? One week in the Armed Forces would teach you more than a thousand years of university rubbish.'

'I've been going up to London quite a bit, visiting

106

exhibitions and concerts and the ballet. I might get into an art school. Hugh Dawson's been taking me round.'

'*That* wet? Can't believe you'll get much education from him, except the wrong sort.'

'You're so wrong,' Heather said crossly. 'Do you know I'd never been to a concert, except for Hiawatha at the Albert Hall, until a few months ago, nor to an exhibition except the Royal Academy,'

'So what's strange about that? Neither have I. Can't imagine anything more boring than a concert anyway.'

'Well I find it very exciting, educational or not. It's like living in a new world; discovering feelings I've never felt before. I'm sure you'd like it too if only you gave yourself a chance to listen to music or really looked at some decent paintings.'

'My precious pet, you are quite wrong. I'm not the highbrow type, and nor are you. You just think it's smart to join up with the dreary intellectual lot that never did anybody any good. Might, in fact, do you a lot of harm.'

Heather's scalp began to prickle and she found herself locked into a frozen vice, half anger, half fear.

'In actual fact,' she said, 'they do me far more good than the dreary people that surround me down here. They're interesting, intelligent, even brilliant sometimes. There's this amazing Indian I've met . . .'

'Oh come now, that's too much. That's not funny. Mix with the low life of bohemia if you must, but brilliant Indians – no. For God's sake, don't get mixed up with that sort of thing.'

'What sort of thing?' Her heart started to thump noisily.

'Well, going about with a black. I mean it's just not done, is it?'

'I can't see why not. And anyway, he's brown.'

'Don't quibble. You know exactly what I mean. You

107

also know damn well it's not done. What sort of a reputation do you think you'll get yourself? I mean suppose anyone we know sees you. Just drop it, that's all, I'm telling you, just drop it.'

It had to be talked out, much as she dreaded the idea of a scene. He had to be shown to be wrong.

'It's all very well to say it's not done, but why isn't it done? What's *really* wrong with black and white people getting together? What are the real reasons for everyone to be so against it?'

'If you weren't so ignorant, you'd have learned by now. What on earth did these damn governess women teach you? The whole world knows that it's insane to allow the races to mix, scientifically insane, apart from anything else. I mean you don't mate a cat with a dog do you? And look at mules; sad, bad-tempered creatures that can't reproduce. Do you want a world peopled by types like that? Do you want a world full of half-castes, neither one thing nor the other?'

The whole world knew these things. Of course they did. She herself had picked up the knowledge. How could the whole world be mistaken? It seemed very unlikely.

'I am absolutely certain you're wrong. And when I'm a little less ignorant about everything, I'll prove you're wrong.'

'You can't, darling, you can't. Even if there were any arguments for it, all the world can't make a case for allowing anything so unnatural. The whole thing has been proved over and over again. Each race is fine in its own way, but don't *mix* them, that's all.'

Heather took up her pen again and read over what she had written. 'He is ridiculously prejudiced,' she wrote, and paused again. 'He told me I shouldn't go out with you because the races shouldn't be allowed to mix, but I couldn't argue properly with him because I don't know enough. What do I say to these people?' She forgot her original hesitation in repeating the conversation as the pen took off, seemingly of its own volition, and she set out Malcolm's prejudices in detail including some of her own with others she had picked up. It became a diatribe, because she felt angry and vicious against Mohendra for putting her in this untenable position. How dare he drag her out of her safe cover and expose her to attack? 'So you see,' she wrote, 'what a useless sort of creature I would be as a friend or lover.' Put him off; show him how impossible it was; stop the whole thing now. 'I am stupid and prejudiced. I am not a fighter, nor do I want to be. You had better let me alone and allow me to crawl back under my stone. I may love your mind and body but I don't seem willing or able to fight for them.'

She sealed the letter quickly without reading it through. If her emotions could change so much during the writing of it, she supposed they could change equally with the reading through. Better to leave it as it was. The whole thing was too big for her. Much better to get out now while the going was good.

The answer came two days later. Pages of neat script in red ink with every part of the paper filled, and insertions crammed between close packed lines and carrying on round the edges of the paper. It was as if he couldn't bear to waste one square inch, nor to leave one tiny word unsaid.

Redcliffe Place
Midday, Tuesday February 24th 1942
My beautiful, much-missed, much-longed-for, much-needed darling, who prefers to spend her time flirting with RAF blokes to concentrating on her faithful adoring London lover.

So you have no time to write to me because you are

busy with your parties and dances and visits to the country and all the other important social happenings in the culturally progressive hamlet of Stoke Poges. Darling, I am teasing you, but I do find it a little strange that all these small events should stop you from writing to me, even though you know how much I wait for your letters, how continuously *you* are in *my* thoughts; can I not hope that *I* might be a little more often in *yours*?

About your prejudiced brother. Darling, don't despair! The most important thing that must be done is to keep the spark of hope alive in our own minds, because most people today are soaked with prejudice and stupidity – they are ignorant and they just don't know. We have to analyse the nature of such prejudices, trace them backwards step by step to their intellectual, theological or religious beginnings, and their economic or class antecedents. That's the scientific method.

When Malcolm, in disapproving of racial marriages, puts forward the cat and dog analogy, is it not all prejudice and stupidity? Is there a jot of clear thinking or a segment of sense in what seems a sensible and popular view?

Even so-called experts write nonsense on the matter. In the first place, no one knows what a 'race' is, what is its constitution, or how many 'races' there are today. The popular mind, of course, thinks in terms of colour: white, brown, black etc. As regards colour of eyes and hair, the Mediterranean stock resembles the Indo-Aryan (Hindus) more than the Nordics. The English are a hybrid race and there are in Germany Nordics as well as Alpines. Stature is no criterion; there are short and tall people in every 'race'.

Again, one must not confuse 'nations' (political

and economic groupings) with 'races'. There are no English, French or German 'races'. Language is no basis for racial classification either. There is no Aryan race, in spite of what Hitler may say! There are peoples who speak Aryan languages, and it was in this sense that the word 'Aryan' (from the Sanskrit) was coined by Max Muller. So the study of language and physical characteristics leads us nowhere (except into the cobwebbed recesses of the minds of Malcolm and co.).

There are no scientific grounds for differentiating people into 'races', so that all these prejudices are a lot of silly nonsense and have no basis in nature or biological facts, yet 'race', colour, etc. still play a dominant role in society. This is reactionary and retrogressive and *must* be fought by well-reasoned arguments derived from a deep study of the problem.

Malcolm's cat and dog theory makes no analogy at all, not even a grain of sense. Tell him to ask the Aga Khan whether he bothers about 'racial' tendencies of his racehorses when he breeds them, or whether he was worried that his son, whose mother is Italian, should have married an Irish lady. I think he probably thought that Guinness was good for him!

So my darling, so much for all these silly people who are so full of prejudices, and how many pages, and how much time it has taken to put paid to their ideas. You see what happens when we don't live together or see each other more often and for longer time. Instead of discussing these and similar things while lounging in big chairs and sipping coffee in the evening, or while lying lazily in bed, I have to write these long, long letters, sitting and sweating alone. And you? Not a word for days until today. Were you so busy with your guests and at your parties that you could not have said to them, 'Now excuse me for half an hour while I write a very important letter'? Do you do that? Even while flirting with all those handsome young men, do you think of me, alone here in my cold room where I have not even a shilling for the gas meter, nor enough at the moment to pay the light bill so that I burn candles! Can you imagine that, Miss Jones?

But I could do without the light and heat if only I had you here to give me both warmth and inspiration. When will you come? Thursday? Friday? And stay for a week so that we have time to talk and so that I have time to quell your silly fears and prejudices about allowing me to make full and complete love to you in the natural, unrepressed way. Send me a telegram to say that you are coming, and I will arrange everything this end.

I kiss you everywhere,
Mohendra

He had not even considered the idea that she should not fight. She put the letter down with an uncomfortable mixture of irritation and shame. Here was someone who was prepared to lay his time, his love and himself at her unworthy feet, while she had been considering opting out of the whole thing because it was too difficult; too much trouble; too uncomfortable. He had bothered to give her the facts she had asked for so that she might tackle the problem. These things had to be done. There was really no question.

And what about the question of her virginity? What was this really all about? So far, she had struggled to keep it, believing – believing what? Was she afraid that he might take further possession of her by that one physical act? Hardly. The danger was not a physical one; he had already engulfed her. There was little point in fighting that fact.

9　Is that It?

There was always the excuse of the bombing for not staying the night in London. Though she had spent one or two anxious and uncomfortable nights on Istvan's sofa, Heather still could not rid herself of the impulse to return, when night approached, to the refuge of home, however insecure that refuge began to appear. She found the step of spending the whole night in Mohendra's flat as daunting as the thought of the loss of her virginity. The two acts were inextricably linked, the implications were quite clear: spending a night together meant that consummation was taken for granted. But it was not only that. How to admit that she feared the bomb that would disclose them sleeping together far more than the bomb that might destroy them? It was absurd.

She did not admit this anxiety to Mohendra, but he was nonetheless impatient and angry. 'You are obstinate and silly sometimes,' he said, 'but you are right to be so against my staying on in London. There is really no need. So I will move out because my beloved insists. If the mountain refuses to go to Mohammed, then Mohammed will move to more congenial surroundings. I will accept that pressing invitation from my dear comrades at Whiteway Colony who have offered me the loan of the small hut they have in their garden. There we can enjoy peace and quiet, and I can arrange lectures in Stroud and write my books and pamphlets without the interruption of guns or bombs or other interferences.' He enclosed her with his arms in a way that made her sense complete protection. His arms were surely longer than normal that they should reach so far round her, and his hands so big that her own shrank to delicate proportions beside them. She loved the bigness of him and the way in which she found herself engulfed in every sense.

So when he moved out of London to the Gloucestershire village where war only served to increase the pacifism of the dedicated inhabitants, Heather's main excuse for evasion was swept away.

'I have made all the arrangements,' he wrote. 'My little hut is more than adequate for my needs, and now only requires your presence to make it complete. I have told everyone here that you are visiting me shortly and they are all dying to meet you. Therefore, please take a whole week off and come as soon as you can. No ifs and buts – I want you NOW.'

There was no way round it.

The hut was certainly small. Heather bent her head to enter the door and saw that there was a large, divan-type bed in the far left-hand corner that took up three quarters of the floor space. There were two small windows on the right with a square oil stove in between them. A kettle and a saucepan stood on top of the stove, and a strong smell of paraffin hung in the air.

'It's nice and warm,' she said, sitting on the corner of the bed. it was piled with blankets, dark grey army blankets, and the floor had several layers of rugs and pieces of carpet spread over it so that it felt soft; almost like the earth, she thought. She felt a sense of excitement as the softness seeped through the soles of her feet, because it reminded her of the idea of camping out.

114

She had always wanted to camp out when she was younger, and her great ambition at one time had been for the family to own a caravan. 'We could have two,' she had suggested to Sylvia at the time. 'One for you and Daddy and the other for Malcolm and Bobbie and Miss Beadle and me.'

The memory passed through her mind as she sat on the bed and watched Mohendra light the oil lamp, squatting down by her feet, with his knees level with his ears. She visualized him in hot sun surrounded by other Indians, all squatting on their haunches, and tried to imagine herself attempting to tuck her own immense length of leg delicately under too short a skirt. The shadows round the hut became deep and soft, and a sense of euphoric comfort, of being enclosed and safe from harm, settled over her.

Mohendra smiled at her as he put the lamp on a small desk beside the bed. 'What do you think of my Englishman's castle? Cosy, isn't it? I have lined all the walls with brown paper, and when that ran out I used newspaper. You can even read *The Times* in bed you see. But I really did it to keep out the draughts because I felt sure that a well brought-up young lady like yourself would not be able to tolerate draughts. Apart from which, the air-raid wardens are very officious down here and do not allow for even one chink of light to show. This hut had so many chinks I am afraid – between every board, in fact!' He sat down on the bed beside her and began to light a handful of scented sticks. 'Never let it be said,' and he waved the sticks in the air so that their pale smoke trails were left hanging, 'that I do not set the scene with the utmost care. Everything must be perfect for my love, nothing left to chance.'

No ifs and buts here. Anxiety flooded through Heather with a discordant rush. Mohendra leaned forward to wind up the portable gramophone on the desk.

'We have the soft lights,' he said, 'now for the sweet music.' The preliminary descending scale of the sitar spiralled downwards into the room to mix with the smoke-scrolls . Heather was momentarily transported, though her panic soon returned. The situation was unreal. It bore no relation to everyday life. It was not happening.

Mohendra pulled her down towards him, kissing her cheeks and her ear and the side of her nose. 'I am so happy to have you here in my own little home, quite away from everyone and all to myself.'

Again this feeling of being enclosed, but this was not the safe enclosure of protection. It had become no-escape imprisonment, and she found herself shaking. His arm encircled her. 'Why are you so afraid? You must stop being afraid.'

She lay quite rigid on the bed with her teeth clenched. 'I can't help it. I can't help being certain that Mummy suspected me and that she'll check up with Louise to see if I'm really staying there, and even though I told Louise, how can she pretend I'm there if I'm not?' Did he know that was not the real issue?

'Silly girl,' he said. 'There's absolutely nothing to worry about. Even if they should find out, it's not the end of the world is it? You make difficulties for yourself with all these imaginings. We will phone Louise tomorrow just to make certain Mummy and Daddy aren't champing on her doorstep. We will go down to the post office just to relieve your silly mind, all right?'

'I hate all these lies I have to tell.'

'Of course you do, my darling, and so do I. If only your dear Mummy and Daddy were nice, sensible people, then there would be no need for all the lies. But darling, it won't last for ever, because with tact and patience we will win them over, these tiresome parents of yours. I adore your uncompromising honesty and if it really bothers you, then we shall have to break the news to them sooner, that's all. Nothing I should like better, though I think a gradual approach might be more successful.'

'You're being ridiculously optimistic. They'll never get used to the idea.' She became intensely irritated with him and his inability to understand the obvious. Why did he continue trying to convince her of such impossibility?

'Perhaps, perhaps – but we must *try*, my sweet, not just give up and do nothing. This is defeatist apathy, and a disaster. Suppose no one fought against the bad things in the world, suppose everyone just shrugged their shoulders and said, "It is impossible, I can do nothing to affect the outcome," what then? Where would we be today if everyone had said that? No Cromwell, no Lenin! We might still be in the throes of slavery or feudal oppression. All the great men of the world have been fighters, my adorable, apathetic sweet. Shame on you!'

He swept her towards him again, and she found herself caught up in a smothering embrace. Excitement began to take over, in spite of her irritation at his overbearing belief in himself. His certainty both excited and appalled her.

She disengaged herself slightly and stared at him. 'Why do I believe implicitly everything you say when I am with you,' she said, 'and then find my mind turns to an amorphous mass when you go away? It's all much too confusing.'

'Because you are an incorrigible doubting Thomas, an ignoramus and a woman of little faith but, thanks be to Budddha, Mohammed, Jesus or Brahma, one of immense voluptuous sensuality.'

So he brought her back, squarely, to the immediate impasse.

'It's going to hurt,' she said. 'That's what I'm frightened of. It's just the physical thing of being hurt.'

'My darling, adorable cowardly person, do you really think I would ever consider hurting you? Do you actually think me capable of that?'

'Yes, I do. It's just that I am afraid of physical pain, nothing more. I mean I don't disapprove, you know how sexy I am, you can't possibly call me frigid, now can you?' His hands pushed away clothes and she felt the mounting ecstasy of skin to skin contact. 'And I do really want to, honestly I do, but you see I'm absolutely petrified, so I . . . ow . . . Oh God is that . . . I mean is . . .'

The sharp pain changed suddenly into an intense, overwhelming arousal and she felt a surge of protective compassion and tenderness flood through her. She cradled his head in her arms, kissing his eyes, his face and his mouth. Was this really the same over-confident giant who had been holding her and reassuring her so recently? This pulsating, vulnerable creature?

'It didn't hurt at all,' she said, wanting to put him at his ease. 'In fact I wouldn't be at all surprised if I'm not going to enjoy it tremendously.'

Mohendra rolled on to his back and laughed helplessly. 'What sort of a girl have I picked for myself?' he said. 'Here am I, pulling out all the stops, and she thinks she might be going to enjoy it in the distant future.'

'Near future I would say. Probably in about half an hour.' What a superlative, incomparable paragon of a lover he was.

The whole of her stay at Whiteway was to have, for her, a marked quality of disbelief. For one thing, the colony was something quite beyond her experience and therefore unreal, and for another, her own status had

118

changed from virgin to non-virgin. A milestone, surely?

'It's rather like being confirmed,' she told Mohendra.

'What do you mean – confirmed?'

'You know, the church thing like being christened.'

'You mean the Bar Mitzvah of the Christian Church?'

Heather had not heard the expression before and thought it was probably an Indian ritual.

'It's when you expect to become immediately filled with spiritual understanding and of course you're not.'

'You mean to tell me you're not now filled with deep sexual fulfilment?'

She laughed and wound her arms round his neck. 'Of course I am. But I don't feel as different as I thought I would.'

'I told you it wasn't an earth-shattering event, didn't I? Merely a normal, natural process.'

'You make it sound so boring.'

'What it *sounds* like is not the point,' Mohendra said, pushing her back on to the bed. 'It's what it does for the body – spiritual, corporeal or carnal – that interests me.'

Mohendra was certainly not unreal in any sense, just his own exuberant self.

'I have asked Reg to dinner tomorrow night,' he said one morning. 'He's the member of parliament for Leytonstone and I've been telling him all about you so that he's most keen to meet you.'

'You've asked an MP to dinner?' Heather had never met a member of parliament before. 'Where are we taking him?'

'We're not taking him anywhere, he's coming here to the hut at seven o'clock and I'm cooking rice and curry.'

'But surely you can't . . .'

'What do you mean, can't? I'm a very good cook and

I got some lamb from the farmer down the road who's a friend of mine because he comes to my lectures at the village institute, so he's kept a bit of lamb back for me under the counter. No coupons or anything. Mary down the road is lending me an extra saucepan; it's all arranged. Tonight you are attending my lecture; let me see, what's it on?' He felt in his pockets for his diary. 'Oh yes, tonight it's the second of three lectures I'm doing for the Workers' Educational Association on the Theory and Practice of Socialism. This one's on the subject of Revisionism, you know, Social Democracy on the Continent and Fabianism over here. I shall probably get heckled by the Communist mob – will you mind that darling? Will you spring to my defence?'

'Me? But I don't know anything.'

'Nor do they; they just feel very insecure, these Stalinists, when they are criticized from the left.'

'Will they throw things?'

'I would hardly think so; eggs and tomatoes are too precious.'

'Do you get paid for these lectures?'

'But of course! I am getting nearly £14 for a course of twelve lectures and when I get the whole thing organized properly, I should be earning about £3.10 a week. Not bad, eh? And as well as that I shall be writing about two articles a week and starting a book on India and the first volume of my three-volume autobiography.'

'If you haven't been able to start these things before, why should you be able to now?'

His irritation showed in the sharp, quick movement he made with his head.

'Why be so defeatist all the time? Now that I am here in the countryside I can quite easily do it. One must have a goal at which to aim and mine is perfectly possible. I have worked out the whole schedule: rise at six, research and write from six to twelve, exercise from twelve to one, work again in Stroud Library from one to five, which makes ten hours work a day apart from my lectures. In ten hours I should be able to write at least two thousand words and at that rate I should be able to finish one book in less than two months.'

'What you *can* do and what you *will* do are not the same thing at all.'

'If it *can* be done,' Mohendra said, 'then we must make it our business to do it.' He regained his good humour at the thought of the possibilities that lay ahead. 'With two or three hundred a year from lecturing and another five hundred or so from my book, we can be reasonably well off.'

Heather thought of the thousand a year she had always considered to be the safe yearly income which could include a car and a married couple living in. Washing up the breakfast cups in a bucket of cold water, the absurdity of the idea made her shake with inward laughter. They wouldn't need anything like a thousand a year, five or six hundred should be ample.

'I want you to meet one of my special friends this morning,' Mohendra said later. 'His name is Bill and he lives in a very nice bungalow that he built himself.' He hesitated. 'He's a bit eccentric sometimes,' he said apologetically, 'but such a kind man. He used to be very rich, but gave all his money away to the needs of the colony.'

All these wonderful people making history and influencing things around them. So much faith and hope, it really was all possible. The frost all round them on the trees and grass was magical. The splitting ice puddles splintered as she stood on them and the visible breath from their mouths made transient mists that hung momentarily in the air before wafting on to nothing. She hugged Mohendra in a sudden wave of pleasure and certainty about her life.

'You're wonderful! I feel as though I could conquer the world at this minute. I feel a complete person with you. Of course you can write a hundred books in as many minutes if you want to. And I can paint superb pictures and write reams of poetry and be hailed as a genius. I know it.'

If he attempted too much, this was not a fault as he so rightly pointed out. With the confidence she felt at that moment, she was certain that she could help him through. She could make it possible for him as well as for herself. It was exhilarating. Words began to crowd into her head with the new sense of self-respect.

'Split ice pools,' she said, treading on one. 'Like stars. Just think of all the lovely words that could describe my present mood and this stunningly beautiful frost everywhere.'

'A poet too? Then you will be able to write poems for the revolution as well as painting pictures for the cause. You must show me all your poetry and I will get it published. I know many people who would be only too pleased to publish it.'

The banality of his words stopped her short in her tracks.

'You're so *funny* too, with some of the things you come out with. If only you had a small modicum of humour in your make-up, you'd see how funny you sometimes are. You don't have an idea about what my poetry's like and yet you talk about getting it published. How do you know it's good enough to be published?'

'Because I know you. You write well, you write beautiful letters to me. You are intelligent. With these attributes, it stands to reason that you would be able to write good poetry if you wanted to. As to your uncalled for remarks about my sense of humour, Miss, I have to agree with you to some extent because I haven't had time in my life to make a proper study of humour.'

Heather gave a shout of laughter. 'You're impossible,' she said. 'You actually mean that, don't you?'

'Of course I mean it.' Mohendra drew his eyebrows together in irritation. 'Humour is, after all, a very regional affair. What is funny in England is not necessarily funny in other parts of the world. One needs to know the habits of people before one can judge what is loosely termed a "sense of humour". For instance I find all this hysterical laughter you sometimes indulge in is very unbecoming and rather vulgar.'

'Oh you're hopeless.' Her shoulders drooped and the brightness dropped out of the day.

He glanced sideways at her and took her hand. 'But these are small quibbles, you vulgar girl, because really I adore you, warts and all, so please don't sulk. Put on your best, and most endearing smile for my friend Bill.'

Bill opened the door to them, and Heather found herself quite unprepared for the fact that he had no clothes on.

'Come in quick, dears,' he said. 'I don't want to let any more of that cold air in than is absolutely necessary. I do hope you'll forgive my informality – you are Heather aren't you? Mohendra has told me all about you.'

They drank coffee in a small, cluttered kitchen in almost stifling heat from a kitchen range, a small electric fire and a paraffin heater. Heather unwound her scarf and took off her coat.

'Too hot dear? But if you disliked clothes as much as I do you'd just have to keep up the temperature. Can't bear the restriction you see; I mean clothes really are chains, aren't they? Actual chains as well as theoretical ones. Like the swaddling bands they always sing about in carols; so restricting, I always think. Stop you moving about, and I find that stops me thinking clearly.'

Heather imagined herself telling Louise. 'There he was, my dear, absolutely starkers, not a stitch, I tell you, not a stitch!' But after all, why should he put clothes on if he didn't want to?

'Why didn't you tell me he wasn't going to have any clothes on?' she said later to Mohendra. 'For all you knew, I might have let out a piercing scream and set off madly in all directions.'

Mohendra looked serious. 'You must be ready to accept the idiosyncrasies of others. I expect he forgot you were coming. But you really shouldn't be shocked. It is only the conventional attitude of the world . . .'

'Yes, yes, yes, I know all that; and anyway I wasn't shocked in the way you mean. It just caught me off balance when I wasn't expecting it.'

'But you should not be caught off balance, that's what I mean.'

She decided not to pursue it, and Mohendra went on to explain the sort of views Bill held. 'Pink socialist, nothing more, and very woolly-minded, but such a good man.'

'Am I a woolly-minded pink socialist?'

'My darling, by birth you are a dyed-in-the-wool, true-blue Tory, but by nature you could not be other than socialist, and by education – my education – you will very soon become a left-wing Marxist, one of the comrade workers working for the revolution.'

'I'm not absolutely sure that's what I want.'

Mohendra put his arm round her waist as they walked back along the road. 'You won't be able to help yourself once you have found out all there is to find out about the way our lives are being run for us at the moment. It's just that you don't know; things have been hidden up for so long by those in power. But darling, you and I together will work as a team to enlighten the world. Just a tiny part of a great team of comrades who will work for the revolution. We will be part of the great organization that will eventually set the world to rights.'

'But how do you know it will set the world to rights? Why should your ideas work any better than anyone else's?'

He hugged her towards him and laughed. 'But darling,' he said it gently and patiently, amused that she could not understand the simplicity of it, 'they are not my ideas, they are the theories of great men. When I was younger, I read all these theories, through and through, and when I had read them all, then I was able to judge which one would work, and which one would not. If there had been any doubt in my mind, then I would not have adopted the Marxist view, would I? I believe in that theory because it is the only theory that will work.'

'That is your view, you mean?'

'My view? No, it's not my view, it's Marx's theory, and it happens to be the only theory that would succeed, otherwise I would not believe in it.'

About twenty people gathered in the village hall that evening for his lecture, and Heather found herself embarrassed and anxious that they would dissent and challenge him. She felt very agitated that they would resent his over-confidence and become angry, perhaps even violent? She sat in the back row in an agony of fear. But he came up to her. 'Why are you sitting right at the back?' he demanded angrily. 'I want you to be in the front so that you can back me up, and so that everyone can see you.' He propelled her to the front row.

'Comrades,' he said, 'I would like you to welcome my companion, Heather, who is staying with me. She is a great poetess and a talented artist and she helps me considerably in all my work. We are a team.'

125

The audience clapped enthusiastically and an old man next to Heather shook her hand.

'A great man and a wonderful speaker.' He smilingly nodded his head up and down several times. 'You must be very proud of him. I should so much like to read your poetry sometime. How do you feel about Rilke?'

Mohendra was by this time launched into his lecture so that Heather was able to evade the task of answering. When she had recovered her composure sufficiently to listen to what he was saying, her anxiety in no way abated. He seemed to be criticizing the armed forces, the Government, the Royal family and the whole conduct of the war. He would surely be lynched. But strangely he was not. At the end of the evening there was a great deal of applause, and the people crowded round him with questions and congratulations.

'So interesting . . .'

'You manage to make things so clear . . .'

'But how do you view Stalin's present attitude towards . . .'

They walked back together in a laughing, talking group, by the light of the full moon and the sound of distant bombardment. It was far away and seemed to bear no relation to any of them there.The searchlights roamed wildly on the horizon. There was a sense of companionship and peace among these people, each one dropping off at their separate houses, many built by themselves. Tiny houses, most of them; could be called hovels by some, Heather thought; but as she bent her head to enter their own hut, she relished the sense, as the others must have done, of coming home.

10 Idle and Suggestive Talk

Stoke Poges
20th June,1942

My dearest Heather,
   I understand from your mother that you have suggested to her you would like to bring your friend, Mohendra, down here for a weekend. I cannot understand why you want to bring him home. You must see that your Mother and I do not like him, and would prefer not to entertain him. Why cannot you face facts, and realize that no good can come of this infatuation? Marriage is out of the question (at least I hope so!), and a white girl going about with a black man is always a subject of idle and suggestive talk by people. It is very painful to both of us and I think you should make up your mind to be done with this friendship once and for all.
   Please think this over very seriously, but take what I write as being to your good.

With best love,
Your loving
Father

My dear Daddy,

Thank you for your letter about Mohendra. I had no idea you disliked him so much as I only brought him to meet you once, but since you do, we will, of course, not ask you to entertain him again.

Even if he were no more to me than an ordinary friend, and if I considered marriage was out of the question, I'm afraid 'idle and suggestive talk' from a certain type of person for whom I have little respect, would not be the sort of thing to make me give up someone I happen to like. He and I have an enormous number of friends and they, luckily, like us for what we are and not for what colour our skins may be.

I can assure you that I am not infatuated by Mohendra, but have considered every aspect concerning our relationship most carefully and consulted every sort of authority about controversial points, so it can't really be suggested that I don't know what I'm doing,

I do realize, and am grateful, that it is my happiness you are thinking of, but I am sure that you must realize by now, that your idea of happiness does not coincide with mine. We are, after all, two different generations. I feel sure that you would be happy if I was happy, and if this is the case, please remember that your present attitude towards me is making me very unhappy. I can only hope that you will eventually be able to see things from my point of view.

With best love,
Heather

Sylvia's pleas were far more poignant and tore at Heather, so that she stayed more and more in London to avoid the pain of confrontation. 'I implore you,'

Sylvia wrote, 'to give up this dreadful liaison you have embarked upon. I am absolutely convinced that the races are incompatible, their ways are not our ways, nor ours theirs. I am being made ill with the worry. The idea of my little girl being ostracized by the world is too much for me to bear. He is obviously proud of being seen with a beautiful white girl like you, but he has everything to gain while condemning you to a life of misery. Don't you see how unkind that is? I cannot stop crying. And all those dreadful ideas, copied, I suppose, from that wicked revolutionary, Mr Gandhi, giving us no credit for all the good we have done in India over the years. My heart is too full of sorrow for me to write more. My darling, do believe me, and don't let this thing go any further.'

Heather wept and sweated over the replies while Mohendra comforted, encouraged and sorted out the arguments for her.

'I am intensely proud to be seen with you, you beautiful white girl,' he said, 'but between you and me, I wouldn't really mind if you were mauve, blue or emerald green. No one would dare to ostracize you if I am anywhere near because I would at once knock his block off. Tell your Mummy that. Darling, *nothing* like that will happen to us, I promise you. It is on the contrary – we will be looked up to and respected by all the people who matter.'

But when he went away for a few days to lecture to troops in the north of England, Heather was alone in the flat and her spirits drooped in the frightening solitude. She wrote up her diary as she sat alone:

Sunday July 20th 1942
   Horribly depressed tonight. Wondering if the whole thing is worthwhile. Parents still think I'm staying with friends in the Boltons, though I

suppose they've probably guessed I'm not. I hate him being away, but these lectures do at least keep him out of the Army. My First Aid work is exhausting and makes me feel both inadequate and frightened. How useless I seem to be. I live in constant dread of being called up and sent off to some far corner of the earth, but Mohendra assures me that I won't be and that if I am, then he'll get me out. When he's here I believe him, but as soon as he goes away I am immediately beset by doubts. So *silly*. They called up women born between 1918 and 1920 last January, so my group will be next. The only way I can see myself getting out of it is by having a baby which is rather drastic, and I can't even consider that sort of solution at the moment.

The whole business of the showdown with the family has devastated me, though of course I really expected it all along, in spite of Mohendra's optimism. All these desperate letters from poor, sad little Mummy who is so pathetically silly. She wrote a 'straight from the heart' letter to Mohendra which we have answered in great detail (thirteen pages!), all terribly rational and trying to keep emotions out of it, but of course she cannot be expected to see reason or accept anything we tell her. I feel so sorry for her, but can't just give up because of that. Mohendra insists that she will come round in the end but I don't think she will. He's so ridiculously optimistic about everything. That really can't be classed as a fault, more an asset; it should help to balance pessimistic me. He is at the moment insisting that he is going to write a complete book in three weeks and be made Ambassador to everywhere in the world after the war! But as he says, is it so wrong to set one's targets high? Of course not. And then this nagging worry I get about not having enough money. He says that this mean streak I have about money is a bad fault. I suppose it is.

Can't write more. Desperately lonely and unsure. Will telephone Hugh, he will probably be able to dispel a bit of my gloom.

Hugh came over straight away with a quarter bottle of gin.

'You can't waste that on me,' Heather said. 'It's precious, and I shan't appreciate it enough.'

'Nonsense.' Hugh poured out two measures and added tonic water. 'Gin is never wasted on a depression. It takes edges off situations and makes them more comfortable.'

'Am I doing the right thing, Hugh?'

'Shouldn't think so for a moment, but who does the right thing anyway? And what is the right thing? All anyone can do is to launch off in one direction or another and then make the best of it. Did I do the right thing shacking up with Istvan?'

'But you seemed so able to cope with family opposition. You just went ahead and did it, no fuss or anything. I just can't bear all this dreadful drama.' Tears started to spill over; she felt hysteria mounting in her.

'Nor could I. And I've lost my family now. None of them will speak to me.'

Heather forced back the rush into self-pity. How could she believe she was any worse off than others?

'How much do you mind?'

Hugh shrugged. 'A lot sometimes because I was horribly attached. I don't know if I did the right thing. But I wanted to be an artist, that's the life I've chosen, and I never could have been if I hadn't broken free.'

'We're trying not to get ourselves cut off if we can possibly help it. Mohendra still thinks they'll come round in the end if we are patient and tactful.'

Hugh smiled a very broad smile. 'That's a side of Mohendra you will have to get adjusted to.'

'What? His not being able to contemplate failure you mean?'

'Yes, that,'he glanced at her quizzically, 'and a bit more than that. A rationalization of all his actions in excelsis.'

'What's wrong with that?' She felt defensive. 'That's one of the things I love about him. He makes me look at things from a logical, rather than an emotional point of view. I mean this whole thing of taking the plunge and getting married and everything, I could never have agreed to it if he hadn't proved how logical and right it was. If there was no reason why we *shouldn't*, then we should.'

Hugh laughed at her. 'That doesn't really sound a very good reason for marrying him, my darling.'

'Don't be so dense.' She threw a cushion at him. 'Shall I tell you why I really want him? It's because I can depend on him, you see, because he knows all the answers. I am proud of him because he looks so wonderful and is so clever and yet has chosen *me* who is stupid and clumsy and gawky and uneducated . . .'

'Here, here – that's quite enough of that. Just be quiet and listen to me for a moment. You, Heather Jones, are the most beautiful, intelligent, attractive and darling woman I have ever had the good fortune to meet. You are worth ten of Mohendra.'

'Oh rubbish, you're just trying to cheer me up.'

'Heather, I mean it.' Hugh took both her hands and looked at her seriously. 'I don't know if you are taking the right step or not, but I do know that whatever step you do take, your own strength of character is the thing that's going to make the best possible job of it.'

'You're so nice to me, Hugh,' Heather found herself embarrassed at the intensity of the conversation. 'But you're quite wrong, you know. Mohendra's worth ten of me. I'm pretty useless and weak without him.' Her eyes suddenly sparkled again. 'And I haven't even mentioned the main thing – he's superbly great in bed!'

As they sat together in the sordid comfort of Mohendra's room, Heather felt the depression lifting and a sense of lazy insouciance take over.

'I feel I can tackle the world with him behind me,' she said. 'It's just when he isn't here that I go all weak at the knees.'

'That feeling won't last, I promise you. You're still in the puppet and master situation that you're so fond of. Before very long you'll find that you're holding the strings and giving the stage directions.'

'How you think I'm going to give Mohendra any sort of directions I can't imagine. And anyway, I don't want to.' She sank lower into the tattered and dirty armchair. 'I just want to be protected from all the nasty things of life by a strong, beautiful, god-like creature exactly like Mohendra.'

The telephone shrilled suddenly, and Heather jumped with such force that she knocked her glass off the table.

'Hallo? Oh darling, it's you, how lovely . . .'

'And who else would it be, pray? Here am I, working my fingers to the bone for a worthless girl who doesn't even remember my existence. Are you missing me?'

'Unbelievably. You can't imagine how depressed I was tonight. I even thought of running home to Mummy because it seemed so silly to stay up here without you.'

'But my darling, you must fight those thoughts. I left you so many things to get on with while I was gone; sorting out those press cuttings into a book, typing that article – and what about the painting you started?'

'I didn't have any inspiration. It was hopeless

133

anyway, and I *have* done quite a lot of things since you left. But tonight I was so depressed because I missed you so much.'

'Silly girl! Don't you imagine I'm missing you too? Talking to all those troops, very depressing sometimes.'

'Must be awful – I know, I'm much better off. I've even got Hugh here to cheer me up.'

'Hugh? Why should he come round?'

'Because I asked him. He's wonderful, I feel much better now.'

'So unnecessary.'

'What?'

'Why waste time in chit-chat when you could be getting on with all that useful work?'

'But Mohendra, I was depressed, I was missing you, I just . . .'

'And I wasn't depressed? Wasn't I missing you, too? Do I therefore ring up some girl or other?' The pips went. 'And I have no more money for the phone. Have a good time, enjoy yourself.'

'But I . . .'

The phone went dead.

'You shouldn't have said I was here.'

'He just feels low because he's so cut off from us all. He just wishes he was with us, poor darling.'

The depression slid back into place.

'I'm so selfish,' she said. 'I was not really thinking of him at all, only my own miserable self.'

Hugh got up and hugged her. 'I refuse to stay in the company of such a fiendishly selfish pig. You don't deserve me, that's all. Want to come and stay the night with us?'

'No, I'd better stay here in case he phones again. He would be so upset if I was out.'

There was really no more to be said.

11   The Straw House

Two things happened during the next six weeks that shook the foundations of the straw house. The first was that Heather discovered herself to be pregnant.

'There's nothing to get upset about,' Mohendra assured her. 'Plenty of girls are a few days late.'

'A week late.'

'Even a week late. Sometimes women miss a month altogether and be none the worse.'

'*I* couldn't.'

'You don't know – all you can say is that so far you have been regular, but that doesn't mean anything at all. With all this anxiety you have been through with the family lately, anything could happen. You don't have to panic. I'm sure it's all right and you're not pregnant at all. Can't see how you could be unless the blessed Holy Ghost's been at work. It isn't as though I took any chances, I was always in complete control.'

The test was positive, and Heather felt the bottom drop out of her world. She had had so many fantasies about the moment when she should find herself pregnant for the first time. It was to have been one of those great moments in life which she would treasure in her memory. It fell into the same category as fantasies about her wedding day which had already been relegated to the anti-climax of reality. Pregnancy now seemed about to join them.

'What can I tell them?' she wailed. 'This on top of everything – it's too awful.'

Mohendra took her in his arms in great distress. 'My darling sweet, don't cry. I feel so bad, really I do, but I was so sure nothing could have happened. I can't bear to have caused you grief like this. So stupid when everything was going so well.'

'What was going well? I can't think of one single thing that was going well.'

'But of course it was going well, they were just beginning to accept the inevitable, and we could have announced the wedding date very shortly. Never mind, we'll solve it somehow, my darling. I'll at once get in touch with the very *best* doctors, I know quite a few, and they will be able to arrange an abortion, don't you worry.'

Heather shot upright in her chair. 'But that's illegal. It's much too dangerous, and to have it done properly costs the earth – at least two or three hundred pounds. There's no way we could raise that sort of money on my dress allowance and your lecture fees.'

'Don't worry about money, I will get it.'

'How possibly?'

'Friends or relations will always help when one is in a jam. Even your Mummy, we needn't tell her what it's for. Or perhaps Louise as an old friend.'

Heather's gorge rose in a sudden agony of fear and disgust. 'I think I'm going to be sick.'

How could she be seriously discussing the idea of getting rid of her baby? 'I don't want to have an abortion.'

'But darling, it would be the most sensible thing. Of course we want babies, lots and lots of them, but wouldn't it be much better to have them when we are a little more settled, perhaps have a little more money and a nice home and everything? And, as you say, it

136

would be adding insult to injury for your poor Mummy and Daddy.'

Why did he have to keep calling them Mummy and Daddy. She pushed past him and made for the lavatory, returning a few moments later.

'I don't want an abortion,' she repeated. 'Our baby is there, now. We can't just throw it down the lavatory and pull the plug.'

Mohendra sighed and turned away from her. 'That's a rather crude way of putting it,' he said with distaste, 'but if you feel so strongly about it, I wouldn't dream of putting difficulties in the way. My darling, let us then bring the date of our wedding forward, how about that? It would be much better anyway, now that everything has been brought out into the open. No sense in hanging about now that they know we do mean to get married.' His voice returned to its usual enthusiasm. 'Darling Miss Jones, will you marry me tomorrow?'

'Couldn't we say that we're married already?'

'Not tactful, my dear, not tactful, because that would make us seem to have been underhand in our dealings and that would make them more suspicious than ever. It would be much better for us in the long run to be open and straightforward with your parents so that we could not be blamed for anything. It would be good to have their blessing. It would not be good to give them the chance of breaking with you completely. You must go tomorrow and tell them as gently as you can.'

'I can't – I could never do it alone, you must come too.' She felt abandoned and desolate. The world was right and she was wrong and now was having to pay for her mistakes. She started to cry again. 'I can't go alone.'

Mohendra stroked her face and kissed the tears. 'Of course you can, my brave love. I can be with you right up to the last minute and then wait for you, concealed in the shrubbery if you like. But you must be sensible and strong. I'm just trying to make things easier for you. Don't you see how it would make things worse if I were to go in with you? After what they've said about me, what they think about me, it would only aggravate them. Don't you see?'

And of course she did, and confronted Sylvia alone the next day. Her very presence was too painful for Robert to face it seemed. He was closeted in his study.

'Mummy, now that you know that we are serious and in love, we would like to get married as soon as possible. On September the first, actually. We thought that would be a nice date.' How lame it all sounded.

Sylvia burst into tears, sobbing loudly and rocking herself backwards and forwards. 'Oh dear, oh dear, how can I bear such sorrow? That I should be called upon to bear it. I was so hoping you might be prevailed upon to wait and then perhaps see the folly and the tragedy of it all.'

Heather fumed, which made it easier. 'For goodness sake stop over-dramatizing the whole thing. Would you rather we lived in sin then?'

Sylvia stopped crying immediately and sat up very straight in her chair. 'How desperately cruel you have become, my darling,' she said. 'A few months ago you never could have said such an unkind thing to your Mother. His influence is wickedly strong.' Tears coursed down her cheeks again. 'You must promise me one thing.'

'What?'

'That you won't start having children for at least a year. Please, darling child, you don't have to rush into that step. For their poor, dear, innocent sakes. At least be unselfish enough to think of them, and consider what misery you would be condemning them to. There is surely enough unhappiness about without adding to it. In a year perhaps you will have realized the wisdom of my words and vow not to bring such poor wee misfits into the world.'

Heather's rage all but overpowered her. 'How can you dare to talk such utter nonsense?' she shouted. 'It's useless to talk to you at all. I tried, but it's useless, I see that now. So let's say that we'll be married as soon as we can get the licence, all right? And I'll send you an invitation to the reception.'

'They'll probably all die anyway,' Sylvia sobbed. 'It's well known that they are always particularly delicate as well as inheriting the worst of each parent.'

'That's all right then,' Heather shouted back from the door. 'At least you can look on the bright side in that direction.'

She was distraught when she reached the flat where Mohendra was waiting for her. 'She can go to hell for all I care,' she said. 'Hateful idiot, fool, selfish beast,' and she put her head on her arms and allowed the tears to flood in a great explosion of grief.

'Darling, darling, don't cry like that.' Mohendra held her and rocked her backwards and forwards. 'Oh Gods, I am a worthless man, causing you all this distress! But my sweet, I will make it up to you, this I swear. Our baby *will* be born in happiness, I promise you, and it will be the most beautiful, the most intelligent, the most adorable girl in the world, just like her mother. I will personally see to that also.'

The wedding was fixed to take place in three weeks' time, on September the first, at the local Registrar's Office.

Heather remembered the time she had first discussed weddings with Mohendra, all those aeons ago – all of six months. The fairy-tale picture she had then, of herself in white – queen bride – in a mist of gauze, lilies, laughter and magic. An anticipated moment looked forward to all through childhood. *The* day – *your* day – when the world revolves around you.

She remembered very well how the dream had suddenly faded as they talked that day. How a grey web of earnest, rational good sense had dropped down over the fantasy picture.

'You dear, romantic thing!' he had said. 'If you want a white wedding, then you shall have one, with all its frippery, trumpery tinsel and its mumbo-jumbo superstition – I swear it. Hand on heart! Put your hand here, on my heart. Is it beating? Then what I say is true, you shall have the whitest, most idiotic wedding the world has ever seen; be it in church, temple, synagogue or mosque – all four if you like. I swear it, my sweet.'

The white wedding dematerialized inexorably and almost immediately. And they had gone on to discuss whether marriage itself was actually necessary.

'If there are children it is,' Heather said. 'And of course there will be children, dozens of them.'

'Marriage is not necessary to children,' Mohendra had argued. 'It doesn't make them into better people to have parents tied together by a piece of paper. But with English law as it is at the moment, it's more convenient for them, that's all. But I'm sure it would please Mummy and Daddy, so my darling, marriage it shall be. You only have to name the day.'

Six short months ago. Heather wondered why the odd formality of the marriage ceremony had remained in the overall plan. But now she did not seem to be at all in control of either her immediate life, or her own feelings. Instead she sensed a frightening vacuum where her feelings should have been. She was in the

140

still eye of a busy hurricane. The centre point, but with no influence on what was going on around her. Quite a restful position, in fact, because everything that was to happen would happen without any necessary intervention on her part.

But on August the twenty-fourth, eight days before the wedding, the second bombshell exploded. Heather's father got up one morning, as usual, and dropped dead in his dressing room from a heart attack.

Heather walked with her mother to the funeral service through the Stoke Poges churchyard which was filled with nostalgia. Why did she feel no sorrow for this man who had been her father? Not even a sense of loss. Why was she not grieving? Or at least feeling sympathy for her mother? Blindly, she tried to put down the real anxiety which was there, lurking, all the time. How would this affect her own plans? She took her mother's arm in a hopeless attempt to expiate her own self-absorption.

Bobbie was back on compassionate leave, but Malcolm was still overseas. Mohendra had wanted to accompany her.

'A good gesture, I think. I would like to show respect to your Daddy, and it would give me a chance to meet the family and friends.'

'You can't,' Heather said. 'It would make things worse, really it would. Specially for me.'

'You are being unreasonable, darling. You cannot keep me hidden for ever. You are still much too insecure. I would have thought it inconceivable for you even to attend if you felt that I would not be welcome. I should never dream of going anywhere that I could not take you. Most particularly to my own father's funeral.'

Heather could only cry in response.

141

'Oh very well then.' Mohendra began clattering cups and saucers in the sink. 'Go – by all means go. I haven't the time anyway. This place is a pigsty, it will take me all day to clean.'

Very few people spoke to her after the funeral. Was she imagining that the indifference was studied? It was difficult to know for sure with those who gave her a hurried, embarrassed smile and turned away. All thoughts were, of course, for Sylvia who was looking, Heather thought, much more dignified and attractive than usual, with her black dress, silver fox fur and a new black hat. Heather looked at her from a distance for the first time, as somebody she had not really seen before, and certainly did not know well. Still no real feeling there for her though.

Heather checked herself angrily. This had gone far enough. She put on what she hoped was a sad smile and wondered whether it looked more like a grin.

Bobbie approached her and she felt her heart flicker. How much did he know about her? Had they discussed her together? Had there been a family conference? Had they asked him to use his influence? It seemed likely.

'Mother's taking it well,' he said. What did he mean? The death or the marriage? 'Thought she might go completely to pieces after what you've been putting her through.'

So he meant both. Heather felt tears prickling behind her eyes. She opened her mouth but could find nothing to say.

'She'll probably get delayed shock reaction,' he said. 'You'll have to watch out for that. I've seen the doctor and he's given her something to calm her down, but she shouldn't be left alone now. So you can't go gadding up to London every five minutes, you'll have to stay and look after her, being the only daughter.'

142

Furious at herself for being unable to control the tears, she turned her back on him. 'You don't understand, Bobbie, I can't even talk to her any more, nor she to me. I just can't come sheepishly back into the fold with my tail between my legs, only daughter or not. It wouldn't work. Anyway, I'm getting married next week, didn't you know?'

'She did tell me you'd threatened to, but I naturally thought you'd put that off now this has happened.'

She turned back to face him, tears or no tears.

'There would be absolutely no point in putting it off,' she said, making the decision as she said it. 'I will come back to her as a married woman or I won't come back at all. If she doesn't want me that way – if none of you want me that way, then you needn't have me.'

She was amazed to see that Bobbie was smiling. 'Good for you,' he said. 'I abominate what you are doing, but I can't help admiring you for doing it.' He squeezed her hand. 'And tell the black bastard I hate his guts.'

Heather smiled in spite of herself and wanted to hug and kiss Bobbie there and then for his admiration. What a complete nightmare this all was. Had she been the cause of her father's death? Could her mother survive both shocks? Could happiness really blossom in the face of all this disaster?

She made her way back to the flat that night in an unremembered haze of exhaustion, doubt and desolation. Mohendra opened the door to her and immediately held her to him. The relief was overpowering.

'My poor darling. How awful this is for you. I have been crying for you all day, and am sick with myself for being so thoughtless this morning when you left. Of course you were right to go alone. You are always right; so wise, so clever, so *won*derful.'

How could she ever have doubted? Here lay

143

strength, understanding, kindness and protection. She hugged him gratefully.

'Together we shall be invincible,' he said. 'And on September the first the first invincible link will be forged. I swear to care for you to eternity, and love you much longer than that. I swear it! Cub's honour!'

The Middle

12   Plain Mrs Hiremath

All through the first month of married life Heather sailed on a daze of unreality. This was not actually happening. She was not waking up each morning in Mohendra's flat, in that harsh little iron bedstead, as plain Mrs Hiremath. Nor was she Heather Jones of Slough. Who on earth was she?

There was no mistaking, on the other hand, who Mohendra was, because he was what he had always been – since the beginning of time. He was the rock on which her small belief was built; cram-full of energy, faith and an awareness of where he was going. So full of certainty.

'Now that we are together, my darling, and you don't have to do any silly war work because of the baby, we must make our own lives work for us. So many opportunities we have, we must make full use of them to impress our little mark on the world.' His enthusiasm was irresistible, she was caught up in it. 'Just now of course,' he said, 'as the adored expectant mother of my eldest child, you will be treated as a VIP, and until that beautiful creature chooses to arrive, I will be your willing slave and wait on you hand and foot. You will take life with consummate ease and not lift a finger. Added to which, there must be absolutely no worrying. I forbid it, you understand? Our baby is to be surrounded by peace and tranquillity both before and after she-he is born, because I insist on it being the most beautiful, and the most balanced baby in the world. All those books you want to read, now is the time. I will ply you with books and with love just so that you can relax and prepare, while I do all the cleaning and cooking and shopping, as well as earning the daily bread.'

It was all so easy to believe and accept. 'I am perfectly capable of pulling my weight, you silly man. I'm not an invalid, merely a rather pregnant lady. And as soon as Daddy's money comes through, we shall be able to look for somewhere else to live. Just imagine how nice that will be! Our own home.'

She told Sylvia about the baby a few weeks later over the telephone.

'Hallo Mummy, I rang to find out how you were.'

'Oh my darling, how sweet of you. I'm bearing up you know, everyone is being *so* kind, you wouldn't believe. I'm being quite spoilt really.' There seemed an unexpected switch to the good old days. Almost as though nothing had changed. 'Alistair and Elizabeth have been here for the weekend. Alistair is so helpful about all the dreadful arrangements that have to be made. He knows just what to do always. But what about you, my pet? Are you managing? Are you all right? I worry about you so much living up there in those dreadful furnished rooms with all those awful bombs. Why ever don't you get a wee place in the country? Plenty of places down near here, I'm sure . . .'

'Well, we . . .'

'I mean it seems so silly to stay up in London when you don't really have to. And I expect it's bitterly cold too.'

'We don't really have enough money to move just now . . .'

'This is what we expected, didn't we? Has he not got a proper job yet then?'

'Yes, he . . .'

'He really should start thinking of you a little, shouldn't he. I mean any sort of job is better than nothing. He can't expect to be kept for the rest of his life. I mean why should he? Why should you . . .'

'But Mummy he *has* a job. He lectures to troops all round the country and . . .'

'Lectures indeed! And where has that ever got anyone? But never mind, darling, Daddy's money will help you out when it comes through; though I want you to *promise* me you'll keep it for yourself and not go handing it over to someone else we both know. It won't be all that much of course, because he did leave the bulk to me for my lifetime, naturally.'

'Mummy, I'm going to have a baby.'

There was a dead silence for a moment.

'My sweetheart – what a disaster! The selfish brute! Couldn't he – but you must have it stopped. I'm sure any doctor would see . . .'

'Don't be so silly, I'm absolutely delighted, and only sorry that you don't seem to be.'

'You're such a brave darling to make the best of it like that – but what a disaster. And after the promise you made me that you wouldn't have any babies for at least a year. But of course it's his fault, not yours. My poor darling, when is it due?'

Heather was ready with her adjusted calculations. 'Sometime round June. And it's *not* a disaster.'

'All right, darling, it can't be helped now, I suppose, so we must put a brave face on it. But it's the shock you see, it will take me a little time. I'm not as brave or as strong as I was.' Her voice wavered. 'My poor baby. Let's hope Daddy's money comes through quickly. I'll send you a cheque darling – you must have extra milk, you know.'

'We can manage. And I do get extra milk and orange juice and cod liver oil, so you don't have to worry. I'm all right.'

'You poor soul, you must try to be brave.'

'Oh Mummy, you're hopeless. I'll ring you again soon, I have to go now.'

Sylvia was crying. 'What a disaster,' she said.

Robert's Will took longer to process than they expected, and six months later the situation was still bleak. Heather almost enjoyed the privations. Housework was a completely new experience to her, and seemed a good way of masking the fact that she was doing nothing with her life. Keeping the place clean, cooking and shopping, were all essential duties, there was no denying that. Mohendra spasmodically washed up and put things away when he was there, grumbling that the place always looked untidy. But he insisted that the housework could easily be fitted into the moments in between their more important work of writing, painting and reading. 'I don't want any wife of mine to be stuck in the kitchen,' he said. 'No one can accuse me of having the Hitler ideology of Kirche, Küche und Kinder.' Heather hoped she would be able to organize her work efficiently in time. Dealing with the restricted amount of money they now shared gave her a satisfactory sense of deprivation. She made lists and kept a meticulous account of every penny spent, so that none should be wasted.

'I'm beginning to feel a real person,' she said. 'A bit more genuine and less superficial.' Dealing with everyday events and organizing life so that the best could be got out of it was new and she found the achievement satisfactory.

'My dear silly one,' Mohendra said, 'you surely need no assurance of your own implicit genuineness? No, it's not that I'm concerned with, but darling, I am concerned that you are not, at the moment, in the best, nor the most serene surroundings for the state of your mind. I don't want our baby to be born in any sort of adverse conditions; we must provide the very best of circumstances for mother and child. None of your stables and mangers for our baby.'

'But I don't feel in the least deprived. The fact of our being together and me being able to do so much reading, it's sort of paradise really, after the upset of what went before.'

'But the raids, it's silly to take such a risk. You would be so much better in the country. Surely your Mummy would see that and have you down there?'

'Go back there?' Heather was aghast. 'You can't mean you want me to go back there.'

His smile was full of teasing good humour. 'Don't be so prejudiced against your own Mummy, my dear. I am sure she would love to have you back in the fold for a bit. She must be very lonely. You really owe it to her to relent a bit towards her. Now that we have achieved our aim, and she sees that we are happy and that all her silly fears are without foundation – now is the time we should slowly start to win her back.'

Heather felt discomfited at her own biased attitude. She had seen her antipathy as a revulsion against asking any favours of the enemy. But he was right, it was just a prejudice. Mohendra had so much common sense. She hugged him to her. 'I'll go and stay with her when you go on that wretched lecture tour next week and see what she says.' They kissed and laughed and kissed again. 'My wise and gorgeous guru,' she said. 'What should I do without you?'

Sylvia was effusively welcoming over the telephone. 'My dear wee thing, how *lovely* to hear from you. I didn't know – I mean I wasn't sure – of *course* I'd love to have you here all to myself for a few days! How perfectly splendid! How long is he away for? You shouldn't be left a moment now; I mean you never know *when* it might arrive, do you? You come straight over and I'll look after you, my darling.'

'Well, I thought I might look after you a bit too, Mummy.'

Sylvia's laughter pealed out over the phone. 'Oh my darling, what nonsense! I don't need looking after. You know I have Auntie Emmy here now – *she* thinks she's here to look after me. At least that's what she *says*. You know Aunt Emmy, it's a question of who's looking after whom, if you ask me!' She seemed to have adjusted to the role of widow without undue tribulation.

It was all so strange, going back to the life that was. It seemed an age ago, and yet it was less than a year since home began to disintegrate and become a non place. Though from the very first talk she had had with Hugh in the churchyard, it had started to change into somewhere to escape from, rather than scurry back to. Sitting on the bus from Slough station, half longing, half dreading, she imagined it must feel like this when you went back to visit an old school the term after you left. You were a big girl now.

The bus left her at the village, and she picked up her case and started the struggle back home, weighed down with the new life – books in her case, baby in her womb. These fatuous similes, why could she never keep things on a more sober level?

The lane was overpoweringly nostalgic. Here was where . . . and there was where . . . and just there was . . . And that was where she saw the firecrest, and there the blackbird had mobbed her when she got too close to its nest. And that was where she fell off her bike because of a thoughtless motorist. And that was where she saw the run-over cat when she was quite young; her solar plexus tingled with the memory; its nose had been

152

bleeding. And there was the stile where she had torn her dress; that was the time Miss Beadle had fallen into a ditch while blackberrying. She laughed out loud. And this tree – she put the case down for a rest – this tree was where Louise and she had hidden so often in the high branches to watch the world unseen. Prodigal daughter, she thought rather irritably, and picked up her case again.

On the doorstep her spirits rose, and she knew exactly who she was: the pregnant, married daughter coming home for a visit, a visit which was anticipated with enormous excitement by the prospective grandmother.

The door was opened by a parlourmaid she didn't know. Another wartime adjustment? But Sylvia was immediately behind, dressed becomingly in grey and white now, rather than the unprepossessing black that she had kept to since Robert's death. She swept through to clasp Heather to her.

'Oh my pet, how lovely; come in, come right in now and let me look at you. My word what a size!'

Aunt Emmy loomed in the background. Aunt Emmy tended to loom because she was so very large. It was difficult to imagine that she was Robert's sister because of the heavy grimness that seemed to hang round her person like a bad smell. Heather remembered her as a part of the background of poor relations that had hovered on the edges of the family at all holiday times. Emmy descended to stay on these occasions as though it were her right, and she always stayed on until marching orders had taken the place of hints on when to leave. She had once been a policewoman and a member of the British League of Fascists. She had found neither to her taste and had left both after a short time to become an official in Our Dumb Friends' League. She felt it her place to serve, she often said.

'Hallo, Mummy. Yes, I am a bit large, aren't I? Hallo, Auntie Emmy.'

Her case was taken, and she was ushered, with tremendous care, into the library.

'Come in, my darling, come in. You must be exhausted with that heavy case. You shouldn't carry heavy things you know. Why ever didn't you take a taxi?'

'There weren't any.' No need to tell them she hadn't the money. She found herself enjoying the novelty of being the guest. Her eyes took in the surrounding luxury with amazement. Could one become unaccustomed so quickly? Everything was so big; the chairs were so soft; the windows so clean; there were no stains on the carpet. She found herself thinking that she was something of a blemish in a lush picture.

'Sit down, sit down, dear one, and tell me how you are. What about a nice cup of tea? You're not off tea, are you? I went right off coffee myself, could not touch it for the whole of the nine months. I had to have things with a clean taste you know.'

'So do I, and I don't like sugar at all.'

Nice, comfortable, pregnant-lady talk. Hard to imagine that she was indulging in it with her mother.

'But precious, you are so *big*, are you sure it's not twins? How far on are you? Let me see . . .'

Heather interposed her adjusted dates quickly: 'Well, September the first to now is seven and a half months, nearly eight really because you count it from the last day of the last period – or is it the first day of the last period?' Make it uncertain, muddle her up a little. But how was it possible that she was discussing periods with Sylvia? They had never been mentioned before. Even the explanation had been left to Miss Beadle after the first one had occurred.

'You should be specially careful now you know.' Sylvia was almost reproachful. 'A little too much

154

extra exertion could easily bring it on and make it premature.'

Heather glanced at her in shock. Was she actually helping her out in the cover-up? Making it easy in advance, just in case?

Sylvia sighed and shook her head. 'I wish you'd waited just a *little*, pet, till you'd got settled at least.'

'Couldn't.' Heather said it with a twinkle. You could actually joke about it.

'It's nothing to laugh about.' But Sylvia had a broad smile. 'You know how people talk.'

Heather laughed out loud. 'Darling Mummy, I know *exactly* how people talk.'

'Yes, of course you do.'

The air of amused agreement between them persisted. Had Sylvia's defence collapsed so completely? Was it because she had lost her back-up? Because Robert was not there to give support? Heather felt her heart lurch perceptibly in understanding. She could have wept. Who was she, to smash her mother's world? Even be partly responsible for killing off her supportive partner; to have hammered away so relentlessly at her comforting little rock of prejudice?

Aunt Emmy sniffed, and Heather remembered her presence with guilt.

'How are you, Aunt Emmy? I haven't seen you for ages.'

Emmy, staid and unrelenting in a tweed suit and a white blouse, looked across at her over her glasses.

'Tolerably well,' she said, 'in the circumstances.'

Meaning, of course, the circumstances of Heather having killed off her father, shattered her mother's existence, and caused her, Aunt Emmy, to take on the responsibility of trying to gather up and restore the smashed pieces. Heather glanced back at Sylvia and met a smile of complete solidarity.

It was some time later that she came up against the borderline of disagreement.

'What nursing home are you going to?'

'I'm going to the local hospital.'

There was a short silence.

'A public ward, you mean?'

'Well – yes.'

'I'm sure you know what you are doing, dear, but personally I couldn't *bear* to be surrounded by so much pain and suffering, nor could I envisage being anything but *private* at such a time.'

'Such a lack of privacy,' echoed Aunt Emmy, 'most unpleasant.'

'I don't worry about that side of it,' Heather said with an assurance she did not feel. 'But I am a bit frightened of the bombing just now.'

'I should think so too. I can't think why you choose to live up there.'

'It's not a matter of choice.' Heather said carefully, so that she did not lose control of her voice, 'but I was wondering about the possibility of having it down here.'

A longer silence.

'I don't know if Dr Brown would have the time to take you on. Doctors are so busy these days, you know, with everyone being called up and all the wounded coming back from overseas and air raid casualties and everything.'

'No, I meant have it here, in the house, with the District Nurse.'

'The District *Nurse*?' Aunt Emmy made it sound a very rude word indeed.

'Oh darling, that's just not possible; not possible at all. I mean how could we be sure she was here at the right time? I shouldn't be the slightest use.' Sylvia gave a high-pitched hysterical laugh. 'I just haven't an

156

idea of what goes on, I was unconscious for all three of you! You would just have to have a doctor here, absolutely essential. I'm afraid you don't quite realize the amount of preparation that would be necessary, how much equipment you need; we just couldn't get it all, not in wartime. We just couldn't take the responsibility.' Her voice rose in panic.

'Quite impossible,' said Aunt Emmy. 'I don't think you should upset your mother by even considering it. She's not up to it. Had far too many shocks lately.'

Heather was numbed. She had imagined there might be difficulties about booking the doctor and the District Nurse, but she had not anticipated this sort of antipathy. She stared at Aunt Emmy in anger. Silly old cow. How dare she interfere? It became immediately impossible in her own mind to stay on, and she longed to get back to Mohendra and the squalor and danger of their attic flat in Fulham. She stayed on for a few polite and affectionate days and then returned to London.

Mohendra was angry. 'Such selfishness!' he said. 'These people have no idea of *real* love and compassion. Can you imagine that happening in my family?'

Heather could not, but his resentment rallied her own sense of defence.

'You've got to think of it from her point of view as well. There's no reason why she should disrupt her life to accommodate me after I have so patently and flamboyantly left home.'

Mohendra snorted with disgust. 'Disrupt her life? What life may I ask? Answer me that, what life? Such unnatural sentiments these people have. In India, mothers would choose to be with their daughters in childbirth; would demand it – it would be their right and their duty. What a people!'

'There are two sides.' Heather was nettled. 'We can't expect her support and co-operation when we have

157

chosen to disregard all that she holds to be right and proper.'

'Not a bit, not a bit.' Mohendra was sternly serious. 'It's just a question of humanity, that's all. I want people to be generous and unselfish towards each other, especially families.'

It sounded so right. She must be wrong in having those misgivings. This exaggerated dread of scrounging with which she had been brought up was perhaps not altogether valid; just another prejudice in fact.

Because of the increased bombing, the hospital where she had arranged to have the baby was evacuating its prospective patients to the Berkshire town of Wallingford.

'A splendid thing,' Mohendra said, 'and I will arrange to lecture to the troops in Reading at that time and to all the schools in the district. I will get all my friends to visit you so you will have great fun, my darling, I promise you. I have doctor friends in both Reading and Oxford which are quite near, and they will look after you personally.'

'I don't believe a word of what you say,' she said, 'but I'm going to pretend to myself that I do, in spite of being terribly frightened.'

'Frightened? What is there to be frightened of when everyone in the county will have your welfare at heart? You will have the best of everything, I shall see to it personally, and I shall be there the whole time.'

'Deliver the baby while lecturing to the troops sort of thing?'

'Yes,' he said. 'It's possible.'

The hospital was antiquated. Bleak, dank and huge from the outside, with *Wallingford Infirmary* written large on a board. It housed the chronically sick, the pregnant, the old, the deserted and the insane, a group to each floor, and Heather's spirits sank when, a week before she was due, she was carried in the cage-like, clanking lift to the top floor. Once there, however, she stepped out into another world.

A starched, smiling sister met her. 'Hallo dear, I'm Sister John. Another one for the torture chamber, I suppose? Splendid. Come and meet your fellow-sufferers.'

She took off down the endless corridor where the sun streamed in shafts into pristine whiteness, and the nurse's feet seemed not to touch the ground at all, they were so quick and light and silent. Taken by surprise, Heather hurried after her at a trot, assailed by the sound of babies crying and the smell of Dettol. Sister John swung open the silent doors at the end of the passage on to a vista of interminable beds, more sunshine and banks of yellow and white flowers.

'Good morning ladies, any pains?' she said. 'Here's another poor unsuspecting innocent come to share the agony.'

The greeting was noisy, cheerful and welcoming, and Heather felt the tautness of both her body and her mind relax into relief. Quite safe here. They would do it all. It was their responsibility.

The actual experience was a milestone. It was just as though she had been foundering in a tumultuous sea and that the act of giving birth landed her fair and square on a solidly triumphant rock.

'I must put it all down before I forget,' she wrote in her diary on the first of May 1943. 'This wonderful, fantastic experience – the birth of our son, Shiva Sebastian Hiremath, last night at twenty past one in the morning. What a stupendous event! I just have to record it all before I lose a single minute. I'd heard such awful stories, I was really frightened out of my wits in case I couldn't stand up to the pain. But I did – I did! Made a terrible noise and shouted at everyone, but it was somehow all so exultant; a sort of inevitable road up to a glorious peak. A triumphant progression. Tremendous, really tremendous!

'Mohendra couldn't get there in the end until it was all over. Not his fault, he tried so hard but all the buses were late and he was terribly upset. But it didn't matter at all, because of course he wouldn't have been allowed to be with me during the birth and anyway it somehow seemed to be *my* triumph. Awful of me but I did feel the achievement and the creation somehow belonged to me, and that I had created a masterpiece all by myself. That first cry! God, I really think something happened to me then – a sort of pride that I don't think anything will ever be able to take away from me.'

13 Another Prop Removed

Mohendra knew that things had not worked out the way he had originally planned, and he realized that this was mainly because of the unnecessary strain imposed by having four children in as many years. In December 1944, nineteen months after Shiva Sebastian was born, Adam Kabir had arrived on Christmas Day, to be followed in another sixteen months by Janaka Jason. Mohendra had pleaded with Heather. 'Only give yourself a chance,' he had said. 'You are giving up too much of your so valuable time to the children. To have them so soon, one after the other, is madness.' He had even tried to insist on taking the precautions himself, but she invariably succeeded in obstructing him at the last moment. Their love-making was still so vitally passionate that he was seldom sufficiently in control to insist when it came to the point. He basked for a moment in the arousal the thought brought with it.

Of course she was a wonderful mother, and of course the children were the pride and delight of his life. When he was with them all and immersed in family existence, his own self, too, was all but swamped. Even away from them he could never fight free of their meshes and only wanted to return to them. But this would not do. There were other things to be achieved; family life could not be allowed to overbalance the ultimate aims.

Heather was unashamedly drowned in motherhood,

161

and almost oblivious to all else. At the back of her mind there was a distant Louise statement: 'Mothers can be terribly boring.' She supposed she was just that, but there was no real belief behind the supposition. There was nothing of any real interest in the world outside. A certain joy and relief at the end of the war, perhaps; the anxieties of the continued privations and shortages; the dawning of a hope for the future, but these things were just a backdrop for the stars of the production – however boring they might seem to the outside world.

Sylvia had become increasingly delighted by her grandsons but utterly confused by their names. Heather told her of the arrival of the third over the telephone. 'Mummy, I've had another boy.'

'Oh my pet – thank goodness it's over, but what a disappointment for you.'

'Disappointment nothing, I can't stand girls anyway. His name is Jason.'

'*What?*'

'Jason, his English name is Jason.'

There was a peal of laughter at the other end. '*James*, how nice. I thought for a dreadful minute you said Jason.'

They didn't bother to tell her about the Janaka until later.

Seventeen months after that, in September 1947, the fourth boy made his appearance. They had taken some time before deciding on an Indian name because Mohendra had been so certain that it would be a girl that he had refused to consider boys' names.

'He should be called Ashoka, bringer of peace,' he said once he had arrived.

'I want to call him Bibendra,' Heather said. 'Bibendra Orlando.'

'Vivendra? That's a nice name.'

'*Bib*endra.'

'That is what I said.'

162

'You have no ear,' Heather said it impatiently. 'Why can't you hear the difference?'

'Viv – Biv – there is nothing in it, he will no doubt answer to both, having both ears perfectly formed. Unlike his poor father who, it seems, has no ears at all.'

Heather laughed, her irritation evaporated at the blatant impossiblity of making her point. 'He's a prince of babies,' she said. 'My best yet.'

'He's very light-coloured,' Mohendra suggested. He sounded deliberately cautious, and Heather glanced at him to see if he was serious. After the blow he had dealt her a few months earlier, could he really be serious? The outside world had encroached suddenly and devastatingly on Heather during the pregnancy, dislocating the balance of her being.

'I had an affair with the milkman,' she said. 'Didn't you know?'

Mohendra frowned. So unnecessary, this sarcasm. Harping on unimportant past events just because her mind was empty of anything intellectual. She would not make the effort to concentrate properly on her art; always this vague, inconsequential approach. No real application in her attitude towards anything. An initial enthusiasm followed by apathy and an unnecessary collapse of self confidence. So undignified. He had always tried to insist on her giving herself time to work by organizing her domestic tasks efficiently, but she had got herself tied up and immersed in useless domesticity. That was the last thing he had wanted for her. Such a waste of a good brain; such a waste. She seemed to have chosen deliberately to burden herself with four children, so that all ideas of serious work had gone out of the window. Thrown away by her own choice. He grew increasing petulant as he thought about it.

'This must be the last one,' he said angrily. 'You have to give yourself a chance as I have so often told you.

You only have to say that you wish me to take the precautions and I will do so. You know that.'

'Yes, I know that.' Heather smiled down at her youngest son. She could easily have stopped this one. She should really have stopped it; done what he wanted. She was self-indulgent and lazy. He was perfectly right. 'I just hate not having a baby round the house,' she said.

'Well no *more*, even though we haven't got the longed-for daughter, there must be no more.' He picked up his son and kissed his cheek. 'You should have been a girl, Vivendra Orlando, but I will forgive you because you are so exceptionally handsome.'

Heather's eyes filled with sentimental tears as she watched them. 'Must he really be my last?'

'Not only your last, but I insist that you get some help with them all so that you will be able to concentrate on important work from now on. All these excuses about no time – you must *make* time. Other women poets, artists and writers make time not only for their children and their work, but for helping their husbands too. Where are all these lovely ideas we had about working together? You would rather wash nappies and play with the children than get on with your own work. So intellectually *lazy* you are.'

He put the baby back in its cot and turned sharply towards the door.

'I met a Danish girl yesterday who said that she would be only too pleased to look after our children. I will telephone her and ask her to call.'

Panic surged up in Heather. Let them be cared for by others? Meaning that she would miss a part of their growing up? Every moment was precious. How could she envisage missing out chunks of their babyhood?

'But we haven't enough money . . .'

'Money, money, always money. It's all you ever

164

think of. There are certain things we have to spend even if, as you constantly point out, I don't earn as much as I might. If we cannot afford these things, then we are lost – our whole lives will be ruined and wasted if we allow ourselves to sink into a domestic rut. I have so much work to do which I can only achieve if you join with me and we work together, like we intended to. Do you remember that time? Not so long ago, but it seems you forget that now.'

'No, I don't. But it was you who always thought I should be able to help, I didn't.'

'So it's all my fault?'

'No, of course it isn't. It's obviously all mine for not coming up to your expectations.'

'Oh darling, don't let's quarrel. You are the most beautiful and absolutely up-to-expectations wife. No one, no one on earth could have produced such magnificent children, nor looked after them so perfectly. Your mere presence is an inspiration to me, so please may I have just a little of that presence with me more of the time? Don't begrudge me that. If you have some help with the children, then perhaps I might claim a small portion of your time – please? With you beside me I shall be able to earn a fortune, I promise you. Anyway, this Danish girl never mentioned wages, I'm sure she would be delighted to help us out absolutely free.'

She melted towards him and put her arms round his waist. This total belief in himself, and his ability to charm the world into supporting him in those beliefs, was an integral part of the man she had married. He was often no more than a fifth son. They kissed and laughed at each other and Mohendra then switched his mind resolutely to the business of the day. So much to do. He walked out of the room, down the stairs and into his own study. Shutting the door against the noise of the children's voices, he felt a certain satisfaction take the place of his undercurrent of irritation. The house, at any rate, had been a good investment. He was glad that he had insisted. Heather had made a great fuss about choosing anything in a district much outside the centre of London – said she didn't want to exchange country gentility for suburban gentility, but he had managed to make her see that one created one's own circle of friends, whatever the surroundings were.

They had found this good solid house in Finchley, a corner site with a garden and a garage. Heather had said that they didn't need a garage as they had no car, but as he had pointed out, her mother now had no need of a second car, and it would be only sensible to allow them to use it. His supposition, of course, proved to be correct.

He remembered the move well, soon after Shiva Seb was born. It had been a very happy time, that. The money from Robert's will had imparted a sense of well-being to both Heather and himself. She was able to be far more expansive and less financially obsessed, he thought. Such a pity Heather had this unfortunate trait; always harping on the subject of money, even talking about it to outsiders; so vulgar. Even among the English it was not considered good taste to discuss money. But she never seemed to learn. Self-willed – and yet admirable in so many ways. Such a lovely girl. He had made an excellent choice when all was said and done.

He telephoned the Danish girl. He had met her on the Danish lecture tour back in the summer and run into her, by chance, at the Imperial Institute the day before. Over here as a student now. He wondered if, perhaps, it was a little tactless to suggest to Heather someone from that particular trip, after the unfortunate incident that had cropped up afterwards. Very stupid he had been to allow it to interfere with his home life, but Heather's

166

over-reaction had also been stupid. She had become almost morbid about the whole thing. So unnecessary, because he never would have allowed the affair to make any difference to his feelings for her and the children. Why could she not see that? After all, she had been very pregnant at the time. She should have had more sympathy with his own predicament and a sense of proportion about a simple, physical slip on his part. She should have been able to realize that the whole thing was an obvious result of an uncomplicated physical appetite. She surely did not expect him to become a total celibate during the last few weeks of her pregnancy? No sense of proportion at all. Such a pity. But this girl had absolutely no connection with Anita, so Heather didn't have to worry on that score. She had just been one of his students in Copenhagen.

'Hallo? Inge? This is Mohendra, who you re-met and reconquered yesterday – you remember? Well, I have spoken to my wife about you and your suggestion that you should look after our children in return for board and lodging – What? Well, *my* suggestion then – but you liked the idea didn't you? And I am sure you will be quite won over by my beautiful boys and my beautiful wife! She is dying to meet you and wants you to come and have a meal with us. What about dinner tomorrow night? But early so that you can meet the children. What about five o'clock? You have the address? Splendid – we shall expect you.'

He opened his diary and ticked the item *Inge Svensen: Enterprise 4911*. He wrote her name on the relevant date page, adding *To tea and supper. 5 p.m.* Then, taking a small notebook from a drawer he wrote *Tasks* at the top of a fresh page, then:

6.30–7. Clear grates. Light fires. Make tea.
8–8.30. Breakfast.

8.30–10. Play with boys.
10–12. Walk or shopping with the children.
12–1.30. Prepare and serve lunch.
1.30–2. Wash up.
Odd times: dusting and cleaning the house.
2–5. Free time.
5–7. Feed, bath and put the boys to bed.
7 to midnight. Free time.

He leaned back in his chair and read it through. Seemed quite reasonable. With all that free time she certainly could not complain about being over-worked. That would give Heather the whole morning and evening to herself – and part of the afternoon too if she would only organize the children properly into playing quietly by themselves; perfectly possible to train them. Plenty of time for work then. No room at all for excuses. He felt pleased and relieved at having solved one of the major stumbling-blocks to their enjoying a happy and productive life. So simple if only some basic concept of efficient organization was employed.

Inge arrived at the door at exactly five o'clock, before Mohendra had returned from the British Museum Reading Room. Heather was tired and angry – with herself, with the children, but most of all with Mohendra.

'Do come in.' She arranged her mouth into a taut smile without attempting to pacify or apologize for the screaming Janaka who was thrashing about in her arms.

'Mr Hiremath, please? You are his wife?'

'Yes, he told me about you. I'm afraid he's not back yet. I expect he will be soon.'

Shiva and Kabir stared with hostile expressions, while Janaka continued to scream and struggle. Heather sat him, rather ungently, on the floor of the hall. 'Try and stop him,' she said to the other two, and hurrying Inge into the kitchen, she shut the door on the noise, and pulled out a chair.

'I've some tea nearly ready,' she said, 'so sit down while I cut the bread.'

Inge was large and brown, with brown curly hair and a rather homespun look.

'You have your hand full,' she said.

'There's a lot to do.' Heather tried to keep the defence out of her voice. 'But I never begrudge any time I spend with the boys, though I do sometimes resent things that keep me from them.' Let her know exactly where she stood as far as help was concerned.

'You must do. If I had children I should want to spend every minute of every day with them and blow to the housework. They are the most beautiful children I have ever seen.'

'I tend to agree with you, of course.' Heather's smile relaxed.

'It is true – no flattery. But then you and your husband have given them a good start, have you not? I so admired this wonderful mixture, and your husband, he is particularly a fine-looking Indian.'

Heather heard his key in the lock and his quick stride across the hall. He came into the kitchen carrying Janaka. 'Why is he crying? Did you not hear him cry? My sweet boy, what have they done to you then?' Janaka's sobs stopped quickly and Mohendra smiled down at Inge. 'You are so punctual! I hope you have been making friends with my wife in my absence. Have you not yet been offered tea? Goodness gracious, where are our manners?' He put Janaka in his high chair and took cups from the dresser. 'Shiva, Kabir, come and lay the table with me, come and help your poor mother.'

Everything was crisply efficient and good-humoured, and Heather turned to pour boiling water into the teapot. There was no reason to take his remarks as implied criticism. Janaka had, after all, stopped crying and the other two were delighted to be involved.

'To be part of this family would indeed be a pleasure.' Inge's voice was full of rapt admiration and awe. Heather found herself liking her childishly appealing veneration. 'Such a wonderfully calm mother and such an understanding and loving father – I so much admire this.'

All right if the admiration was for the family unit, but too much adoration for Mohendra might be all wrong. Heather castigated herself for being a jealous harpie. Not yet over the Danish incident, obviously. Danish incident? It sounded like an international crisis; prelude to war. Was that what she was going to allow it to remain? She was surely over it now; everything had been ironed out – as Mohendra put it. It had meant nothing at all, he said. It had not *in any way* affected his feelings for her, he said. Had he not, in fact, been a reformed character since then? Was he not really trying to be less irritable, more patient, more understanding – the prototype of the loving, ideal husband? Could she not let it rest? Just because this girl was Danish as well, was there any reason to mistrust her? It was ludicrous. She switched her mind and heard arrangements being made.

'We have a splendid spare room and would love to have you making use of it. It's only going to waste.'

'It would be so nice to look after these lovely children.'

Again the panic. 'I need help with the chores rather than with the children,' Heather said. 'I like to look after the children myself.'

'Of course you do, darling, so do I.' Mohendra was understanding and loving. 'But it is the time, my dear,

170

that these demanding young gentlemen take up. We must not allow them to tyrannize us completely so that no time is left for our serious work. Heather is a writer and an artist,' he told Inge. 'She needs a little peace and quiet for that sort of work. She is also a wonderful typist into the bargain. I cannot really do without her help. She is a constant inspiration and an invaluable partner to me.'

Kabir rushed to Heather and clung to her legs. 'She's not your Mummy,' he said angrily to Mohendra. 'She's mine and I shall marry her as soon as I can.'

'You can't,' said Shiva, 'she's married already.'

Kabir looked at him in disbelief, 'Who to? Who's she married to?'

Shiva collapsed into shrieks of mocking laughter in which Janaka joined with delight.

'*Daddy*, you stupid boy!' shouted Shiva.

Heather hugged Kabir to her. 'Thank you for wanting to anyway,' she said. But Kahir shrugged her off furiously.

'I don't want to,' he said. 'You're horrible and so is Daddy.'

'Are you Daddy's girlfriend?' Shiva asked Inge. 'Is he going to sleep with you? He does sleep with Danish girls, you know.'

How did he know? Heather felt a rush of guilt because it must have come from her. What had he heard? He must have heard her say something.

'Give me a chance, sir, give me a chance!' Mohendra was laughing naturally and easily. 'I sleep with Mummy, she would be lonely if I left her on her own.'

Indeed she would, thought Heather, and poured out the tea.

Hugh, who, with Istvan, had remained a supportive neighbour and friend over the passing years, phoned her the next day when everything, it seemed, had been

171

arranged and Inge was joining the family for a trial period at the end of the week.

'I am very down,' Hugh said on the phone. 'Very sad indeed and much in need of support.'

'*My* support?' Heather was amazed. 'Would I be any good?'

'Of course, you would be of immense good.'

How strange, she thought, he wants my support when really I am needing his. 'Then come over straight away. Mohendra is out and I will give you coffee, or even tea, my divided attention, and anything else you may need. You just have to promise that you'll listen to my troubles too.'

'I find it hard to believe that you have any troubles,' he said.

Later that morning they drank coffee in the kitchen, while Shiva and Kabir were at kindergarten and, by some miracle, both Janaka and Bibendra asleep at the same time. They sat amid a welter of washing up, drying nappies and general confusion.

'Of course Inge is a good idea,' she said. 'I do realize I'm not able to cope, but I've just got to make sure that she does the things *I* want, and nothing else.' She repressed the real reason for her anxiety because it was really so silly, and anyway, Hugh knew nothing of the background. He had come to discuss his difficulties. 'What's your problem?'

Hugh looked down into his cup desolately and silently for a moment. Heather wanted to hold him to her and kiss away the distress. She had never seen him like this.

'It's Istvan,' he said at last. 'He's found someone else and he's gone back to Hungary.'

Heather's desire to unburden her own anxieties melted in a rush of sympathy. What an extraordinary coincidence, she thought. 'Is it forever,' she said

172

carefully, 'or only a passing isolated thing?'

'I don't really know. Not even sure if I care. I'm just so bloody jealous I want to die.'

So did I, Heather thought. 'Poor dear Hugh,' she said. 'But it probably isn't forever, you know.' And what sort of use was that remark? It was now he had to deal with. 'Even jealousy gets better with time.' Does it?

'With pain like this,' Hugh said, 'I don't feel I have the time. It's not a bearable pain.'

She was frightened of the way he looked; there was a kind of grey despair in his face.

'Even if he does come back, I shan't be there. I have pills and things. I know how to do it – it's quite easy. I can't sit alone in that studio.'

'You're not going to sit alone in the studio, you are going to stay here with us, and don't say no because I can't possibly spare the time to come dashing over to Fulham to see if you're dead or not.'

'I can't just sit there and wait.' Tears were coursing down his cheeks and dripping into his coffee. 'I never thought I'd be thrown like this. It's ludicrous. I keep saying to myself if only I could be sure of the relationship then perhaps I could sit back and wait for it to return to normal. If only I could be like you and Mohendra are sure. I keep saying to myself, if only I was Heather, I would be forgiving and understanding and *strong*, whereas I find myself consumed with doubt and despair and hate, and only wanting to die.'

'Dying on purpose really makes it worse,' she said, without believing herself. 'Agnostic as I am, I don't feel you would be allowed to escape so easily; hell and damnation would certainly be meted out to you and that would be much worse than your present pain. And you would deserve it just for causing *me* such unbearable grief.' Why on earth does he think me forgiving, understanding and strong, she thought; I am none of those things. 'Anyway, it would be a great pity to die before you'd had time to recover your balance. I know it's a cliché, but things can only get better.' I couldn't die because of the children, she thought, but he hasn't got that sort of lifeline. She felt increasingly inadequate and fraudulent in her false position as the strong, understanding supporter. She wanted to tell him her story so that he could understand how inadequate she was, but decided that this would be self-indulgent. She could perhaps lend herself as a temporary prop. She took his hand in hers.

'Don't think of dying, please,' she said. 'My problems may not be in the same class as yours.' They are, actually, just as bad. 'But I do need your support. I can't help feeling perfectly certain that a Danish girl Mohendra has just invited to live with us is a thin end of a wedge. She is obviously going to replace me in Mohendra's life.'

It took a few seconds for Hugh to bring his thoughts and his eyes back from nowhere to stare at her with the beginnings of recognition. His face relaxed a little, and he gave an explosive and rather strangled laugh.

'What an idiot girl you are,' he said.

'Maybe I am, but you have to spare at least some of your mind to help me out of my anxieties.'

She talked on without telling in a stream of petty grievances and inconsequential patter, because the anxiety she felt for Hugh released her tongue in the irrelevant way moments of stress always had done. It almost reminded her of the recitations of their first meeting; keep talking to cover up the inadequacies of her true inability to cope with the situation. How did one deal with the agony of loved ones? It was all quite beyond her.

As she talked, he gradually emerged a little from the

greyness which had seemed to engulf him. It occurred to her, as she spoke, that she had never really considered Hugh and Istvan as having a permanent relationship. It was not, was it, the real thing, only an alternative to reality. God, she thought, and it stopped her conversation momentarily, that is exactly the sort of mindless prejudice we had to contend with. How could I be so obtuse?

Mohendra's reaction to Hugh's presence, when he came in, was unpredictably warm.

'You must certainly stay with us for a few days, dear boy. We will put you back on your feet, never fear. Until our Danish maid comes, you can stay in the spare room, and after that we can easily fit you in somewhere; plenty of room, no trouble.'

Maid? Heather felt a bubble of laughter well up, but suppressed it.

'Perhaps you will be able to inspire my dear, unsystematic wife to get on with her real work while you're here. You mustn't feel too depressed you know. I am sure things are not so bad as you think. Istvan wouldn't do a thing like that. I'm sure of it. Must be some misunderstanding somewhere. Anyway, I shall be going to Hungary next month to lecture, so I will be able to look him up and bring him home, I promise you. Don't you worry, I will knock a little sense into him – tell him where he gets off!'

Heather was embarrassed by his jocularity and shocked by the statement. Going to Hungary? She glanced at him in amazement, but saw that he obviously believed what he was saying, so why shouldn't she? He might have arranged a trip to Hungary that very afternoon for all she knew. The important thing was to get Hugh through the next few desolate days or weeks. Get him on to everyday things like breathing and living.

175

Though despair and crying were at first only just below the surface, she found that he grasped with relief at any material help he could give with the children, the cleaning and the cooking. At the same time their understanding of each others' problem began to involve itself more deeply. As a means of giving Hugh a chance of liberating himself out of his despair into another's life, Heather talked, without discrimination, about whatever came into her mind. She found her own surface anxieties spilling out in a way that surprised her. Was there really so much underlying dissatisfaction in her life? Hugh emerged very gradually from his depression into an almost continual hubbub of crying, shouting, laughter and disorder.

'It's all so therapeutic,' he said, 'because you have no time to think.'

'No time to stand and stare,' Heather said briskly.

'Exactly. Thank you, good friend. I think I'm going to be able to cope, and now that Inge's come I'm sure Mohendra finds it difficult to understand why, with two maids, Inge and me, working in the house, you should not have become his permanent private secretary and political partner.'

Heather smiled at the idea of the two maids. How do I dare to worry about my small problems, she thought, when his are so much greater? He had been left quite alone.

'I am beginning to feel sane and human again,' Hugh said, 'and rather ashamed when I see you sailing through apparently insuperable difficulties with such enthusiastic poise. Thank you for restoring my sense of proportion.'

Heather found a prop to her own existence had been removed when he left.

14 Just a Loss of Face

The following weeks continued to be filled with frustration for Mohendra. His work was not going well because his time was taken up with matters of organization. He spent much time arranging lectures in various parts of the country as well as overseas, and he resented this continuous struggle to bring in immediate ready money. 'I should really only be concentrating on the more worthwhile things. This lecturing business is only a stopgap, you know, until I can get down to my real work of writing books,' he told Heather.

She was grateful for the stopgap fees, small as they were, which eked out her own income. She was having to sell capital every year in order to keep the overdraft down. But soon it would be all right, she felt sure. When he got down to those books and as long as she was able to keep the family going until he did. He knew so much, had so much to say, there was no way he could fail to succeed in the end.

'I have enough material now,' he said, 'for fifty books, and I have talked to several publishers who are pleading for them. But I have first to make every possible effort to get some sort of paid employment with the Indian Government. With all my overseas experience there is bound to be a place for me somewhere or other, so I have to be on the alert so that I do not miss making all the necessary contacts. This is very important.'

He sat in his study and looked again at the list of books he would write; one on the emerging India, one on Trotskyism and Stalinism in the war years, and a critical treatise on Churchill which he intended to call *The Other Side of Churchill's Medal*. Good title that, might put a few cats among a few pigeons. What a charlatan the man was! His mind flashed from subject to subject and he clicked his tongue in angry impatience at all the things that prevented his getting on with his life. It was as though everyone in the house was deliberately against him; Heather through sheer obstinacy and Inge more through an inability to understand what he expected of her. She could possibly be trained, but Heather was more difficult to control.

Coming into the kitchen one morning, he found Inge struggling with washing up from the previous day's supper, as well as the morning's breakfast things. There was a mountain of dirty clothes on the floor, toys were scattered randomly, and an unemptied pot stood in the doorway.

He snatched up the pot and emptied it with violence out of the window into the garden. 'Where is Heather?' he shouted. 'Why is she not here?'

'She walked the boys to school,' Inge said apologetically.

'Walked? *Walked?* Why did she waste time by walking when she could have taken the car?'

'She said it was a beautiful day and that the air would do them all good.'

'What use is good air when there is all this washing up to be done? Why was it not done last night?'

'Well, I – I had my class . . .' Inge felt upset that this poor man had so many difficulties to contend with. So brilliant a scholar with so much potential should be shielded from everyday frustrations. She felt a great desire to relieve him of all his difficulties. He should not have to worry about domestic details. 'I will finish here very soon. There is not so much. Please don't worry.'

He took a tea towel and started to dry the stacked china, then pushed a pile of dirty clothes to one side and picked up several bricks, four books, a stuffed elephant and a wooden lorry. These he placed on a chair and took a broom from the cupboard to sweep the floor.

'It's not your fault. Heather should have organized things before she went. She should have gone quickly and come back in five minutes so that all this could have been finished by now.' He swept quickly and aggressively. 'I wished her to type this article for me – most urgent it is. Should have been in by yesterday. She *knew* this.'

'I could type it for you, perhaps.'

'You could? That would be most helpful to me. I would be so much obliged.' They left the kitchen together.

Heather meanwhile strode through the spring sunshine in an elated mood. March weather could be the most stimulating experience, and she felt an internal explosion of energy and pleasure. The day made her feel that life could not be better for her than it was at that moment. The weather and the absurd pride she felt at being able to display her creative achievements for all to see and admire. Better than any painting in an exhibition or any slim volume of poems, these living examples of a combined genius. They were certainly beautiful children, no one could deny that. It was not just the indulgent mother's eye that saw that. Their progress through the streets was like some triumphal parade, with passers-by stopping to stare. The big old pram had Bibendra at one end and Janaka and Kabir at the other with Shiva walking beside. Heather's hair was loose and rather long, and she wore light corduroy trousers with a camel jacket and an orange scarf. The three older boys' black hair was long over their ears and cut square, with thick fringes.

'Don't know why you can't have them looking like

179

other little boys,' Sylvia had complained. 'The long hair makes them look like girls. Very pretty but so effeminate. I think short hair looks nice and tidy and clean.'

'But that shaved up the back, short back and sides look is dreadful,' Heather said. 'It would make them look like lavatory brushes.'

Only Kabir's hair was straight, the other two older boys had deep waves and curls. Bibendra's head was covered with a soft down that was unmistakably red.

'What beautiful children!' It met her everywhere.

'How wonderfully sunburned they are!'

'Well, well, you little boys must have had a good holiday in the sun!'

Sometimes she felt bound to explain, almost as though they were accepting praise under false pretences. 'Actually, they do have a head start.' But that, more often than not, caused intense embarrassment to the admirer, so it was more discreet to keep quiet. The whole performance gave her great pleasure.

As she walked, she forgot to temper her pace, and Shiva had to maintain a steady trot to keep up. How to keep the pleasure of these exhilarating times alive for ever? She kept a diary, but felt the need to share her intoxication with others. To spread it abroad a little. Publish something? An article in a magazine? A book about children? The idea filled her with excitement, but of *course* a book! A book on the one thing about which she knew, as much as, if not more than, others.

She charted chapter headings in her mind – there was so much she could say that might help women to see what excitement and satisfaction the whole process could bring. She had to share her euphoria with the world. Mohendra *must* approve of the idea of her writing a book. He would be so pleased to know that she was embarking on something really worthwhile, some really intellectual work.

She dropped Shiva and Kabir at school and kindergarten and raced home with the other two, full of heady ideas and an impatience to share them.

'I've got this wonderful idea,' she said, hurrying straight into the study when she got home. 'I'm going to write a book on babies and baby-management from a new point of view. Very few women think of childbirth as a superb creative experience, and I want to . . .'

'My dear, disorganized wife, you have not the medical knowledge to be able to confront doctors and nurses and those who have made it their business to study the subject. It would take years of research. You are an artist and a poet, my darling, and very good at both those things, if only you would concentrate on them and do a little background study. Until you feel inspired to carry on with either of these talents of yours, you would do better to help me in my work rather than going off at a tangent on some entirely new fancy plan. Poor kind Inge here has stepped into the breach to help me with my most urgent typing this morning, so perhaps you could go and clear the kitchen, it's in the most appalling mess.'

'I have to feed Bibendra.'

It was the only possible thing she could contemplate doing at that moment of deflation. Whether he wanted feeding or not, her peace of mind required his dependence upon her. His gimlet eyes said quite plainly, 'I am the only thing that really matters to you.' And she believed them.

But when she put him back in the pram and wheeled him into the garden so that he could watch the sun through the first green of the leaves before he slept, morose thoughts seethed again in her head. Was the mild, pliant Inge a new threat? Did it matter if she was? The constant memory of the Danish affair uncovered itself as clear and sharp as it had been the day she had read the letter during the pregnant months before Bibendra was born.

Why had she been reading the letters in his Danish file? Was it really by chance, or an underhand descent to his level of listening in on telephone calls just because she had chanced to see a certain entry in his diary? 'Anita 8 p.m.' stared up at her and then some writing in Indian script which she could not understand. She found the letter in his file by design, not by chance. 'Darling,' it had said, written in a flowery handwriting and purple ink, 'I could not talk to you on the phone because there was someone there, but I tell you now how much I look forward to the Aarhus trip. To work for you by day and to love you by night is all I ask.' It had taken some time to read completely, because the 'darling' and the last sentence had been scibbled out in a different coloured ink.

The memory of that moment of discovery was still torment to her mind, it was a feeling of wild panic and complete loss of control. Her heart beat unremittingly with sledgehammer intensity for a full hour after she read the letter, and she found herself walking round the house during that time in a state of total abstraction. Wandering from room to room, picking things up and putting them down again; walking in circles and forgetting what she had just done. And all the time shivering uncontrollably.

Thinking back on it now, on this smiling March day and as she looked down on the satiated red-headed baby in his pram, she marvelled at the tranquillity of the creature who must surely have reeled a little at the violent shock to both their systems a few weeks before his birth. But although the memory of the incident was still vivid to her, the emotionalism seemed to have evaporated. There was now only a cold apathy where before a tumultuous jealousy had been mixed up with despair. Mohendra's arguments were so rational, she had begun to see the sense of them quite soon after the first crisis point.

'My love, I am mortified by my own baseness and weakness. To have caused you unhappiness at this time is unpardonable.' Tears started in his eyes at the idea. 'I abase myself before you and ask for forgiveness for my silly slip, but please, please, let us not make mountain out of molehill. You remember we have talked long ago so much about this possibility occurring? You remember?' She well remembered hours of earnest and stimulating discussion they had had. Such sensible conclusions they had come to. 'And do you not also remember what we agreed? That if the possibility ever did materialize, then as long as it did not interfere with our *real* love for each other, then it must not be allowed to matter. You remember that?' Again she remembered. 'We were agreed? Yes?' He took her hands and clasped them in his own. 'So now, do I have to convince you that you are my only love, however weak the flesh may be?'

There were no real arguments. She would be crazy to doubt the truth of what he said. All she had suffered was just a loss of face and some security, but confrontation and antagonism at this point might mean a collapse of the more important aspects of their life together, and this she could not contemplate. They had talked about it daily for weeks after the incident. Thrashed it all out amicably, Mohendra said. He had been contrite, affectionate and disarming, and she found herself loving him with an even greater depth.

'I suppose this extra love I am feeling for you just now, little as you deserve it, has come about because I found myself face to face with the possibility of losing you.'

'Losing me? Darling how can you possibly say that? There is not even one small chance of you ever being able

183

to get rid of me. Don't you realize that yet? Be sensible, please.'

'How can anyone be sensible about the sort of emotional earthquake I've been through these last few weeks?'

'And all so unnecessary, my dear beloved wife, wasn't it?'

'But if I went to bed with anyone else, no matter how extenuating the circumstances were, you would go beserk.'

'I would only be upset because it would make you look a cheap and vulgar type of woman.'

'A description that can apply equally to men.'

'Ah no, not in the same way. It is far less understandable in a woman.'

'You prejudiced, Indian-type pig! There's an irrational statement if ever there was one.'

'Not at all, not at all. There is a most definite difference between the male and the female sex.'

Heather found herself suddenly shocked by his attitude and a small core of dissent lodged itself unexpectedly within her mind. 'Well, nothing you say will ever convince me that the sex act is not the most important and emotional part of marriage for both men and women equally. Companionship comes a poor second, because you can feel companionship to a greater or lesser degree with plenty of people, so I think that emotional climax and intimacy should, with a little effort, be reserved for a husband or a wife.'

'Exactly, dear, emotional one; sex on its own should not be allowed to disturb the complete emotional climax you so eloquently talk of, which one has with one's partner.'

She lost the thread of her argument and her mind became infuriatingly blank. She returned to bland platitudes. 'But if it's more than one isolated incident,

184

then it becomes an affair and that's not right. It's morally wrong, whatever you say.'

He laughed at her. 'But darling, I have said nothing on that count; I plead not guilty and, in the context of our contemporary conventions and historical traditions, and also in view of our mental and psychological make-up, I agree it is "wrong", in that it can lead to unhappiness. Only in that sense is it "immoral". But you must allow for extenuating circumstances, you intolerant woman you. Being far away for a long time when abstention might cause stultification of thought and creative action, and particularly if such an affair doesn't lead to any decrease of mental or physical love towards the other partner – the exact contrary in our case it seems – then a longer, one might say premeditated affair shouldn't multiply guilt on repetition.'

'You talk like the *Encyclopaedia Brittanica*.'

'And I adore you in *Encyclopaedia Brittanica* terms.'

The very complexity of the discussions mingled with the affection, the protestations, and his gentle, teasing attitude towards her anxiety, combined to lull her back into the comfortable state of certainty that everything was all right. It was only her stupid jealousy getting the better of her. It was quite possibly true, as he insisted, that he never actually went to bed with the girl. She felt so much love and affection for him at this time, and his love for her was obvious; he was constantly showing it.

'I absolutely agree, my darling, that if any action or opinion of mine causes you all this unhappiness, then I am miserably at fault for being the unwitting cause. From now on, I will make it my business to avoid all temptation, this I swear. Cub's honour.'

This time, it was not an embarrassing attempt at humour, it was a dear, childish part of his innately absurd make-up that she accepted, along with other silly little irritations. And when he left for Paris to attend a conference a few weeks after the original debacle, she was full of the same sort of certainty that was only occasionally tinged with small stabs of anxiety.

'No more sex orgies remember.'

'How could I forget, my sweet? You have won me over with your wise and clever theories, I have no taste for orgies any more. Quite given them up, I *swear*.'

The shock of the second letter, although no greater, was intensified by the sense of despair that drowned her. Was it her imagination that the baby writhed inside her with some sort of agony at that moment? She picked up the letter from the hall floor and immediately recognized the writing and the purple ink. The fear inside her crept quite slowly through her being like a paralysing injection, and she walked awkwardly and stiffly through the house into the kitchen which felt warm and familiar like a welcoming friend. The purple ink said PRIVATE in the top left-hand corner, with *Forward Please* written underneath. How did she know he was going away?

It was some forty minutes later that she steamed open the envelope with an acute sense of guilt. 'Darling,' she read, 'I am nearly crying. After buying my ticket for Paris and arranging with my office, I cannot now leave. I cannot get my passport in time. Don't be cross with me. I did my best. I am longing for seeing you. Much love, Anita.'

Heather's love, her trust and, it seemed at that moment, her whole life dropped into a pit.

But her day was filled, as usual, with children's meals, children's tumult, fetching and carrying from school and shopping, all done automatically and totally without feeling.

'Come along, darling,' she said to Shiva, 'eat up your

supper and then I'll read to you for a little bit.'

'For a big bit,' Shiva said. 'I want to be read to for a big bit.'

'All right, for a big bit.'

Kabir upset mashed banana on to the floor with studied deliberation and there was no irritation to contend with. She remembered thinking that she would have shouted at him the previous day, but the further memory of the putting to bed ritual and returning downstairs to the shambles of the uncleared house and the unwashed dishes had gone. She could only now remember the pain of the return of sensation; that hot deluge of anguish that submerged her quite suddenly as she stood by the sink, and put all her dead reactions in motion again. She was still crying painful, moaning sobs some two hours later when the phone rang.

His voice sounded further away than Paris; it was floating and unreal. 'I suddenly missed you all,' he said. 'I wanted to hear your voice. Are the boys all right? Things are going very well here – lots of possibilities . . .'

'There's a letter from Anita,' she said. 'She can't come over to join you. She can't get her passport.'

'What?' There was a silence and she replaced the receiver slowly and deliberately. It was far too expensive to argue over the phone to Paris. Before going up to the bedroom, she took the receiver off so that he could not ring back and lay sleepless until early morning when she drifted into a short nightmare. In it she dreamed she went to Paris, met them together and tried every method of persuasion, cajolement, threats and fury without being able to make any impression. She walked out of the dream, leaving them together, and woke to be sick on the floor beside the bed. It was degrading and disgusting, but the physical, repellent act appeared to clear her system of the tumult of emotion that had returned so suddenly the night before. She found herself again drained, passive and completely blank. It was a great relief. Just like a black curtain being held very close to her face. Stifling and blinding, but quite insurmountable. There was absolutely nothing she could do about it.

She was still in this empty state when he dropped everything and returned the next day. As he hugged her to him, she noticed his familiar smell, that his coat was wet (so it must be raining) and that he had not shaved that morning. He tried to kiss her but she turned her head away and saw at the same time that he was crying. I should be crying, she thought, not him.

'My darling, darling, what must you think? Oh Gods above, what a mess up. But it's not a bit like you must be thinking, darling, you must have got completely the wrong end of the stick. She mentioned in Denmark that she might be in Paris the same time that I was, but it wasn't an arrangement, if that's what you think. Is that why you put the phone down last night? My God, what do you take me for? Some sort of monster? You know quite well how much I love you; how could you imagine that I would do a thing like that?'

A small flicker of hope emerged. Could it possibly have been a mistake?

'You silly girl, did you really think I would have betrayed your trust like that?'

Her tears started to flow again because he was there, holding her and loving her. Absurd to imagine he was a monster. There must be some other explanation. The boys rushed in from the garden and clung to his coat and his legs.

'Hallo, my lovely boys,' he said, releasing Heather to gather them up altogether in one armful. 'Are you pleased to see your Daddy so soon again? I could not keep away you see. I missed you all so much. Do you know last night I just couldn't stop thinking of you all and I telephoned Mummy all the way from Paris to say that I was coming straight home again.' It was all right to tell children lies because they were only little white lies to make them laugh. 'Now what shall we all do today? Shall we take Mummy to the Zoo? What about that? I am going to spend all day with all of you and we will go to Lyons for lunch. Would you like that?'

'Can I have fish and chips?'

'Of course, of course you can, and I will have elephant and chips.'

Perhaps the whole thing might become just another upsetting little incident. Nothing really to worry about. Keep off the subject as long as possible; pretend it never happened.

But when they were alone the pretences fell away and she was left with herself as a person and not as part of a landscape. Wrapped, as she was, in a deep fear of confrontation, there was nevertheless something here that had to be faced.

'You must have arranged it all,' she said. 'You must have been writing to her all the time you were swearing undying devotion to me. You *must* have.'

'Beloved, I swear – there was absolutely nothing arranged. She had said she would be coming to Paris while I was there. So what to do? Tell you about it so that you would worry? Silly idea; if she came, she came – and could do all my typing into the bargain! Don't say there is no method in my madness! But it had nothing to do with you and me, nothing at all. Would I risk all that I have for one night of love? Or even two or three nights, come to that.'

'But that's just what you did.'

'Darling, in your imagination only; it's always playing you tricks. My life with you and my work is everything to me, there is no room for anything else at all, not one small Danish or French or Chinese or Eskimo girl. I promise you.'

So it seemed she was just being silly. Why should she let doubts and suspicions and emotional reactions ruin their life together? He was there, her children were there, her home was there. Could she possibly risk losing these? Or course not. Hold on to what you have, through thick and thin.

'There was just no need for all this fuss, darling,' he said. 'It was all a silly mistake made by my silly, darling wife. But all the same, I am going to devote my whole time, from this actual moment on, to reassuring her, to loving her, to looking after her, and to ensuring that our new baby – which is going to be a girl by the way – will have the very best possible pre-natal life. I will, from this day forwards, look after the boys, cook the meals, do the shopping and I will not nag you about one single thing. This I promise, so that you can just rest, and be peaceful and do Yoga and meditate.'

For the last weeks of her pregnancy he kept the promise with exaggerated care and she found it impossible even to remember the doubts or distrust. He neglected his own work in order to care for them all; it was a miracle and she loved him for bringing it about.

In that same indulgently quiescent mood, Bibendra Orlando slipped easily and quickly into the world in an aura of love and understanding, and he immediately became the focus of Heather's life. The experiences of the previous months converged into a giant volume of love which fastened itself on this, her latest masterpiece. The passion tended to overwhelm her to the exclusion of the rest of her life. She found herself behaving like the parent swans they so often watched on Regent's Park lake, driving off last year's progeny in the spring. Feed times became sacrosanct, though her books and her common sense told her that she should guard against the likelihood of the other children feeling rejected.

'Take them away!' she shouted to Mohendra. 'Take them right away or I'll go mad!' and he hastened to obey, even though the excessive devotion he had lavished on her during those last weeks now had occasional lapses.

Quite unreasonable, he told himself, she is really being quite unreasonable, and with no cause at all. I have done my best to see that she should have everything she could possibly want, that she should be petted and looked after all through her pregnancy; given up my own work to do so, and yet she behaves in this bad-tempered way. No thought for others. I have given up so much of my time to help her and yet she does not seem to appreciate it one bit.

He picked up Janaka and herded the other two out of the room. 'Come along, come along. Mummy seems to be tired for some reason. We cannot seem to please her at all, however much we try.'

I really cannot waste my time any longer, he thought; if she can't manage the children any more without neglecting our work which we should together be doing, and without becoming bad-tempered, then we must employ a maid.

He dressed the children and put Janaka and Kabir in the pram and then strode off towards the park with Shiva running beside him in an effort to keep up. All those articles still to be written, he thought, not to mention the books. Must really get down to work again. Have to get a maid. The obvious answer. That's what we must do.

And so Inge became a part of the family.

15   *Living in a Shoe*

As Bibendra adjusted himself to the life around him, he remained the focal point of Heather's existence. Whether it was the memory of their shared trauma or because the period of his birth coincided with the birth of some allied new beginnings in her own person, her life became inextricably bound to this part of her, even after the division of birth. The change was so subtle as to be scarcely noticeable, but it was nevertheless there in the back of her mind. Life moved into a different phase as he grew.

Mohendra continued to drive himself on relentlessly, constantly frustrated and furious at the incompetence which surrounded him. Still no real recognition from the Indian Government for all the invaluable work he was now doing to promote Indian philosophy, music and dance over here. Giving up so much of his own lecturing and writing work in order to promote the cultural side of the Indian heritage, the Government was bound to recognize his contribution sooner or later. So inept, these people were, with no real sense of what was important in overseas diplomacy; India House was full of incompetents and sycophants; a disgrace.

He thanked God for a solid home life and children who were proving to be such a credit to him. The pity was that Heather still did not seem able to pull herself together, but remained disappointingly negative in her

attitude. She had so much talent but failed to recognize
it in spite of all the encouragement he gave her and
failed also to give him the support he needed in his own
work. He was lucky to have Inge still helping him. Such
a good, devoted worker; a little dull, perhaps, but he felt
that he himself was able to put a small amount of outside interest into her life. She believed completely in
what he was attempting to do and gave her unstinted
support. Fascinating too, that gentle, pliant co-
operation she offered – she was so quick and eager to
learn. It reminded him of Heather as she used to be. A
stab of resentful disappointment pricked him. Heather
had so much more to offer under that hard, obstinate
exterior she seemed to have built up. All the talents
that Inge lacked. How much more of a satisfactory
partner she would be if only he could persuade her to
channel those splendid energies towards combining
with him in more worthwhile ventures. Together they
could still achieve great things. Instead, he felt his own
energies were being sapped by her lack of response and
support. He turned the page of the *Daily Worker* with
an angry snap and uttered a grunt of exasperation.

Inge, at the typewriter, looked up quickly. 'You
would like coffee? I brought in some of those biscuits
you so like.'

He smiled at her radiantly and took her hand.
'Always the thoughtful Inge! How nice to be considered in this way. You know all my needs, do you not?'

'I try to learn them.'

'And an excellent student you have proved yourself
to be, if I may say so. First class honours in thought-
fulness.'

She smiled at his joke. 'I like to do things that
please.'

'And this is one of the things that makes you so
nice – and so tempting.'

She withdrew her hand sharply. 'No, I do not want to be tempting. I only wish to serve, not to tempt.'

'Can I help it if I find that service tempting?'

She rose from her chair and pushed her hands through her hair decisively. 'I will get us some coffee,' she said, and took a packet from the large basket beside her chair. 'Here are the biscuits, you open them.'

'So, it seems I will have to content myself with biscuits.'

Heather remained wrapped within her own sufficiency, such as it was. Bibendra was the immediate remedy for her present ills, which began gradually to recede into a vague, glossed-over memory. The Anita affair started to take on the rather rueful air of an almost unbelievable historic incident way back in the past. What had the fuss been about? She wondered why she had not confided in Louise at that moment of crisis. Their letters were full of intimacies after all. But there was no comfort in relating failures. Particularly not to Louise who was forever doing the right thing.

Hugh's crisis and subsequent visit had also helped to dissipate the intensity. She kept reminding herself that Hugh's position was a great deal worse than her own. He was left alone with himself, while she was still surrounded with all the trappings of family life. And even apart from the children, her relationship with Mohendra was not really changed. Though his initial contrition had gradually worked itself out, they seemed to be outwardly back to where they were. So there was only her unreasonable jealousy left rankling quietly in some shrouded corner of her mind. It was clear that this was the only fly left in the ointment. She smiled to herself as she heard Sylvia's expression emerge from her childhood.

Sylvia was a constant visitor to the house, usually

194

for Sunday lunch and sometimes for a few days' stay. It was difficult to remember that she had once spoken of her prospective grandchildren as miserable, sickly outcasts or considered the imminence of their arrival as a disaster. 'So good-looking and intelligent they are,' she constantly told her friends, adding on one occasion, 'Such a happy family you know. Just been on a lovely holiday in Cornwall and come back brown as berries.'

Heather marvelled at the changes in her feelings for her mother, just as though that bleak, black war between them had never taken place. The love she now felt for Sylvia was genuinely warm and tolerantly benign. Rather motherly really, she thought. How odd, we seem to have changed places. And how right Mohendra had been to foresee that Sylvia would eventually accept the situation. He was constantly being proved right all along the line. His predictions for his own future must eventually also be fulfilled.

Sylvia still guarded her right of motherhood and protection of her chick. 'You work far too hard, my darling, you'll kill yourself if you don't take a little more care. And the house is a complete mess you know. I shall trip over something one of these days and break my neck. That Ina or Enid girl, whatever her name is, is useless, hanging round Mohendra the way she does. You must really get some proper help in the house. Just wearing yourself out. It isn't good enough. Why doesn't Mohendra do something about it?'

'He does, he helps a lot with the children and the washing-up and often with the cooking too, but we can't actually afford it at the moment.' She thought anxiously of the mounting overdraft and a recently increased struggle to keep expenses within tighter limits.

Sylvia clucked impatiently. 'It's just not good enough. I shall personally see to it by giving you an allowance *just* for your own relief. You must get a daily and not let her do *anything* for Mohendra.'

Thus it was that Heather later found herself answering the door to a stream of applicants for the job. Mrs Bonnet was under five foot tall and over sixty years of age. Heather rejected her instantly in her mind, but asked her in for a cup of tea and an offer to pay her fare. She had an incomplete set of over-large false teeth and bad feet. There was no way she could possibly be suitable.

'I think there's probably a bit too much . . .' Heather started to say, but got no further.

'I expect you're going to say I'm too old to manage all this, aren't you? But don't you believe it. When I saw your notice in the shop window, "Mother of four needs help," I said that's for me, mother of four needs help, that's for me I said. But mark you I was thinking of a poor frail little woman at her wits' end when I read it.' She gave a great cackle of laughter. 'So when this great huge woman answers the door to me you can just imagine the shock I got! But appearances are sometimes deceptive as they say and now I'm here I might just as well show off me paces and you can judge for yourself. You see I was the eldest of nineteen and me mother passed away when I was twelve so I had me hands full till me stepmother come along and I went out to work at fourteen and I bin in service all me life since then.'

Are there still such people? Heather thought confusedly as cups, teapot and anything else that happened to be lying around were whisked away into the sink with remarkable speed. Two exhausting but hilarious hours later, the kitchen had been cleared and cleaned and the boys were sitting down quietly and cheerfully to their lunch. Mrs Bonnet was established beyond question as an integral part of the household.

196

She called Heather Madam and Mohendra The Master, and the boys were Master Shiv, Master Caber, Master J. and Master Bib. She came to love the whole family fiercely from the moment she took them on, with the exception of Mohendra with whom she fought intermittently. 'I never did get on with blacks,' she said thoughtfully, 'begging your pardon of course, and no offence meant.' She cooked, cleaned, mended, baby-sat and talked from early morning until such time as she could be persuaded to take the bus back to her furnished room in Wood Green. It could have been tiring, but Heather found she did not have to listen all the time. It was sufficient to catch a word here and there to be able to get the gist, and give sympathetic answers now and then.

But she watched with anxiety over the next few years as the money sank lower and lower in spite of Sylvia's allowances. Mohendra started to turn his attention and his energies into the arrangement of recitals of Indian music, where the takings seldom seemed to cover the expenses.

'Don't you see,' he said, 'if we get a really good organization going to promote Indian culture, it will not only bring in a good income but also give me a chance to show the Government what I can do in the way of putting India on the map over here. That is of paramount importance to my landing a worthwhile job. The British people, God bless them, are absolutely ready to accept all things Indian now that their sense of superiority has been brought down a peg. This is the time to show them what Indian culture is about.'

All very reasonable and really quite possible, but not the sort of thing she herself wanted to join in. Indian music had had a deep effect on her from the first time she had heard it in Istvan's studio, but taking part in the organization of amateur but earnest recitals filled her with dread.

'All these good people come to help me,' Mohendra said, referring to the continuous stream of ardent, and often very odd enthusiasts who seemed to wander in and out of the house at different times. 'But my own wife does not want to lift a finger. What a shame!'

She felt he was quite justified in using the expression as he did – to express shame at her lack of zeal. 'I'm being a snob,' she told Hugh once when she had escaped from a leaflet-folding party to drink wine in his new studio. 'I do realize this, but I feel it's all so second class. Suits Inge beautifully. She couldn't be happier.'

Hugh's studio was neither so large nor so luxurious as Istvan's had been, and it did not have the chaotic appearance of decadent bohemianism which Istvan's had managed to convey, but it was warm and welcoming. Hugh had carved an elaborate name board with 'The Haven' on it and nailed it to his door. 'Expressly for you,' he said. 'I considered *Notre Repos* but didn't think you were educated enough to understand the French.'

'I seem to have been seeking havens all my life,' Heather said. 'I so appreciate somewhere to run to now and then.'

'Don't we all?'

'You seem to be able to make your own refuge.'

Hugh shrugged. 'Well, now I'm alone I've decided to become rich and famous. I'm doing up someone's flat and being paid a vast amount of money to do it – murals and all.'

'I've got to do something too. Our money's dwindling alarmingly. I've written down a lot of little stories I've told the children over the years, and I've illustrated them. I'm going to try them out on some of the publishers.'

'What about Mohendra? Does he approve?'

'He won't know, because of course he wouldn't approve if he did. Inge is terribly useful because she can keep him fairly happy and supply all his needs.'

'*All* of them?'

She smiled. 'Not absolutely sure, but she's so high-minded that I think she would have quite a struggle before she could bring herself to accede to any immoral proposals.'

'Do you mind? Remembering our reactions a few years back. Are we moving into a new sphere of tolerance? You know Istvan is back in England and wants me to live with him again, but I find I need to be on my own. Still love him of course, but he's only a part of my life now.'

'We do change,' Heather said slowly. 'Here is Inge becoming the second wife that I was warned about on my wedding day, and here's me finding her most extraordinarily useful. Mind you, I am not of the opinion that she is actually sharing the marriage bed. I might have an unreasonable and uncalled for reaction if I was confronted with that.' She laughed. 'But then again – I might not.'

The progression of the family through their life was swift, with time hurrying by almost unnoticed. There was so much to do, it was all so absorbing. Sylvia, Mrs Bonnet and Inge were all integrated into the fringes, with Hugh and Louise just outside the circle. This was how Heather liked to think of them. It was a hiatus kind of period, and even when Heather's children's books were accepted and became a modest financial success, she did not feel that a really exciting step had been taken, rather that a satisfactory support system had been instituted.

'Splendid stopgap work,' as Mohendra said, 'but darling, why oh why can you not put your mind to something worthwhile and serious? I could so easily get many important people to sit for you.'

'But I'm not a portrait painter, I'm an illustrator of children's books.'

'Darling, don't think that I am not immensely proud of your achievements, whatever they are. But can't you see that you could be doing something much more important than these little books, something to make the world sit up and take notice.'

'They wouldn't take notice if I did a whole lot of bad portraits of all these important people – which I would, because I'm not interested.'

Mohendra banged his fist on the table, making her jump. 'But you *should* be interested. And a good painter doesn't do bad paintings, he makes sure they are all good, whatever they are – illustrations, landscapes, portraits. He makes it his business to be good at everything through dedication and serious study.'

Heather turned away from him and stacked cups and saucers angrily and noisily on a tray. 'But I'm not a good painter, merely a hack illustrator of worthless and very unimportant children's books, quite brainless and stupid and no good to anyone. And if you don't like me you'd better lump me.'

He laughed and caught her round the waist so that the cups and saucers slid from the tray to the floor. 'Teach me how to lump you,' he said. 'It sounds amazingly sexy.'

The children were delighted by Heather's new-found success. 'Mummy's an arthur,' Bibendra told Mrs Bonnet when the first one was published. 'She used to tell us stories and now she's made them for other children too.'

Mrs Bonnet cackled with laughter. 'So Mummy's an arthur, is she? That's comical I must say. So funny how these little ones get their words mixed. I remember when my Freddie was small there was a lot of words he couldn't get his tongue round. Ever so comical he was. I had an Uncle Arthur once, bit of a rip he was and no mistake. Died of drink at ninety-four.'

The boys grew and went to school and became individual personalities. Shiva the practical intellectual, Kabir the rebel, Janaka the musician and Bibendra the bright star. Mohendra began to grow a little more frenetic and Heather sank in balance into a more static, obdurate attitude. Sylvia grew older and a little sillier and Mrs Bonnet went on talking. Inge's role as the second wife seemed to become more comfortably established.

'I've never made any actual discovery,' Heather told Hugh. 'I suppose because I didn't really want to. I have this feeling that it would be a shame to deprive her when it doesn't seem to affect me, or Mohendra's and my relationship either. Isn't it strange?' She said it with great interest. 'Shows what a good idea polygamy is.'

'Bit one-sided at the moment. Not absolutely fair.'

'Yes, I suppose I do tend to feel resentful sometimes. But I don't think I could stand up to a confrontation and I can't really hope to entice young and eager lovers to my lair when I'm so house- and child-bound, now can I? And it's not that I am sex-starved, you see. He's as ardent with me as ever.'

'Splendid stud.' Hugh's eyebrows were raised with what might have been distaste, and Heather rounded on him with laughter.

'Don't be mean to him. It's just that it's not done over here, in a lot of other places it is.'

'I can't tell if you're being impossibly intellectually tolerant or merely resigning yourself.'

'Nor can I.'

*　　*　　*

Heather and the boys went away that summer on a wet, steaming camping holiday in a Cornish field, so when Mohendra returned from a conference in Stockholm it was to a dark and empty house. He realized with a pang of guilt that he had forgotten that they would already have left before his postponed return. He remembered that he had not told Heather that he would be arriving five days later than he had originally planned and now that Inge had moved out into her own bed-sitting room nearby, the house was deserted. The shock of the emptiness brought a bleakness when he walked into the silence. He turned the lights on and found nothing in the fridge to eat. Anger at once beset him and swamped his unease. Fancy her not having the imagination to leave something for him. He went to his study and dialled Inge's number, glancing at his watch as he waited for the reply. Past eleven; she might be out or gone to bed.

'Hallo, Inge? Sorry dear, did I wake you? My goodness, but you go to bed early these days. Just arrived back, yes, to find an empty house and – much worse – an empty fridge! They're all away you know and nothing made ready for the poor hard-working husband. Could you really? That would be most kind. Anything at all would be welcome – bread, cheese, anything at all. Thank you so much, you are an angel. I mean it, dear, I really do.'

She arrived some fifteen minutes later with bread, cheese, salami, tomato and a tin of soup.

'But what a feast! You have saved my life quite literally – I should have died of starvation by morning. And I have been able to find some fine brandy tucked away in my secret store. We will celebrate together.'

Inge served the food up to him with an earnest solemnity that began to relax only when he had persuaded her to drink a good measure of brandy with him. 'I

202

cannot drink alone. It's not decent at this time of night.' He poured some into a glass for her, and pulling her down on to his lap in the big armchair, he held the glass to her lips. 'Medicine,' he said, 'to lessen the shock of being dragged from bed to feed a ravening monster. How nice it is to be cosseted and looked after. I don't get as much of it as I should these days.'

Inge struggled a little to get up, but he held her back. 'No, please don't move. I need to be cosseted just a little more – and you excite me so much, lying on me like this.'

She scarcely resisted the kiss and was soon overwhelmed by many years of pent-up longing. 'I have loved for so long,' she said. 'I do know I should not allow myself, but it is too much to resist forever.'

'Much too much,' Mohendra agreed.

'It's not,' he said the next morning, 'as though we were doing anyone any harm. If Heather had been here waiting for me, it would not have happened. But she does not have much time for me these days, and she need not know about this. It would be very unkind to tell her, and I don't want her to be hurt.'

'Of course not,' Inge pulled him back on to the bed. 'We must be very careful not to cause any hurt to Heather or those darling boys.'

Mohendra travelled down to Cornwall the next day and was met with screams of excitement and delight.

'My goodness, but you have grown into giants in a few weeks,' he said. 'So all these things I have brought back I had better give to someone else. Where are those puny boys I left behind me? You are obviously much too old for the toys I have. Better throw them all away,' and he gathered up all the parcels he had taken from his bag and put them in the rubbish bin.

203

The boys clustered and clung and shouted with laughter, snatching at the parcels, and Heather stood aside and watched them delightedly.

'It'll make so much difference to them now that you're here,' she said. 'You can take them to the beach while I do the shopping.'

'Will you take us in a boat, Daddy? Mummy was afraid.'

'But of *course* I will. I'll take you in a submarine to America.'

'You can't drive a submarine.'

'Not able to drive a submarine? How dare you, Sir – I can drive *anything*, didn't you know that? Submarine, airship, tank, pony and trap – anything at all.'

The glow she experienced as she saw him take up his share of their responsibilities so enthusiastically was one that had love, relief, pride and happiness all mixed together. *This* was what it was all about. That was why you suffered the bad bits, why you let things slide when they were good, and failed to face up to, or even remember, the disappointments and disillusions that might have gone before.

As they lay huddled together in the small caravan bunk that night, they were both still mellow from the pleasure of coming together again.

'Quite like old times,' Mohendra said. 'So cosy in this little bed. I like it.'

'Good to be on our own, isn't it? Wish we could live on a desert island just with the boys. I've missed you so much down here, a holiday is really incomplete without you. The boys need you. So do I. Been feeling very sexy and broody the last few days.'

'I will attend to it without delay.'

'I hate not having a baby about the house, you know. The boys are practically adult. I think we should have another one. Just one more.'

204

'You absurd, unrealistic girl. It would be silly just now, when you are at last able to have some time to yourself with the boys at school, leaving you with nothing to do.'

She pushed him away and held him at arm's length. 'Nothing to do? Do you really believe it leaves me with nothing to do?' Her anger seized up quickly.

He restrained his own irritable reaction. Showing anger tended to make her more obstinate.

'Nothing is of any real importance if it doesn't concern our work together, darling. I just want the best for you, you know that. I want so much that you should achieve the things you are really capable of. Another baby would be a disaster just now, when we have a real chance of doing something with our lives. Opportunities are everywhere, just waiting to be snatched up.'

Some of the warmth and pleasure faded, but she found herself loving this silly optimism, and the homecoming atmosphere was far too good to spoil. He was actually being perfectly reasonable, it would be mad to start up again after a three-year gap.

'Well, you'll have to do something about it because my cap isn't safe any more, it doesn't fit properly. I have to get another.'

His annoyance surged up again. Why had she not attended to this matter while he was away? So inefficient. Later, the thought occurred to him that the whole thing was some sort of excuse, because that same night the French letter split. Mohendra stared at it in fury.

'Did you do this?'

Heather was convulsed with laughter. 'Me? Of course I didn't. God, how funny! Seems *He* decided to take a hand in the matter.'

Mohendra was never absolutely convinced. As she had obviously wanted a child at that time . . . he had

205

been away some six weeks ... supposing she had had some affair and then found herself pregnant? It wasn't so far-fetched. He took no chances at all for the rest of the month. It was unlikely that anything could happen after just one slip like that. But it was all to no avail. A daughter, India, was born nine months later, looking exactly like him; everyone remarked on the likeness, so there could be really no question.

16   Proverbially Happy Couple

India arrived in the world bald and hideous, like an unfledged pigeon, and in spite of the uncertainties of her conception, at once became Mohendra's *chef d'oeuvre*. Heather, on the other hand, found it difficult to provide as much time for her as she had been able to do for the boys. It filled her with guilt, and she could not imagine the reason, nor really admit to the feeling. There somehow seemed to be far less time now than when Bibendra was born. Why? Her children's books, now beginning to bring in a small financial return, occupied all her spare time, but Inge and Mrs Bonnet cooked and cleaned and took the boys to and from school. There should be more time, not less, for the new baby phenomenon, and yet India slipped methodically into the situation of one of the daily chores which either Heather, if she had time, or one of the others attended to. She was shocked at herself. It was not that there was any lack of love, she was just as infatuated with this plain little baby as the rest of the family seemed to be. But there was this small sense of incompleteness in her thinking which began to creep up on her and would not go away.

The holiday atmosphere of the summer in Cornwall never quite returned. Mohendra's work over the next three years became a more fanatical and concentrated occupation. But in spite of the increased stress, the satisfaction of the family atmosphere still diluted, for Heather, the bitter taste of disagreement and anger. Bath-times were admirable moments for reconciliation, and during the school holidays the bathroom became one of the main venues for family fraternizing. Heather sat at the tapless end with India on her lap, and Bibendra and Janaka crowded into the middle between Mohendra's legs. Shiva usually managed to snatch his turn before the others got in, and sat on the edge wrapped in a towel. Kabir refused to take his clothes off in front of anyone, and bathed privately, when Heather could persuade him to do so at all. He was, however, anxious not to be left out, and would sit, fully dressed, on the lavatory. The bath water always overflowed and there were rubber ducks, boats and sponge animals scattered in the water and on the floor. It was a funny, noisy, good-natured time. One of the highlights, Heather thought, and then realized the idiocy of considering a bath-time session as being one of the highlights of her married life. But it was so happy, and wasn't happiness one of the important things? Ah but – said her better self – you *should* get happiness from the more significant elements of life.

'Grandma's coming for lunch today,' she said on one of these occasions, 'so remember to restrain the noise because it gives her a headache.'

'Will she bring us presents?'

'Can I play her my clarinet piece?'

'Are we having a joint? And not cabbage, *please* not cabbage.'

'And why not, sir? Cabbage is very good for boys, gives them muscles – think of Popeye.'

'That's *spinach* you stupid Daddy.'

'How dare you call your eminent father stupid, you impossible Janaka Jason boy.'

'Janaka Jason, born in a basin . . .' Kabir sang, and

dripping sponges flew across the room.

'I'm going to arrange a talking match between Grandma and Mrs B.,' Shiva said, 'and I shall be the commentator.'

The competition took place as they were finishing lunch, with the commentary carried on in whispers under the table.

'Of course, things aren't like they were when I was a girl. You can't get the quality these days like you could . . .'

'Mother B. comes out of her corner in good fighting trim,' whispered Shiva into the back of a spoon, 'and goes straight into the attack. Grandma Jones retreats in confusion, bobbing and weaving.'

'And writhing in coils,' added Kabir.

'Take vinegar . . .' said Mrs Bonnet.

'Take vinegar indeed,' Shiva continued, 'but isn't this a bit below the belt, we ask ourselves? We even ask the referee Janaka, do you not think that taking vinegar is below the belt?'

'Oh, indubitably, Mr Commentator. A foul blow I would say.'

'. . . in the old days you could rely on vinegar to make a good pickle. My mother always said . . .'

'We made ours with green tomatoes . . .'

'A counterattack! A counterattack from Grandma Jones. Can this stop Mother B.'s onslaught?'

'. . . you must have first class vinegar, else it's no good my mother said, always insist on first class vinegar and she was . . .'

'But alas, a further body blow with first class vinegar, the green tomatoes have absolutely no effect on the champion.'

'We grew them in the garden but they never ripened properly and so . . .'

'But Grandma Jones doesn't give up, back she comes into the fray.'

'. . . last time I made it the vinegar was bad and the jars exploded all over the ceiling . . .'

Heather came in with the coffee.

'And there goes the bell for the end of the first round,' Shiva said, crawling out from under the tablecloth. 'And only just in time to stop Grandma Jones being floored by the exploding pickle jar, I would say.'

The other three rolled out from under the table, convulsed with laughter and Janaka rushed to Sylvia, flapping a table napkin in her face.

'Deep breaths now,' he said, 'you're doing fine. She may have it on points at the moment, but you can easily score a knock out in the next round if you don't panic.'

Kabir offered Mrs Bonnet a glass of wine, and Shiva mopped her brow. 'Rinse it round and spit it out,' he said. 'You've got her cold, sister, only got to wade in and finish her now.'

Mrs Bonnet took a sip of the wine. 'Well that's nice, though I don't go all that much on wine really. Much prefer stout myself. My mother always said that you can't go wrong with stout. They do say Queen Victoria was quite partial to a glass now and then. I don't take it regular, mind, but I do like a drop now and then, specially in winter and of course when I was nursing our Harry then the doctor said it was the best thing. I suppose it what you might call changes into milk in your chest. Wonderful really when you come to think of it . . .'

'Coffee Mrs B.?' Heather said, without any real hope of stemming the flow.

Sylvia was laughing. 'Whatever are you boys playing at?' she said. 'Stop flapping that thing about Adam, I mean Jason. This house is cold enough already without you creating all that extra draught. I have decided to put central heating in for you, Heather, because otherwise I shall have to stop coming to see you. I invariably go away with chilblains, and I can't think why these children with their background aren't all dead from pneumonia by now. I don't understand why you economize on heating like this. Anyway, it's false economy because you'll find doctors' fees are far more expensive in the long run.'

'. . . had to have the whole place done up,' said Mrs Bonnet, 'because once you paint the ceiling everything else looks dirty, have you noticed that? Everything else looks as though you've never done any spring cleaning, in fact my cousin Connie once said to me . . .'

'Daddy, Daddy,' shouted Bibendra through the door. 'Grandma's going to give us central heating, so you won't have to get up and do the fires every morning.'

'How very kind.' Mohendra was smiling expansively as he came into the room drying his hands on a teatowel.

Sylvia stared at him angrily. 'The children are at risk in these freezing conditions,' she said. 'It's for their benefit.'

Heather's guilt surfaced. They should be able to afford their own central heating. Why should her mother have to pay?

'It's certainly very kind of her,' Mohendra conceded later, when they were alone, 'but darling, remember she enjoys doing it. Gives her a sense of satisfaction and of doing good. Your mummy is not the sort of selfless person who gives her all to others. She would never be able to thread herself through the eye of any needle. It's not as though she'll have to deprive herself in any way. And of course we *could* afford it ourselves, there's no question of that. It's just that we choose to spend our money on the more essential things of life.'

'You're quite wrong,' Heather said. 'We don't have that sort of money, and we certainly couldn't afford it.'

Mohendra wheeled on her in a fury. 'Always money!' he shouted. 'You are obsessed by it, never tired of reminding me that you are the great provider.'

'I didn't say that.'

'Not in so many words, but isn't it implied all the time?'

'If you choose to read things into what I say . . .'

'Choose? Choose? What choice do I have? It's not as if I waste my time. Never waste a minute, always working – unlike you, just sitting around and enjoying yourself.'

'Worrying about money isn't a particularly enjoyable pastime, but someone's got to, and since you don't . . .'

'So I don't worry? This is some new idea of yours? That I am irresponsible and spendthrift? Do I spend on myself at all? Everything I do is for you and the children and yet you complain. I am never idle from morning till night. You are the spendthrift. You it is who wastes money and makes no attempt to achieve what you are capable of. If you're so keen on money, why don't you help me in my efforts to earn it?'

'You *mean*, vicious, tyrant!' Heather screamed at him. 'How *dare* you say that to me when I . . .' Words jumbled themselves up in her fury. 'How *dare* you . . .' She swept past him and out of the house in a black rage. Let him stew. Let them all stew. She'd had enough. Let him bloody well try to run the house and the family without her. Let him just *try*. Thank God for the car. Or rather, thank Sylvia for the car. Where would they be without her help? She found herself shaking with a quite uncontrollable passion, and once in the car, she put her foot down and sped up the Great North Way. How *dare* he call her spendthrift? How *dare* he say she just sat around enjoying herself? Louise would take her in. She would drive up to Yorkshire. Should get there by morning.

It took about two hours' driving to get the anger out of her system. Real life then began to ebb back into the confusion. How did one get to Yorkshire other than by just following the signs to the north? She searched among the debris in glove compartments and side pockets. Paper bags, chewing gum wrappers, lolly sticks, dirty handkerchiefs, one glove – but the maps were in the bookcase in the sitting room. The petrol was low. She had one pound with her and no cheque book. It was raining, and already one o'clock in the morning. She stopped the car and allowed herself an exasperated session of crying, before turning round and following the signs back to London.

It had not been an entirely wasted exercise, rather a release of stored emotions. She realized, with shock, that this was the first time that such an outburst had actually taken place between them. Mohendra had often exploded with rage about something. But the usual effect on her had been an agitated retreat into herself, and a consequent short sulk. Short, because she was never able to hold on to the anger for any length of time. However hard she tried, the sense of injustice and fury that originally overpowered her invariably evaporated, just as it was evaporating now. Why had she been so angry at his accusations? She *was* always nagging him about his lack of income, she *did* spend freely on the children. The money she brought in was really so much chicken feed, quite probably she would earn far more if she painted big important portraits. At least he was doing his best to provide for them and must surely succeed in the end. So – perhaps her outburst was unjustified and unnecessary.

The journey back was a nightmare of exhaustion and

anxiety. The thought that Bibendra might have been racked with worry if he had heard the argument and subsequent slam of the front door, nagged at her. Mohendra might also have been angry enough to storm out himself and leave them. Could he have done that? Would he have gone round to Inge? Or called her round there? Shiva would have dealt efficiently and calmly with India and the younger ones. He loved dealing with situations and enjoyed taking responsibility for the family at any time, but Bibendra might have sensed the danger.

She reached home at three-thirty and found her heart beating quickly as she let herself in. Why be so afraid? Why shake like this? Was she afraid of Mohendra? There was no sound as she crept upstairs to the children's rooms. All were sleeping except for Bibendra who was sitting upright in Janaka's bed, next to his own.

'I didn't know where you were,' he whispered. 'You didn't tell me where you'd gone. Where did you go?'

'I just went for a very long drive because I got very angry and I wanted to get over it on my own.'

'Did you get over it?'

'Yes, I did.'

'I didn't know, you see. I thought – I thought . . .'

Heather lifted him out of Janaka's bed and found that he was shivering. He put his arms round her neck and his head on his arms.

'You wouldn't ever go *away*, would you?'

'No, of course not. Except for a holiday or something like that. You wouldn't mind that, would you?'

'No. Janaka said I could sleep in his bed, but I don't need to now that I know you are home.'

So no running away again.

Mohendra lay on his back in the middle of their bed, snoring softly. He awoke as she got in beside him, and looked at the clock.

'What a time to come back. Where did you go? Why

214

did you make off in that silly manner? Where have you been all this time?'

Heather was silent because the argument within her was dead, and he banged over on his side, away from her, and was immediately asleep again. She lay absolutely still on the edge of the bed, as though it were a precipice. If she moved he might wake and continue the questions.

But in the daytime of breakfast pandemonium, normality returned as though it had never been away. Nothing was said about the previous night. Heather was unsure why, but was again unwilling to disturb the uneasy peace. If only she could get away somewhere to think it out and relax some of the continuous tensions of trying to pour oil and keep her temper with the world.

'I'd like to go away and stay with Louise for a bit,' she said suddenly on impulse.

Mohendra looked round from his desk where *The Times* and *The Daily Worker* were spread out in separate sheets on every side. There were piles of stacked newspapers on most of the available space on the floor, on the table and on several chairs. The walls were lined with books from floor to ceiling. Mohendra had been making cuttings with a razor blade, and he seemed astounded by her suggestion.

'For what reason would you want to go there?'

'Because I would like a few days off and because I haven't seen her for a long time.'

'I haven't seen many of my friends for a very long time, but that doesn't mean I go gadding about all over the place paying wasteful visits. It's up to them to call on me. Why doesn't your friend come to see you? Does she think you are at her beck and call?'

'For God's sake – she hasn't even asked me yet.'

'Then why this urge to go? How undignified to have

215

to ask someone to take you in. You are surely not in need of a holiday – a few days off from what? It's not as if you're exhausted from hard work, is it?'

'Not exhausted, just fed up with the lot of you.' Dangerous talk; if he lost his temper there would be no hope of any sort of reasonable communication.

'So am I fed up with all of you – and with much more cause I would think. Go, by all means go. But if you do, then so will I go off somewhere. That is only fair, isn't it?'

The telephone rang.

Oh blessed telepathy, or coincidence or second sight or whatever you like to call it: it was Louise. '*Darling* Heather, I just felt I had to phone. I haven't seen you for a hundred years or so. Why don't you come up and stay with us for a while? Could you possibly? I would so like it.'

'I don't believe in magic,' Heather said, 'but Mohendra and I were just this minute discussing the selfsame thing. He *just* said that our friends ought to visit us more often. What an incredible coincidence!' She turned her back on him to avoid looking at the furious scowl on his face. 'I think he might find it difficult to spare me at the moment as he's frantically tied up with work and couldn't deal with the children. But can't you come down and share our chaos here for a few days?'

'My God, that would be heaven.' So quick to agree; was there something desperate in the voice? 'Exactly what I need. Are you sure you can deal with me? I could come tomorrow.' And she did.

Their meeting was unaccountably emotional this time, suppressed as it was into a pricking of the eyelids and a constriction of the throat. Heather put it down to her generally run down state. When they sat alone together with coffee, she marvelled at the ease with

216

which they slipped back into the fireside or treetop conversations of childhood.

'It's so good to see you, Heather. You're still such an essential part of my life, you know.'

How to answer without sounding trite or maudlin? Heather felt she would like to hug Louise to her and cry on her shoulder. How *silly*. 'It's really pretty odd how it carries on,' she said, keeping a firm control of her voice.

'You can't imagine how much I wanted to come. Right from the first when I rang you up, but I couldn't say it then because Johnnie was there, so I asked you instead. He hates me going away, you see.' She broke off suddenly and collapsed, equally suddenly, into a storm of weeping. 'Oh Heather, it's been so awful, I don't know what's happened to us. I can't seem to do anything right. I'm so utterly ineffectual and hopeless and Johnnie is being the absolute end. You just can't imagine.'

Heather stared, flabbergasted, as another of her certainties fell about her ears. Was this Louise the secure traditionalist being overcome by everyday living? The perfect couple in disharmony? How could that be? She was amazed.

'But I thought – I mean I always looked on you as . . .'

'The proverbially happy couple? Well I suppose we are in a way, or at least we ought to be. We're so well-suited. Like the same things, do the same things, same sort of people really. I suppose it's just me being impossible. You see, I'm beginning to feel I want to explode out of it all and not do what's expected of me all the time. Johnnie's a complete dictator sometimes. Everything's got to be just so and the same as yesterday and what his father did. Mustn't change a bloody thing. I suddenly envied you doing all those exciting eccentric things, all wrapped in Eastern calm and everything.'

217

Eastern calm? Heather thought. That's a laugh for a start. 'But we are horribly uncalm,' she said, 'and not at all eccentric. Terribly conventional and ordinary. Mohendra's just as conventional as Johnnie and probably more of a dictator.'

'You're mad! Surely he was always a dangerous anarchist – at least that's what everybody said. Isn't that why your family made such a stink?'

'Not an anarchist, a Trotskyist. And it wasn't so much because of that, it was because he was Indian.'

'Well anarchist *and* Indian. I mean if he'd been a Maharajah it wouldn't have mattered.'

'Oh it would, but not so much. And do get it right, he's Trotskyist, not anarchist, and only a theoretical one at that. Though he'd kill me for saying so.'

'To ignoramuses like me, it's all the same, they are all supposed to carry bombs in their pockets, theoretical or otherwise. But I do so admire you, Het, I always have.'

'Admire *me*? But why for heaven's sake?' Heather found her values again being upended. What was all this admiration? She had thought of Louise as the loyal friend who stuck, through thick and thin, no matter how crazy you were. But admirer? That possibility had certainly not occurred to her.

'Because you were so incredibly brave and strong and determined to do what you thought was right. Whereas all I could do was toe the line, not put a foot wrong, and look where's it's got me. Instead of being ecstatically happy and grateful for all my good luck, I'm just a bloody failure, that's all.' Tears started to flow again. 'I sometimes feel I can't go on, but I wouldn't have the guts to run out on it. Just isn't done, is it?'

So all the same in the long run. 'I was half-way to Yorkshire the night before you rang,' Heather said.

'Running away like mad to my safe, solid, conventional friend who always does the right thing and who would be able to look after me and tell me what to do.'

'You *weren't!* How bizarre! But why? You mean it hasn't worked out after all? Were all the doom forecasts right then?'

'The doom forecasts were as wrong as your success forecasts. How *suitable*, they all said to you, and how *un*suitable they all said to me. And what's happened? We've both arrived at pretty much the same conclusion for pretty much the same reasons. We have started questioning what our husbands expect from us. I really resent things being expected of me, don't you?'

'Absolutely. It's that maddening innate superiority line, isn't it?'

'Johnnie too? I thought that was just a Mohendra failing. He's always so certain he's right. Looks on me as the poor misguided idiot.'

'Really? Does he really? But I always thought you both were so emancipated and progressive and sort of – together.'

'Well, we are really.' Heather retreated a little, on the defensive and feeling disloyal and perfidious. 'Together, I mean.'

Yes, of course, so are we,' Louise said unhappily, but if the feeling of disloyalty was acute, the desire to share the repressed dissatisfaction was quite overwhelming. They had both imagined themselves alone in their failure.

Heather gave a giggle. 'I made a list the other day,' she said, 'of all the things I'm expected to do and to be. Mind you, I was in a furious temper when I wrote it, so it's probably frightfully unfair and one-sided and everything.'

'Oh do tell, this sounds exactly like me and Johnnie. What does he expect?'

219

Heather unlocked her diary from the desk drawer, feeling rather like a criminal. 'Making a list of someone else's faults gives you a sense of smug satisfaction, doesn't it? I did it to restore my self-esteem, you must understand.'

Louise laughed. 'Stop feeling so guilty. There's nothing wrong in being honest with ourselves for once.'

'All right,' said Heather, taking the bull by the horns quite firmly. 'So, first, I must run the house perfectly, and that includes (a) ordering the most nutritious, cheapest and varied food, and above all the sort he likes.'

'Otherwise it's not nutritious and therefore a waste of money,' Louise added.

'Right, and (b) seeing that not one single scrap is wasted, ever.'

Louise nodded.

'(c), keep everything perfectly tidy, perfectly clean and perfectly mended.'

'His things as well as ours and the children's.'

'Of course, and see that anyone we employ does the most work for the least wages in the quickest way.'

Louise's depression began to lift, and she laughed. 'So right, so right,' she said. 'Why do they always expect perfection? This sort of well-oiled machine business, you mustn't be *seen* to be doing the washing, but it must nevertheless be done.'

'Absolutely. Second, all this must be done without your taking any time over it, because of course, third, you must always be passionate, understanding and calm at all times – otherwise how could you show constant affection towards him and *never* get cross or upset? Because remember it's your job to inspire and support him in his work.'

'Oh God, what did we take on? Do you think it's just us or do other women find this too?'

'You haven't talked about it to anyone else?'

'No, because it just isn't done, is it? I couldn't possibly talk to any of my friends up there, and anyway they all seem blissfully happy and able to cope with things.'

'I thought you were too.'

'And what about affairs? I bet he doesn't have affairs, does he?'

Not possible, Heather thought, surely Louise would never tolerate it. Johnnie would never – would he? 'But I thought it was just my husband,' she said. 'Because of me being inadequate as usual.'

'Just what I thought.' Louise fell back, laughing. 'Aren't we *green*? Oh Lord, it's marvellous to feel other people are in the same boat, don't you think?'

They both basked a little guiltily in a sense of smug solidarity, however ignoble that sentiment might be.

Mohendra was effusively genial with Louise. So unpredictable, Heather thought. What does he hope to get out of her? This contradiction of left wing theories and the opportunism of not letting go the main chance. She felt ashamed of him. Louise would surely see through the false charm. But he seemed so genuinely pleased to have her staying with them, she even found herself being convinced.

'Are you going to join our yoga class this evening, Louise?'

'I thought we'd go to a film,' Heather joined in quickly, sensing the embarrassment of putting Louise in a spot, making it difficult for her to refuse without seeming rude. Never present people with awkward situations. Never embarrass them.

'A tuppenny hapenny film? You underestimate our guest's intelligence, my dear. I am sure you would like to try out yoga, wouldn't you Louise?'

'Well, I have never . . .'

Heather saw Louise groping, anxiously. 'She wouldn't, Mohendra . . .'

221

'Let her answer for herself. Stop telling her what she would or wouldn't like. So bossy, my wife.' The confidential, amiable smile beamed out. 'Do try, dear Louise. We have a wonderful teacher who teaches the Queen of the Belgians and Yehudi Menuhin. All the *best* people learn yoga, my dear. You will try?'

'But I shouldn't be any good.' There was already a note of excited anticipation. How persuasive he was.

'How do you know if you've never tried? And no one is any good to begin with. It's the first steps that are all-important. Soon people will be practising yoga all over the country, not just in a Finchley back garden, you'll see.'

After the class Louise was enthusiastic. 'Heather, it's tremendous! You never told me about this. I must take it up, I *must*. Just what I need to keep the old shape supple. I've been seizing up for years. And that relaxation period is just wonderful.'

'You see?' Mohendra was visibly triumphant. 'What did I tell you? And you thought she would not be wanting to try! I tell you,' he turned to Louise, 'my dear wife is barmy and a wet blanket into the bargain. Of *course* you should take it up. I will make arrangements for someone near you to instruct you. We will have branches of the class all over England very soon and I will see to it that there will be someone to teach all the Yorkshire people. You may live in the frozen north, but our missionaries are willing to brave every danger in order to spread the gospel according to the yoga swami.'

'He's so funny,' Louise said later. 'You may find him tiresome to live with, but at least he's a lot more fun than Johnnie. You're alive down here. I have the feeling that we died some time ago in Yorkshire, only no one noticed.'

Life with Mohendra was certainly not boring,

Heather conceded. In spite of everything, she had much to be thankful for. And at least he didn't drink.

The Indian opportunity surfaced some three years later. Mohendra felt his vitality was being sapped by the uncomfortable fact that Heather and he seemed to be drifting apart. He wrote a note in his diary: 'Control of myself will induce co-operation in others which in turn will produce mutual success and therefore happiness.' And underneath he wrote: 'Make special effort to control impatience and bad temper.'

He clenched his teeth with exasperation at the thought of so many chances missed and so many years wasted. An eternity since the innocent had ventured abroad. He cursed the memory of his lack of relevant education at that time; so green, so unwitting. All that wasted time. How many years? Ten? twenty? Perhaps thirty? He did not like to calculate. Even letters from home had stopped.

Heather was always nagging him to write home. 'Why cut yourself off completely?' she said. 'You must have some feelings for them and they for you.' How little she understood! And how could she talk of family feeling? She, who had not shed even one tear at her father's death! He remembered vividly the display of family grief at his own father's death. The sound of wailing was still in his head. How could she then understand the shame of a return home without achievement? It was impossible to go back or even retain contact in shame. He had first to achieve before returning, no matter how long it took.

Then suddenly, out of the blue, a letter arrived to say that a troupe of dancers with Government support wanted to make a European tour and needed someone with the right sort of European knowledge to co-ordinate the trip. Just my cup of tea, he thought. A direct result of getting to know the daughter of that official from Bangalore when she was in England last summer. Justification, he thought complacently, of his unceasing work in the social sphere. You could never let up, it was only by accident that he had discovered she was a distant relative of his own family. Quite a bit of luck that, leading directly to this offer which could be considered as a real breakthrough. He would be able to promote her and her troupe throughout Europe. All those contacts he had made over the last few years would now come in useful. Added to which they were willing to finance his air fare to India, so killing two big birds with one stone. You only had to be a little patient and things would turn up.

Heather was swept up in the optimistic rush of preparation and the confident belief that here, at last, was the opportunity for which they had waited so long.

'Could lead to all sorts of things, once I get in on an official level. I could get a job as an overall organizer of the arts in the UK. They should make me cultural attaché. Once back there I can meet them all, give them an idea of what is needed over here. They don't really have any idea how to organize things.'

'So good they're actually paying your fare.'

'Fare? Oh that's a detail, they will pay a great deal more than that.'

'Yes, but it does mean we don't have to borrow money to get you there.'

It was difficult to be patient. Always homing in on irrelevant details and making an issue of them. He remembered her unexpected burst of temper over their last disagreement and his earlier vow to control his own irritation.

'They won't pay the fare in advance.' He said it quite gently. 'It is included in the general expenses which they have promised to meet, and of course I will be able

224

to include a great deal on the expense account once I get out there. You don't have to worry about that, my dear.'

Heather's pleasure of anticipation evaporated with dramatic suddenness. 'But we have an enormous overdraft already.'

'And has the Bank Manager complained?'

'No, but I hate owing money.'

'My darling wife.' No exasperation, no irritation. Much better to reassure rather than castigate. 'Much as I usually respect your likes and dislikes and bow to your better judgement, my darling, this time I think the Bank Manager's opinions are the ones to take note of. If he doesn't mind, then we shouldn't. It's just a question of a small loan which we will be able to pay back ten-fold – a hundred-fold – just as soon as I get paid myself. It's a business arrangement, a capital investment.'

She wanted to laugh – or cry – at the idea of Mohendra talking about a business arrangement; and the realization that this chance, after all, would probably go the way of all others crushed the remaining flicker of hope.

'I have grown up with the idea that borrowing money is wrong – discreditable in fact,' she said stonily. The battle was already lost.

He was silent for a moment in the effort to contain his anger. Then he pulled her on to his knee and put his arms round her, kissing her neck and her ear. 'Darling, darling, don't give up on me yet, please. I know I've let you down right left and centre. I know I'm a hopeless case but please be a little sensible and a little understanding. Remember that in your family everything was safe and secure. Your daddy didn't have to borrow money, so, naturally he would say it was a discreditable thing to do wouldn't he? If he had ever been in a position

225

of not knowing where his next meal was coming from, of having pawned his watch or any other little thing of value he might possess, even his overcoat – then don't you think he might have had a rather different view of life?'

There was, of course, no satisfactory answer. He just might be right this time. Useless to quibble anyway.

On the way back from taking Mohendra to the airport, the confusion, the turmoil, the emotion of his departure and the past few days gathered into a ball of pain in Heather's left eyebrow, the start of a migraine which would shortly wipe out all thought in waves of anguish. But in the tense clarity of the preliminary, half-blind vision, she found herself questioning the direction of her life. What had she left herself be swept into this time? Was this another beginning of an end or end of a beginning? The engulfing wave of nausea was flowing and ebbing rhythmically as she rushed home along the Great West Road; she could hear the painful hiss of the sharp shingle in her ears. By great good fortune, the traffic was light enough to ensure that she reached home before she was sick.

17 Letter from India

New Delhi, November 1956

Dear Boys and one, beautiful Girl,

I have not the time to write to each one of you, so
please put up with my lazy ways and accept one letter
to you all. But please, all of you read it – best, perhaps, if Shiva calls you all together (Mummy too) and
reads it to you. In that way each can make comments
or ask questions, and you can discuss together one
with another, some points I put forward.

'OK everyone,' Shiva waved his knife at the breakfast
table, 'prepare for the letter-reading session.'

'Bibo's pinched the last piece of toast, Mummy.'

'There's plenty more, stop fussing.'

'*Quiet!*' shouted Shiva above the clatter. 'Are you
sitting comfortably?'

'No,' Janaka was on the floor, doing up his shoes. 'I
am most uncomfortable as it happens.'

'Then I'll begin.'

'That's what they say on *Listen with Mother*,' said
India. 'They say, "Are you sitting comfortably? Then
I'll begin." '

Kabir turned to her, 'No – really? But that's
amazing. Did you hear that, folks? They actually say
that in *Listen with Mother*. Isn't that fantastically
interesting?'

227

'Stop being nasty, Kabir.'

'Mummy, Kabir's being horrible to me.'

'QUIET!' roared Shiva. 'Here beginneth the first lesson according to Father. He suggests I should call you together to read, mark, learn and inwardly digest what he writes.'

'Hurry up then, or we'll be late for school.'

'All right, pin back your lug'oles then: "Well here I am at last! In the year of our Lord 1956, in India for the first time for some *thirty years*! Think of that, you children!" Shiva glanced up, 'Have you thought of it? Yes? Then I'll proceed (and I bet they don't say that on *Listen with Mother*). "Back in my native land! (i.e. land full of Natives, as you British conquerors called us! Ha ha!)." ' Shiva looked up again. 'Joke,' he said. 'Got it? Good. "And what a welcome I got too! It was so moving and I longed for you all to be here to share it with me. There was really an emotional upheaval, and so many presents offered for me to bring back to all of you. All your aunts and uncles and cousins galore are asking about you and demanding that I should bring you over here. They want to know so much about you. 'Why does not our dear Heather Auntie accompany you on this trip?' they ask. Why indeed?

' "Of course I could not come straight to the village because so much work had to be done in Bombay, and then in Bangalore. I was kept hard at it for many days before I could make the longed-for visit.

' "Tell Mummy that the work is going very well. I have been asked to found a cultural society here and to be its organizer at a nice big salary. We shall have to talk about it when I come back. Meanwhile I am meeting many important people who will be able to do me much good." Paragraph, quotes, colon, exclamation mark, dot dot dot, etcetera etcetera.' Shiva glanced round the table. 'And all the rest of the rubbish that

228

makes you come top in the English exam, let it not be forgotten. And this is where the story really starts, folks. "(a) The Government officials, both of the Union Government at New Delhi and the State Governments in Bangalore-Mysore and Bombay, have been most helpful, besides receiving me with great warmth. I have been able to secure promises and assurances – some of them in writing – of financial support . . ." '

'Boring,' interrupted Janaka. 'Can I go now?'

'Are you taking me to ballet tonight or do I go straight from school?' Bibendra was practising pliés with one hand on India's head.

'I'll be taking you.' Heather handed out plates of bacon and fried bread. Bibendra's ballet class was one of the highlights of their week. A period of relaxation, and with the Royal Ballet School scholarship a very real possibility, he needed all her support and encouragement.

'That's not fair,' India wailed. 'I wanted you to help me make a cake for the school bazaar. You said you would.'

'Mrs B will be coming. She'll help you.'

India continued to cry loudly. 'It's not fair, you always do what Bibendra wants, you never do what I want.'

'But Bibo is much nicer than you,' Kabir said. 'Can't you understand that, my hideous little sister?'

'*Kaybeer!*' Janaka hit him with a spoon. 'Desist, I beg of you. We all love you really,' he said to India, 'particularly when you stop crying.'

'*B!*' yelled Shiva, holding the letter in the air, and filling his mouth with bacon. ' "I have been promised quite big sums of money by really important people." ' He lapsed into an Indian accent and wagged his head from side to side. ' "Such rupee donation will be paid into our Indian Bank at New Delhi, but some will be

229

paid in sterling. I am now negotiating with the Finance Ministry. Thus, the net result regarding finances, though most promising, means that I have, as yet, no sterling to bring home." '

Heather's disappointment did not show in her face. She scarcely allowed it to surface at all. But by now no one was even making a pretence of listening, and Shiva flung the sheets of airmail paper into the air so that they fluttered back on to the table among cups, saucers and bacon. One settled in the marmalade and Heather collected the pages to read later. What happened to the dance troupe, she wondered. That had seemed so definite somehow. Was everyone like this in India? How could life be carried on with promises only? How did things get done?

When they had all left for school, she sat down and read the part of the letter which began, 'My most-missed-children's Mother Darling. Many thanks for your letter, which brought me both pleasure and depression. I am very glad Bibendra is doing so well with his dancing – he is really a star that boy, quite the genius, and we must do all in our power to encourage and promote his efforts. You yourself get in touch with all the big ballet dancers – Margot Fonteyn, Beryl Grey etc., they will surely help him. We must leave no stone unturned in our efforts to give him the very best of chances. I have already contacted various people here and am arranging a tour for him in Delhi, Bombay, Bangalore – all over the country.' Heather jerked her shoulders in irritation. 'I am so glad that the other boys are progressing well with their studies and hope you are giving them daily assistance with their homework. If they need to know anything specific from me, let them write express and I will telegraph a reply.'

She skimmed the lines impatiently. 'The "depressing" part of your letter concerns (a) the work I left you to do in England during my absence and (b) what you say about the suggestion I made before I left that we should all visit India sometime next year. With reference to (a), I am enclosing a list of the things I asked you to do to make it easier for you.'

Heather picked up four typewritten sheets of lectures, dance recitals or concerts to be organized, all neatly divided into alphabetically listed points such as halls to be booked, films to be ordered, programmes to be printed and invitations to be issued. 'Tell Inge to help you with this and get the boys to address envelopes and stick on the stamps, they should really enjoy doing this, with perhaps some of their friends. I shall be back in a few weeks, and can take up the rest of the work then, but it takes away all my energy and zeal when I find you have not been doing the things I asked you to do, adopting instead a kind of *laissez-faire* attitude. In contrast, ever since I reached India, I have been getting an average four to five hours' sleep in between meeting important contacts, writing out reports and long official letters and so on, in fact crowding my day with action and important business.'

Heather felt the fury mounting within her, but forced herself to read on with a masochistic desire to pile up the irritation.

'As to your own reactions regarding your proposed visit to India next year, I really cannot understand your negative attitude about this. Would you deprive the children of a chance of visiting their own kith and kin? Everyone wants you to come, they ask all the time why you are not all here now with me – it is really quite embarrassing trying to answer them! I am bound to be able to find some group or some interested party to put up the money for the fares. They wish me to lecture here at many universities and you too could give lectures. Bibendra will dance in many towns and cities and Shiva

231

will be able to lecture to schools and colleges on education in England. We can all pay our way, you see!

'So please consider all this carefully. This visit to India might mean the break I have been working and waiting for, but I need you all here with me to support and help me with my work.'

Heather put the letter back in its envelope carefully, as though the slow deliberation of putting at least one thing back in its proper place might help her to organize her feelings into some sort of logical order within herself. There was such disorder all round her; a holocaust of disorder on the breakfast table alone, and what more would she find in the rest of the house? Resentment against his expectations of the way she should arrange her life seethed inside her. And yet, as she continued to remind herself, there was a certain amount of justification. The children *should* go to India, there was really no argument to that one, but the circumstances had to be right. The idea of them all taking off and just hoping for the best was a recurring nightmare.

'I want to consult the oracle, Hugh.' They had arranged to meet on Hampstead Heath where snow was sprinkled sparsely on the ground and shone in the sun. 'Being a rich and successful businessman now, you are obviously the right one to advise me. But first, how's Istvan?'

'Impossible, but devoted and completely reliant.'

'Will you ever have him back?'

'Oh, it's not really a question of him coming *back* because I moved out. We choose now to be together but separate, so much better that way.'

'He'd move in with you tomorrow if you let him, though, wouldn't he?'

'Very probably.' Hugh smiled, 'But it wouldn't work. He has to have his little flings with beautiful young men and I shouldn't like that, not under my nose. And they would tend to clutter up the place.'

'Dear Hugh, you've become so strong and wise – but then I suppose you always were. You could always make decisions and then follow them up. But I did think when you first moved in with Istvan that he was the dominant one, you seem to have changed places somehow.'

'Just adjusted a bit. Relationships do tend to sort themselves out with time if you let them. And it has been quite a long time.'

'Over fifteen years – a lifetime. But I don't seem to have sorted my relationship out yet.'

They walked quickly through the sharp cold sunshine and paused by the pond to stare down over London, a tiny model city set down comfortably within the bowl of distant hills.

'I love it,' Heather said. 'Couldn't possibly leave it – not ever.'

'Does he want you to?'

'Not sure. But I shouldn't feel so negative, should I? I should be ready to pack up and adjust. I don't even want to try, mainly because of the children – and yet it's because of them that I should at least make the effort.'

'If there's a possibility of your going for a short time, then I think you should, in spite of difficulties, and I think you should take as many of the children as you can. There – a concrete suggestion for you, offered straight off the top of my head. They must be given the chance of choosing.'

'Choosing?' Heather's voice was sharp with criticism. 'What do you mean, choosing? How can they be expected to choose *now*, in the middle of their developing lives? We can't disrupt their lives half-way through.'

'But is all this relevant? Aren't you jumping the

gun? Isn't he just suggesting that you might make a visit there? It seems reasonable enough. Why are you fighting it?'

'Because I want to be ready . . .'

'With guns spiked.'

'Well, sort of. Really I think I want to be sure of my own mind and my own feelings before I let myself be carried away into some mad scheme I might regret. I could, you see, have some scheme of my own which didn't include living in India.'

'Up the rebels.'

She shook her head. 'I feel a little desperate at the moment because the money's running out and my children's books don't bring in enough to support everyone. I might just be able to rustle up enough for all our fares now, but we shall be down to the rock bottom of Daddy's money soon.'

'That's lot of money to have got through.'

'It wasn't much use saving it for a rainy day. I was so lucky to have it. But now I just have to think of a way of earning something more – just in case things don't turn out the way Mohendra hopes they will. Maybe I could teach, or help in a kindergarten or something.'

They walked on down the hill towards the Vale of Health, and she found herself crying uncontrollably. 'What am I going to do, Hugh? Suppose I can't make enough to support them all, and suppose he does get a job in India, then I won't have any choice, will I? And suppose the children all fall in love with the place as soon as they see it and want to stay there.'

'For a start, you can stop supposing here and now and begin to sort out your own life.'

'He says he's coming back in a week or two to "discuss all the exciting possibilities" and then take us back with him.'

'So polish up your armour and be prepared.'

234

'To go to India?'

'Of course. *You* might fall in love with it, you never know.'

But the weeks went by and Mohendra did not return. He wrote in January. 'Every day a new and very important engagement crops up and this might mean my staying here in Delhi till February 10th or 11th. A few more days' stay might mean a great difference in our fortunes. Yet I am torn, when I hear that the work I set in motion in London does not go well. If only I could be assured that you would hold the cultural fort for a couple of weeks longer, then I would have the heart and the energy to stay behind here and get as much work as possible done so that I could return to London with some concrete financial results. Please, therefore, try to understand and let me have details of all the meetings you have arranged.'

She put the letter down and telephoned Inge.

'He wants to know what meetings I've arranged, Inge.'

Inge's laugh over the phone deafened her with its raucous quality. Mohendra was always complaining of that laugh, calling it vulgar and unattractive.

'Why does he bother you with this?' Inge said. 'He knows quite well what I have arranged because I write and tell him. I have done my best, which is not very good, to do things the way he wants them, but it is difficult. But you do not have to worry at all, I will write and tell him. You have much too much to do with the children and your books.'

'You're such a good person, Inge.' Again the laugh and Heather held the phone away from her ear. 'I do appreciate you.'

So she quelled the irritated anxiety and started to make use of the clearer and peaceful period that

235

Mohendra's continued absence gave her, by joining evening classes on creative writing and poetry. Her own children's books suddenly seemed to her to be petty and irritating. The writing trite and the drawings facile. She wanted to experiment with words again. There was an immediate sense of blossoming evident in her life as March moved into April, and still Mohendra wrote of important meetings and engagements that could not be missed. With each week she felt as though she was unfolding a little further. It was exhilarating, but accompanied by a slight sense of guilt. His letters nettled her because they allowed the guilt to resurface.

'Do you miss Daddy very much?' she asked India, who was even more sulky and petulant than usual with her, and resentful of her brothers.

'Yes, because he's kind to me.'

'Aren't we kind to you?'

'No you are not. Everyone is very unkind to me except Daddy.'

'Oh India, what a fib, we are all terribly kind to you.'

'Kabir isn't. Kabir is horrible to everyone, specially me.'

'Kabir is a bit like you, he thinks everyone hates him.'

'So? I do hate him. Like you hate Daddy.'

Heather felt the blood rush to her face. 'I don't hate Daddy. Why do you say that?'

'Because you always fight when he's here. You're always saying he's stupid.'

'I never say he's stupid, India.'

'But you think he is, don't you?'

'No, I don't think he is at all. I think he's the cleverest person I know.' If he could only put that cleverness to some use. 'I think he is about as clever as anyone could be.' If only he could have a modicum of practicality wrapped up in that cleverness.

'He thinks you're stupid too. So do I.'

236

'India! Why are you so rude and horrid?'

'Because you are nasty to Daddy and don't let him come home.'

'He is coming home, you know he is, you read his letters.'

'He says he is, but then you must write and tell him not to because he doesn't.'

Heather was shocked, and full of anxiety. Later that day, she approached Shiva who, at nearly fourteen, seemed unusually full of wisdom and sanity.

'What do you think about Pa being away so long? Does it worry you?'

He looked at her to see if she was serious. 'Of course it doesn't worry me. Why should it?'

'Well – not having him around with all of us. A sort of splitting of the group.'

'You're mad, Mother. Totally potty. Why this sudden Victorian-type anxiety? You know it's much more peaceful without him. We can all get on with our lives so much better when he isn't bossing us around.'

'India seems upset by it.'

'But India is upset by everything, isn't she? I mean you can't do right by her at the moment. She'll probably grow out of it. She's just absolutely the end for the time being, whether he's here or not.'

'So you wouldn't mind if he never came back?'

'I didn't say that. Yes, I would mind that. It's all very illogical, I suppose, but I do like the idea of our family, even if I can't usually stand the reality.'

'He wants us to go over there for a visit – or perhaps even to live, you know.'

'Now, that *would* be something, a visit I mean. Can we go?'

'Two problems, basically. Disruption of school and lack of money.'

Shiva was visibly excited. 'School doesn't matter . . .'

'But what about O levels?'

'Oh come on, what's a bit less swotting compared to a trip to India? I mean you can't compare, can you? I shall get them anyway, you know I will, and the others are all too young to bother about. As for the money, couldn't I cash in on that legacy Grandpa left me?'

So what had she been fussing about? There were no real practical hindrances, only inner doubts in her own mind.

'If we went on a visit,' he went on, 'we could at least see for ourselves what it was like, and then decide if we wanted to live there afterwards, couldn't we? I mean we don't have to make awesome decisions immediately, do we?'

'Of course not.' Not immediately perhaps, but some time.

Janaka and Kabir came in together. 'What awesome decisions don't we have to make?' Janaka asked. 'I vote for fish and chips anyway.'

'Pa wants us to go to India.'

'Oh God, that means injections. I can't stand injections.'

Kabir dropped his school case on the floor and sat down suddenly. 'To live?' he said. 'I don't want to live in India. I hate Indians. Ghastly greasy wogs with no sense of humour.'

'Nor have you,' Janaka reminded him.

'Not to live, fool,' Shiva said. 'Just to have a look.'

'Can we go in school time?' Kabir brightened at the thought. 'That would be good. I wouldn't mind going then.'

Bibendra made a sudden, explosive entrance through the back door and the kitchen. 'I've got the lead,' he said. 'They want me to play Puck!'

'That's not the *lead*,' jeered Kabir. 'Why do you always have to show off?'

'How lovely!' Heather felt Bibendra's excitement rather more intensely then he did himself, and she lifted him off his feet in a hug of satisfaction and pride. 'I'm so *glad*!' She felt as though the achievement were her own. Each audition she had taken him to had seemed a stimulus for him but an ordeal for her. This success made it worthwhile.

'You won't be able to come if you're in a play,' Janaka said.

'Come where?' Bibendra looked from one to the other of them. 'Where are you going?'

'We're going to India to see Daddy,' India said smugly, 'and you won't be able to come if you're in a silly old play.'

'I said that,' Janaka glared at her. 'Why do you always have to repeat everything?'

Heather saw Bibendra's excitement and triumph shrivel and die, and she felt a sensation in her solar plexus as though it had suddenly iced up. 'For goodness' sake,' she said angrily, 'nothing at all has been fixed, certainly not the time, and we probably haven't enough money anyway. It's only a vague idea at the moment, nothing more. I just wanted to see what you thought of it.'

Bibendra was looking at her with an expression of despair. 'You wouldn't go away without seeing me in the show, would you?'

'No, of course I wouldn't. At the moment it's just a suggestion. Dates haven't even been mentioned. It's probably quite impossible anyway.'

But as she was saying it, there welled up inside her a sudden flicker of excitement. A trip to India? The whole idea was sensational! What an opportunity, if it could be arranged. The objections dwindled by the minute.

'It would be great adventure, wouldn't it?' she said.

18   The Benefit of the Doubt

'I felt I just had to come down for Chelsea,' Louise said, arriving in a welter of homemade jam, vegetables and flowers from the garden, a large goose from their farm and a suitcase stuffed with clothes her children had grown out of. 'I have become a fanatical gardener over the years of boredom. Thought these things might come in. You don't mind do you?'

Heather was overwhelmed. The clothes looked as though they had never been worn, she did not have vases enough for the flowers and had never cooked a goose, but was moved by the thought behind all the easy generosity.

'Oh Louise, you shouldn't have – but how wonderful – you are an angel of mercy, really you are.' She stared in wonder at all the clean-cut hacking jackets, jodhpurs and lace-up brogues as though they were from another world, which of course they were.

'Sure you don't mind or anything?' Anxious not to give offence.

Heather hugged her. 'Mind? You're mad. I'm delighted. You're so good to me.'

Anxiety lifted from Louise's eyebrows. 'You see I look on you as such a haven. I tell Johnnie "Heather needs me" or "Heather is overworked and starving, I must go and help her out of her difficulties" and then he can't really say a thing about me coming away. At least not much, because it makes him feel terribly justified about your marriage. "It never works," he says, "poor girl, everyone told her," and that makes him good tempered because he thinks he's been proved right.'

Heather gave a whoop of laughter. 'He does? *Really* does he? How priceless. You don't think that do you?'

'Of course I don't.' Heather heard embarrassment in her voice. She did think it. In spite of everything, the suspicion was there. 'All I want is a slight respite from the sameness in my life. A few days steeped in the stimulation of your mad, exciting way of life sets me up for another few months.'

They struggled into the house with the cases and parcels, and flower petals and cabbage leaves strewed themselves on to the floor as they went.

'It's so good to have you here,' Heather said. 'So much I want to tell you, ideas I want to sound out on you, like the possibility of us all going to India for a visit.' And the possibility that you think mixed marriages are doomed, she thought to herself.

They went together to the flower show the next day and Heather was at once transported back into the pre-war era when 'Chelsea' in her diary meant the beginning of summer with tennis parties and dances and coming up to London to buy long evening dresses. For the Eton and Harrow match at Lords, for Henley and cocktail parties and for Ascot in long dresses and floppy hats. Where was that life now, she wondered as they fought their way round in the mud and in between the showers.

'This takes me back,' she said to Louise. 'I haven't done this since before the war. It was always a must for Mummy.' How impossible it was to get out of saying Mummy and yet how embarrassing it sounded.

'I *know*, and I was always dead bored, weren't you? So absolutely different now I find. I want every single

241

flower to plant in my own garden. Gardening is really the most satisfying and relaxing thing in the world, along with yoga. I absolutely dote on it. Win all the prizes locally, which just shows what a competitive old sod I am.'

'I don't have time to do it.' Nor yoga either when Mohendra wasn't there to insist. Or was it just an excuse?

She broached the subject of marriage as they drove back in Louise's car through the traffic jams.

'You do think some of my marriage problems are due to Mohendra being Indian, don't you?'

'Not *just* because he's Indian. But you have to admit your upbringings were so completely different, that must make it more difficult to adjust.'

'So what about you and Johnnie? Your upbringings were almost identical.'

'But that's not the same thing, that's just me being impossible and not being typical. Not toeing the line.'

'But that's just what you did do! That's just what you were saying last time. Praising me up because I didn't. It doesn't have all that to do with upbringing and background. It's what each individual becomes afterwards.'

'But background's always there. You can't throw it off completely and he is terribly Indian and a bit sort of haremesque and everything, isn't he?'

'No more than Johnnie is terribly English and conventionally overbearing.'

'You're absolutely right, of course. People are so prejudiced; so anxious to insist that things they don't approve of must fail. But you're not going to live over there are you?'

'Not on your nellie said she from the bottom of her heart which is absolutely full of prejudices. But I don't know. I might love it, and he might get a marvellous job there.' She had mustered all the reasons against Hugh's responsiveness to the idea. Now list the arguments against Louise's antipathy. How perverse. But it was always the same; if anyone showed hostility to Mohendra, it was impossible not to spring to his defence.

'I find it interesting,' Heather said later as they sat in the unkempt Finchley garden after supper, drinking coffee and eating chocolate cake, 'that we should both have taken our frustrations into other, therapeutic activities; you with your gardening and me with my creative writing classes and book illustration. All wonderful remedial experiences, very good for clawing back a bit of self-esteem.'

'I must admit that I get a great sense of superiority in taking people round the garden and sounding off with Latin names: "Have you seen my *polyganum balschuanicum*?" I say, or "It's not a good year for *corylopsis spicata* this year, is it?" And all these cups I get, takes me right back to schooldays and success. I love it.'

These meetings with Louise had become a safety valve, Heather decided. A time for outpourings, sortings and reflections. She deplored her own lack of self-sufficiency in her desire to outpour. So cheap, so vulgar, so undignified as Mohendra was always telling her. She had always longed to be pale, interesting and remote, but somehow never achieved it.

With red-faced humiliation, she recalled embarrassing moments where she had allowed her inexhaustible flow of words to get the upper hand. She could never forget the incident in the hospital ante-natal clinic before Janaka was born. Sitting next to an unknown pregnant woman for hour after hour, moving up, seat by seat, to the top of the queue, and spilling out her life to the stranger beside her. When they reached the surgery door the stranger knew her intimately, but with the calling of her name 'Mrs Hiremath, please' the intimacy dissolved and they never saw each other again.

On the next monthly visit to the clinic, she considered taping her lips and sat, firmly controlled and mutely smiling away her anxiety, searching tensely for the one who knew her inside out. Instead, the new unknown beside her spilled her own soul into Heather's mute ear.

'I didn't need this baby,' she heard, 'but he gets drunk you see. Terribly remorseful afterwards he always is, but that's all very well I always say . . .'

Two hours of it as they played their musical chairs in the waiting room. She remembered, with some relief, that she had given her confidante more chance to reply, there had been a slight bond of accord between them. Was her unburdening to Louise any different? she wondered. It was still considered discreditable and slightly ridiculous to bore others with one's own problems. Much more creditable to be self-sufficient.

'It's so nice to be able to use each other as a sounding board, isn't it?' she said. 'Puts things in perspective somehow.'

'Bit like a confessional box. Get it off your chest so that you can set off in a new direction – if only there was a new direction to set off in.'

Illogically, Heather felt, at that moment, half convinced that her own new direction might conceivably be somewhere in the offing.

Mohendra started his day at four-thirty in the morning. That gave time for a full half-hour of yoga. He took the lotus position and closed his left nostril with the third finger of his right hand. Breathe deeply – two, three – and out, slowly, slowly, through the left nostril, blocking the right with the thumb. Clear the head, clear the body of all detritus.

All going very well. Great possibilities opening up. Really good progress yesterday with that official in the ministry. Good preparation for a possible meeting with the Prime Minister; should be easily arranged and then, of course all doors would be opened, no more truck with silly officialdom. So puffed up with their own importance; not an ounce of intelligence, most of them. He prepared for shirshasana pose, bringing his legs slowly into the vertical with the weight squarely on his shoulders. A talk with the Prime Minister and then perhaps they would sit up and take notice. His own family already respected him, he had won back their respect when they found out how much good he had done with his life, examinations or no examinations. Just had to prove himself to Heather now. Such a lack of faith she had. Mostly through her own sheer obstinacy to believe in him. Silly girl, such a childish lack of faith.

Sudden irritation seethed inside him and made his breathing uneven and difficult. He came down from the pose and took up sarvangasana. Why did she have to be so opposed to everything he suggested? It was bound to affect the children's attitude, in fact this could already be seen in their lack of respect for him and their silly, frivolous view of serious problems. What a shame. Much too much of this English habit of playing down the deep, important things of life. It was essential that they should spend some time in India before it was too late. Two or three years over here would adjust the balance. Only then could they be trained into a more positive way of thinking.

The tinny sound of Latta Mangeshka's recorded voice wafted across cock crows, motor horns and human voices, and he frowned angrily. These stupid Indians! Why did they have to ape Western sound in trashy film music when they had such unprecedented traditions of their own to choose from? No sense of values, none at all. So many beautiful ragas and all they could produce was this dreadful hotchpotch.

Later that day he went to the office of Shushila Gopal to get her to type some letters in her lunch hour.

'A letter to my family, please,' he said, 'or they will think I have deserted them.' He smiled down at her. 'And when you look as beautiful as you do today, it makes that quite a possibility. You modern Indian girls are a constant temptation you know.'

He switched his mind and his expression quickly back to the work that had to be done and looked at his watch. 'Tch tch. So little time and such a lot to do. Leave the beginning, please, I will fill that in later. Let us start straight away with paragraph one.

'I am very sorry that I myself haven't written to you lately,' he dictated. 'It's entirely my own fault, though I was rushing around from place to place, I had told members of the family to let you know of my movements. But on returning from Bangalore the other day I was shocked to discover no one had written to you. Very sorry about this.

'I am sending with this letter a formal printed note on all the work I have so far accomplished over here. Not bad, eh? What financial good all this is going to bring me now, I will enumerate for you in this letter, but the note will give you a picture of my movements, and the most probable date of my return home. Re the possibilities of getting financial grants etc., the following steps have been taken (for what they're worth):

'(a) I have set up numerous sections of a cultural (musical, literary, artistic) society to be known as the Indian Cultural Circle, and these are now being registered and tax exemptions obtained (from donors' point of view). After that they've planned to raise funds from public and business firms. One Congress Leader and a Chief Minister of Mysore talk of raising £40–50,000 –

in rupees of course – and trying to get permission from the Delhi Finance Minister to transfer 20–30% of this into sterling. All this does take time.

'(b) I am being made the Director of an International Society honouring a great 12th century thinker-reformer on whom I was invited to deliver this year's annual lecture in Bombay. They've promised to pay me £1,100 a year in pound sterling in London. (The *final* conference about this will be held a little later in the year, but it is 100% certain).

'(c) In the meantime, the Mysore State Government have already announced that they would invite us two as State Guests to attend the Daseera Festival in October at Mysore. They'll be, as far as I can gather, sending two return air tickets (from London to Bombay and back) to stay for three to four weeks (hospitality, internal travel given).'

He paused for a moment. 'I think that's all for that one,' he said. 'Now I have a few more for those damn big-wigs back in Delhi, God bless them!'

His wide smile was not returned by Miss Gopal. She did not feel it was her place to share pleasantries with such an important man. She was highly honoured to have been chosen to work for him, and was only too pleased to give her services and free time to help him in the work he was doing. But she would not presume to do more than that. She adjusted her sari on her shoulder, kept her eyes fixed on the typewriter and folded her hands submissively in her lap.

Irritated by her lack of response, Mohendra decided to find a different typist as soon as he could. But meanwhile time should not be wasted, and he dictated six more letters to members of Congress for her to type in his absence. He took the family letter to the main post office, and sat there to finish it off. Looking first at his watch and then at the post office clock, he wrote '5.16

247

'p.m., Tuesday, May 25th 1957' at the end of the type-written page. By the time he had finished the letter, the spaces in the two typed pages were completely filled by his small, neat writing, with the final sentences crawling round the margins of each page. It was not worth taking a further sheet.

'You tell me in your letter,' he wrote, 'that you are attending lectures on "creative writing", and that you are thinking of taking a job! Thus, you state, you cannot possibly envisage a trip to India in the near future! What nonsense is this? Some local class on creative writing, whatever that may mean, given by some nincompoop not one hundredth part as qualified as you yourself are! This is more important than the chance of visiting India? Then this unexplained bombshell – *you are thinking of taking a job!* Not once did you discuss with me this new idea – just calmly announce it out of the blue! My darling, I do know how you worry about money (unnecessarily I think), but now that I have written down all the new possibilities that are building up over here, do please give up this silly idea of yours.

'My darling, mistrustful wife, please return to what you once were, a strong and supportive partner, the light and centre of my life, without whom I would be of no account. And for my part, I promise faithfully to reform my Oh so wicked self! I will not nag, I will not criticize, I will merely work and slave for you and the children so that you may enjoy all the luxury that this life can provide. So please no more talk of some job which is not worthy of you. No wife of mine should have to work in some nine till five employment! What a waste! How undignified! Please be more proud, and love me always as I do you.'

Heather read the letter in a turmoil of uncertainty and consequent anger. What right had he to disturb that fragile, new-found equanimity she had been so

248

busy building up? The schemes and possibilities he laid before her, because they were new, all seemed quite plausible. Perhaps the jobs and the income really would be forthcoming this time. Surely he could not be so definite about them otherwise? Quite likely it was possible to get financial backing in present-day India. It would be most unfair of her not to give him the benefit of the doubt just one or two more times. Would the return tickets really be forthcoming? That, perhaps, could be the test case. If they materialized, then everything else would, or at least *could*. But did it really matter whether they were forthcoming or not? Had she not decided to go anyway?

It was surely silly, even if more comfortable, to rest one's decision on the materialization of two air tickets. Just a ploy to shift the weight of a decision. Like the tossing of a coin; heads I go, tails I stay. Cowardly and ridiculous.

'So, my dear, fatherless chicks,' she told them that same evening, 'We burn our boats and set sail for India in October – just for a short visit, mind you – and devil take the hindmost.'

There was a jumbled hubbub of excitement from everyone.

'I can't see,' Janaka said, 'how we can set sail if we burn our boats.'

'Don't be silly, dear,' Shiva said, 'it's just Mother mixing her metaphors again.'

'What's a hindmost?' asked India. 'And what does the devil do with it when he's taken it?'

'It's an arsehole,' Kabir told her, 'and the devil . . .'

'KABIR!' Heather shouted, 'be quiet at once. I forbid you to continue.'

The four boys rocked with gales of laughter, with India scowling in their midst.

'Why can't he tell me what he does?' she said. 'I want

19 Indian Adventure

The initial enthusiasm waned as the weeks went by and neither Mohendra nor the tickets materialized. The festival they were supposed to be attending was to be held in mid-October. The travel date had been fixed for October 10th, and by the end of September, Heather was taut with anxiety and disillusion. Though she kept telling herself it was of no real consequence that all promises had not been kept, there was still the feeling of let-down and disappointment. Damn and blast him, why did he have to pretend all the time? What was the point? But then to him it was no pretence, it was assured confidence that what he predicted would undoubtedly come about. Just a different way of looking at things.

She approached Hugh. 'I can raise half the money at once,' she said.

'And I can raise the other half,' Hugh said.

'Oh Hugh, could you? Just a loan, mind.'

'But of course, what else? I shall charge enormous interest and hope to make my fortune out of you by foreclosing just as soon as you come back.'

Elation returned in an explosive wave as she walked from the travel agents with the package of tickets, travel documents and labels. How satisfactory it was to write out a cheque for six air tickets from London to Bombay and back! The relief of taking such a practical, irreversible step was exhilarating.

Three days later, two return tickets from London to Bombay and back arrived with a letter from Mohendra.

My darling wife, so soon to be united with the whole family!

Here, at long, long last are the promised tickets! Such trouble I had, you can't imagine. First they insisted that they were only meant for you and me, so they could not transfer one to my eldest son. I finally persuaded them, but it was most difficult, and they would not fork out further tickets for the other children. Mean, isn't it? But some of these Indians are most mean, and the inefficiency is a complete disgrace. So lackadaisical and lazy! It has been one great struggle from start to finish. But now – what joy! It is all about to happen! Darling, you cannot imagine how excited I am! In fact the whole family is agog! It might be Queen Elizabeth II (God bless her regal majesty) who is arriving!

I do sincerely hope that you have been able to raise the money for the other fares without too much difficulty. I am sure your Mummy or even Hugh or Louise would help you out for a short loan – we shall pay them back very soon, this I can promise, you dear, ever-doubting Thomas, you, or should I say Thomasina? Don't forget that India and Bibendra and Janaka (who is only just over age, so I am sure they would not mind) can travel for half fare, and you could get some cheap flight for the other two. It should not be at all difficult, and I am sure they would find it a great adventure to travel on their own on some mysterious Eastern airline with many exciting stops on the way. I will meet you at Bombay airport, we have a Government car at our disposal and will be staying for some nights at the home of a high-ranking official in Bombay, so you see you are being treated like the VIPs you undoubtedly are!

Heather felt the tenseness of anger and anxiety stiffen her neck muscles and hunch her shoulders, so she closed her eyes and blotted her mind with imposed relaxation. The effort to relax turned into a fierce struggle which was more exhausting than the original tension, so she switched instead towards attempting to control sudden, inexplicable tears that welled up behind her eyes and gave the familiar, restricted pain in her throat.

Why *cry*? she thought furiously, the exasperation spilling out along with the tears. What is there to *cry* about? She could perfectly well cancel two of the tickets she had booked, and even if he was not finally coming back to take them over, there was really no reason why she could not manage the journey on her own.

'I'll never get there, Hugh,' she wailed over the telephone. 'Not only will I lose at least *one* of the children on the way, but we shall obviously crash as well, and anyway he won't be there to meet us at the other end, I know he won't.'

'Well, a crash would solve the other two problems, so I should concentrate on just worrying about the one if I were you,' Hugh said. 'Will you please stop getting into a frenzy, darling, and start your packing. I will take you to the airport and make sure you at least *start* with all five children.'

Sylvia had been crying over the telephone ever since she had been told of the visit. 'I can't think why you have to do this to me,' she sobbed. 'You'll all be killed, and *then* what will I do? Robbed of my only daughter and five of my grandchildren in one fell swoop. First he deserts you all and then orders you to join him in all that poverty and dirt, with everyone killing each other all over the place.'

She is old, Heather kept reminding herself. I must remember she is over seventy so is bound to be even more unreasonable than she used to be. I must not lose my temper. I must be patient.

'Always very demanding, these Indians,' Mrs B. told her. 'When we was in India with the regiment you could see it. None of them Indian wives didn't have no say in anything, just did what they was told. But then it's the same all over, isn't it really?' She gave a loud, toothless laugh, having forgotten her teeth that morning. 'Man commands and we jump to it, whoever we are. My mother always said it's a man's world and no mistake, and she was right, you know. I mean like you going over there when he calls you, no matter how inconvenient. But you don't have to worry about nothing in the house while you're gone, Madam, because I shall be here every day and see that no harm comes to it whatever may happen to you over there. I never did drink the water myself because of what it does to your belly – Delhi belly we used to call it, if you'll pardon the expression. Just runs all the time you know, no stopping it. Dreadful it was . . .'

It was not until they were actually flying over Bombay that the full revelation of the reality of the situation began to catch up with Heather's disordered thoughts.

'Look Mummy, look . . .' India's voice rose shrill. 'Palm trees – on a beach!'

And there it was, beneath her; to anyone else, India, the subcontinent, but to her, possibly another slice of her life. 'Of course he won't be there,' she thought, 'and then what shall I do?' The Indian heat struck her like a dragon's breath as they stepped out of the air-conditioning, more intense than anything she had imagined. But he was walking across the tarmac towards the plane so other impressions dissolved. How had he got permission? No one else was there. She had forgotten how handsome he still was; striding towards

254

them in a white shervani and a tight white chudidar pyjama; a Gandhi cap on his head.

'Ah, darlings!' he said and swept India and Bibendra up into a hug. Again the tears welled. Heather was enraged with herself and dropped the baggage on the ground to clasp him in a long emotional embrace. He held her so that she could neither move nor breathe properly and made no attempt to stop his own tears.

'My love, my love – why so long?' he said. 'How could I stay away so long? Don't leave me, will you? Don't ever leave me again.'

The children were startled and watched them with such interest that he released her.

'You see children? How your silly, sentimental father appreciates your marvellous, wonderful mother. I can only hope you do the same. Never forget, as Keats was wont to remark, a thing of beauty is a joy forever.' He wiped his eyes with a handkerchief and picked up some of the luggage. 'So now let's set off. I am going to show you the whole of India and show India the whole of you, down to your very toenails, just you wait and see.'

The Government car did not turn up and they waited an hour-and-a-quarter before taking a taxi.

'These damned Indians,' Mohendra fumed as he paced up and down the forecourt. 'No sense of duty or reliability.'

As they drove into the city through some of the shanty-town Bombay slums, Heather could only feel that she was watching some television documentary on India. The sense of reality that had momentarily touched her as they were approaching the airport had evaporated again; she was back in her seat, watching the show, not really involved.

'We are staying tonight with a charming family,' Mohendra told them. 'He is a big man in the railways, able to give us worthwhile concessions on our fares.

255

Most kind and co-operative. He has four daughters who are dying to meet India – plenty of little girls to play with you see!' He poked a finger at India's chest. 'What about that then, eh?'

'Are there any little boys for me to play with?' Shiva asked. 'Or can I play with the little girls, too?'

'Still the family wit I see!' Only a trace of impatience showed. 'I'm afraid you will find the well brought up girls in India are far too shy for boys like you.'

The flat of the big man in railways was in a large Victorian house which would not have looked out of place in suburban London. They were welcomed, after ringing the bell twice and waiting long enough to fear another disappointment, by Mr Chandra himself. He was effusive and charming.

'How very delightful to meet you, Madam. Mr Hiremath has sung your praise very highly to us. Will you please come in and be at home with us, please sit down now. Your journey was passable?'

They filed into a big, dark room with a fan rotating in the ceiling, and ranged themselves rather awkwardly on the chairs and sofas he pushed towards each one. Mohendra was still telling the taxi driver where each piece of luggage should be put down.

'It's very kind of you to put us up like this.'

'Please, please! We are only too happy to do so.'

Having seemingly completed his speech of welcome, he sat silently opposite Heather, smiling expansively, his hands folded in his lap. She cast about wildly in her mind for something to say but could think of nothing, so smiled back at him in embarrassment. The smiling silence continued to the sound of outside argument between Mohendra and the driver.

'You've got some little girls?' India asked, looking round.

Mr Chandra wagged his head from side to side, still

smiling. 'Yes, indeed,' he said, and remained still sitting, still smiling and still silent.

Kabir and Janaka began to giggle. Bibendra sat, serious and upright in his chair, his feet in third position with the left at right angles to the right.

'Lovely weather you are having,' Shiva said.

Again the head wagged and the smile widened. 'Very hot.' And again silence.

Janaka and Kabir, who were sitting behind Mr Chandra, side by side on a sofa, pulled grotesque grimaces at the back of his head, their tongues out and their fingers in their ears, and India let out an explosion of laughter in which Mr Chandra joined. It might have got worse, but Mohendra burst into the room at that moment, exuding excitement and good will.

'You have introduced yourselves then? Good, good. These drivers! Such crooks isn't it, Chandra? Always on the make. And where is your dear wife then?'

'She is in the kitchen.'

'And all the lovely daughters?'

'They also are in the kitchen.'

'What? So shy?' Mohendra strode from the room to return with Mrs Chandra pressing her hands together in a namesthe greeting, and attempting to back out of the room again. Mr Chandra addressed her sharply, and then returned to his smiling and head wagging. 'She will be fetching refreshments immediately.'

The four daughters came in with sweet tea, already mixed with hot milk in the pot and stood, silent and serious, in a corner of the room. Heather took a cup of tea, and watched anxiously as India bit into one of the sweets. She saw an expression of agonized embarrassment build up and passed a tissue furtively so that the sweet could be spat out.

'You will be needing a bath,' Mr Chandra said some time later. 'Please come with me.'

257

The bedroom was shuttered and almost completely dark with one double bed and five mattresses rolled up on the floor. The bathroom was an adjoining large room with a Victorian-type bath at one end. The bath gave the room an oddly western touch, until the plug was pulled out and the water ran out on to the tiled floor and down a drain in the centre. An air of hysterical and exhausted amusement overtook the whole family which manifested itself in helpless laughter as they moved between bedroom and bathroom, trying to cool themselves under the fans. Even Mohendra smiled indulgently at the reaction.

'You must forgive my countrymen,' he said. 'They mean well.'

The next days were a forgettable mêlée of sweat, warm boiled drinking water, curry for breakfast, endless smiling, traffic noise and being introduced continuously to innumerable people. Shiva and Janaka veered between witty sarcasm and bad temper, Kabir sulked, Bibendra was reverent and intense in his admiration for everything he saw and India refused to eat anything but tomatoes and eggs. Mohendra's enthusiasm and delight in having them there was boundless and irrepressible. Heather was both touched and exhausted by it.

'Tomorrow we go to Mysore,' he said. 'There we shall be guests of the Maharajah for his Daseera Festival and will stay in the Government guest house. He will ride on an elephant,' he told India.

'So did I ride on an elephant at the zoo. It was horrid.'

The Government Guest House was palatial with liveried servants to greet them.

'Cor, something like,' Janaka said. 'Will they have fish and chips here, do you think?'

'But of course,' Mohendra assured him. 'You can have absolutely anything you want here.'

There were no other guests and they occupied a suite of rooms decorated with decaying opulence and splendour. In the bath there were six huge cockroaches which meant that India and Bibendra refused to enter the bathroom for the few days that they stayed there.

'What about all our lovely relations?' Shiva asked. 'I thought they were all panting to see us?'

'That comes next,' Mohendra said. 'They cannot afford to travel even as far as Mysore to meet you, so we go to our village after Mysore. But I have to warn you children, it is a little primitive there, you know. Nothing like the princely luxury we are enjoying here.'

'Good,' Shiva said. 'I have an overriding desire to get down to some real living because I can't feel this is India at the moment. Everything is so false; we're not seeing the real things at all.'

'Well said, my good socialist son!'

How can he be so breezy about it all? Heather thought. If he disagrees with the style of life, why does he follow it so avidly?

'But while you are in Rome,' Mohendra continued, 'you know you must do as the Romans do, or you won't get anywhere.'

'So where do you want to get?' Janaka asked. 'Do you want to be like Mr Chandra? A beeg man in railways?'

'Of course not. I have no interest at all in railways. But you must understand that in India, unless you attain some sort of position, or at least are in with all these bigwigs, you can get nothing done at all. It's a rotten system, but while it's there, you have to live with it in order to improve it.'

'Are you improving it?' Bibendra asked.

'I'm doing my damnedest. Nothing much to show for it yet, but just you wait, in a few years' time you won't recognize the place. Prime Minister Hiremath will be making all sorts of splendid reforms.'

259

'Will you really be Prime Minister, Daddy?' India was ready to believe.

'But of course! What do you take me for? Some sort of ninny or something? You think I can't be Prime Minister of a little country like India? Now what do you bet me?'

'Five shillings,' India said. 'I bet you five shillings you won't be Prime Minister of India.'

'Done.' Mohendra shook her hand. The charade was being charmingly played out.

Mysore was not a success in spite of all the seedy luxury. Their reserved seats for the parade had been taken by others who refused to move, so they stood or sat on the ground for some three hours in unbearable heat to view the procession. It was delayed by two hours, but the Maharajah finally rode by on an impressively caparisoned elephant, preceded by small contingents of army and police and large contingents of boy scouts and girl guides accompanied by painful bugle bands. The boys were bored and India was sick. Even the lit up palace at night, surrounded as it was by over a thousand light bulbs, did not make up for it.

Heather felt depressed and guilty at their lack of enthusiasm. Was this what they had come to India for? How can I admit to not enjoying myself? she thought. What inadequacy is there in me that makes me feel I am hating this? Other people are bowled over, enamoured, besotted, and yet I remain unmoved, except in the wrong direction. The children one might excuse, but her own defect was unpardonable. She was full of encouragement and good humour towards Mohendra in order to make up for her own deficiencies, and urged the children to show a little more good will for his sake.

'Tomorrow it may be more difficult for all of you.' Mohendra showed his anxiety as though he sensed her own and yet was not conscious of the cause. He was too taken up with the pleasure of assembling together his background and his family; a final knitting up; the last bit of the jigsaw. The idea of completion gave him a sense of satisfaction and achievement.

'We are going to the village and I think we shall have to stay the night there.'

'But of course we'll be staying the night there,' Heather was startled that there should be any other arrangement. 'Surely we shall be staying much longer than one night? Isn't that the point of the whole trip?'

'One of the points, but by no means the only one. India doesn't just consist of villages, you know. There are many important things to achieve in this first visit; so much to be done in such a short time, though if we can prolong the visit, then we could spend much longer catching up with just family matters. Important in themselves, I agree, but not, perhaps, the most important thing on this, your first visit.'

Heather looked at him incredulously and said nothing.

'Why I was a little anxious about it,' Mohendra went on, 'was because it is a bit primitive, you know. No lavatories, for instance. You know there are no lavatories don't you?'

'Of course we know,' Janaka said. 'You've told us often enough. One field for ladies and one for gentlemen.'

'I can hold it back for six days,' Kabir said. 'I did it once at cub camp.'

'I like doing it in a field,' Bibendra said.

'What about all the scorpions waiting to sting your bottom?'

'Are there really scorpions there?' India asked.

'Only in the gentlemen's field,' Shiva said. 'They don't like ladies bottoms, they think they're rude.'

It was a long train journey to the nearest small town three miles from the village.

'The railway runs right beside the village,' Mohendra

261

told them, 'but we are so small and insignificant that the train doesn't stop there, so we have to walk across the bridge over the river. Quite exciting. You boys will enjoy that, because you can see the river way down in between the gaps in the railway sleepers.'

'Can't we take a taxi?'

'My dearest, pampered boy, you cannot drive a taxi along the railway line and there is no road that crosses the river there.'

There was a sharp silence and Heather suddenly had the picture of an isolated collection of huts in the middle of a dense jungle.

'But I wrote and told them when to expect us,' Mohendra went on. 'I am sure they will come to meet us at the station.'

They did.

As the great steam train slowly pulled into the very small station, Heather looked out on to a sea of faces; about three hundred of them. And as Mohendra leaned out of the window, the mass moved forward with a cheer of recognition and ran, pushed and jostled its way along the platform to keep abreast.

Three replicas of Mohendra stepped forward as the train stopped and doors were opened, their hands in namesthe greeting and their faces creased with smiles.

'Welcome! Welcome home, dear Sister Heather.'

'Amiable and propitious greetings, dearest sister.'

'We are oh so happy to greet you thus.'

Children ran forward with flower garlands for everyone and Heather felt her heart bound with a wave of affectionate recognition and love. She hugged the three brothers who were just other aspects of Mohendra she had not seen before. Here it was no disgrace to cry – everyone was crying and laughing at the same time. The Indian children were laughing aloud and leaping round India and Bibendra, and Heather saw, with shock, that both Shiva and Janaka had tears spilling over their smiles.

A railway official pushed his way through the crowd. It seemed unlikely that he, too, should be both crying and laughing.

'Come please, we must get going now,' he said. 'The train has to go now.'

The brothers became alert at once. 'Back on the train,' they said. 'Quickly back. We have arranged everything.'

They were herded back into the compartment with no time for questions, and many more of the crowd now in there with them. The brother ran forwards towards the end of the platform and climbed on the footplate while the rest clambered and clung to the side of the train as it glided slowly forward towards the river ahead. Children ran cheering along the track beside the single line.

Mohendra looked contentedly round at his relations and their friends. 'They have arranged for the train to stop at the village,' he said.

'Just for *us*?' Kabir expressed the awe that the others felt.

'What do you mean, *just* for us?' Mohendra was steeped in complaisant pride. 'Are we not all-important? I told you, Indians will move heaven and earth for VIPs.'

After crossing the wide yellow river on a frail-looking bridge, they slowed to a scarcely moving crawl beside the village on the other bank. A line of newly white-washed stones lay either side of fresh-dug steps down the embankment. The clinging passengers peeled off the side of the train and dropped randomly down the incline. Children took up positions beside the stones, standing smartly to attention, and Heather found herself flanked by two brothers guiding her out of the compartment. Other passengers hung out of the windows, waving, shouting, smiling encouragement and goodwill. What an extraordinary dream sequence it all was.

The procession through the village was a triumphal one. The old bowed and waved from their doors and the young danced alongside, small boys shouting and laughing and small girls clinging in groups and collapsing into paroxysms of giggles whenever they caught an eye to eye glance. At the entrance of the central house, which was the only one to have a second floor, they stopped and were greeted by the three wives and the older female relatives. From a plate bearing a small lamp, flowers and kum kum, the red powder mark, or tillak, was pressed on to Heather's forehead by the thumb of the eldest wife. She took Heather's hand.

'Right foot first over threshold,' she said. 'It is propitious for the daughter-in-law.' And they entered a small, cool entrance hall with a raised platform at one side. She saw the flicking tails of cattle in the inner, larger room.

'Sit, sit.' And they sat, Mohendra and Heather together, crosslegged on the raised platform as though they sat on thrones. Mohendra gave a nudge and a wink.

'To receive the plaudits of the multitude,' he said.

The multitude certainly came, one after the other, with garlands, fruit and nuts and everlasting smiles of welcome. They seemed never ending.

'Who are they all?' Heather whispered in between smiles and gifts. 'Where on earth do they all come from?'

'They are all the relations,' Mohendra told her, 'come in from other villages to meet you. They must have been arriving here every day for the past week or so. It's an occasion, sort of delayed wedding party.'

The long-delayed wedding party was no less enjoyable for being some fifteen years late. There were parties and feasting all that day and the next. Meals were taken in various houses, with different branches of the family. Expeditions to surrounding temples were undertaken, picnics arranged, school children assembled in the village school to be addressed and to sing songs of welcome.

The contrast with the previous week was prodigious. The whole family was excited and yet relaxed. The smiles were suddenly genuine and the feeling suddenly profound. Too good, really, to be true. There was a distinct sense of transience woven through the exhilaration. This was today's delight; tomorrow it might disappear. In spite of that, tremendous efforts had been made for this possibly ephemeral interlude, however long it might or might not last. The lavatory question had obviously been considered in some depth before the visit, and Heather was approached on the first day by one of the unmarried nieces.

'Auntie, I am Uma. I am looking after your comfort. If you wish to . . .' pause; a dip of the head with a smile behind a raised sari. '. . . wish to – *relieve* yourself – visit toilet isn't it – you please tell us and we will take you. We have something arranged for you.'

At the indicated signal, she was led by Uma, carrying a bucket of water, a small cloth and a black umbrella as a shield against the sun, through the village. They collected a train of interested children in their wake, and came to a field where three or four sick-looking buffalo stood motionless apart from rotating jaws and switching tails. Uma led on towards a shoulder-high palisade in the middle of the field, where was hidden an aged commode, resplendent in mahogany dignity. Heather exploded with laughter as did Uma, convulsed behind her sari. After handing over the water, the cloth and the umbrella Uma retreated back across the field to wait, respectfully, with the group of squatting children outside the gate.

The visit stretched on from day to day, like a successful party where no one wanted to go home. Guests had brought their bedrolls and laid these down wherever they happened to be when night fell. There were two very small bedrooms on the upper floor of the Hiremath house and one other room which held a table and two chairs. Mohendra and Heather slept in one of the bedrooms where the luxury of a makeshift mosquito net had been unearthed for their comfort. India and Bibendra occupied the other bedroom and the rest of the family unrolled their bedrolls next to their cousins, aunts and uncles wherever there was floor space.

The nights were noisy with the whirring of crickets, children's cries, the snoring of the elders and howls of the pariah dogs of the district. Sounds which came back to Heather so vividly in the years that followed and kept the atmospheric memory of the Indian visit nostalgic in her mind.

It had been arranged that they would fly back to London from Delhi.

'You have to see the Taj Mahal by moonlight.' All the relations insisted on this. It would have hurt their feelings to refuse.

'Need we?' Shiva asked Heather. 'It'll obviously be a terrible let down.'

'And we've seen millions of photographs of it,' Janaka complained.

'And millions of awful models in millions of awful cabinets in awful Indian houses in awful Indian towns where a lot of awful Indians live.' Kabir said. 'I *know* what it looks like. I don't have to see it.'

'Do we have to, Mummy? It's much better here. I'd

quite like to stay here for ever.' India had found herself to be the centre of universal admiration among the villagers and ruled her kingdom with a degree of old-fashioned colonialism that amounted to unashamed despotism.

'I'd like to see it,' Bibendra said. 'I'm getting quite bored of –'

'Bored *with* . . .' Shiva corrected.

'Hindu temples and things. I mean you just can't go on looking at all those statues even though they are very nice to begin with.'

'Specially the sexy ones,' Kabir said.

Heather rather agreed. The Hindu temple sculptures she had found overpowering and far removed from the single bronzes she had admired and collected back home. Strange that although the thought of seeing these masterpieces in situ had been one of the anticipated excitements of the Indian visit, actually to be surrounded by them she found oppressive and somehow self-indulgent of their creators. The surfeit was overpowering.

'Of *course* we must visit something that is one of the seven wonders of the world,' Mohendra insisted. 'It would not be right and proper to miss it out.'

'It's not one of the seven wonders,' India said. 'We learnt them at school. I can't remember what they were, but the Taj Mahal wasn't.'

'Moslem architecture is much nicer than Hindu,' Bibendra said with an air of detached precision. 'So much more – sort of – sensible somehow.'

The older boys groaned and Kabir held his head. 'Oh God, here we go,' he said. 'Lord lah-dee-dah Orlando Bibendra Muck throwing his genius about.'

Bibendra blushed and Heather felt enraged with Kabir.

'All right, moron,' Bibendra said. 'So you're not as

clever as me. We can't all be top of the class, you know.'

Leaving the village was a major upheaval. At first everyone seemed astonished that they would not actually postpone their flight back to England.

'But surely you will not want to leave so soon – when you have just come?' they said. 'Such a short time in India is not thinkable.'

Most of the relations had taken six weeks to two months off from their work for the visit and could not understand that other commitments could be classed as of even approaching importance. They were hurt by the insistence. 'We are not interesting enough for you,' they said, and as many as possible packed into the three cars hired to take them to Belur airport for their flight to Delhi.

The journey was a nightmare of dust, furious driving and overpowering heat. The drivers drove as fast as the ancient cars would allow, in the middle of the one track road. Their hands stayed continuously on the hooters whenever any other usurper could be seen on or near the road, but they did not slow down, and in consequence ran over two dogs and hit an old man, a buffalo and several chickens. They only stopped to feed a troupe of monkeys which had invaded one part of the road.

If the departure from the village had been distressing, then the leave-taking from the close relatives who had accompanied them to the airport was harrowing. Everyone clung and kissed and cried, and the young children wailed. One of the drivers whom they had not met before that morning sobbed uncontrollably in the back of his own car. The London family was quite caught up in the emotion, and Heather was neither embarrassed nor irritated by this extraordinary display. It was all part of the moment she found herself in.

'You will come back soon?'

'But of course, very soon.'

'You could come and finish your education in our school. You can do A levels in the sixth form.'

'I will come.'

'And Pritam could come too and do O levels, and you could stay with us.'

'You will write to me?'

'I don't want to go,' India howled, clinging to one of the uncles.

They made their hysterical way to the plane, and one of the cousins had to be dragged out, struggling and crying, before they could take off.

In Delhi they stayed in a small hotel which was hot and cramped and not at all comfortable, but the money was running low.

'I have plenty,' Mohendra insisted, 'but at the minute not quite sufficient to travel on the Taj Express. But don't you worry, I shall arrange everything. The only way to travel to Agra is by the Taj Express. None of your common, low class travel for my family if you please.'

They left Delhi early the next morning to spend the day in Agra, and met an English couple from Manchester at Delhi station. Mohendra not only exchanged pleasantries and addresses, but asked them to stay in Finchley whenever they came to London and persuaded them to cash one of Heather's cheques.

'I may not have enough in the Bank to cover it,' she whispered, but he shushed her impatiently, and they climbed into the luxury of the most superb train any of them had ever seen.

'You see?' Mohendra was triumphant. 'We Indians can do some things in style. We are not all stuck in the mud of pre-historic times.'

It was on that journey, in quiet, air-conditioned comfort, that Heather looked out at last on the beauty of India itself. The colours of the flying countryside seemed suddenly to burst upon her. Hundreds of butterflies swarmed in profusion and birds appeared to decorate every tree. Glimpses of Indian women in bright saris working in the fields or carrying pots on their heads no longer seemed just another coloured illustration in a glossy magazine.

This place is wonderful, she thought. Why do I have to realize it only in the last few days of the visit?

The Agra trip was a spell of relaxed fulfilment formalized in a dramatic way by the impact of the Taj Mahal itself. It looked exactly like all the photographs they had ever seen, but the magic was unexpected. There was no moonlight, there were seething crowds, there was a great deal of commercialism, but the magic emerged and engulfed them all.

'I never thought you could look at it from anywhere else except the front,' Janaka said, viewing it from Shah Jehan's palace and tomb down the river, 'or that it would look far *more* beautiful from here.'

'Thou still unravished bride of quietness,' quoted Shiva. 'Keats hit the nail on the head, didn't he? Even if he *was* talking about a Grecian urn, and even if I never quite know whether he meant still meaning immovable or still meaning up to that time; but then of course . . .'

'What does a Grecian earn?' Kabir tried to bring the conversation back from the embarrassing. 'I don't know, man, what does a Grecian earn? Oh, about two and six a day. Ho ho ho.'

Shiva refused to be sidetracked. 'I feel exactly like stout Cortez, with or without all his men, silent upon a peak in Darien. At least I think I do.'

'All right all right,' Janaka groaned. 'So you're doing Keats for O level, so what else is new?'

Mohendra hit Shiva on the back with unrestrained delight. 'Good boy! Splendid! Literary analysis with apt quotation. And you are absolutely right, though

270

one could equally quote and subsequently analyse Tagore or Basava on the same theme.'

'Why can't I paddle in the fountains?' India moaned. 'It doesn't say you're not allowed.'

'Uncultured ghoul,' Kabir said. 'You should take notes when one of your learned brothers speaks. But paddling in the fountains is not such a bad idea. I might join you. I should enjoy telling people that I paddled in the Taj Mahal fountains – or even *piddled* in them for that matter, that might be even better.' He sat down on the floor and leant back against the wall yawning. 'I'm bored with all this sightseeing anyway.'

Bibendra showed his distaste in his expression. 'But how can you be bored? I mean just imagine poor Shah Jehan sitting here and crying and crying about her. And then being killed off by those awful sons of his, it's all so sad.'

He moved away from the others and stood behind a pillar to cover up his feelings. The idea of being bored among such drama was unthinkable and upsetting. The story of Mumtaz and Shah Jehan would make a wonderful ballet. He saw himself dancing tragically across the stage to the accompaniment of sitar music.

The final departure from Delhi airport for London was an anti-climax to all that had gone before. Mohendra cried unrestrainedly but they did not. Almost as though they had taken their leave before. They had retreated back into their own reality and were looking back, with some disbelief, at what they had been such a short time before. Unmoved, unemotional and slightly embarrassed by the weeping Mohendra.

'I shall be coming back *definitely* in two weeks' time,' he sobbed. Heather felt no flicker of response. They were just words, after all. 'There is no reason for me to stay after the conference in Delhi, and I have several things that need urgent attention in London with all the contacts I have made here.' The tears dried as he talked. 'Such a lot of good things I have achieved over here. I was absolutely right to stay on as I did. But now we must consolidate our gains. A great pity you declined to stay on here with me so that we could all have returned together. You could have given me help and support instead of rushing back as you are doing.' He shrugged his shoulders and the tears flowed again. 'Why all this silly separation, my darling? So unnecessary.'

Heather looked at him from a distance, and the irritation began to worm its way back into her consciousness. Even the acting in this tragi-comedy she was watching was lamentable.

The End

20 Forty Year Itch

It was not that home life after the Indian adventure was a let-down. In fact the trip in retrospect was more pleasurable then the reality.

'Coming home after our stay in India is like coming home after going to a play,' Bibendra said. 'Sort of cosy teatime with hot buttered toast and curtains drawn and everyone discussing it.'

'It wasn't a bit like an adventure when we were there,' India said. 'It was like ordinary living most of the time, but now we're home again it seems like it was something special.'

'Mostly because people keep asking and then saying, "Fancy going to India, aren't you *lucky*." '

'Distance lends enchantment,' Shiva said dreamily.

'And the higher the fewer,' Kabir added. 'And the nearer the bone the sweeter the meat.'

'And diamonds are a girl's best friend,' Janaka pointed out.

They crowed with laughter, carried the game further and forgot the adventure.

Mohendra stayed on for a further three months after their visit. Nearly two years away, and time's positively flown, Heather thought, with a tinge of guilt. He finally returned in January 1958 with an Indian dancer and no solid financial commitments. Sitha was plump and pretty and stayed in the Finchley home, 'Until I find her a decent place to stay,' Mohendra said. 'No longer, I promise you. Once I can organize a few concerts for her she can afford to stay in a hotel. But I did tell her mother I would keep an eye on her.' He smiled at Sitha. 'So suspicious, these Indian mothers, isn't it?'

Heather realized quickly that this was the third wife; and she was pleasantly surprised to find that jealousy was not there. Inge, who had become stolid and dutiful by that time, came back lovingly and faithfully to the typewriter. She was far more affected by Sitha's presence, and Heather felt an unreasonable sympathy for her, and was amused by the odd situation. Mohendra and Heather still shared a bed while Sitha occupied one of the single spare room beds. Much more sensible if he moved in there with her, Heather thought, with a spark of internal laughter, but this, of course, could not be done because nothing was admitted to or discussed. Did he really think she did not notice these things?

The lack of jealousy was strange, but it was tied up with a complete sexual indifference towards him. An indifference which did not seem to be connected with either Sitha or Inge. Even stranger was the enhanced affection she felt for him, as though he was an impossible but charming child, whose kisses and caresses and absurdities she could relish, just as long as it went no further than that. There could be no inevitable and taken for granted conclusion to the love-play. That would be improper. With all the insecurity and imponderables still hanging over her, she could not feel sufficiently intimate to allow herself to be taken over and possessed again. There was somehow no necessity. If there was any possessing to be done, there was an impression hovering around that she might be the one to do it.

'I'm not attuned to you after all this long time,' she

said, wriggling away from him a little in the bed, yet not wishing to hurt his feelings.

Mohendra was stunned. 'But what is this nonsense? In India it was all right, wasn't it? A bit of all right one could say. What has happened to change things since then? It was all so wonderful over there. To me the long absence, which was much against my will, as you well know, has made the heart all the fonder. I need to make up for all that lost time.'

'We're back home now, and things are different. You are different. Over there the whole thing was like a sort of unreal holiday, with you relaxed and happy, just like we were in Cornwall. Here we only seem to have time to make love in the short respites in between work and disagreements. Sort of tap-like turning on and off to order. Not part of life at all.'

'But my darling, with a life as busy as mine is, we have to make use of snatched opportunities. You know I would gladly drop anything to make love to you, wherever we were – Victoria Station, Buckingham Palace, the House of Lords – you only have to give me the sign and I would halt Piccadilly traffic immediately.'

Yes; there was certainly no lack of sensuality. He was undeniably lustful whenever his mind switched on to the subject, no lack of enthusiasm at all, even after all these years. So how genuine were her excuses? Or was she rationalizing her reluctance? Could she possibly have been influenced by the flattering admiration, hope and love which had recently been showered on her by the young Persian student at her writing class? She dismissed that possibility in some confusion, because it would have been a childish, immature reason.

'I just don't want to,' she said, and felt guilty. It was not even consistent, because she was uneasy and apprehensive of the persistent sex she found seething inside

277

her at the same time. There were constant dreams of affairs with strong, sophisticated lovers. Jubilant dreams, where she confronted Mohendra in triumph with the new love. Shameful, of course, showing the tit-for-tat attitude so near to the surface underneath all that bravado. But it was not conscious bravado, surely? There should be no room for retaliation in the present blossoming attitude towards life around her. With her rather humble wage-earning efforts, there were the beginnings of growing financial security. She had managed the children, the house and herself on her own for the past two years. Her own efforts were boosting her self-confidence: there suddenly seemed to be an independent way ahead.

She found the attraction she felt for Darius, the boy at the writing class, most difficult to contain. Rather as though she had been transported back into adolesence when sex and men were a constant challenge, his interest in her was both stimulating and seductive.

'You look just like the Shah,' she said when she first met him.

'Oh please no. It is because of him that I cannot go back to Teheran. He would shoot me and my family. We are exiled.'

She felt a flicker of disappointment. Another political rebel? She had absurdly hoped that he was what he looked – an elegantly polished sophisticate, full of charm, wit and good taste. How was it that hope sprang eternal, even when one had passed forty? He was certainly handsome, the shape of the head giving her particular pleasure. Out of the blue she visualized a painting she suddenly wanted to create. Not the naive little illustrations she was so good at, with their childish detail, but a huge canvas of Darius, the beautiful, in profile against a window. Tight, black curls rising flat from collar to crown which made her want to clutch a handful for the pure sensuous pleasure of it. Aquiline nose and fringed black eyes.

There was a muted excitement as she thought about him. Strings of words rushed back into her mind from the distance of twenty odd years. The poet had lain dormant all that time, drowned in the everyday things of everyday life and only now resurfacing. How strange that she had not missed that part of herself, but there had been so little time for anything beyond keeping pace with life. She had forgotten the pleasure of inspiration during that long, infertile period. Why should it now be rekindled by this gauche youth who looked like Mohendra once looked? At least I'm true to type, she thought, with a wave of amusement. She experienced a small spark of desire to break away from the doubt and anxiety of today, in a hesitant belief that she could perhaps achieve a more exciting tomorrow.

They began to spend occasional time together, though Heather kept a strict hold on her feelings because of the improbability of the idea that a boy of twenty should wish to do more than flirt amicably with anyone of her age. She even resisted the temptation to start a painting of him while Mohendra remained in England, though she wrote several poems, which were dominated by the theme of rebirth and reincarnation and new days dawning. How childish I'm being, she thought, do I really need this sort of morale boosting?

Mohendra had stayed in London for seven taut months before returning 'to follow up some of the important leads' he had initiated in Delhi. During the seven months, he had swung between buoyant satisfaction at the mild success of Sitha's dance recitals and explosive frustration at Heather's sex embargo and lack of support.

'I am not the Mahatma you know, God bless him. Wonderful man that he was, I do not go the whole way

279

with him. Celibacy does not agree with me at all. So what do you expect me to do? Hire a prostitute or something? Darling, what has happened to you? What has happened to us? The fact that you may be off sex for some time, that is understandable, it happens to the best of us. But surely, during that time, we put up with it for the sake of the one we profess to love, do we not? The really loving wife wants to please her husband in the same way that he would want to please her. Do you think I was always "in the mood"? Of course not! But I was never so selfish as not to respond to your sweet seductions, was I? Do, please, pull yourself together, dear.'

But there was no way she felt capable, at that time, of pulling herself together as far as love-making was concerned. In fact, the situation that confronted her seemed to be pulling her apart. Before, sex between them had been so satisfactory and stimulating that all problems dissolved once they were in bed. So in spite of the infidelities – or perhaps because of them – it had been imperative for her to hang on to the physical side because it was one of the satisfactory realities of her life. It was absolute, overwhelming and total – the one sure thing. The arbitrary inconsequence with which she now rejected this certainty made her deeply uneasy.

Both Sitha and an enraptured Inge, who had taken to wearing a sari regularly, went back to India with him. Heather found the concept of Mohendra setting off with his harem vastly amusing, and she saw them off in a whirl of gaiety. The relief was dramatic. A relaxation of tension that made her sink, mentally, into a comfortable vacuum. And yet it was not that she felt she and Mohendra were irrevocably split. This was something she could not admit to. The relief came from easing up on the effort of smoothing things out. When she was with him she was constantly watching her step.

Checking on her words in case they might lead to more disagreements. It was the confrontations she still dreaded. Anything to avoid them; keep the peace today and tomorrow would be all right. This continuous watching of herself was exhausting, and freedom of letting go was intoxicating. In the first few days of being on her own after the exodus to India, she basked in the joy of being able to do and say exactly what she liked when she liked. The gratification of having the freedom to concentrate on her own world of inspiration, appreciation and personal achievement, and the unlikely, but intoxicating anticipation of a lover.

Darius came for a sitting the week after Mohendra had left. He wandered through the house in a haze of appreciation. How strangely foreign he looks in this place, she thought. Something not to be shared with the rest of the family. Something uniquely to do with and belonging to her. He infiltrated the empty house, which at that moment was streaked with sun and looking unreal and ethereal, with billowing curtains and warm summer air blowing through morning open windows. Poetry she had never noticed before had suddenly and inexplicably wafted into that solid, surburban residence.

'A house full of you,' he said. 'Your smile is all over it.' He stopped in front of a painting of Bibendra. 'And this is your painting, and your son.' He paused. 'He is a spirit, so beautiful. I am already jealous of him, and of your painting. You never told me how well you painted, did you? I didn't know till now the sort of person I was dealing with. I am filled with humility. Before I had considered us as almost equals. Forgive me. How can anyone have so many talents?'

'Stop swelling my head.' How good it was to be worshipped, even by someone who knew no better. He was, after all, very young.

'I want you to stand by the window, the one that's open where the curtains are blowing. Just lean and look out.'

The paroxysm of inspiration almost suffocated her with excitement. So long since she had felt anything like it. It surged feverishly back from the heady, early days with Mohendra. Such certainty of knowing exactly what she was about to do. Then, it was the certainty of Mohendra's support, now it was, surprisingly, her own conviction. These moments of joy, so few and far between, that seized you through your life were so magical: one certain duet in Figaro at one certain time; a view from the South Downs or Yorkshire Dales on a particular day; a sudden understanding and appreciation of a poem or a painting.

The painting proceeded through the day with intervals for bread, cheese and wine, and the magic did not abate. Even as the children returned from school they seemed, for Heather, to be swept up into the unreality of a new beginning. India was first.

'Mummy it's not fair. Penny got the best part in the play and I'm much better than her.' She ignored Darius. 'They always choose Penny for everything. I hate her. What's for tea?' She went into the kitchen without waiting for an answer and put the kettle on.

Bibendra ran straight into the room where they were painting, breathless, and stopped dead. 'Oh, hallo.'

'This is Darius.'

'Daroosh? How do you spell that?'

Heather spelt it out.

'Oh Dar-oosh. Is that really how you pronounce it? I always thought it was Dar-ius or *Dar-i*us. Are you from Persia? I think Persia's a much nicer name than Iran don't you? It sounds rich and sort of sumptuous, don't you think? Iran and Iraq sound like Castor and Pollux. Is tea ready?'

So they obviously did not consider him as a foreign body – just another piece of furniture. Shiva was impressed by the painting, and stared at it for quite a long time.

'That's super,' he said. 'Quite outrageously super. You are a very clever mother, and I never noticed before.'

'Nor did I,' Heather said.

It was the beginning of the transformation scene. Heather could just remember the old pantomimes of her childhood where gradually, and with spellbinding subtlety, lights glowed, gauze curtains faded, scenery ascended and descended, and the magician's dungeon changed into the fairy palace.

The painting was a startling success and was accepted for exhibition. It was the first of many in which Darius was the pivot. Sometimes he appeared in them; sometimes it was just the straight back of the head that ordered the design, sometimes the line of the profile, over and over again. They met more and more often.

'You know I am in love with you.' He turned to look at her.

'Keep still; turn your head back. I'm just doing something important. What do you mean by being in love?'

'I mean I am obsessed by you. I think you, I eat you, I am incomplete without you.'

I don't feel like that, she thought, but I love the situation. I *am* a bit obsessed by that. This hard-to-believe circumstance of having a young boy, not much older than Shiva, in love with someone like me; it's incredible; and wonderful.

'And very good for the ego,' Hugh said when she told him.

'I shouldn't be so easily flattered.'

'Yes you should. We need boosting at our age.'

'But I don't love him, I just love the conquest. I want to tell everybody about it. Sort of shout it from the house-tops: look folks! I can still knock 'em cold. I'm still attractive to men, aren't I clever? That's absolutely disgraceful and awful and shallow, isn't it? But I can never understand those women who think they are insulted by men who make passes at them. I *love* it! Why should it be considered insulting if someone wants to go to bed with you?'

'Something to do with men being such wicked, wicked creatures, and bed being probably all they want.'

'And probably in nine cases out of ten it is all I want.'

'Then that makes you promiscuous and a wanton.'

'Silly isn't it?'

'Very silly.'

He suddenly pulled her down on to his lap and hugged her. 'Oh you dear, dear promiscuous wanton. I do love you, too, you know.'

She put her arms round his neck and kissed his cheek and his ear and his nose. 'It's mutual,' she said. '*Tremendously* mutual.'

As time marched on, she found the affair, which was not yet an affair, with Darius a little hard to control.

'You know I have to have you,' he said. 'Not just hole and corner, up to the point and then stop; it's got to be everything.'

'I know. Trouble is it's a step for me. Really quite a big one.'

'And for me.'

'Yes, but not so much. I'm stepping out of marriage, which I haven't done before. Sex is one of the big things that still locks me in this marriage. I'm a bit afraid of letting that go in case the baby gets washed down the plughole with the bath water. With you it's just a new experience.'

'Why are you so tiresomely moral?'

'I'm not. Not at all. This is just a rather selfish clinging to something I know. The devil I know in fact. Quite
a lot to do with cowardice and also because I really like
the marriage-family situation and I don't want to lose
it. I went into it with the conviction that we could make
it work, however much adjustment it took.'

'Couldn't you look on me as just another
adjustment?'

She put her palette on the table and sat down.
'Mohendra could have done where his lovers were concerned – still does in fact. But I'm not sure that I could
view it that way. Suppose sex with you is ultra, ultra
successful . . .'

'Which of course it would be.'

'So then what would the marriage be left with? It
would be a sort of sterile second best affair.'

'Isn't it already?'

'Not really. It has a lot going for it, which included a
very good sex side.'

'You put it in the past?'

'Temporarily. Just a passing idiosyncrasy of mine
that's probably only a superficial whim. A step like this
might put paid to everything for good and all. I'm not
sure that's what I want.'

'But I want you,' he said, 'and you want me.'

'I don't know, I really don't know.' She stood up and
rocked from one foot to the other. 'Let's go for a walk on
the Heath.'

'Outdoor exercise and cold baths being the English
answer to sex.'

She laughed. 'Possibly, but perhaps trees and long
grass on a summer day might be a stimulant rather
than a suppressant.'

'I need no stimulant.'

'But I might do.'

They walked, hand in hand, across Kenwood slopes

285

and sat deep in grass in a private world. People passed distantly with muffled shuffle and murmuring. For Heather, the stimulus of hay smell and the buzzing of outside summer flies mixed with the anxiety of the outer world intruding.

'Suppose someone comes.'

'Let them.'

His hand found and held her breast, and she was breathlessly transported to a forgotten depth of pleasure.

'Oh Darius, Darius . . .' She used the true pronunciation which was soft and made a whisper of the word. 'I had forgotten this – I didn't remember this . . . this tumult.' There was no outside, no world beyond; just the sky, the tall grass above them and an ocean of ecstasy.

'So much more wonderful,' he said, 'so much better than I had ever imagined.' He buried his face in her blindly in a way that was childlike and belied his words. There was no time to waste, only urgency to touch and take in case the moment slipped away.

Heather slid breathlessly back into the world with a sensation of disbelief. It had never been like that before – had it? Perhaps she had forgotten, or perhaps she had never envisaged such abandon.

'Delight will have a whole new meaning from now on,' she said. 'I think I never really met it before.'

He lay sprawled and motionless, his eyes shut.

A dog barked in the distance, and sounds floated back from the end of the world. She sat up, and pushed her hands through her hair. 'I must be mad,' staring out over the long grass, 'stark, staring bonkers, taking a risk like that – we could both have been clapped in gaol.'

He rolled over on to her lap and clasped his arms

round her. 'It was worth a thousand years of hard labour,' he said.

The ground she trod after that day and for many days to come was endlessly cushioned with pneumatic mattresses, and everyday life was painted a permanent shade of rose pink.

21   Loss of Prized Possession

This time Mohendra stayed in India for eighteen months. Letters arrived sometimes daily and sometimes weekly, but always full of incident; recounting exploits either just about to happen, with spectacular results, or which had already happened, with equally spectacular results. Success was always just around the corner.

'And of course it may be, you know,' Heather said to Hugh. 'There is every possibility that it may be. I mean *finally* all these tremendous efforts of his must give a modicum of success. Surely. Mustn't they?'

Hugh shook his head, 'I do realize that I haven't got your unshakeable faith. Nor am I the charming, if slightly brash, optimist that you are, but I cannot see Mohendra as a success – not ever. He just couldn't cope with success. It would ruin him.'

'Don't be ridiculous, of course he could. And it would solve so many of his problems. Just give him a little real success and he'd lose all these frustrations that make him impossible at the moment. I mean it's obvious – he feels a failure so he has to blame everybody. Particularly me. And of course it is partly my fault, I realize that. I'm just not giving him the support he needs.'

'Finished?' Hugh said. 'Come to the end of your sin-list? All ready for the priest, are we? We're talking of *his* failings, not yours. Two different things. Support's all very well, but the main plant has got to be there in the first place. You're trying to support a hole in the ground.'

'You're very unkind about him, you unsympathetic pig. And anyway, a hole in the ground might come in very useful one day. I could hide in it.'

'Just what you have been doing for a good many years, you dear idiot.'

'Well he's coming back soon. When he starts saying he's arriving next week, that usually means within the next two months or so.'

'So what is your plan of campaign?'

She shrugged. 'Wait and see, I suppose. I usually do. At least I've had a bit of success while he's been away with all those exhibitions and things. He can't say I've been wasting my time, can he? He should be pleased about that.'

'Nonsense, he'll be devastated. You're beating him at his own game. You're achieving something. And what about Darius?'

She smiled in satisfied and affectionate contemplation. 'What about Darius?'

'Don't pretend to be obtuse. Have you got your puppy husband-trained?'

'More or less. He's petrified at the thought of him.'

'Will you tell Mohendra?'

'Good God no.' Her face took on an immediate expression of alarm. 'He'd kill me.'

She paused to consider just why she should be so afraid. Afraid of what? Being caught out? Showing up in a bad light?

'You're still frightened of confrontation,' Hugh said. 'You crumple whenever you contemplate it.'

'I suppose I'm frightened of what he might do.'

'He wouldn't beat you up would he?'

'I suppose he might. He's so unpredictable.'

'Perhaps I could tell him for you.' Hugh laughed out loud at the thought.

'Don't you dare. Anyway, I'm thinking of giving up all this illicit love, especially when he comes home. It would be too much of a strain.'

'Giving it up?' Hugh said. 'What a rash thing to do.'

'Oh I know, I know. I mean where is a geriatric like me going to find this sort of opportunity again?'

'That's not what I meant.'

'Dear Hugh, I know you didn't, but it's a thought that constantly occurs to me. One shouldn't look gift horses in the mouth, specially when they're as lovely as Darius, but I have this mad, illogical female feeling that I am being taken advantage of yet again.'

'Don't worry, it's just your self esteem attempting to raise its cheeky head.'

'It's just that things seem to be taken a tiny bit for granted. I find myself feeling guilty if I don't hop into bed whenever there's a free moment, kind of thing. Oh *men*, how do they manage to make us feel so guilty? Why do we always find ourselves in the wrong where they are concerned? Can't we ever kiss and cuddle them and be nice without their thinking we are in need of everything else?'

'Try me,' said Hugh, and he clutched her to him so that they rolled over together on the sofa, screaming with laughter.

'I wish there were more around like you,' Heather panted as they untangled themselves.

'Well there are really, but we tend to get locked up,' said Hugh.

Mohendra returned to England in February 1960, and the seesaw existence of coming and going kept up its air of unreality. When he went away, life for Heather started up in earnest, and when he was in England she seemed, in her mind, to be sitting back and waiting for him to leave again. Her emotions and inspirations folded themselves neatly away until she could take them out again. Almost like keeping themselves out of harm's way.

Mohendra was happy that the situation seemed to have improved greatly in the interim. Good that he had been patient when she was so obstructive about sex the last time he was back. Perhaps she had been jealous of Sitha, though it was difficult to see why. What could she expect if she denied him like that? But much better this time; she was far more co-operative and sensible right from the first day.

He had arrived at Heathrow on a bleak day amid a confusion of misunderstanding and pique. Heather had been to the airport to meet him the day before on the information he had given in the P.S. to his last letter. The following day she was handed a telegram which read: 'Arriving Heathrow tomorrow 11.35.' The telephone rang as she was reading it.

'Why aren't you here?'

'I've just this minute got your cable.'

'Just *now*? But I sent it in plenty of time.' The tongue clicked furiously.

'Shall I come now?'

'Well, I suppose – come to the terminal – I have so much to carry. The plane was very late and the customs are impossible.' The pips went. 'I have no more money, you should leave straight away or very soon . . .' and the dialling tone. She replaced the receiver thoughtfully. After eighteen months apart and that was all? Amusement mingled with apprehension. How was life going to change this time? She almost felt that it was retreating from her already as she got into the car.

But apart from the terse start, it was really quite a joyful homecoming. Inge, complete with caste mark and her hair scraped back into a tiny bun, had accompanied him on the journey but was despatched to her own flat, so he and Heather arrived at the Finchley house to an enthusiastic and boisterous welcome. India and Bibendra had strung a sign over the front door which read 'Welcome Home' and Janaka had typed a neat notice, pinned underneath, saying 'Fathers are welcome in this home only if they wipe their feet and their noses and promise to be obedient to their offspring at all times.'

Mohendra overcame his original displeasure at not being met at the airport, and exuberance took over.

'So you've missed your poor hardworking father, have you? I should hope so indeed. Come here the lot of you and let me look at you. My God – but you are all taller than I am.' He hugged Shiva in an emotional embrace. 'And what about my future Cambridge under-graduate? How goes it with you?'

There were a few moments of gauche embarrassment as the older boys adjusted themselves to the cliché humour they had grown unused to in his absence.

'Stop making Indian-type remarks, Dad,' Kabir said. 'Do remember we are all sophisticated, super-intelligent geniuses now, not drooling infants.'

'I beg your pardon, sir.' Mohendra stood to attention and saluted. 'From here on I will remember not to make bad jokes, and to treat you all with the respect you don't deserve. But you will have to forgive me if I make mistakes. I left you all as infants and I return to find you all men.'

'And ladies,' India said.

'And of course ladies.' He squatted down in the familiar haunches posture and started rummaging in one of the cases. 'Now let me see, I believe I have some-thing here for ladies called India.'

He will never stop treating us all as infants, Heather

292

thought. I wonder if they will be indulgent towards him. I wonder if *I* will be indulgent towards him; you need to be very adult to be indulgent.

The presents he brought with him were numerous and extravagant; Indian sandals, shirts, Gandhi caps, shervanis, saris, bronze figures, toys. Often quite inappropriate and in appalling taste.

He was the old, effusive, all-embracing Mohendra this time without any new accompanying lady companion. Heather was not sure whether she felt freer or more restricted. There was greater sense of responsibility having no one, apart from Inge, to share him with, and Inge had somehow become more like a second typewriter than a second wife.

'No lady friend this time?' she asked, and wondered at once if he would resent the remark. Silly to start a disagreement for no good reason. But Mohendra was still in a relaxed, expansive mood. She caught herself wondering why, but immediately suppressed the thought in case it might be uncharitable. Indulgence is adult she repeated to herself. He put his arm round her and kissed her.

'Ever the suspicious wife, I see. My darling, I have left all the adoring ladies behind this time, there were just too many to bring. And anyway, I wanted you to myself.' He kissed her passionately and lingeringly. 'Let's go upstairs *now*.'

'Can't possibly.' Heather was pleasantly brisk and feeling suddenly perfectly in control of the situation. 'It's lunch time, and there are ravening hordes to cater for.'

'Can't Mrs B. give them their lunch today?'

'Mealtimes are family get-togethers, as you have so often told me.' She took his hand and pulled him up. 'So come and be *pater familias* for a change. It will do you the world of good.'

It was not for an hour after the uproarious meal that the subject of her work surfaced.

'You've got to see what Mum's been doing since you've been away,' Kabir told him. 'It's super fantastic.'

'You'll be amazed,' Shiva said. 'It's really great stuff.'

'She's quite famous,' Bibendra said.

'Hung on all the best railings,' added Janaka.

'We went to the private views and heard people talking about her.'

'And there was a bit in the paper.'

'Goodness gracious me,' Mohendra smiled benevolently. 'And why was I not told, pray? Am I married to a star without knowing it? Lead on MacDuff, I say.'

They all crowded into the studio to watch the effect. Darius looked down at them from every angle and from canvases propped on the floor, interspersed with family groups, sketches of the children singly or together, and drawings scattered and pinned everywhere.

I've done as much in the last eighteen months as in the last twenty years, she thought with some surprise. A release of the floodgates indeed. The influence that Darius had had on the short spell of life they had so far shared struck her forcibly only at that moment. Surrounded, as she was then, by both paintings and family, she suddenly realized her own output. Before then, the glut of work she had turned out seemed just a natural progression. Rather the same sort of phenomenon that had amalgamated Darius into the family circle to become part of it. But standing there with the Mohendra-based family she realized, with a jolt, how odd the whole thing was. She glanced at Mohendra apprehensively, but then remembered that he was never troubled by perceptions, only facts. He would not be bothered by any hidden psychological subtleties.

'Well, well,' he stared round, smiling, while the family watched and waited. 'Well, *well*! What a gallery! You have certainly worked hard, my dear. Very good – very good!' The words were without heart and uttered with only a show of enthusiasm that did not ring true. He stopped in front of the first portrait of Darius.

'And which of the boys is this? Not such a good likeness as some of the others, perhaps?'

India let out a giggle of rather embarrassed laughter. 'That's not one of *us*,' she said. 'That's Darius, Mummy's boyfriend.'

There was a hushed silence. The only one unaffected by the remark was Mohendra.

'Boyfriend, indeed – is this something else I don't know?' He put his arm round Heather. 'I shall obviously have to get to the bottom of this, but if you ask me, I would say he's just a little bit young for Mummy, isn't it?'

'He's a young Persian student who has adopted us lately,' Heather said. He did not believe in her boyfriends any more than he believed in her art. 'I found him very paintable. He's very like you used to be.'

'What's this "used to be"? Am I still not the most handsome man you have ever seen? Tell her, children, stick up for me please. Anyone would think I was growing old.' He had lost interest in the paintings. 'Now let's go and find what else I have in my bags and I want to see how all of you have been getting on with your studies. This is most important.' He turned to Heather as they left the studio. 'And what about all those portraits I suggested to you. Did you write to the Prime Minister? Persian students are all very well, but how much better to paint one really important portrait. *This* is what will get you known you know.'

*   *   *

The next few weeks proceeded easily and lazily. Mohendra seemed to be taking one of his occasional rest periods. His nature changed when he was not working frenetically towards a definite target. Practically a normal being, Heather thought, but checked the uncharitable thought; much too biased.

Darius telephoned once.

'Heather?'

'Yes? Oh hallo . . .' Mohendra was in his study and was bound to have picked up the phone; he always did, and listened in. Always. She had warned Darius of this. How could he be so silly?

'I'm very depressed.'

'Oh really? I'm so sorry.'

'Can I see you?'

This fear that surfaced, how ridiculous it was. Why should it make her heart beat so quickly and almost painfully?

'Why don't you come round then? We shall *all* be here most of the time.'

The dream; showing off the lover to the husband, only the triumph wouldn't be there. Or would it?

'Oh – yes – I see. Well . . .'

'Come to lunch on Sunday. A family lunch. My mother will be here too.' The more the merrier; and probably the safer; and certainly the crazier.

'Well I – er – I . . .'

'Please come,' she felt in control again now and amused at the anticipation. 'I want you to meet Mohendra – who is listening in on the other phone.' There was a slight sound but no word. He would never admit to listening in.

'All right,' Darius sounded miserable. 'Thank you very much. I'll see you on Sunday then.'

There were thirteen of them eventually, as Hugh and Inge had joined the party too, and Mrs Bonnet had come to help. The table was stretched to its limit but Sylvia would not sit down.

'But we're thirteen, darling, you know we can't sit down thirteen. Surely you remember that. We sat down thirteen the day before my poor dear father died you know,' she told Hugh. 'My mother did her best but Father insisted because he hated the idea of superstition. But he died just the same. Such an obstinate man you know.'

'My mother always said the same thing,' Mrs B. joined in. 'Not that I grew up what you might call superstitious; couldn't really call myself that, though I do cross myself whenever I see a black cat, but then that's habit I would call it, I mean I don't really *think* about it, just comes natural really. But I walk under ladders and that . . .'

'India, could you and Bibendra sit at a little table.'

'That's not fair, I want to sit at the big table.'

'I'll sit at a little table,' Shiva said. 'I would love to sit at a little table.'

'But you're too big to sit at a little table, your legs will get in the way.'

'Why can't I sit at a little table by myself, I'd much rather,' said Kabir.

'Mummy said I could sit at a little table with India. You'd have to sit with *me*.'

'Uuuu-ugh – I don't want to sit with *you*.'

'I'll sit at the little table,' said Heather. 'That will solve it.'

'What about Grandma sitting there with Mrs B.?'

By this time the whole company, except Sylvia, Mohendra and Mrs B., was convulsed with laughter and the noise was over-powering.

'. . . and in the East of course they believe in all those things much more than we do over here, what with their witch doctors and things and when we was in India –

my husband was in the army you see . . .' Mrs B. explained to Sylvia. 'We was out there for four years or more but that was when it belonged to Britain of course and it was like living in Neasden really when you came to think of it because there was such a lot of us and of course we did tend to keep ourselves to ourselves and not mix with the natives or anything . . .'

Sylvia put her hand to her head and sat down heavily at the table. 'I can't take the noise,' she said faintly above the din. 'I didn't mean to cause such an upheaval. I'm really very sorry but I just can't sit down thirteen. Perhaps you could serve me mine in the kitchen?' She looked severely at Mrs B., who was saying '. . . and we always fried ours in butter because I didn't hold much with that Indian stuff . . .'

Mohendra sat down next to Sylvia. 'Of course we won't let you sit in the kitchen. You will sit next to me as the guest of honour and because I have not had the pleasure of talking to you for so long. Inge will sit at the little table, won't you Inge? And would you please be good enough to fetch the table from my study and put it up so that we can all get on with the meal. Let me give you some wine.' He filled Sylvia's glass and his own. 'Sit down everyone, what a lovely family party, this is. Mrs Bonnet, will you please serve us, Heather has started carving. To Mrs Hamilton Jones first, of course.' He not only pacified her but charmed her as well, Heather noticed with satisfaction. She smiled over the heads at Darius, sitting like an oasis in a sand-storm and for a moment there was the pleasure of the shared secret between them.

There was no opportunity for much more than that. A few words as they cleared the table. 'I miss you – it's unbearable,' he said, then Mohendra came into the room with the coffee.

'Come into the sitting room,' he said, looking from

one to the other. 'We will have coffee in the sitting room.'

Heather saw Darius start fractionally and watched his confusion with a feeling of tenderness. She took his hand and squeezed it in hers as they followed Mohendra obediently out of the door.

In bed that night she lay wide awake, watching the shadowplay of street lights, trees and wind on the ceiling of the bedroom. From distance and memory there was surely another such calm before storm somewhere, but she could not remember when. The shadows all seemed grossly and obviously symbolic; gentle and fluttering one minute, turning the next into wild ravages of tempest with the accompaniment of hissing sound effects.

She turned over impatiently and Mohendra immediately stirred and felt for her.

She felt she could afford to be tolerant now and sex could be very satisfactorily soporific. The imponderables and the insecurity had diminished. Sex had become a way of celebrating affection and gentle familiarity. At least with Mohendra it had. With Darius now, that was something different. With him the stimulant effect was uppermost and carried her through days of wide-awake intensity. Both reactions were tremendous, so why the overall disinterest in the initial approach? Was she really just the hostile female being offended by winks and wolf whistles? The one with whom she professed not to be in sympathy? Once set in motion, there was no denying the pleasure. However doubtful the approach, she found the outcome invariably superb and satisfying.

They lay entwined and spent, and loving each other.

'And does your other boyfriend satisfy you like that?' It was a gentle, mocking question, with no hint of accusation, but her body tautened like a wound spring.

'No,' she said; and then, because she sensed the

299

disloyalty to Darius of the reply, added, 'Not like that.'

She listened to the ensuing silence, noticing that it was full of unknown quantities. It lasted too long to be innocuous.

He propped himself on his elbow.

'Has he made love to you?'

There was no use even to think of lying. It was just not possible for her to do so with any modicum of success. No sliding round that one. The fear came back with a rush.

'Yes,' she said, and waited, quite rigid.

He lay back on the pillow and said nothing for what seemed to be a very long time.

What was he thinking? Why didn't he say something? Was he going through the same agony that she did all those years ago? Assuredly not. He had always said that she had made an absurd issue out of something supremely unimportant. But he would have forgotten all that by now, because to him it *had* been supremely unimportant. This silence might mean that he was already thinking of something different.

'I can't believe it,' he said at last.

Was that just a jokey figure of speech, thought Heather, used as Louise might utter it. But no, of course it wasn't. He was actually finding her statement impossible to believe. To him it was not true; couldn't be. She was lying, just making it all up. It had obviously not occurred to him that she would ever countenance the idea, nor – and much more insulting – that anyone would ever consider her seriously as a lover. An unforgivable assumption. Was this really what he thought? Her fear of a few moments before evaporated instantaneously.

'Is it as unbelievable as all that?' she said, sitting up and looking at him. 'Eighteen months all on my own, is

300

it so strange? You tell me plainly that you cannot remain celibate for so long – well perhaps I can't either.'

'But it's just – just – not done.' He sounded embarrassed. 'I mean a beautiful girl like you allowing some callow boy . . .'

'What do you mean – *allowing*? Maybe he did the allowing. Maybe I found something lacking in my life and went out looking for it.'

Mohendra became angry. 'No, no – I cannot accept that. You would not have taken the first move. This would be unforgivable. With so much to lose – someone like you? No, no; not possible.'

'How can you be so illogical?' She fumed with resentment. 'When you go off with all and sundry.' This tit-for-tat element surfacing again, she thought crossly. It was despicable and petty.

'But it's different for a man, it's different. For a girl it is cheap, undignified, unfeminine.'

Her temper rose like a red suffocating fog. How *dare* he? Poised to retaliate, she turned towards him, and saw his eyes were full of tears.

'But you cannot really think anything of this boy – you cannot think more of him than of me?'

How could anger turn to pity so quickly? 'I didn't say I thought more of him.' He was like a child who had lost a prized possession. You couldn't be angry with such naivety.

She had not bargained for this sort of reaction, and it took her by surprise. She had expected resentment, fury, a diatribe of vituperation; anticipated even the physical retaliation which had occasionally exploded on to the boys – misplaced swipes when they had been at their most irritating, immediately followed by tears of mortification at what he had done. 'Unforgivable!' he would moan. 'That I should raise my hand against them through sheer idiotic bad temper. What is life coming to?'

Her defences collapsed, and all she felt like doing was to gather him up, comfortingly, with there, there, don't cry; Mummy kiss it better. It was ludicrous, because the fury was bound to follow sooner or later.

But it never did, and for the rest of the time that he stayed with them in London, Mohendra's whole character took on a different guise. It couldn't last, she decided. He had been like that after the Anita affair too – but it hadn't lasted then either. He was bound to revert in the end. However, she relished the respite because it was time to recuperate; took her right back to the early days. It gave her time to sit back and consider. It started to become difficult even to remember the bad old days of disagreement and rancour. Memory was strangely selective; one remembered the sunny days and forgot the rain. But why not? It could, perhaps, be set fair indefinitely. It was just possible. If things started to go right for him in the future, this was how life could be for them both. How it possibly was for the majority of married couples.

But before very long, the ureal situation of Mohendra behaving like a frightened child began to unnerve her. It was so out of character. Because he was not teetering on the brink of some exciting project just out of reach, but concentrating, it seemed, on going out of his way to please and appease her, he appeared unnaturally passive – moribund almost. He had become depressingly humble.

But somehow she could not feel remorse, only a certain degree of pity. He was endlessly patient with the children, spending hours talking to the older boys and taking the younger ones out. He helped in the kitchen and spent time sweeping the paths and pulling up weeds in the garden. His own work dwindled to the writing of a few letters and making cuttings out of the papers, so that Inge became embarrassingly redundant. Was this, then, the sort of partner she had dreamed he might be? She should be happy with the loving, reformed character who had taken the place of her husband.

'What in Gods name *do* I want?' she said to Hugh in disgust. 'I don't like him dogmatic and I hate him submissive, so what am I looking for?'

'The impossible,' Hugh said. 'Like all of us in our varying degrees, searching away diligently for Mr or Mrs Right, our Prince or Princess Charming.'

'So life is one long compromise, as if I didn't know that already.'

He will have fair hair and be able to play the piano very well, floated back to her over the years. *A thousand a year and two maids and he will adore me.* Oh well, Inge could after all be considered a sort of maid, and presumably she, Heather, was still adored.

'It's not very nice to have to admit it's a compromise,' Hugh said, 'and you should only do so very occasionally, otherwise it tends to stop one striving.'

'And hoping for better things.'

'So don't let's admit to it.'

'The happy ending is just round the corner.'

'Of course it is.'

Darius was never mentioned again by Mohendra. Obviously something not to be admitted to. An unacceptable threat which could not be allowed to surface again. He almost become a figment of Heather's imagination as well, although she met him regularly at classes, and often went back with him to his room to bask for a while in his admiration and love-making. The whole thing was more like an illusion than anything else, but she could pretend, couldn't she? Back in the stalls again, watching the farce which was meant to take you out of yourself for a while. More tangible evidence of him lay blatantly round the studio walls, but even these seemed unreal – something she had achieved in another life, or a dream, but had no place in the present. She made herself paint at well-ordered intervals, out of a sense of duty, or habit, she was unsure which. But now all the paintings she turned out were total failures, all unfinished.

'Just a phase,' she told herself. 'I'm bound to come through this unproductive period.'

The cycle ended as suddenly as it had begun, with a letter from Delhi. Mohendra brightened as he read it.

'Splendid news,' he said, 'Splendid news at last. This could be what we have been waiting for. A small return for all the work I've been putting in all these years. You remember my telling you about one Begum Khan, that rich old lady in Delhi?'

Heather had no recollection. 'Yes,' she said.

'It seems she wants to employ me to organize the cultural functions she holds in her house. She entertains constantly, you see. All the big noises end up in her house sooner or later. Great friend of the Prime Minister. Very useful person, and she also plays the sitar, so she is a sponsor to all the best musicians in the country. What a great chance that would be. When I met her, I was suggesting that we could make her house – really more of a palace than a house – into a cultural centre for all India, and now you see how that suggestion has borne fruit. She says I could occupy a suite of rooms in her home, and she also invites you to come, and most especially she would like us to bring India as she has grandchildren of her age. What an opportunity! We should start making arrangements straight away so that we do not miss the season. We should be able to go in about two weeks from now if we arrange things properly.'

She invites me to come, that's nice, Heather thought. 'It would be difficult for me to go away just now,' she said cautiously, unwilling to damp down the obvious change of mood. 'I mean for any length of time, at least, because – well, for one thing, Bibendra's performances are coming up. I have to be there for them.'

A bit of the old irritation showed. 'Yes, yes, that is important, of course. But think beyond today, my dear. If this idea succeeds, then how much better for him to be principal dancer of the Delhi Cultural Centre for the Arts, than to have to work away for years as some tuppenny ha'penny member of an English ballet chorus.'

And he really believed it to be better. There was no sense in putting another point of view.

'But perhaps India could go with you for a while.' India would actually enjoy it, so Heather should not have to worry too much about the idea of using her as a decoy against her own resolution not to go. Then a terrible twinge of conscience. Sending her off into the unknown? Who was this woman? An immediate panic assailed her. How could she be so irresponsible? How could she consider entrusting her daughter to some strange old Indian eccentric? Anything could happen.

'But who is this woman? Could she look after her?' she asked. 'Suppose you were busy all day or had to go away or something?'

He hugged her in the excitement of the moment. 'My darling, of *course* I would look after her. What? Neglect my adored daughter? How could you imagine such a thing? I shall see to it that she will be waited on hand and foot by all Madame's servants – she must have dozens – and of course, with her charm she will win everyone's hearts. They will all be her willing slaves, I promise you!'

The depression dropped off him like the wicked magician's cloak in the pantomime, and he emerged, the dazzling hero-prince again. Heather's own spirits lifted with the absurd simile, and she laughed in spite of herself.

Panic preparation started at once, with India wild with excitement and the others infected with varying degrees of covetousness. Kabir was incensed.

'Why should *she* go? Why can't *I* go? There's absolutely no reason. Everyone knows I'm a dunce and I'm not going to get a single A level.'

'That's not because you're a dunce,' Shiva said, 'it's because you choose not to get them.'

'Well, whatever, I'm not going to get them, we all know that. In fact, as my headmaster is so keen to point out, I am wasting both the school's time and my own. And anyway, I shall be sixteen in a few weeks so I can really do exactly what I like then. Thus, dear Father, I would like to accompany you on this trip.'

Mohendra thumped him on the shoulder. 'Splendid! Splendid! Nothing I should like better. And I will fix you up with a job as my second in command. I will write to Madam Begum straight away and say that I have to have one more air ticket for my invaluable assistant. Money is no object to her. She will be delighted.'

Heather wondered just how delighted the Begum would be with Kabir, and whether he and Mohendra would be able to tolerate each other for long enough to cover even the journey out there, but it was not altogether a bad idea, for Kabir, at that time, was reacting fairly violently to the successes of the other three boys. She harboured the guilty impression that she might just be offloading some of her difficulties in an irresponsible way. Making things easier for herself rather than considering what might really be best for the children. But they were his children as well. The reminder gave her a slight shock. Of *course* they were his children too, and his responsibility. But as the conflicting and disturbing doubts flicked over in her head, she also

306

glimpsed a long, unfraught vista of peaceful living unfolding ahead of her. It was as tempting as a warm feather bed, though she controlled the pleasant anticipation smartly. This was no way to face up to the challenges of life. There could be lots of unforeseen disasters round the corner. Shouldn't take anything for granted. You never knew.

22 Grandmother's Steps

Even though the return to peace was not quite as intense as she had envisaged, this third departure was nonetheless dramatic. There was an ominous sense of finality about everything. Heather found that her own feelings were too confused to experience the overwhelming relief that had been so dominant the last time. Things were not at all simple. As the plane took off with her husband and two of her children, she found herself crying uncontrollably as though she had irretrievably lost a part of herself. A bit of her was being torn away and lifted into uncharted space. She was frightened by the speed, the scream and the roar of the jet. It was like some inexorable dragon threatening her security. The nightmare concept of a crash kept forming in her head. But that fear always surfaced at take-off when you were personally involved with a traveller. So why all this uncontrolled shivering? There was no real reason to imagine a final curtain. It was just another interval.

The house was distressingly quiet without India and Kabir. Did they really cause so much disturbance when they were around? But the lack of tranquillity that accompanied the quiet seemed more to do with the menacing something unknown simmering away just over the horizon of consciousness. The emptiness hung about like a deflating balloon. Without India there,

Heather felt a physical void in the centre of her body. Was it an absurd need for the feminine in a male-dominated environment? Did she actually, unknowingly align herself to this small nine-year-old in a position of female defence? What nonsense was this? But India's absence did certainly make her realize how little time she had given her daughter in relation to the others. A further cause for guilt?

She did not have long to ponder, as a new phase of her life overtook her very soon after they had gone. She was offered an exhibition of both her children's illustrations and her big oils by a London gallery. The elation she felt was sharply tempered by shock and anxiety.

'They want the children's stuff as well,' she told Hugh. 'They must be mad. Do they really consider that art? And how on earth can they think of combining them with those great big oils of Darius? Those pictures are so personal and part of me. I can't imagine anybody being interested.'

Hugh and she were sitting down to a celebration lunch in the kitchen. He had brought champagne and numerous bunches of flowers.

'I'm trying to be conventional,' he said, 'as befits a gentleman given the honour of lunching with a celebrity.'

'But Hugh I can't possibly do it. I'm not ready for such a thing. Supposing the whole show is a ghastly flop. I should die of shame. And there'll be so much work and expense with framing and carting to and fro. I shan't have time to look for a proper job, and then I shan't have enough money and I . . .'

'Shut up you weak-kneed drip.'

'It's all very well for you, you think I'm capable of anything.'

'Practically anything.' He opened the champagne inexpertly and it flowed everywhere. 'Whereas I can't even open champagne properly.'

They ate brown bread and smoked salmon and played Vivaldi on the record player. 'Just to prove to ourselves that we are now the intellectual middle class and not the upper class dregs that we used to be,' Hugh said.

'Up the intellectuals,' Heather said, raising her glass. 'Though I don't know that I've changed a great deal. I still think pretty much along the same lines that Louise does, and she hasn't defected.' She poured herself another glass and held it close to her nose to watch the bubbles. 'That's not strictly true,' she said. 'In some things I don't think along the same lines Louise does. Her family and their whole set don't consider any of the arts as a part of real life. You know what my uncle once said? He said, "I read a lot – not novels or poetry of course, but biographies and history." ' They both laughed complacently and comfortably in their combined superiority.

'They can only consider reality,' Hugh said, 'nothing else counts.' He laughed again. 'But that's just what Mohendra thinks too.'

Heather was shocked into a moment's silence, 'Mohendra?' she said. 'But he's the intellectual of all time. Brilliant, scintillating . . .' She held her glass aloft.

'And totally devoid of intuition, insight and instinct.'

'So I exchanged one barren desert for another.'

'Something like that.'

She slid down among the cushions of the sofa. 'Why do I struggle so to make a go of marriage?' she said. 'I feel very confused by it all at the moment. It was much clearer the first time he came back with that dreadful dancer, we were so obviously on opposite sides of the fence then. But his reaction to me and Darius has thrown me. All the things I seemed to be fighting against appeared to collapse, so that I just fell on my face, fighting nothing.'

'So pick yourself up and take stock. Why are you fighting?'

'To keep things going, I suppose. To make sure that I don't lose my house and my children. If I ran away from him I would lose both because I would be the guilty party, wouldn't I? The divorce laws would see to it that I was very properly brought to my knees.'

'Doesn't apply any more. The children are all perfectly able to take care of themselves, the house is yours, and you are financially independent.'

'Stop putting things so logically. I can never deal with logic, it lacks humanity. Just because Mohendra seems to have become transformed from my saviour and defender into another dependent son, it's not really very moral to throw him over because he's no longer any use, is it?'

'My darling, I'm not suggesting that you should throw him over, I'm merely pointing out certain facts.'

Her eyes filled with tears. 'I'm a louse, aren't I? Throwing him out in my mind even if I'm not doing it literally. It's the same with Darius. I get him to build up my self-esteem, then my mind tosses him overboard as well.'

'Don't be so bloody self-critical. It isn't ever one-sided, you know. You've given them twice as much as either of them ever gave you.'

'Do you really think so?'

'Of course I think so. I think you're way up on the credit side with Mohendra. Quite time to stop doing the feminine thing of trying to make a go of an unbalanced match.'

'Is that a feminine thing?'

'A bit I think. Males tend to remain pampered sons all their life, and women tend to pamper. All a question of upbringing.'

'Not maternal instinct?'

311

'Might be a bit of that too – especially where you're concerned. You do treat most males as sons.'

'Oh God, do I really? Even you?'

'Not so much me, perhaps, but then I'm not particularly male, am I?'

She smiled at him tipsily. Pleasant how even a small amount of alcohol tended to blur the dividing line between impetuosity and restraint. 'I feel madly maternal towards you at this minute.' The champagne burped down her nose, and she sprawled back on the sofa in a haze of relaxation. 'I feel wonderful,' she said. 'Come and sit beside me, sonny, and let me give you a motherly cuddle.'

Hugh rolled on to the sofa beside her. 'You make me feel alarmingly heterosexual,' he said. 'But then *all* homosexuals are in love with their mothers, aren't they?'

She held him at arm's length and felt the charged atmosphere of sexual attraction surge between them.

'Are they?' she said. '*All* of them?'

'Practically all of them.'

'And the mothers return the affection?'

'Invariably.'

Things became hectically and urgently out of control.

'But won't it spoil everything?'

'Might do, might not.'

'But should we risk it? I mean – after all this time?'

'I don't see,' he said undoing the buttons of her shirt, 'that we have any choice.'

'I suppose,' she said between frenetic kisses, 'that you are ambidextrous.'

'Must be.'

They lay quite silently for a long time afterwards, side by side on the goatskin rug beside the fire.

'What an absolutely amazing thing,' Heather said finally.

'I've wanted to for ages. Years really.'

'I've sort of felt like it too, but I couldn't admit to it because I thought you didn't – I mean I thought I wasn't – I mean . . .'

'Well I did and you were.'

There was another brief silence as they stared at each other, lying prone, with their fingers entwined.

'It could be slightly embarrassing,' she said, with a short burst of laughter. 'I don't think we ought to make a habit of it.'

'One should never make a habit of it.'

'The exception rather than the rule.'

'Exactly.'

She sat up suddenly, still and straight, with her back to him.

'Am I using sex as an easy answer, Hugh? A sort of daily tipple, a tonic pick-me-up? I mean, first Darius and now you. Am I becoming some sort of harlot or something? What does it mean? Am I just paying out Mohendra for not being the perfect husband?'

'You insult me, you whore-like woman. Am I to be considered as merely the paying-out-Mohendra instrument, then?'

She lay back against him again, and found the pressure of his cheek against hers to be reassuring. She took his hand and held it against her other cheek. 'I don't want to start looking on sex like Mohendra does. I still want love-making to be something special.'

'Something to be kept for best in fact.'

'Yes, Sunday best – like wearing gloves for church.'

He wound strands of her hair round his finger and let it spring back into a curl. 'It can be wonderfully therapeutic if used with discrimination.'

'Makes everything so *rosy*, doesn't it? Transforms things. I feel as though I've grown an aura in this last hour. Don't you feel like that?'

'Of course. My aura is a kind of chain mail, keeping

313

me safe from outrageous fortune with all those slings and arrows and things.'

'You and Darius have somehow managed to make me feel worthwhile – restored my self-esteem and given me a self-respect I never had before, much more than the success of the exhibition could. Silly isn't it?'

'Being loved is a great soul restorer.'

'I never really think of you being in need of restoration, you're always in mint condition.'

'Just a fake veneer, that's all, but I do feel extremely restored at this moment.'

'A kind of rebirth.'

'Or a resurrection.'

'Or a reincarnation.'

'We must make sure we keep it like that.'

And suddenly the atmosphere cleared and reverted to pure pleasure, and they clung together and kissed and laughed.

'So, just as long as it's not habit-forming,' she said. 'It's quite the best thing that ever happened to us.'

'You took the words straight out of my mouth,' he said.

During the ensuing weeks Heather immersed herself in a feverish period of painting, framing, mounting and planning for the exhibition. The preparations filled her mind and brought a great wave of energy within her.

'The efficient woman has finally surfaced,' she told Shiva. 'I bet that surprises you, doesn't it? Your untidy, impractical dithery mother seems to be able to tick over like clockwork when she tries. Isn't that amazing?'

'Darling Mother,' Shiva said, 'nothing you did would ever surprise me. You never cease to give me inferiority complexes.'

'Really?' Heather switched to her role of concerned

314

mother. 'I didn't think you had any inferiority complexes.'

'You're such an idiot,' Shiva said kindly. 'In fact, you are awful, but I *like* you.' He pushed her firmly backward into a chair and sat on her lap. 'And that reminds me, I haven't had my September cuddle.' He folded his long legs and arms as small as possible and Heather hugged as much of him as she could.

'You're a fool,' she laughed. How wonderfully funny and lovely her children were. Bibendra and Janaka appeared from nowhere and piled on to the chair on top of her, shouting with laughter. 'Not fair.' 'My turn.' 'Get off, you goons.' But why weren't they complete? She felt a sharp stab of pain at the incompleteness.

'I'm far too busy to waste my time with a lot of silly babies like you,' she said. 'I have frames to make. Yes I can,' she insisted at their derisive jeers. 'Darius taught me and I'm *extremely* good at it.'

'Can we help?'

'Don't tempt me, I might agree and then I shouldn't be able to brag about how efficient I am, doing it all by myself.' Discovering one's own abilities was exhilarating. She wanted no outside help, but Hugh's support was different. It was not that she relied on it, it just seemed a natural part of her own effort.

'You do complement me so beautifully, Hugh. A sort of right arm really. Do I presume on your good nature too much?'

'Far too much. I love it.'

In spite of the build-up, Heather was quite unprepared for the success of the show and the publicity it brought.

'I've sold twelve of the illustrations and two of the big ones,' she whispered to Hugh at the opening. 'Can you believe that?'

'I told you, didn't I? You're a success.'

315

'Or as Mohendra would put it, I'm a beeg heet.'

Just a cable from India: 'Deepest love congratulations and prayers for success all happy here.' But it wasn't *real*, it wasn't *real*. He should have been there. He should have brought them back. Or was that too much to expect? She supposed it was.

Shiva, Janaka, Bibendra and Darius were stiff with pride at the private view.

'You're famous, Mummy, I heard people say so. Will we be on telly?'

'Wish the others could have been here. Kabir hates to miss things, he'll be wild.'

'But Father would have cocked it up and been embarrassing.'

'I don't know. He would have added his own eccentric, eastern charm. Very fashionable sort of thing to have at a smart private view. All the rage really.'

Bibendra was shocked, but laughed with the others. He had never considered one could look on a father as a smart asset.

So again, a large stride forward. It was just like Grandmother's Steps. You advanced a little and then she turned round and caught you and sent you back to the beginning again. When was Grandmother Mohendra going to send her back to the beginning again? The astounding Hugh development remained where it was, without further incident, but it had now been transformed into a tender, intimate affinity by the magic wand. Pumpkin into coach, kitchen drudge into Princess Charming. Much too sugar plum fairy, she thought, can't be real. 'And the little girl turned over and opened her eyes – she had been fast asleep in her own little bed all the time.'

Heather's life was now filled with painting and illustrating. There was no time for writing classes or bread-and-butter jobs, and not a lot of time for lovers either. Darius complained a little, but Hugh brought her food to eat and wine to drink whenever he could spare an hour or so from his own work. Her enthusiasm and inspiration seemed to have returned with a rush, and kept her constantly at her easel. Commissions were steady and the bank balance began to right itself.

Occasionally she sat back and marvelled at it all. A forty-three year-old painter, quite successful, with one husband, a nice home, five children and two lovers. What an extremely lucky person I am. Then she remembered that part of her was in India and quite unresolved, so the good fortune was quite likely to be only temporary. Chickens should not really be counted so soon.

Letters from Mohendra arrived regularly. She found herself skimming through them to find news of the children. She was told that Kabir had soon taken off, and that his whereabouts were obscure. This she had read between the lines as Mohendra had not actually admitted that it was so. 'That questioning son of ours is so interested in the philosophies of India that he wanted to go out and see for himself. Silly boy, I told him that he could find out far more in the libraries of Delhi but he wished to travel. So I gave him some money and my blessing and sent him off to some friends of mine who live in Varanasi. They will look after him. He is very remiss about letterwriting though. We really should have trained him better, he should keep us better informed.'

India, he told her, was ecstatically happy with Rani Kumar's grandchildren, and attending a private convent school in Delhi. Prim, school-written letters from her were sometimes enclosed, or scrawled messages written round the edges of Mohendra's letters. 'I miss

317

you, Mummy. They are very kind here. School is very nice. It is very hot.' What didn't they say?

She had expected Kabir's breakaway, but she was nevertheless anxious, in a distant sort of way, that he would most likely be experimenting with drugs and become involved with some possibly unwise philosophy, adapted to his own way of thinking. The idea of a convent education for India seemed absurd from every point of view, but taking responsibility for the other side of the world was difficult. To interfere from this distance would not do much good. India was his child too, she reminded herself yet again. Shared responsibility was finally being achieved. This was undoubtedly a Good Thing.

But event followed event in an inexorable way, and another large Grandmother's Step was about to be taken. It could be said to have started on September the twenty-third, Heather's forty-fourth birthday. Sylvia had made a trip from Stoke Poges to take her out to a birthday lunch.

'Just you and me, my darling. I thought Aunt Emmy could jolly well stay at home this time, so that I could have you all to myself on your birthday. She's such a miserable old curmudgeon.' The word took Heather back to childhood; everyone was an old curmudgeon to Sylvia when they were over sixty. At nearly eighty, Sylvia was frail and pretty and, surprisingly, in high spirits. 'I want to let you into a little secret too,' she said. 'It's really my birthday present for you this year because I haven't been able to get you a real one. Instead, I had old Mr Whojamacallit, the solicitor, over the other day and we made an arrangement.' She sat back in her chair complacently. 'You're going to get *all* my money when I die. Bobbie and Malcolm are far too rich for their own good, and anyway, they're not a bit nice to me these days. Hardly ever come to see me, you

318

know.' Heather knew that they both visited her regularly, more often than she did herself. 'And I've never taken to those children of theirs; not a patch on your little darlings and not nearly so clever.'

Heather was shocked. 'But Mummy you can't do that.'

'Yes I can. You need it and they don't, and anyway, Daddy left them far too much. I told him it was unfair and I've just adjusted the balance, that's all. They can fight over the jewellery if they want to. I've left Aunt Emmy the big diamond brooch so she won't be able to complain.'

She looked very smug and happy, and any guilt still haunting Heather for all the pain she had once caused her took off into thin air. She squeezed Sylvia's hand and kissed it. 'You're so sweet, Mummy,' she said, 'you really are. But I absolutely forbid you to dwell on such a morbid subject. You know perfectly well that you're going to live till you're ninety-nine, and that's another twenty years.'

'Heaven forbid,' said Sylvia. 'I couldn't stand Aunt Emmy for another twenty years.'

On reaching home that afternoon, Heather found a letter from Mohendra which she opened guiltily, because she owed him three already.

'Beloved wife,' she read. 'Why do you not answer my letters? It is most unfair and heartless of you, when I write so much and so often myself. You know how anxiously I thirst for news of the children – how Shiva does at Cambridge, for instance. I want to know exactly what he is studying so that I can provide him with any information and books he may need. I cannot imagine you troubling yourself about these matters. I have had no reply to mine of the 16th, nor of the 24th of last month nor the 7th of this month. Can you not tell the boys to write? It is really too bad.' And of course it was. Inexcusable. She sighed, and skipped the next few paragraphs. At the top of the following page there were several lines underlined in red.

'*But now for the great news!* I will not nag further (thank goodness you say!) *Darling, our great chance is really here at last!* Yes, I promise you, it is all *signed, sealed and delivered!* None of your airy fairy promises this time. I know you will not believe me after such a time – you disbeliever! – so I will tell you. Begum Rani Khan has employed me, at an agreed salary of £2,000 a year *plus* all living expenses! This means we shall live here in her sumptuous palace with our meals provided and cooked for us. Such luxury that even you and your rich family has never dreamed of! Oh darling, I am so very happy to be able, at last, to provide for you like this. You know how much I have always longed to do so, but circumstances were ever against me. Can you please forgive me for making you wait so long? Because now all that long wait is over.

'Rani Kumar is really very pleased with the way I have been able to run things for her – in fact she has become really fond of me!! Hmm, hmm! Are you jealous, my dear? I hope so!' If there is one more exclamation mark, Heather thought, I think I shall scream. But she read on unhappily. '*Now* – so much has to be done that I cannot write it all here. Just the most important I will jot down so that you can start straight away to make all the arrangements.

1) I think first of all you should put the house on the market. This should fetch a good price (put it with the very best house agents) and we shall need the money over here to buy our own house. You had better start making arrangements with your bank for transferring this money as it may take time. We might keep a little in London because we are sure to want to make visits back and forth.

2) Shiva, of course, will stay on in England until he has finished at Cambridge, after which he's bound to be able to get a good lecturing job over here. I would advise Janaka, too, to pursue his attempts to get a scholarship for either Oxford or Cambridge. Do try to advise him against doing music but to concentrate his efforts on history or English. Music is not useful as a career, and of course he will be studying Indian music once he gets over here. It would be useful for him as Rani will certainly employ him in her Music Centre.
3) Bibendra will be able to finish his dance training over here in both Indian and European dance.

Such opportunities now we all have!
4) As for you, my darling, you will at last have all your real talents recognized – and not just by me this time! You have had to wait so long to get just *one* exhibition in London, but over here I will be able to arrange for at least one exhibition every year and probably more. Also, there are so many Maharajahs queuing up, waiting to be painted. I have told everybody about you, so you will be able to earn a great deal of money and become famous all over India.'

The letter went on for another two pages, but she folded it and put it back in the envelope. What more could he possibly say? Nothing, she felt sure, that she could bear to read. She walked, instead, into the studio and sat down in the chair she had used for so many of Darius's portraits. Running her hands over the carved arm rests, she stared bleakly out of the window where the sun was setting in a translucent sky. She made an attempt to analyse her feelings but found it difficult. The overall coldness she felt was probably fear, she thought.

This, then, was the parting of the ways. No more pretending. The breakdown, the failure was absolute and admitted at last. Everybody had been right and she was wrong. She felt a warm flood of relief as she sat there and a sense of contradictory satisfaction. The way was still not clear, but at least the decision had been taken.

The next day the i's were dotted and the t's crossed. A tiny scribbled letter from India lay on the breakfast table.

'Dear Mummy, Happy birthday. I will bring you a present. I hate it here. Please fetch me home. I am very unhappy. Daddy is being horrid and Mrs Kumar wants me to marry her son. He is at least forty and I am only ten. He is also very nasty and spits in the mornings. It is all too awful and I have been crying for two days. Daddy says I shouldn't sulk. I miss you most terribly which is funny because I never thought I should. Please tell Daddy that he is to send me home. He won't listen to me and gets very cross. This is a completely secret letter. Best love from your suffering daughter, India.'

Heather wept, but it was more from relief than anything else. She had several years of neglect of India to make up for, and now she was being given a second chance. Immediately she started to make plans. Send her a ticket now, today; cable it before sending her reactions to his letter. Would he agree? Her heart started to pound. She must think of some reason that he would consider valid to get her back. Hugh would think up something. She paced the room, biting her knuckles with anxiety. Suppose he refused to send her? Panic caught at her. Oh God, suppose he refused to let her go?

The telephone shrilled close beside her and she started violently. The shock was painful and the way her heart was beating made her breathless. Suppose he refused to send her. She clutched at the receiver with both hands in an attempt to control the shaking. 'Hallo?'

322

'Oh Heather, Heather my dear.' It was Aunt Emmy. 'Some very bad news for you, I'm afraid. Your dear mother passed away very suddenly this morning. In her sleep, my dear, no pain it seems – such a wonderful way to go – and she was so specially happy yesterday after she had seen you. It did so cheer her up. But such a shock to those left behind.'

'Oh no – oh *no* . . .' the storm of crying overwhelmed her utterly and she gave way to it. 'I'll come, I'll come at once.'

End of chapter? End of performance? What a complete and sensational finale it was, she thought. Fairy godmother dies and hero exits in a puff of smoke. Garish melodrama, in which she was totally involved. The house lights would go up any minute now, and she would be revealed with red, crying eyes and a soul laid bare.

23 Harlequinade

After the initial hours of shock, she became more and more convinced that Sylvia had made her final bid for her daughter's happiness by dying when she did. She could not have arranged it better. Heather was swamped in guilt. She had not done enough; she had been insensitive; she had not loved enough. But it was out of her hands now, too late to do anything. All part of the inactivity of sitting back and watching the story unfold around her.

'So you think Mummy knew best all the time?' Hugh said. 'Even managing to save her daughter from the wicked villain?'

Heather smiled wanly. 'You could say that.'

'And now you're going to stay to watch the harlequinade?'

'But I always took part in that,' Heather said, remembering quite clearly the very last scene in the pantomimes of her childhood. 'I always pushed my way right down to the front of the stalls to be sure I got a cracker or a balloon from Pantaloon.'

Hugh kissed her. 'So start pushing,' he said.

A cable was sent: 'Mummy died suddenly this morning cabling tickets for Kabir and India to attend funeral.' He would never deny the right of children to attend their grandmother's funeral. She knew that. She herself, would have laughed at the idea, would have thought it psychologically unwise for India to be there. But there was still much ritual in his make-up, thank God. Playing a trick on him really, she thought. Mean, but imperative in this case. Kabir could make up his own mind, if Mohendra managed to contact him, but India was safe. Thank you dear Mummy, along with God – be he Jehovah or Rama.

Would Mohendra come too? She waited, apprehensively, to see. Her unfinalized and in some senses uncertain decisions could possibly be thrown into confusion if he did. If she had to discuss the future rationally, face to face, eye to eye, she might still be over-powered to the point of surrender. He still held the magic sword; confrontation could still defeat her. But the cable came back: 'India flying Air India tomorrow contacting Kabir forgive absence impossible leave now deepest sympathy and love writing.'

So the struggle was over. She knew the way ahead. No longer any uncertainties.

It took a considerable time to come through the traumas of grief and guilt and, later, the anxieties of decision and explanation. Hugh and Heather wrote her letter to Mohendra together. There was nothing final in it, only rational and reasoned statements of facts. She had decided, tempting though Begum Rani Khan's offer had been, that she was bound to base her life in England, at least for the time being. 'With so much starting to take off for me at this time, I don't feel I can throw it all up and start somewhere else. I would first like to make a go of it here. Perhaps later I will want to move on and out, but not now, not yet.

'I am hoping to buy a house in Hampstead with a studio because Mummy left me some money. It has to be big enough to give everyone a room of their own.' That was sufficiently vague. She did not exactly know, herself, what it meant. Leaving all possible doors open perhaps? Avoiding making actual decisions?

Mohendra expressed, by turns, his astounded anger and deep disappointment, and supposed that she was still suffering from the shock of her mother's death. This he could understand, but he hoped that very soon she would feel better in herself and be able to see the error of her present way of thinking. If she had not been obviously distressed by the loss of her mother, he would have found her behaviour incomprehensible, and it would have been most embarrassing for him to have had to explain away her perversity to Rani Begum. To waste money on a new house in London when all those possibilities awaited her in Delhi – it was sheer madness. Buy a small place somewhere in England if she felt she must, where they could spend their holidays – in Cornwall, for instance – but to buy a big house would just be throwing good money down the drain. He did not wish to pile on the agony in this period of obvious sorrow, so would say no more now. However, he begged her to consider seriously what he had said. 'We will shelve the whole matter for the time being, darling, until you feel more yourself and have wound up your Mummy's estate, and then we'll discuss it all when I next return – probably in about six months or so. Meanwhile, Rani and I are making splendid progress in this internationally important work we are doing here.'

So he's not going to admit to the possibility, she thought. He doesn't believe I would do it, any more than he believed I could have a lover. That at least swept away a few vestiges of irresolution. The way seemed clear ahead.

Heather and Hugh found the house together, stumbled on it really, after listening to lunchtime carols in St John's Parish Church with the whole family, which included Darius. They had streamed out through the elegant Georgian doors into December sunshine with frost and robins and Christmas cheer all round them. Another churchyard, she thought, scanning the tombstones, with Constable buried in this one. She laughed at the comparison – she had moved from Gray and poetry to Constable and painting. How crazy these coincidences were.

'Let's watch the sunset from the Whitestone Pond,' she said, and they moved off in an ambling, companionable group. Kabir had finally been located and was now temporarily with them, looking rather like an Indian sadhu with long hair and a Kashmiri jacket. This, thought Heather, looking round at them all, is happiness. Like the poem-reciting dance with Hugh, like the security of the first few Mohendra years, like the early pram-pushing days, like the Darius paintings, like Hugh – all peaks in Darien upon which to stand silent.

The house was in one of the tree-lined roads leading up to the Heath. Hugh and Heather noticed it together and stopped simultaneously.

'Isn't that beautiful,' Heather said. 'That's where I want to live.'

'So do I,' said Hugh. 'I would like it in my Christmas stocking.'

'Well, we can't both have it,' Heather laughed. 'We can't both live there.' There was a long silence as they looked at each other. The others stared up at the castle-like mansion. The estate agent's board read: 'Magnificent Residence with Studio. For Sale Freehold.'

'I wouldn't mind living there too,' Darius said.

'Nor would *I*,' said Bibendra. 'I would have room to practise.'

'Make a neat London pad, man,' Kabir said.

'Can we buy it Mummy?' India asked.

'It will be much too expensive,' Heather told them.

'Couldn't Hugh share with us? Then it mightn't be,' Janaka suggested.

'What an idea!' Hugh smiled.

'Out of the question,' Heather agreed, laughing.

They collected the key from the agent and spread out from the panelled and stately hall into the dusty rooms and up the baronial staircase.

'Late Victorian, I suppose,' Shiva said. 'The height of decadence and presumption.'

'And absolutely wonderful,' Heather said. She climbed to the studio floor and knew at once that it was perfect. A north light and a view over London, her heart lurched as she stared out over the magic. It was much too good to be true. Even a gallery in the studio with room for a bed up there, and there were two rooms on the same floor. India in this one, she thought to herself, and my bed could go here, against the wall in the other one, and that cupboard could be made into another bathroom, and there's even an attic for storing canvases and lots of wall space for bookshelves. But of course it's impossible, much too expensive and I couldn't cope with a house this size. It would be madness to buy it. As she came slowly down the stairs, reluctant to drag herself away from such a fantasy, she met Janaka and Kabir, darting from room to room on the next floor down.

'I want the tower room,' Kabir said. 'It's just great with that recess-type window in the corner. It's like a little watch tower, you could keep a look out all round you. I mean just no one could creep up on you.'

Janaka was standing in another of the rooms with his arms held out straight on either side of him. 'It would be perfect – I could even have a piano in here and there are enormous cupboards down each side for instruments and things. It could probably be soundproofed.'

Hugh came up the stairs. 'Can I have the ground floor?' he said. 'I do realize that it is possibly the best part of the house, but I'm rich and famous, so I actually do deserve it, don't you think? It would make a wonderful studio and office where I could impress all my rich and famous clients and entertain all my poor and infamous friends. Does anyone mind? We could make part of it into a vast dining room-kitchen area for all of us to eat together if we want to, so that the house can be used in the way it was meant to be used – as a big, warm, welcoming family home.'

'Can we have a mat with *Welcome* on it?' India asked, jumping up and down. 'And can we call the house "Sweet Home" like in the song?' There were screams of protest and a lot of laughter.

'Quite a lot of reconstruction work to do,' Hugh said, looking round and making notes in a notebook. 'More bathrooms and things. We can probably get a grant from the council.'

'I'm booking a bedsit on the first floor,' Darius said. 'Next to the one Bibendra's dancing in at this moment. A business arrangement, of course,' he added. 'I mean I'll pay rent and everything.'

'We can all pay,' Shiva said. 'Once we start to earn, I mean. I'll do the books and organize everything. We shall even have some rooms left over. Let's be a lodging house and make a lot of money by being wicked landlords.'

'Your father will need at least two rooms,' Heather said sternly, and there was a general burst of laughter.

'Let's put him in the cellar,' Kabir suggested, 'and then we can brick him up if he's naughty.'

'No,' Shiva said, 'we'll allocate the whole of the basement area for him, with that big room that leads out into the garden. It's even got its own front door, so it could be a separate flat.'

'And we could let it out on a weekly basis when he's not here,' Janaka added, 'because otherwise it would be a wicked waste of valuable space, and you know how he would hate that.'

So the stage was set, and the whole production was put in motion. It took endless time planning, in which Heather, Hugh, Darius and Shiva joined, in enthusiastic co-operation. Mohendra wrote regularly, but did not arrive. He almost ignored the news that he was given of the progress of the house plan, and spoke only of his own achievements.

'Almost as though he's put us and our mad ideas out of his mind,' Heather said. 'Something he doesn't want to think about.'

'Rather like you used to do with him,' Hugh said.

'Still am doing, I suppose,' She thought about it for a moment. 'Odd you know, but I can't really feel that Mohendra and I were a failure,' she said.

'Thank God for that at least. Of course you weren't a failure; people usually grow apart as they grow up, don't they? Do a bit of dividing and then spend most of their married life trying to get together again and balance things out.'

'I didn't quite balance Mohendra's work obsession, did I?'

'No, can't say you did. You were a sort of humanizing element at first, but sadly, it didn't last. You lost out to work in the end.'

'I could have been much more supportive and sympathetic. I wasn't really what he needed.'

'You weren't an amorphous prop, no, but then neither was he the prop you were looking for.'

'If he had been a prop, I probably would just have leant, and then I never should have discovered what I was actually capable of, would I? I might still have been the vaccillating, vacuous monstrosity I used to be.'

Hugh put his arm round her waist and kissed her ear. 'I rather liked you like that,' he said. 'Made me feel masculine and competent.'

'Well, I didn't like me like that, so I have every reason to feel undying gratitude to Mohendra for rescuing me from the morass.' She leant her head back on Hugh's shoulder. 'The simple answer to a happy marriage,' she said, 'is to accept each other's individuality, and then proceed, side by side. There's a clever, corny philosophical statement for you to go away and brood over.'

'Very restful,' Hugh agreed, 'A comforting, fairy-tale picture of euphoric married bliss, seldom, if ever achieved.'

'One day he'll come along,' sang Heather. 'The man I love.'

'And he'll be big and strong – exactly like me.'

'Can you feel me leaning?'

'You won't lean, my darling, however big and strong I may become, because you will be much too busy turning into a great big octopus, sitting on top of your great big house in which you shut up your great big family of adoring sons.'

'You foul fiend,' she said furiously. 'How can you be so unkind?'

'But I'm not being unkind,' Hugh argued. 'An octopus is really a beautiful creature with a heart of gold that is thoroughly misunderstood. All it wants to do is to wrap its arms round people and love them. It's an everloving creature that enfolds you with its many arms and keeps you safe from harm. Of course it may eat you in the process, but never mind – *tant pis*.'

'But an octopus is hideous, am I so ugly?'

'On the contrary, you are one of the most beautiful octopuses I have ever met.'

331

They were sitting in the new, empty studio at the top of their tower house, and hearing the hammering, sawing and general building commotion drift up from below. The sun was setting far too prettily into pink fluffy clouds and azure remoteness. Very trite and obvious, Heather thought, as she wound her arm round Hugh's neck and wondered if it felt like a tentacle. They stared out together at the unlikely sugary backdrop through the window.

'Happy ending?' she said.

'Not exactly,' he replied, 'But we've at least set the scene.'

THE END

The Governess
Patricia Angadi

This is a sophisticated book, so confident in intention and execution that the long shadows of THE TURN OF THE SCREW do not dim its effectiveness
VICTORIA GLENDINNING, SUNDAY TIMES

How should Mable Herring ('Herry'), governess and heroine of this intriguing first novel, be regarded? Is she a saint or a devil? Did she manage, against considerable odds, to hold the Lane-Baker family together for many years, or was she the instrument of its destruction?

Herry is engaged as governess by Eleanor Lane-Baker in the summer of 1918, and her appointment is itself the conclusion of a battle between Eleanor and her husband, Edward. The couple have six children and for his growing, pleasant, middle-class family Miss Herring, so calm and competent, seems the ideal companion. Yet from the start, Eleanor has her misgivings. She has the uneasy feeling that she engaged Miss Herring against her better judgement because of some inexplicable power.

But is it really this which causes the destruction of the family, and is it based on reality or a distortion?

'I had to read on, mainly because Mrs Angadi has such an acute knowledge of the habits and foibles of youngsters *en familie*.'
DAILY TELEGRAPH

0 552 99201 1

BLACK SWAN

Ellen
Ita Daly

'A startling first novel. Initially the charm, sharp
observation and slight self-mockery are reminiscent of a
Jane Austen heroine. By the end Ellen has become
something far more sinister'
JULIAN ALEXANDER, LITERARY REVIEW

An only child of Catholic Dublin parents, Ellen was a
strange, solitary girl. She was lumpish and dull, she was
lonely. But she had resigned herself to this, and wanted
nothing more from life than to be left alone in her
isolation, to carry out a quiet typing job without
interference, without change. If only her mother would
stop entertaining such ambitious fantasies for her. When
Ellen's hopes of an academic career fell through, Mrs
Yates moved on to visions of a glittering social success,
inviting strange girls around for elaborate teas and
friendships which never materialized.

Then Ellen met Myra. Pretty, rosy Myra who wanted
Ellen to be her friend, to meet her family, to share a flat!
A new world unfolded, a world which Ellen found
completely voluptuous; evenings by the fire, fish and chip
suppers, secrets shared with a friend – even if that friend
could sometimes be casually brutal. Throughout the
summer months, there were lazy days spent in the garden
with Adrien, Myra's stockbroker boyfriend and his cousin.
Bobbie even paid attention to Ellen. She had never
imagined that life could be like this, and she wanted it to
go on forever. Who would have thought that the idyll
could be violated – let alone in the shocking way it was?

'A first novel that is formidably subtle and fluent'
GILLIAN SOMERVILLE-LARGE, THE IRISH TIMES

'An intriguing and disturbing picture of a moth in the
glare of a flashlight'
COSMOPOLITAN

'ELLEN is a deftly promising first novel'
CHRISTOPHER WORDSWORTH, THE GUARDIAN

0 552 99251 8

BLACK SWAN

Cobweb Walking
Sara Banerji

'A book which exercises a compelling fascination and reveals an original and highly imaginative mind at work'
THE LONDON STANDARD

As a child – so tiny and delicate that her father calls her fairy – Morgan has a special relationship with nature, for she can hear the Silence – the humming of the Silence is her secret, even from her beloved father, as is the day that she walks along a cobweb.

But with adolescence comes a loss of childhood innocence and the intrusion into her perfect world of an unwanted stepmother and baby sister. Her privileged position in the household is usurped. She begins to learn the uncomfortable truth about her strangely sheltered existence, and slowly her thoughts turn to revenge.

'The inner depths of this creature are explored with skill. The change from hate to love is a hard chemistry to analyse but Banerji succeeds'
SUNDAY TIMES

0 552 99220 8

BLACK SWAN

As We Forgive
Barbara Neil

'Obsessive love, loneliness, despair, guilt and incest are all deftly brought into this ambitious work, which would be a praiseworthy achievement even for a seasoned writer; as a first novel it is an extraordinary accomplishment.'
PUBLISHERS WEEKLY

The happiest moments of Lydia's childhood had been those spent at the home of her wealthy friend Nathalie. Nathalie, with her rosebud nightgowns, her governess, and her magnificent father, Ben Wavell, was everything that Lydia longed to be – and never could be.

When the adult Lydia met Ben Wavell again she found him a sad, middle-aged man deserted by both wife and daughter but still, for Lydia, he shone as the glamorous figure of her childhood, still exerting the sexual pull that she was now old enough to recognise. Once more her life was to be dominated by the Wavells as she was sucked into an obsessive and sexually overwhelming situation.

'This first novel is heady and forbidden fruit. In immaculate and at times inspired prose, the taboo act of incest is gradually revealed.'
BOOKLIST

'She has taken on two difficult problems, a delicate theme and some aggressively articulate characters. The theme she handles with exquisite control, establishing an almost psychic relationship with her readers.'
NEW REPUBLIC

0 552 99260 7

BLACK SWAN